# THE FALL GUY

*Charles Holborne Legal Thrillers*
*Book Ten*

## Simon Michael

SAPERE
BOOKS

# THE FALL GUY

Published by Sapere Books.

24 Trafalgar Road, Ilkley, England, LS29 8HH

**saperebooks.com**

ISBN: 978-0-85495-706-4

# ACKNOWLEDGEMENTS

My thanks go to the following. Firstly, the musicians and those in the music business. In addition to having made some very good movies, Robert Rosenberg and his co-director Bill Curbishley of Trinifold Management Ltd manage such great bands as The Who and UB40. Robert's experience of the British music industry in the late 1960s was invaluable in writing *The Fall Guy*. I didn't remember, for example, that in 1969 groups of musicians were not commonly referred to as "bands" but "groups". I would also like to thank Andrew Davis, former chorister at Temple Church, who wrote to remind me of the choir to whose practising I used to listen while sitting at my desk. He would have been singing at the relevant time (albeit not in the mornings) and it was he who suggested Bach's Mass in B minor.

As to the legal professionals, I am very grateful to Paul Bleasdale KC of No. 5 Chambers, whose experience of judicial obituaries given in open court is greater than mine, and provided most of that which finds its way into the final paragraphs of the penultimate chapter. Rex Tedd KC, also of No. 5 Chambers, provided a hilarious memoir of his taking silk, which might find its way into the next book (no spoilers here). David Lister, a detective sergeant employed by the Met during the relevant period, has helped make sure the police procedural aspects of this book are accurate. Any legal or procedural errors that remain are mine alone. Finally, I am grateful to Neil Cameron, whose encyclopaedic knowledge of all matters is always an invaluable resource.

I deal with the following in more detail in the Historical Note, but worthy of mention here are Peter Watts's wonderful book *Denmark Street, London's Street of Sound*, Don Black's *The Sanest Guy in the Room* and *Mr Big*, the autobiography of Don Arden, born Harry Levy, legendary manager and father of Sharon Osbourne. I have relied on all of these books in creating this confection.

Those of you who have read the previous book in the series, *Death, Adjourned*, may remember that Big Kev Lane is in fact my accountant and Shirley Titmarsh was an administrator at my former chambers. Both requested to be in the book. That made me wonder: would readers/listeners like me to name a character after them? I sent a mailshot to the members of my reading club, inviting the first five to reply to be a character, anywhere from a walk-on part to evil genius. I was absolutely stunned to receive over 100 replies within minutes of the email landing, together with some really heartwarming praise for the series.

Thank you to all who took the trouble to reply. The five winners, all of whom have a part in this book, are: Karen Bailey (sister of the deceased), Nicola McDonald (a doomed singer with the voice of an angel), Adrian Benson (a Home Office pathologist), Sarah Bruce (the deceased's teacher) and Paul Feder (a corrupt Detective Sergeant — sorry Paul!). It goes without saying that these readers' fictional equivalents are just that, fictional.

However, there were a century of disappointed applicants and so I take this opportunity of expressing my heartfelt thanks to you. You are wonderful, and I love hearing from you. I'm so sorry you didn't make the cut, but watch out for book eleven; you may well find yourself in it as a corpse, a stripper or a corrupt copper!

My thanks go to the following unlucky respondents (in order of response to me): Adele Vanderkar, Martin Oldham, Alex McEwan, Dave Anand, Nigel Turner, Nick Whear, Claire Mealing, Barry Hadden, Robert J. Marlowe, Ian Thwaites, Gerry Madden, Tracy Smith, Lynn Madeley, Clive Woolfe, Janet Martin, Steve Keauffling, Jeff Greenwood, Amanda Streatfeild, Greville Waterman, Lee Carson, Steve Caplan, Rebecca Roberts, Max Wiseberg (who, lest we forget, is already a major character in *Corrupted*), Chris Glasbey, Ian Jacobs, David Lister, Rebecca Roberts, Judith Blake, Maria Truscott, Alan Humphries, Diana Dunn, Susie Woodward, Pat Gowdie, Susan Graham (Chisholm), John Caplin, Polly Dymock, Steve Frewin, Lee Watkinson, Charlene Capodice, Hilary King, Malcolm Sunley, Bernadette (Bernie) Rowe, Susan Baines, Anthony Holt, Vivien Saunderson, Karin Schlüter Lonegren, Peter McCann, Rob Abbott, Mike Walker, Ian Martin, Sue Hancock, Marc Nagel, Glenys Steedman, Caroline Sargisson, Alexander Avidan, Russ Powell, Graham Carr, Bill McAllister, Karen Goring, Tony Papanicolaou, Lesley Cox, Phil and Sandy Chapman. Jon de Gray, Pauline Wilcock, John Harvey, Jane Bromfield, Anne Nurse, Jill Doyle, Rory O'Mara, Phil Mitchell, Mark Dempsey, Linda Leary, Peter and Susan Amies, Ian Worthington, Penny Hacking, Vince Weldon, Karen Ingless, Russ Scott, Sharon L. Faye, Marion Caldwell, David Tate, Joan Hillman, Pam Levy, Dennis Stimpson, Amanda Launchbury-Rainey, Jonathan Baumber, Pam Lidford, Sharon Clarke, Steve Fanthorpe, Tim Hiles, Peter Kuhfeld, Ian Robertson, Maggie Henshaw (on behalf of Elsie Starke), Mark Frey, Doug German, Elizabeth Cytra, Vivianne Atkin, Tim Lane, John Cloney, Mark Dobson, Steve Goodier, Mike Dickinson, Chris Milton, Debbie Barker, Harrison Barker and Nigel Benson.

As always, I thank my beta readers for their insightful comments. Those not already mentioned are David Beckler, Louise Blackburn, John Keane, Peter Barnes, Patricia Cunningham and Charlie Sangster, the very talented members of the South Manchester Writers' Workshop group.

Lastly, as always, my thanks and love go to Elaine, my most loyal fan and always my first reader.

# PART ONE

# CHAPTER ONE

The woman in the witness box sobs. Tears stream down her cheeks. She buries her face in her handkerchief, unable to respond.

Charles Holborne, the barrister facing her across the well of the court, is about to repeat his question, but he looks up from his notes and checks himself.

The packed courtroom falls silent but for the quiet distress of the witness and the scratch of reporters' pens.

After a moment the coroner again asks if the witness would like some time and, again, the woman shakes her head. Charles's impression is that if she were to accept the offer of an adjournment, she might not find the strength to return to the witness box. The poor woman's only function in the proceedings was to identify her daughter's body, and that she has already done. But Charles has further questions.

She gave her details as "Mrs Fairfax, school cook" and judging from the way she speaks, she has little education. To Charles, a Cockney himself, her accent places her origin as just east of London — Essex probably, possibly Kent.

The grief of this simple, dignified woman has affected all the actors in the drama. It is the gold dust sought by the reporters and journalists now thronging the back of the court and, Charles is sure, will feature large in all the morning papers. Even those paying for Charles's attendance, insurers whose aim it is to ensure that she loses her proposed case, no longer believe that this is the opening gambit in a cynical money-making strategy. Whatever might be the motives of Mr Fairfax, stepfather of the deceased girl, or the ambulance-chasing solicitor who sits beside him, the mother is certainly genuine: a grieving woman, doing her best to comprehend the pointless death of her beautiful daughter.

And the girl *was* beautiful; Charles has seen the photographs. Not the ones showing her lying in the corner of a rather grand bedroom, froth on her lips and dead eyes staring at the camera, but those taken only a month earlier on a family holiday. They revealed a slim girl in her early teens on a sandy beach, one hand on her knee as she laughs and points at something out of shot. She sported a bikini and a pixie cut to her blonde hair — she looked like the sort of youngster you might see on a television advert for a wholesome family holiday at Butlin's.

Charles's heart is not in this case — he hates having to trample on a bereaved family's grief — but at the same time he doesn't believe any liability attaches to Gold Management and Talent Ltd, the tenants of the mansion where the dead girl was found or, accordingly, to their insurers. It's Charles's job to bring out the evidence which, it is hoped by everyone on his side of the fence, will halt in its tracks the threatened, unmeritorious claim for damages.

He doesn't anticipate any difficulties. The coroner released to the interested parties a summary of the post-mortem report produced by the pathologist, and all the signs are that the girl died from a heroin overdose. Charles fully anticipates a verdict of "death by misadventure".

He sees the flow of tears ebbing. Mrs Fairfax blows her nose, tucks the saturated hanky into her handbag, takes out another just in case and lifts her blotchy face to Charles.

'I'm sorry,' she says. 'Could you repeat the question, please?'

When Charles speaks, he does so in even gentler tones than those he was already using. 'You told us that you had no idea that Christine had gone to the concert that evening.'

'That's right. We knew she was at Karen's for the weekend, but we didn't know what they planned.'

'Karen, her older sister, is eighteen, I believe?'

'Yeah.'

'Can you explain how Christine was found with Karen's identification?'

The woman shakes her head. 'I can only suppose she took it 'cos she was planning on going to a pub. Chrissie looked young ... well, she *was* young, only fifteen, but the two girls looked a lot alike.'

'Had Christine ever done anything like this before?' asks Charles.

Mrs Fairfax hesitates. She answers without looking up, and her voice drops. 'They're very independent.'

'Would you mind explaining that a little? How was Christine independent?'

'Well, from age six she wanted to walk herself to school. When she was twelve she decided to decorate her bedroom herself. I got home from work to find purple paint everywhere. And we were called into school a few times 'cos she was cheeky. Nothing serious. But once Karen moved to London, she used to nag and nag to be allowed to visit her. Karen promised to look after her, so eventually I'd give in and let her go up on the train for the weekend.'

'Do you know if this was the first pop concert Christine ever attended?'

Mrs Fairfax shrugs. 'I dunno.'

'Do you know if she ever had contact with pop stars in this way, before that night?'

'I couldn't tell you. We used to ask what she and Karen got up to, over the weekend, but...' Her voice falters again and she shakes her head.

Charles feels even more sorry for her than he did before. Mrs Fairfax is obviously struggling with the knowledge that she gave her independent-minded teenager too much freedom, and disaster followed.

'Just one last issue. Were you aware that Christine was a fan of Johnny Blaise?'

Mrs Fairfax nods. 'Yeah. Her bedroom's covered with his posters.'

'And that didn't worry you?'

Mrs Fairfax frowns. 'Why would it?'

'Well, the Hellraisers have quite a reputation, for booze and drugs, smashing up hotel rooms, that sort of thing.'

'Yeah, maybe, but this was a teenage crush,' replies Mrs Fairfax defensively. 'She just liked their music.'

'So if she managed to meet him at the stage door after the concert, or perhaps in some other way, it wouldn't be surprising if she accepted an invitation to go back to his place for a party afterwards?'

'I suppose not.' She looks up and adds, with defiance, 'But she'd never take drugs. Never! She was just a kid, and needles terrified her.'

'Thank you, Mrs Fairfax. I'm sorry I've had to ask you these questions.'

Charles nods to the coroner and resumes his seat. There is a stirring in the court, as if the one hundred or more observers have let out a collective breath held for the last ten minutes.

'Dr Benson?' says the coroner, addressing a man sitting on the bench behind Charles. Benson is the Home Office pathologist tasked by the coroner to carry out the post-mortem. 'Would you like to come forward and take the oath, please?'

The man rises. He is in his sixties and wears a three-piece suit, a dark blue bow tie and gold-rimmed glasses. He carries a file under his arm. As the oath is administered Charles leafs through his papers to find the summary of Benson's findings.

'Now,' starts the coroner. 'You are Dr Adrian Benson, yes? And you are a pathologist on the Home Office-approved list, practising from St George's Hospital, is that right?'

'Yes, sir. I have held that position for twelve years and have been medically qualified for twenty-nine.'

'Thank you. Now, on the twentieth of July I asked you to conduct a post-mortem for the court. Detective Inspector Pilcher has already given evidence that the body was found the previous day, at around four in the morning, in a bedroom at Kingston Grange, Kingston upon Thames, where Mr Blaise and his entourage were staying, and where this party was apparently held. Please could you summarise your findings?'

'Certainly, sir.' Dr Benson consults his notes. 'The body delivered to the hospital was that of a girl in her mid-teens who at that time was identified as Karen Bailey, date of birth second of January 1951, which would have made her eighteen years of age. My initial evaluation of the body was that it was of a younger woman, and we now have confirmation from Mrs Fairfax and from dental records that the deceased was in fact Christine Bailey, Karen's younger sister, born twenty-second of March 1954, which made her fifteen. When I first saw the body it was in the pathology suite at St George's Hospital, and was unclothed. The evidence I received from the police indicated that when the body was discovered it was in the same state of undress.'

'Leaving aside the blood analysis, to which we will turn in a moment, did you discover anything of note about the body?'

'Yes, sir, I did. It was apparent that the deceased had engaged in sexual intercourse. Samples taken for analysis revealed semen and a small quantity of blood.'

Charles looks up sharply and there is an audible gasp from Mrs Fairfax, who is now sitting towards the back of the court. A few seconds later the sound of renewed sobbing is heard. This is new evidence to Charles and, apparently, to the family.

One of the aspects of coronial law Charles finds most unsatisfactory is the fact that the usual rules of evidence do not apply, and each coroner approaches his task differently. A tiny minority, usually the practising lawyers amongst them, give the interested parties full disclosure of all evidence they have collected prior to the inquest. The vast majority, however, offer little or nothing. They guard their inquisitorial function jealously and treat other parties as unwelcome guests in their court or, worse still, observers who should be seen and not heard. Quite often Charles has had to resort to threats of judicial review even to be permitted to question a relevant witness.

'What did you conclude?' the coroner asks.

'The analysis, together with mild bruising and inflammation and a recently torn hymen, all suggested that the deceased engaged in sexual intercourse shortly before death and, probably, was a virgin prior to that.'

'Very well. Had she suffered any injuries that would have contributed to her death?'

'No, sir, unless you count the injection site. There was a puncture mark in the left antecubital fossa, in other words, the inside of her left elbow.'

'Did you carry out blood analysis?'

'Yes. She had ninety milligrams of alcohol per one hundred millilitres of blood. That is slightly over the legal limit for driving, which is eighty milligrams of alcohol. She was a slender young woman and therefore one might reasonably conclude that she would have been quite severely intoxicated unless, perhaps, she drank frequently and had a higher than expected alcohol tolerance.'

'Thank you. Anything else?'

'Yes. The lab found heroin metabolites in the deceased's blood, together with free morphine of zero-point-one milligrams per litre.'

'And what does that tell us, please?' asks the coroner.

'In layman's terms, it means that the deceased took intravenous heroin, probably no more than two hours before death. Furthermore, although that amount of morphine is certainly enough to cause an overdose, it is unusual. So, someone more habituated to the drug would be unlikely to die from that quantity.'

'Were there any other signs that death arose from heroin use?'

'Yes. She had miosis, that is, her pupils were extremely constricted. Heroin also causes respiration to be depressed, so breathing is impaired and a frothy fluid accumulates in the lungs, the airway and the mouth. I found some frothy liquid in the mouth, but a relatively small amount. Lastly, there was mild cyanosis. That is a blueish tint to the skin caused by a lack of oxygen in the blood, or hypoxaemia. That too arises from respiratory depression.'

'So, all these signs would indicate that she had taken heroin and died as a result of an overdose, correct?'

'Yes, sir. But it is a little more complex than that. I need to return to my dissection findings.' The pathologist leafs back several pages and runs his finger down his notes. 'Yes, here we are. I found an unusual pattern of bruising on the upper and lower left arm. Rather than show you the photographs, which might be a little distressing, I made a sketch last night. May I hand it up?'

'Yes, please.'

'My assistant has made some copies,' adds Benson, and he hands a sheaf of papers to the usher, who distributes a copy to each of the advocates.

Benson continues. 'You will see four small round bruises on the outer aspect of the left forearm, and another, slightly larger, at the same position but on the inner aspect.'

'They look like fingerprints,' comments the coroner.

'Exactly so, sir. These indicate that someone gripped the arm, that is the arm into which the hypodermic was inserted, hard enough to cause bruising. That must have occurred before death. I found similar, although less characteristic, bruising on the wrist of the right arm. One cannot be certain, but it seems likely to me that the deceased's upper limbs were forcibly restrained.'

'Does that mean that this young girl was subjected to violence? An assault?' asks the coroner, apparently also surprised at the turn of the evidence.

Charles notices a change in the quality of the silence in the courtroom. The death of an underage girl from a drugs overdose at a party at the home of a well-known American rock star on the verge of world fame is a big enough story in itself. The newspapers have been full of it for weeks. But the suggestion that the death might not, after all, have been an accident, is breathtaking. This will be worldwide news.

'It's impossible to be certain beyond reasonable doubt, but that is a possibility. She definitely died from the heroin overdose. However, the pattern of bruising suggests that she might have been held down while the injection was administered.'

The coroner pauses to make a note of what he has just been told. His puts his pen carefully down on the desktop and rubs his face with both hands as if suddenly tired. He says nothing for almost a minute.

'Very well. Mr Niblett?' The solicitor acting for the family stands. 'Any questions for this witness?'

'No, thank you.'

'Mr Holborne?'

Charles also stands. 'I don't think so, sir.'

'Thank you. In those circumstances I have no alternative but to adjourn these proceedings. All the evidence will be passed to the police for further investigation and prosecution, if there is to be one. Inquest adjourned *sine die*.'

Charles feels a tap on his shoulder. He turns. Sitting on the bench behind him is the young solicitor instructing him. Both he and Charles are being paid by the insurers of Gold Management and Talent Ltd, Johnny Blaise's UK promoters and managers.

This lad looks little more than a teenager himself and Charles has already established that this is his first court appearance since qualifying. When a senior counsel like Charles is being instructed, it is usually thought only necessary to send a junior to support him. On many occasions Charles's "support" has been an untrained dogsbody from the solicitor's office who knows absolutely nothing about the case and even struggles to make a note of the evidence.

'What's that mean?' asks the young man.

'It means,' whispers Charles in reply, 'that Christine Bailey might have been murdered.'

'That's bad news for the clients, right?' offers the young man.

Charles does not dignify that contribution with a response.

# CHAPTER TWO

The home of Bobby Gold is a large, draughty and chaotic house in Brixton in need of renovation. It is, now and always, full of noise, music and the smell of dill and paprika, so characteristic of western Romanian cooking. Gold, born Florian Popescu, arrived in Manchester in 1948 with Mihaela, his eighteen-year-old girlfriend, having decided to sidestep Gheorghiu-Dej's secret police and start again in the West. He had the heart of a capitalist and Romania was not the place for a boy with dreams such as his.

The couple, known as "Bobby" and "Mickey" for the duration of their twenty-year marriage, now have two entirely English daughters, Jessica and Susannah, fourteen and twelve respectively, who presently sit at the long breakfast table in the house's enormous kitchen, talking loudly and excitedly.

In addition to the Gold parents and children, the household includes Bobby's nephew, Dragos, a more recent immigrant to Britain, and a diverse and fluctuating group of musicians. The Golds frequently give house room to waifs and strays of the music industry and one such, sporting shoulder-length hair, torn jeans and unnecessary round-framed sunglasses, is presently entertaining the girls while finishing his lunch. Another is upstairs in the attic room, still sleeping off the previous night's excesses. Sitting at the far end of the table is a large middle-aged man with deep rings under his eyes, quietly drinking a mug of tea.

Bobby enters the kitchen wearing a white three-piece suit, a gold medallion and an open-necked white shirt. He is carrying a leather attaché case and rifling through the documents inside, apparently looking for something. He is a small man, no more than five foot five, with broad shoulders and a large square head.

'What time will you be back?' asks Mickey from the stove, where she is stirring a pot of mămăligă, polenta Romanian-style. Bobby looks up and snaps the attaché case closed, satisfied that he has all he needs. 'It's not those horrible Hellraisers, is it?'

'They aren't all horrible. Johnny's a proper gent. You shouldn't believe all you read in the newspapers.'

'I don't. I'm getting it from the horse's mouth,' replies his wife, nodding at Bobby.

'Well, you needn't worry. I'm taking the boys from Willesden, to see if I can get them on. And, to answer your question, I'll be back late.'

'It's a long way to go on spec. And the girls are back at school tomorrow morning.'

'I know, but I've heard that Aynsley Dunbar's vocalist's lost his voice. The venue doesn't know yet, so I'm hoping I can get The Dose on to fill the spot. I'm taking a load of singles too. It's a good opportunity. And there's someone I want to see.'

Mickey shakes her head, her wooden spoon still stirring. 'They don't deserve you, those louts.'

'They're okay. Just young.' Gold looks at his watch. 'Did Dragos get off on time?'

'Yes. I've never seen him so smart. Did you buy him that suit?' Gold is not concentrating on his wife, and doesn't respond. 'Bobby?'

'Eh? Oh, the suit. Yes. He can't go to the coroner's court in T-shirt and jeans.'

'I still think you should have gone,' says Mickey.

Gold shrugs. 'The lawyers said I wasn't needed, and you know how busy it is. Dragos'll report back. Listen, I must go. Ready, Stan?'

The big man at the end of the table knocks back the dregs of his tea and rises. He picks up the car keys beside him. 'Ready, boss.'

'Wait a moment,' orders Mickey. 'Jess, come and stir this, please.'

The older girl leaves the table and takes the spoon from her mother's hand. Mickey crosses the cracked floor tiles and goes to a large ancient refrigerator in the corner of the room. She opens it, takes out something wrapped in foil and hands it to Stan.

'What's this?' asks the big man.

'Sandwiches.' She nods at her husband. 'I know what he's like. He'll have you in the limo all day, and you won't get so much as a bite of food.'

'Thanks, Mrs G,' he replies, and he bends to kiss her cheek.

'You coddle him,' says Gold.

'No more than anyone else,' replies Mickey, taking over stirring duties again. 'Drive safe.'

'Have you managed to get hold of Sean yet?'

It is early evening in Clerkenwell, on the opposite side of London.

Sally calls down the stairs to Charles as he closes the front door behind him. These are the first words she has addressed to him since they parted that morning. It's also the first thing she has said to him on every occasion he has returned home over the last week.

The inquest having adjourned early, Charles decided to head back to Chambers and deal with the growing pile of paperwork on his desk. He got engrossed in a difficult medical negligence case and left the Temple much later than he had planned.

He hangs up his coat and calls up. 'Had a nice day, dear?' His sarcasm is good-natured.

'Yes, thanks, Charlie,' she calls back. 'And?'

Instead of answering, Charles puts his briefcase down on the hallway floor and climbs the stairs towards his partner's voice. On the first-floor landing he passes Greta, Leia in her arms, on her way down to the kitchen. The Swedish nanny stops long enough to allow Charles to kiss his daughter and inhale the scent of her freshly washed hair. Greta winks at him. Ever diplomatic, she senses another difficult discussion and is making space for her employers to have it.

Charles finds Sally in their bedroom on the top floor, having apparently had a shower. She is wrapped in a towel, hair wet and skin pink from the hot water. Charles lifts her bathrobe off the hook on the bedroom door and holds it open for her. She discards her towel and moves to put her arms into the robe but, as she does so, Charles steps back, out of reach.

'Don't play silly buggers, Charlie. I ain't got the patience for it. Now, what's the answer?'

Charles moves in close and holds open the robe. She inserts her arms and he hugs her from behind.

'I tried him twice,' he says softly into her ear. 'As far as I can tell he's still with the regional crime squad 'cos they're still taking messages for him, but he's never available. Have you thought of calling Irenna?'

'She's on nights. And you know what it's like at Chancery Court in the afternoons. It's completely manic, and by the time she's up and about I can't spare the time. In any case, you're asking her fiancé, not her. You need to speak to Sean.'

Sally is the senior clerk of Charles's former chambers in the Temple and manages a team of four clerks and, now, almost forty barristers. The afternoon is when court diaries and returns are managed and fees are negotiated. Sally will spend almost all of that time on the telephone.

'I'm trying,' protests Charles.

'Try harder. Or write him a letter,' suggests Sally, disengaging and reaching for a hairbrush. 'At least we'll be sure he's got the message.'

Charles sits on the bed, watching her. He still thanks his lucky stars every time he sees her afresh, even when they've only been apart for the working day.

Sally has almost completely regained her pre-pregnancy shape — what Charles calls her "old-fashioned" figure, hourglass-shaped and voluptuous; not for him the current generation of skinny waifs such as Twiggy, Farrow and Shrimpton. He wonders idly, but without much optimism, if they might get to bed early. So far the demands of maternity combined with working full-time (even with the assistance of a part-time nanny) have meant that the second Sally's head hits the pillow, she is asleep.

'You can get that out of your head too,' she says, reading his mind, ''cos I'm not in the mood. We need this sorted.'

'I know, I know.'

'And we've already lost the best of the weather. I'm beginning to wonder if you've persuaded Sean to disappear.'

'Why would I do that?'

'To buy time. It's always the same with you, Charlie Horowitz. You and commitment are like oil and water: they don't mix.'

They are planning to marry before the end of the month — a small registry office affair — and Charles wants Sean Sloane as his best man. The problem is, they haven't been able to reach him, which is unusual. The detective was working with Superintendent Read's team out of Savile Row in central London but, despite shift patterns and long hours, he and Charles always found time for a weekly pint and a game of snooker. Charles can't remember a period this long when Sloane's been uncontactable.

'I hope you're joking,' he says, his soft brown eyes registering some surprise.

'Of course I am,' she says, sitting next to him on the bed. She reaches over and brushes a wayward curl from his forehead. His hair is still glossy and dark but there is an increasing amount of grey. 'But this is so frustrating! I need to make plans.' She pauses. 'Look,' she says, more gently, 'I know how close you two are. Believe me, I do. You saved his life, he saved yours, all that.'

'Well, then.'

'But if you can't reach him, the solution's obvious: go back to Plan A and ask David.'

This has also been discussed before. Sally is worried that Charles's brother will be hurt when he's overlooked for the role of best man, and she doesn't believe Charles has thought it through sufficiently.

'David'll be fine,' replies Charles. 'If it was a synagogue wedding, then yes, obviously I'd ask him. But a non-religious service at a registry office? I'm not even sure he'd consider it a proper marriage. You know how important the Jewish thing is for him.'

'You're wrong,' she answers, firmly. 'But right now that's not the issue. If you want Sean, then you need to ask him. And soon.'

'I agree. I suppose I could pop down, after we've eaten.'

27

'Good idea,' says Sally, standing. 'Right. If you'll read Leia a story, I'll start on supper.'

While Charles settles his daughter in his lap and re-opens *The House at Pooh Corner*, a little over one hundred and twenty miles north, Bobby Gold waits at a table at Mothers nightclub in Erdington, Birmingham.

Gold gave his name to a guy behind the bar ten minutes earlier, but nothing seems to be happening. Fans lining the bar, waiting impatiently for the support band to finish its soundcheck, seem to find his appearance comical, as they have been staring at him, pointing and laughing. One of their number is presently imitating his slightly grandiose strut.

Finally the barman returns and directs Gold to a door leading backstage. With some relief, he heads through it. He is presented with a short corridor and three doors opening off it. He walks past two empty dark rooms. The last door is open and lit and there, behind a small desk, sits the young bearded DJ he has come to see.

The DJ has long hair at the back of his head and a prematurely receding hairline at the front. His name is John Peel.

Peel returned from a decade working in the US with a big reputation and secured a late-night slot at a pirate radio station. When the BBC belatedly realised that the world had changed and that without its own dedicated pop programmes it would be left behind, the only people with the required expertise were the pirates. With some trepidation, Peel was hired.

In the two years since, his rise has been meteoric. He now fronts Top Gear, the BBC's flagship music show, and is considered by many (particularly himself) to be the high guru of the British music scene. When he says a new band will be the next "Big Thing", it is invariably a self-fulfilling prophecy.

Gold knocks on the open door.

'Mr Peel?' he asks.

Peel looks up and his eyes widen at the sight of Gold. A slight smirk bends his lips. The Bold meeting the Bald. Gold swallows more irritation. This is an opportunity he can't afford to waste by losing his rag. Tonight's headliners, Group Therapy, are supported by Deep Purple. Gold, who prides himself on knowing everyone worth knowing, knows their manager. A slim connection, but sufficient to get him through the door or, at least, a foot in it.

'I listened to the tape,' says Peel, coming straight to the point. He speaks with a soft Liverpudlian accent, but something about it sounds odd and Gold wonders if it's fake or, perhaps, exaggerated.

'Well? They're fantastic, right?'

Peel is running through stapled sheets of paper — a set list, guesses Gold — striking through some entries and amending others. It takes him a moment to reply. 'I did like them, actually,' he says in his soft, downbeat voice. 'But there's no way the Beeb'll let me play 'em.'

'Why not?'

'With a name like that? I can do pretty much what I want, but there are limits.'

'The Dose? It's just a name. What about The Lovin' Spoonful, for heaven's sake?'

'It's not just the name. The title of the single is "Was It You?"'

'What's wrong with that?'

'Mr Gold,' replies Peel patiently, 'it's a revenge song aimed at the girlfriend who gave him the clap.'

Gold shrugs. 'That's what the kids sing about now. What about "Why Don't We Do It in the Road?" or "Happiness Is a Warm Gun"?'

'That's the Beatles, and different rules apply. Sorry. I'll keep an ear open for The Dose, if they record something a little less … provocative. Sorry you've had a wasted journey.'

'We were coming up anyway. I've got the lads outside. We're on our way to the Golden Eagle in Hill Street.'

'You're not playing there tonight, are you? They've got Aynsley Dunbar and a support act.'

Gold smiles. 'They do. But I hear Aynsley's a no-show. His vocalist's lost his voice.'

Peel shakes his head, but smiles. 'You're a trier, I'll give you that. Good luck.'

# CHAPTER THREE

After they've eaten and Leia is settled for the night, Charles changes out of his suit into jeans and a T-shirt and jumps in the car.

It's dusk, a rare night of warmth and clear skies. For the first time in a long while he wishes he were not in the Rover. It's a lovely car, quiet and comfortable, but at times like these he misses his battered Austin Healey convertible, sold a couple of years ago when Sally demanded something more reliable.

Sean and Irenna live on the third floor of a faded Georgian terrace in Notting Hill, a two-minute walk from Portobello Road market. All the housing in these streets has been divided and sub-divided into multiple-occupation apartments and the area is generally run-down, but it's one of the most vibrant in London. Charles loves it. It houses the largest West Indian community in the capital and is increasingly popular with trendy young people. Particularly at this time of year, life is lived on the streets. Cruising in the sportscar through Notting Hill with the top down, catching snatches of Caribbean music from shops and stalls — almost all still open — and savouring the cooking smells from doors and windows, always lifted his spirits.

As soon as he hits Notting Hill Gate he opens the driver's window, slows down and immediately, from the open door of Musicland, hears the voice of Marvin Gaye explaining that he is, apparently, too busy thinking 'bout his baby and he ain't got time for nothin' else. Charles hums along.

He pulls up outside Sloane's building. Half a dozen young West Indian lads are sitting and smoking on the flight of stone steps leading to the front door. The door itself is, as always, open. Charles climbs out of the car.

'Hey, Errol!' he calls, recognising one of the boys. Charles represented the lad's father the previous year. It was a run-of-the-mill case of police corruption — the usual planted drugs and fabricated confession — and Charles was instructed pro bono by the North Kensington Law Centre.

'How tings, boss?' replies the boy, standing and ambling over to the car.

'Great, thanks. Jesus, you're getting tall! How are your parents?'

'Good. Me father started him new work pon de buses.'

'That's great news. Give them my best. Would you mind the car for five minutes? I'm just popping up to see Sean.'

'Sure.'

Charles looks up at the top floor and Sloane's living room, and for a moment there is a suggestion of movement from behind the drawn curtain. He manoeuvres between the youths still sitting on the steps and enters the building. He passes half a dozen doors on his way to the top floor, different conversations, music and cooking smells emanating from each.

Reaching his friend's flat, he knocks on the door. There is no reply and no sound from within.

'Sean?' he calls through the closed door. He waits a few seconds and knocks again. 'Sean?'

Still no response.

Charles considers the envelope in his hand. He really wanted to speak to Sloane rather than leave a letter but, with no other option, he bends and slips the envelope under the door. He waits to see if his action might cause the door to open. When it doesn't, he turns and retraces his steps down to the street. Errol is leaning against his car.

'Not dere?' he asks.

'I thought I saw someone at the window from down here, but I must've been mistaken. They're still living there, right? Sean and the doctor?'

'Me nuh see dem fi a day or two but, sure, me tink so.'

'Okay, thanks,' says Charles and, taking a final look up, he gets back in his car.

Sloane watches through a crack in the curtains as Charles pulls away from the kerb, executes a neat U-turn, and heads back the way he came.

'Well?' asks Irenna from the far side of the room.

'He's gone.'

'He's your best friend, Sean.'

'I'm aware of that, and I hate doing it.'

'But you can trust him.'

Sloane shakes his head. 'He's still got one foot in the East End criminal fraternity.'

'Not since the Krays went down,' protests Irenna. 'You're being unfair.'

'Okay. Perhaps not one foot, but a toe certainly.'

'You can trust him,' she repeats.

'The inquest's over. It won't be long now.'

The tall Irishman moves away from the window and picks up the envelope left by Charles. 'Put the light on, will you, sweetheart?'

She does so. 'Well?' she asks again.

'I'll be damned,' mutters Sloane to himself.

'What?'

'He wants me to be his best man.'

'When?'

'Soon.'

'Oh yes? And how are you going to manage that?'

It is well past midnight when Bobby Gold's white limousine cruises back into Soho. He has already dropped the band off at their new home. The gig went well, and they are all happy and buzzing.

The Willesden house, one of several used by Gold to house his young charges, is a bit tatty, but he doubts The Dose will notice. Only one of them, the bassist, is over the age of twenty and none has lived away from home before. The first time Gold returned to the property, three days after the band moved in, he couldn't believe his eyes. Every cup, plate and saucepan had been used and left, unwashed, on a surface. The living room was littered with beer cans, overflowing ashtrays and vinegary fish and chip paper. Not one bed was made and, despite the availability of wardrobes, the belongings of all five members looked as if they'd simply been tipped onto the floors. None of them apparently knew how to flush a lavatory. The better he knew The Dose, the more appropriate their name seemed to him.

The car passes the 2i's Coffee Bar on Old Compton Street and, on a whim, Gold leans forward.

'Stan?'

'Yes, boss?'

'Pull over, will you?'

The driver slows and moves into the kerb. 'Everything all right, boss?'

'Yeah, fine. The 2i's still open and I'm going to pop in and see who's playing. Want to come? If not, you can get off home.'

'What about you?'

'I'll walk to Denmark Street and kip on the couch. I don't want to wake Mickey and the kids, and I've got an early morning meeting anyway.'

Stan brings the limousine to a halt. 'If it's all the same to you, boss, I'll head off. What time do you want me tomorrow?'

'Midday will do. The Wild Boys have a recording session booked at two, so we'll go wake them.'

'Want me to collect Todman from Kingston?'

'No, he'll meet us at Abbey Road. I want the cover shots done there.'

Gold gets out of the car. For a heavy, thickset man, he moves surprisingly lightly on his feet. 'See you tomorrow.'

He walks back up Old Compton Street and opens the door to the café. Only a couple of tables are occupied on the ground floor, but music comes from below.

The 2i's is a London institution. It has a tiny basement stage which, for a while, was home to a selection of skiffle bands who queued to take its open-mic slots and play for fun. Then, as rock 'n' roll became more popular, it started to attract a much larger and hipper clientele. There was frequently a crowd hanging about on the pavement waiting to get in. Dozens of acts who are now well-known were discovered there, including Tommy Steele, Adam Faith, Cliff Richard, Joe Brown and Georgie Fame. TV and film actors, poets and musos, as well as celebrity criminals like the Krays started frequenting the 2i's, and it became one of the places to be seen in London. A decade earlier, shortly after Gold moved the family to London to pursue his new career in management, he was told to go to the 2i's and check out the talent on offer. He has since signed three groups and a female singer, all discovered playing there.

He heads for the staircase leading to the basement when someone calls his name.

'Bobby?'

He turns towards the voice. It's Brenda, one of the young women who work the espresso machine. She is wiping it down, about to close up for the night.

'Yes, love?'

'Some bloke's been all over Soho looking for you. Been in here twice. I don't know what it is, but he says it's bloody important.'

'What's his name? Did he leave a message?'

She shakes her head. 'He was a square, speccy, wore a suit. Said if he didn't get you here he'd leave a note for you at Denmark Street. Told me, if I saw you, you should get round there, soon as.'

Gold swiftly retraces his steps to the door, but Stan and the limo have gone. He reaches for the door handle. 'Thanks, Brenda.'

He strides down Old Compton Street. All the cafés, pubs and shops are closed and in darkness. There is no traffic and few pedestrians. As he walks, he runs through in his mind all of the other groups and artists in his charge who might have got themselves into trouble. Other than the poor girl who overdosed at Blaise's party at Kingston, he comes up blank.

He turns left onto Charing Cross Road and right into Denmark Street. Here, despite the late hour, the lights are still on in half the buildings, and even now he can hear a group practising in the basement of number 9, opposite his offices. Tin Pan Alley is to aspiring musicians what Hollywood is to aspiring actors. It's a magnet for every wannabe pop and rock star in the country.

He finds the door locked. There are only four people with the main door key: himself, Mickey, Butcher, his chief plugger and office manager, and Dragos, the office junior. He unlocks the door, lets himself in and re-locks it. The ground floor is where the receptionist and typists sit. It's in darkness, and he can see that the basement door, beyond which expensive musical instruments are often kept overnight, is still padlocked. He climbs the stairs, passing framed billboards and black-and-white photos of his twenty-year stage career as he ascends. The first floor houses the obligatory piano and the second, the pluggers. He continues climbing to the top where his own office and occasional bed is situated. Before he reaches the door he sees faint light shining from his office. He looks through the window before opening the door.

Dragos is asleep on the couch. It was Brenda's description of the suit which misled him; he had momentarily forgotten that the boy now owned one.

Dragos couldn't have been deeply asleep because as Gold opens the door he sits up.

'*Bună, unchiule,*' he says in Romanian, rubbing the sleep from his eyes. '*Te-am căutat peste tot.*'

'English, Dragos, English! How many times do I have to tell you?'

At Christmas 1965 Bobby's younger brother and his wife were killed in a car accident in Romania, leaving their thirteen-year-old son, Dragos, an orphan. A meeting was convened in Bucharest with the extended family to decide what should happen to the teenager. Bobby and Mickey couldn't attend but they offered to take over parental responsibility if Dragos could be got to England. The Romanian government seemed to have no objection and granted an exit visa, and Dragos arrived in London shortly thereafter. A bright boy, his English is now almost perfect but, particularly at the end of the day when he's tired, he prefers Romanian.

'Sorry. I thought it's okay when it's just the two of us.'

'At home, if you must, but not outside. It's no good for business. So?'

'I've been looking for you everywhere.'

'What's the matter? Is Mickey okay? The girls?'

'Yeah, yeah, it's nothing like that. It's that case today, the inquest. They reckon she might've been murdered.'

'What? The lawyers said it was an overdose, death by misadventure.'

'Yeah, I know, but it wasn't. All sorts came out, boss! I was there early and got a seat. No one knew who I was. Right at the end, when everyone had gone, I was in the loo and the copper doing the investigation came in with someone else. They didn't see me. So, they was there, you know, having a piss, and I heard that copper, DI Pilcher, say they was going to arrest *you*.'

Gold has come to a halt just inside the office door, stunned. 'Me? No, you've got it wrong.'

'No, boss, I haven't. I heard him clear as day.'

'But ... I don't understand.'

The boy shrugs.

Gold walks to his desk, sits heavily in the chair and stares out of the window at the night sky, thinking.

'Shall I make you a coffee?' asks Dragos.

Gold doesn't answer for a moment. Then, belatedly realising that his nephew has spoken, he shakes his head. 'No thanks. Go home. I'll take it from here.'

'Righto. What're you gonna do?'

'Don't you worry, son. Get off home. And be quiet when you go in.'

Dragos collects his suit jacket and departs. Gold looks at his watch, picks up the telephone and dials. He waits. It takes more than thirty seconds before the phone is picked up at the other end.

'Victor?' he asks. 'It's Bobby … Florian.' He hears a man clearing his throat at the other end. 'I'm sorry to call so late, but it's an emergency.'

'Mickey all right? The girls?'

'They're fine, thank God. But I need some help.'

'At two in the morning?'

'You're the only solicitor I know.'

'Wait a minute.' Gold hears movement at the other end, the sound of a lamp being illuminated and a woman's voice. 'Okay, what's happened?'

'You remember that case in the papers about Johnny Blaise? The fan who died at a party?'

'Yes.'

'The inquest was today. The coroner thinks it might've been murder, and the police are going to arrest me.'

'What did you do?'

'I hope you're joking! Nothing! But I need a solicitor. Can you get down here?'

'When?'

'As soon as possible.'

'But, Bobby, I don't do crime.'

'Yes, you do! You told me all about that theft case.'

'It was shoplifting! And I told you about it because it was the only criminal case I've done in ten years. I can't represent you on a murder! Apart from anything else, you're my cousin.'

'I know. That's why I called you. You're the only solicitor I trust.'

'Bobby, it's always a very bad idea to represent someone in the family. Believe me, it causes nothing but trouble. If it goes wrong, no one ever speaks again.'

'If it goes wrong, Victor, you won't be speaking to me again anyway. Please, I'm begging you. Come down and help me through this. It's all a load of nonsense. I had nothing to do with it.'

Gold listens to his cousin's breathing at the other end of the line as he thinks.

'Wait a moment,' says Victor eventually. 'Didn't you tell me those insurers of yours hired a barrister for the inquest?'

'Yes, but I never met him. I don't know him from Adam.'

'What's his name?'

'I don't know. Holroyd? Holding? Something like that.'

'Not Holborne? Charles Holborne?'

'Yes, that's it. Charles Holborne.'

'Do you know who he is?' asks Victor.

'Haven't a clue.'

'Then let me tell you. Firstly he's good, very good. Should be in silk already. His name's in the press all the time. His real name is Charlie Horowitz. He grew up in the East End, a Jew, very clever, but from a poor family. He served with the British in the war, got a decoration and then a place at Oxford or Cambridge or somewhere. I can't believe you don't know this.'

'Why would I know? I'm a song and dance man, not a lawyer. Anyway, I don't need a barrister. You'll do it fine.'

'Sorry, Bobby, but I won't. I don't have the skills. This barrister already knows the case. He's perfect! If you let me instruct him as counsel, I'll do what I can. Otherwise, you'll have to look elsewhere. Now, let me get back to sleep.'

# CHAPTER FOUR

Charles opens the front door of his home on Wren Street, looks out and considers the weather. It looks promising. It is chilly — autumn is just around the corner — but he decides to chance it. Shouting a final goodbye to those within, he leaves his raincoat and hat on the hook by the front door, and steps outside.

He heads south down Gray's Inn Road and then Chancery Lane. There are several entrances to the Temple on its northern boundary, and Charles likes to vary the route to his workplace by using a different one each day. He grew up in the deprived East End and, twenty years into his career, he still experiences a thrill every time he walks from the bustling twentieth-century streets into the peaceful courtyards and tended gardens of the Temple. Here he is surrounded by English history. His desk sits in a building named in the works of Dickens and, on days when he is not in court, he dines under a magnificent hammerbeam roof in a spectacular Tudor hall. He knows how lucky he is.

He crosses Fleet Street at Temple Bar and checks his stride briefly while deciding which entrance to use. Today it will be the gate at the top of Inner Temple Lane. The sound of footsteps on flagstones echoes about him as he strides through the narrow stone tunnel. Above him, now sandwiched incongruously between taller and more modern structures, is the gatehouse to the Honourable Society of the Inner Temple, replete with magnificent balustrade, relief-carved timber frontage and two storeys of leaded light windows — the sole timber-framed Jacobean building in London to have survived the Great Fire.

As he passes Goldsmith Building he is startled by a sudden burst of loud music, an organ accompanying a considerable number of voices. He pauses. The sound is coming from Temple Church. When he is working late, especially on summer evenings, there's nothing he likes more than to open his windows to the gentle breeze blowing off the Thames and to hear the singing of the Temple choir floating over the roofs of Francis Taylor Building. He has never heard them practising this early; perhaps there's a concert coming up.

Charles listens to little choral music but, to his surprise, he recognises this piece. It's Bach's Mass in B Minor, and he knows it because he has actually heard it performed in the "Round", the Temple's round church. Some years earlier, in company with other members of his former chambers and surrounded by stone effigies of the Knights Templar, he attended a candlelit charity performance here. It was magical, and he has never forgotten it. He resolves that, if it's to be performed again, he will try to persuade Sally to come with him. He listens for a minute or two until the music stops abruptly before hurrying on towards Chambers.

He runs up the old oak staircase to the clerks' room and enters. Jennie and Jeremy, the two juniors known throughout the Temple compendiously as "JJ", are already there.

'I tried ringing your home, sir,' says Jeremy.

'Why?'

'New conference this morning.'

'We've just had a call from the secretary to a Mr Victor Serban,' says Jennie. 'He's arriving at Euston in a few minutes for a nine o'clock con.'

'New case?' asks Charles.

'Sort of,' replies Jennie. 'It's for Mr Gold, from yesterday's inquest. The police have already tried to arrest him, but apparently he didn't go home last night. He's also on his way here, although he'll be late.'

At ten past nine Jeremy knocks on Charles's door and shows in a balding man in his fifties with olive-coloured skin and an impressive bushy moustache that hides most of his mouth.

'Mr Holborne, sir, this is Mr Victor Serban, from Berkeley, English and Co. Mr Serban, Mr Charles Holborne of counsel.'

The two men shake hands. 'I understand you've come down from Manchester this morning,' says Charles. 'You must have had an early start. Can we offer you anything?'

'No, thank you. I bought breakfast on the train,' replies the solicitor, 'although only the British could call a sandwich made of buttered cardboard "breakfast",' he adds. He speaks with a Mancunian accent, but there is something else underlying it — Eastern European, thinks Charles.

'Take a seat,' he says. 'I've been told that Mr Gold won't be here for a while. Shall we wait for him?'

'Well, actually, I'm glad we've a few minutes before he arrives. I've no papers for you, I'm afraid, so I need to fill you in on some background.'

'That would be helpful. I do have some questions, like why does Mr Gold think he's wanted by the police? There was no evidence at the inquest to suggest responsibility on his part. That's why I advised he needn't attend.'

'His nephew was in court throughout. He overheard a police officer in the toilets afterwards talking about arresting Bobby for murder.'

'He said that? Murder?'

'That's what he says. Bobby thinks it must be a mistake and can be sorted out in a few minutes. So he plans to walk along the Embankment and simply hand himself in at Scotland Yard.'

'When?'

'This morning. I couldn't dissuade him. I think I should explain, Mr Holborne, that I don't do much crime. Almost none, to be honest. I tried to persuade Bobby to instruct someone who does, but he wouldn't have it.' Serban smiles. 'He's a man of strong opinions and he doesn't trust anyone.'

'But if you don't do crime —'

Serban interrupts. 'I know. I have no suitable experience or qualifications except one: I'm his cousin.'

'Ah. I see.'

'Even then, I agreed to help only if you were instructed.'

'Okay. But I thought he wasn't present at the party where the girl died, right?'

'Not quite. He was at the property, briefly, earlier in the evening, but not when there was any party. The coroner decided not to call him, presumably because, like everyone else, he assumed it was a straightforward drugs overdose. But Bobby doesn't have an alibi for the later part of the evening. He left Kingston Grange at about ten-thirty and went back to his office. He got home very late and slept in the spare room so as not to wake his wife. No one saw him until the following morning.'

'But unless they're going to say he actually injected the girl himself, this won't be an alibi case. The girl and the drugs could have been brought to the property at any time, whether Mr Gold was there or not. It's probably more to do with how they got there. And there must be other more likely candidates, not least everyone who was present at the party when, presumably, drugs were taken.'

'I agree. But Bobby thinks the police are interested in him because he's been in trouble before. He has a rather cynical view of the police — actually, of the whole world. It's out to get him.'

'So he has a criminal record?'

'I don't think so. Not here at least.'

'Not here?'

Serban pauses, staring out of the window. He seems to be deciding how to answer. Charles waits patiently. After a moment Serban addresses him.

'We come from Romania, Mr Holborne. Bobby's birth name is Florian Popescu.'

'Okay,' replies Charles, awaiting more.

'What do you know about Romania after the war?' asks the solicitor.

Charles shrugs. 'Nothing. Except it fell under the sphere of the Soviets.'

'It was, and is, run by the Romanian Workers' Party, the communists. Their secret service, the Securitate, had a worse reputation than the KGB. Thousands disappeared, especially those suspected of being capitalists or having ties to the West.'

'Did that include Mr Gold?'

'My cousin was not politically motivated, but he wanted to make money and he saw no prospect of that at home. He made several attempts to leave. It was a dangerous journey, through Hungary to Austria. If you made it to a safe zone controlled by the Americans or the British, you could apply for asylum. Then you went to a series of refugee relocation centres. It often took months, years.' He looks down and continues softly. 'I myself came via a similar route. My father was killed making the attempt.'

'I'm sorry to hear that,' says Charles sympathetically.

'We were betrayed by a friend to the secret police.' He looks up again. 'Our family do not trust the police.'

'I see,' says Charles. 'And after Mr Gold got here?'

Serban's face brightens and he smiles. 'Have you never heard of Bobby Gold?' Charles shrugs apologetically. 'He used to be on the stage, on the northern variety circuit. He had a great voice and was a wonderful mimic — he sang and danced — but it was really tough to break in. There was a lot of prejudice.'

'Prejudice?'

'This country seems to have problems with foreigners.'

'You don't say.'

'There were a few punch-ups and rumours of his bribing various theatre people to get a foot in the door. He was very determined, and he got a bit of a reputation. He upset a few people. He was dumped by an agent and banned by a couple of the venues following altercations. You've heard of the Manor Boys affair?'

'The pop group?'

'Yes. This was after Bobby set up in London. He discovered them, his first real success. So, the story goes that another manager tried to steal them from him. Told them they weren't being paid enough, Bobby was taking advantage, that sort of thing. Bobby went round to his office with some heavies and hung the man out the fourth-floor window by his ankles.'

'Was he charged?'

'No, the other manager made no formal complaint and the group stayed put. Bobby says the story was exaggerated, but it went round like wildfire. In fact, he encouraged it. It enhances his tough-guy image, so people don't mess with him. I've even heard people claim he carries a gun.'

Charles looks up from taking notes. 'Does he?'

Serban laughs. 'Of course not! Under all the bluster, my cousin's a complete softie. You should see him with his family.'

'I've seen Mafiosi with their families,' points out Charles drily. 'All right. What am I being instructed to do?'

'Come to the police station and make sure Bobby doesn't put his foot in it. As far as he's concerned, a five-minute chat with the police will sort everything out. I told him I wasn't qualified to do it. I'm supposed to be in Manchester County Court to defend a possession action on behalf of a corner shop tenant. That's my practice, mostly conveyancing and a bit of contentious civil work. So, I'm instructing you to accompany us.'

'I don't think both of us can do it. He's entitled to legal representation, but there's nothing to say they have to permit solicitor and counsel.'

'Then it'll have to be you. Is that okay?'

Charles considers for a moment. 'It's unusual, but not unheard of. Pupil barristers sometimes stand in for solicitors on the police rota when they're too busy. It's good marketing. But there are risks.'

'Risks?'

'If there was ever a dispute as to what was said during the interview, the barrister might find himself, or herself I suppose, being called as a witness, which would disqualify them from continuing to act for the defendant.'

'Does that happen often?'

'A dispute over interviews? I don't know what it's like in Manchester, but down here, if an accused isn't represented at the police station it happens on a daily basis. Police routinely make up confessions. But it's less likely with a lawyer present, and I take a decent note. I sometimes ask the interviewing officer to initial it before I leave, which makes it difficult later to fabricate anything. And coppers don't like to get into an argument before a jury with a barrister who has a different account of an interview.'

Serban blows out his cheeks. 'I had no idea.'

'My rule of thumb is never go into a central London police station voluntarily and never without a witness.'

There is a knock on the door.

'Come in,' calls Charles.

Barbara McIntyre, Chambers' senior clerk, puts her head around the door. 'Your lay client has arrived, sir. Shall I show him up?'

Charles raises his eyebrows to the solicitor sitting opposite him, who nods. 'Yes please, Barbara.'

A minute later she opens the door for Bobby Gold, who is carrying a cup of coffee, and introduces him to Charles, who shakes his free hand. Gold is wearing a creased three-piece suit in white which shows signs of having been slept in, and has shadows under his eyes, but he looks as if he has shaved.

'Pull up a chair, please, Mr Gold. Have you had anything to eat this morning? I can send out for breakfast if you like.'

Gold lifts the cup of coffee. 'I got something to eat before I left the office, and your Scottish lady gave me this, thank you.'

Charles had been expecting a trace of the Romanian accent that he detected in Serban, or perhaps some Mancunian, but he hears neither. If Charles had met Gold without knowing anything of his background, he would have imagined him to be a Londoner. He remembers Serban saying that his cousin was a good mimic.

*He's learned to be a chameleon*, thinks Charles, *just as I did.*

'Mr Serban and I have been discussing the dangers of going into police stations in London,' he says. 'I understand you propose surrendering to arrest.'

'I've done nothing wrong. I'm sure it's just a mix-up. The sooner I go, the sooner I can get on with the rest of my week,' says Gold confidently.

'I understand that's your position,' replies Charles, 'but the police don't usually arrest people without grounds. They need reasonable suspicion of an offence. So, we should be prepared. May I ask a few questions first?'

'Sure, fire away.'

'Firstly, this house where the deceased was found.'

'It's a big house in Kingston upon Thames. I have several properties I use for my groups. It's cheaper than hotels, and I can keep an eye on them more easily. This one was bigger than normal, as Blaise has a large entourage and it's a long tour. He needed a semi-permanent base in the UK. And it has a recording studio in the basement.'

'So you rent it?'

'My company does.'

'Is it normal for promoters like yourself to rent accommodation for their groups? One sees photographs in the papers all the time, rock groups pushing through crowds and entering or leaving hotels,' says Charles.

'I don't work the same way as other promoters or managers. With my own groups I provide them with accommodation, transport, drivers, in some cases even a housekeeper or cook. I decide on their look, I buy their clothes, I decide what should be recorded and when, and I book their gigs. All they have to do is roll out of bed into a limousine, be counted in, and do what they do best.'

'That sounds expensive.'

Gold shrugs. 'Not at all. Renting a property is much cheaper than having twelve people on room service at the Hilton. The rest, yes, it's an expense, but it comes out of their end.'

'So they pay for it? Surely they complain?'

'Sure, some do. But I'm breaking my back for them. They've no idea.'

Charles raises a sceptical eyebrow. He knows little about the music industry, but even he has read enough in the *NME* to pick up that many up-and-coming groups complain about being ripped off by their managers and promoters. The Rolling Stones' dispute with their former manager, Andrew Loog Oldham, and later with Allen Klein even made it out of the music press and into the broadsheets.

Gold must have seen his expression, because he starts justifying himself. 'Look, I know the business like no other manager. I was in it myself for twenty years. So I fight like a tiger for them, and I look after them. You need to understand, most of these kids are hopeless, and I've seen it go horribly wrong. Take some scruffy kid from a council estate in Stoke, or Watford, straight out of school sometimes, or off the dole. Never had money. Playing in pubs with his mates for a couple of pints on a Friday. All of a sudden he's rich and famous, living the high life in London, and surrounded by people offering him booze, drugs and sex. Too many of them go off the rails. I've had them turning up at gigs so stoned they can't even lift their instruments. They get arrested. They miss studio time. It's expensive. And there's always trouble with women, or men. In one case, both.'

'Tell him about the Geordie girl,' says Serban. He turns to Charles. 'One of Bobby's early acts died from an overdose. What was her name?'

Gold answers. 'Nicola McDonald. The voice of an angel and, boy, could she write songs! Heartbreaking stuff. I met her when I was still performing. She would've been bigger than Joni Mitchell.' He shakes his head sadly. 'But that one was already lost when I met her, God rest her soul. I never want that happening again. This way I keep some control.'

'And this is what you're doing for Johnny Blaise and the Hellraisers?'

'It's a bit different for them as I'm their European promoter and booking agent, not their label. Their records are produced in the States and shipped over. But I provide accommodation, transport and security. I arrange the advertising, venues and ticketing, and I look after them. Johnny's older than average, but most of the musicians and his group aren't. Nor is Wyatt.'

'Wyatt?'

'Johnny's younger brother. He travels everywhere with them. He does the admin: daily expenses for the crew, the techies and so on. I don't have much to do with him as he reports to the US label.'

'And you operate this system even when you're taking groups to Europe?'

'More or less. I pay for everything that Wyatt doesn't cover — all the major expenses at this end. I take all the risk, and I keep all the profits, if there are any. And I have to pay the American end upfront or they won't let their guy leave the US.'

'Okay, thank you. Now let's talk about this young woman and how she got into the property. At the inquest we heard evidence about fans who hang around the groups. Are they generally allowed into the accommodation?'

'The Grange has tall fences and electric gates, and the security team have instructions to keep the fans out, but it's almost impossible. The musicians are young, but over the age of consent. If they take a fancy to someone at a concert, what can I do? I can't stop them. Sometimes the musicians bring them in, and sometimes the girls sweet-talk the men on the gates.'

'Is it always girls?' asks Charles.

'Depends on the artist, but in Johnny Blaise's case, yes, it's mostly girls.'

'What do they want? Is it merely fame, bragging rights for having slept with one of the musicians?'

'Mostly,' answers Gold. 'Others are just freeloaders, up for a good party. They see these handsome young men in trendy clothes with fame, money, lots of free alcohol and drugs, and want a good time. A few are more mercenary. They're looking for a kiss-and-tell story to sell to *The Mirror*. And a small handful set their sights even higher. They're hoping to be the next Mrs Mick Jagger.'

'I don't suppose you have any idea into which category Christine Bailey fell?'

'No idea. I never laid eyes on the girl. When I left the Grange there was no party. Johnny had gone to bed early and Wyatt was sitting around the lounge smoking and drinking with about a dozen others. It was all pretty tame, actually.'

'Were you at the concert?'

'Yes.'

'So how did you travel back from the venue to Kingston Grange?'

'I should have been in the limo but Stan, my driver, wasn't expecting to pick me up until gone midnight. Then we had all the electrical problems, and the concert ended halfway through. So I came back on the coach.'

'Did you see her there?'

Gold shakes his head. 'No. There were a few random people, and I think one or two of them were girls, but not Christine Bailey. But, remember, there was another bus. She could have been on that.'

Charles makes a note and then looks up. 'Tell me about the drugs.'

Gold sighs. 'It's a bit like the girls. I do everything I can, but it's impossible to stop them getting in.'

'Are we talking about hard drugs like LSD or heroin?'

'Until that young girl died, I'd have said no. I know most of the group smoke weed, and all of them drink, but I've never seen any hard drugs. Cocaine, perhaps, but even that only rarely. Certainly nothing like heroin.'

'But his stage persona,' points out Charles. 'What's the album called ... yes, *Inferno*. He has hair down to his waist, paints his skin black and wears devil's horns.'

'You're obliged to keep this confidential, right?'

'What?'

'It's all an act. And the hair's a wig. Under all that gear he has short blond hair and a perfect complexion. He looks like a high school teacher, the sort of chap you'd bring home to meet the parents.'

Charles smiles to himself and makes a note. 'So you didn't see her at all?'

'No, I was busy. We got back to find there'd been a flood. One of the idiots left a bath running. I helped the housekeeper mop up and then I left.'

'So, if you had nothing to do with her, why are they about to arrest you for her murder? The house was full of potential suspects and yet for some reason they've plumped for you.'

'I don't know,' replies Gold, raising his voice. 'That's why I want to get down there as soon as possible. There's been a mistake.'

'They'll have interviewed everyone at the house. Someone must have pointed the finger at you. Can you think why? Is there anyone with a grudge?'

'Grudge? No. Until all this blew up, this has been one of the smoothest tours I've done.'

Gold looks at the heavy wooden clock on the wall between the two sash windows. 'Look, should we get going?'

'One last question please, Mr Gold. Who do you get to do the security? This fifteen-year-old kid — good family background, no suggestion of involvement in the drugs scene — manages to overdose on heroin in a house leased by you and used by your clients, a bunch of rock musicians with too much money and easy access to drugs. It's odds-on that someone in the house supplied her. We need to find out how.'

'They're called Celeb Security. They do lots of groups, film stars, even politicians. I had my own guys but they didn't have the skills, so I got proper advice from the police.'

'Okay,' says Charles. 'And remind me, who was the officer who took your statement after the body was discovered?'

'A man called Quigley.'

'Rank?'

'Not sure. Detective Chief Inspector, maybe? He's based at Scotland Yard. Can we get going now? I want to nip this thing in the bud as soon as possible, and I've got to be at Abbey Road at twelve.'

'Yes, yes,' says Charles, frustrated by his client's impatience. 'And does Quigley know you're coming?'

'No. I just thought I'd go down…' He tails off as he sees Charles shaking his head.

'He won't be hanging about waiting for you. He could be anywhere.'

'Let's try anyway. The longer I leave it, the more chance it'll leak to the press, and that'd be a disaster.'

'If you just turn up at the desk, you'll be kept waiting for hours, at best interviewed by a junior officer who won't make a decision. You could spend most of the day there.'

'All right then,' replies Gold, somewhat belligerently. 'What do you suggest?'

Charles picks up the phone on his desk. 'Barbara? Please could you put a call through to Scotland Yard and see if you can locate a chap called Quigley, possibly a DCI. If you manage to get him, or anyone involved in the Bailey case, please say I want to speak to them about Mr Gold coming in to be interviewed.' Pause. 'No, don't tell them he's here. We don't want the police turning up mob-handed if we can avoid it. Thank you.'

Charles hangs up. 'Let's see if we can locate Quigley, or at least one of his team.'

They wait, and when it becomes clear that the phone is not going to ring immediately with news, Charles leaves the room to organise further drinks.

Still they wait. Gold paces around the room, examining Charles's law books and complimenting him on the view. Charles comes over to the tall sash windows to look down on the manicured gardens and the choppy waters of the River Thames. They make polite conversation but Gold is becoming increasingly irritable. After a while he asks if he can make some phone calls to rearrange his morning, and Charles allows him to sit in the adjoining room whose usual occupant is out at court.

Just under an hour later the phone on Charles's desk rings and Gold hurries in from next door. Charles picks up. He says little in response to whoever is at the other end, but makes notes before hanging up. He turns to Gold, who has resumed his seat in front of him.

'As I suspected. You'd have had a wasted trip. Quigley's been in court this morning at Lewes, but he's on his way back now and heading to his office at New Scotland Yard. We can meet him there. I suggest you clear your diary for the rest of the day.'

'Already done it. Saw the way the wind was blowing.'

'Good. And it is my very strong advice that you do not answer any questions. None.' Charles raises his hand to forestall Gold's protest. 'I know you want to get this cleared up as soon as possible, but you've no idea what you're dealing with. From *their* perspective they're going to want to tie you down to admissions when they have evidence in their back pockets which will show you to be lying. From *our* perspective, we want to find out what they have. So we listen to the questions, and we say nothing at this stage. Do you understand? No comment.'

# CHAPTER FIVE

Charles and his client walk down the crooked wooden staircases of Chambers. On his way down Charles pauses briefly to put his head into the clerks' room, where Barbara leans in and whispers a few sentences in his ear.

Barbara is teetotal, a Scot, and a woman. Accordingly, she is only an *ex officio* member of "The Mafia", the network of boozy, English and predominantly male criminal clerks responsible for half the barristers' sets in the Temple. Nonetheless, she was able to tap into the organisation's unrivalled knowledge of the runners and riders in the criminal justice system. DCI Quigley, Charles learns from her, is a regional crime officer on detachment to Scotland Yard, and his prestigious secondment arises from a reputation as one of the "Golden Boys" of his generation. He is said to be a diligent and cunning copper, with a spectacular clear-up rate.

Charles thanks her, rejoins his client and leads the way through the Temple and out via Queen Elizabeth's Building to the Embankment. There they turn right and walk parallel to the great river towards New Scotland Yard. Once there, Charles and Gold wait for half an hour in the interview room to which they are shown on arrival. They are offered, but decline, further drinks.

Eventually there is a knock on the door and a tall, thin man enters. He has large sunken eyes and a pale complexion. He wears a black three-piece suit which, together with his demeanour, give the impression of an undertaker.

'I'm Detective Chief Inspector Denis Quigley,' he announces. 'And this —' he indicates a younger man who is at that moment following him into the room — 'is Detective Inspector Pilcher.'

Quigley offers his hand to Gold, which surprises Charles. Gold shakes it willingly. Quigley turns to Charles.

'And you are Mr Gold's solicitor?' he asks.

'Charles Holborne, of counsel,' replies Charles, not offering his hand.

'Counsel?' says Quigley with some surprise. 'Can't say I've come across that before. Your client isn't under arrest, so why would he need a barrister to represent him here?'

'He's entitled to be accompanied by his lawyer, isn't he? I'm that lawyer. I was instructed for the insurers at the inquest, so it was convenient to ask me.'

'I see,' replies Quigley, still frowning. 'Take a seat then, gentlemen.'

Charles and Gold take seats on one side of the small table, with the officers facing them on the opposite side.

'Thank you for coming in. I repeat, Mr Gold, you're not under arrest. You may leave at any time. For the moment you are simply assisting us with our enquiries into the death of Christine Bailey. Do you understand?'

'I'm very keen to help.'

Charles shoots a warning look at Gold. 'I need a moment with my client,' he says.

'We've not even started,' points out Quigley.

'Nonetheless...' says Charles, standing.

The police officers remain in their seats, looking up at him. Charles waits patiently. With evident reluctance, the two men stand.

'We'll be outside,' says Quigley, and he leads his junior officer out. The door shuts.

Charles turns to Gold and whispers, 'Remember what I told you. Assume that anything you give them will be turned against you.'

'But they haven't arrested me,' whispers Gold in return.

'Did they go to your house last night?'

'Yes.'

'They woke up your family?'

'Yes.'

'So that you could *assist with enquiries*? Does that sound likely? Mr Gold, whether you are formally under arrest or not, I strongly advise you to say nothing until we understand what we're dealing with.'

Gold nods reluctantly. 'Okay.'

Charles takes out his notebook and fountain pen, ready to record what's about to be said, and opens the door to allow the officers to re-enter. Everyone retakes their seats.

'Right,' starts Quigley. 'Would you mind telling us where you were on the night of this party, Mr Gold?'

Charles answers. 'Is my client under suspicion of murder?'

'We're asking the same questions of all of the people who were on the premises that night. Someone supplied that young girl with drugs, maybe even administered them.'

'Administered them?' queries Charles. 'You mean someone else injected her?'

'Christine Bailey had no history of drug use. Even dope. It's a big jump from nothing to heroin, so we have to keep an open mind. Mr Gold, where were you that evening?'

Gold does not answer.

'Other witnesses tell us you were at the party.'

'That's not true,' replies Gold. 'There was no party when I left —'

He breaks off as Charles puts a gentle restraining hand on his arm.

Quigley addresses Charles. 'If your client wants to answer the questions and help us sort out what actually happened, why are you so keen to prevent him?'

'I've given my client certain advice, which you are not entitled to hear,' says Charles.

Quigley turns back to Gold. 'Do you know a man named Frankie Perry?'

Gold starts to shake his head but Charles intervenes. 'In what context?'

Quigley ignores Charles. 'It's a simple question, Mr Gold. Do you know anyone named Francis Perry, yes or no? He usually goes by the name "Frankie".'

Gold draws a breath to speak but then sees Charles's stare, and shuts his mouth.

'I don't understand,' continues Quigley. 'You've come in voluntarily and say you'd like to help us with our enquiries but, apparently, you've been told not to answer any questions. How is that helping anyone?'

'In what context do you say Mr Gold might know of this Frankie Perry?' repeats Charles.

The two police officers look at one another. Quigley tries again. 'We have multiple witnesses who say that you hired the security team at Kingston Grange. So you would know the men manning the gates, checking people in and out and so on.'

Gold fidgets in his seat, but does not answer.

Quigley changes tack. 'Can you throw any light on the heroin used at Kingston Grange? How could it have entered the property?'

When Gold doesn't respond, the junior officer, Pilcher, has a go. 'We've all read about beatniks like Mick Jagger and Keith

Richards using drugs,' he says with contempt. 'Is that what it's like at Kingston Grange, Mr Gold? Sex parties and getting high? Have you seen Blaise using drugs? Or members of his group?'

Gold bites his lip.

'You see,' says Pilcher, 'it's your company name on the Kingston Grange lease. You provide the security. We're told that no one and nothing gets in without your approval. And we're told you also provide all the food and booze. So, when a young girl dies of an overdose in the property for which you are responsible, you can see why we need to ask you these questions. How could that have happened without your knowledge?'

Gold looks at Charles.

Quigley tries again. 'It's in your interests to tell us the truth. Mr Holborne here will tell you that the courts are much more favourable to defendants who admit their part early. You're just making things worse for yourself.'

'I don't know anything about it!' blurts Gold. 'I'd never allow drugs into the property. I wouldn't allow fifteen-year-old girls in either!'

'Then how did they get in? Because they did, and Miss Bailey ended up dead.'

Gold looks at Charles, his eyes pleading to be allowed to respond, but Charles shakes his head.

'Maybe,' says Quigley reasonably, 'you were acting on someone else's orders. I imagine these pampered rock stars can be very demanding and you have to keep them sweet. Maybe you didn't know who the drugs were for. Is that it?'

Gold looks down at the desk and manages to remain silent.

The younger police officer tries again. 'You told us you weren't there when the party occurred. So, where were you? If you can show us you were definitely somewhere else, we can eliminate you from our enquiries.'

Charles flashes another warning glance at Gold. He'd intended to repeat to his lay client what he had said to Serban, that this was unlikely to be an alibi case, but he got diverted and hurried out of doing so. Gold holds his tongue.

'I'll give you one last chance to tell us where you were at the relevant time, Mr Gold,' says Quigley, 'but I should warn you that you are not helping yourself by taking this attitude.'

Gold turns to Charles, who shakes his head slightly.

'Very well,' says Quigley. He stands. 'You are free to go for the present. Are you going on tour with Mr Blaise?'

Gold looks at Charles, who nods. 'I would do, normally,' replies Gold.

'When do the band leave the country?'

'Monday week. They've got two more gigs to do here first.'

'Don't leave the country, please, until we've spoken again. We will continue with our enquiries, but we'll certainly need to speak to you further.'

'But I need to go with them. I've organised everything — venues, hotels, transport.'

'If you push me on this, Mr Gold, you will leave me with no choice but to arrest you now on suspicion of murder and confiscate your passport.'

Charles frowns at this. It's bullshit. If Quigley had evidence sufficient for reasonable suspicion that Gold committed murder, he would arrest him now and read him his rights. He certainly wouldn't allow him to retain his passport. Whatever the nephew might have heard at the coroner's court — and Charles is assuming he heard correctly — Quigley has decided to continue getting his soldiers in a row, and that suits Charles.

It gives him some breathing space; preparing Gold's defence will be a lot easier if he's out of custody.

'I'll make sure that Mr Gold understands the position,' he says.

A few minutes later, Charles and his client are escorted out of the building and find themselves on the pavement at Westminster. Gold turns to Charles angrily.

'You should've let me speak.'

'The more you give them, the easier you make their job. Believe me, Mr Gold, it's what any decent criminal lawyer would tell you. Don't say anything until you know what they've got.'

Gold takes a deep breath. 'Well, what now?'

'Is Mr Serban at your office?'

'Yes, waiting for me.'

'Then I suggest we go there now and decide on a strategy.'

'But maybe that's the end of it? Obviously my idiot nephew misunderstood. If they were going to arrest me, surely they'd have done it.'

'I don't agree. They're still collecting evidence. Quigley made it clear that this wasn't over, and you're in the frame. At least now we have a chance to find out why.'

'How do you know I'm "in the frame", as you put it?'

'He told you himself. He called you the "defendant" and said you were making things worse for yourself. He wouldn't say that if you were only a witness. Nor would he threaten to arrest you. But what I don't understand is why? There have to be more likely suspects than you, but he's ignoring them. Why are they targeting you, Mr Gold? Or, to put it another way, who are they trying to protect?'

# CHAPTER SIX

Despite his refined accent and polish, Charles is a Cockney, a Londoner through and through. So he's aware of Tin Pan Alley, the heart of the British music business, but he's rarely had cause to go there. His thing is jazz, and he'd take Miles Davis, John Coltrane or Art Pepper over any of the new generation, even the Beatles. However, living with Sally, sixteen years his junior, and Greta, who is younger still, makes it impossible for him to avoid current music. Radio 1 plays constantly at Wren Street.

As Charles and his client walk into Denmark Street from Charing Cross Road, he pays closer attention to the buildings than he has before. Every one of them is dedicated to music in one form or another. Above every doorway and stencilled across all the windows are the names of music publishers, booking agents, managers and instrument retailers. There are a couple of restaurants but he notices that even these have music-related names, such as The Melody. Almost every business has the name "music" in its title.

There is a buzz of energy and excitement in the street. Young people hang about on the pavement smoking, looking through windows and entering and leaving doorways. Some wear flares and flower-patterned shirts; others are more like Mods, with crisp suits and haircuts; a few are rockers in leather and jeans.

As they walk down the narrow street, Charles hears the sound of wailing guitars, drums and keyboards emanating from several doorways. Gold sees his enquiring expression.

'Rehearsal studios, and some for recording. The Stones recorded their first album down there,' he says, pointing at the basement of number four. 'Regent Sounds. Cheap and cheerful — and filthy — but surprisingly good acoustics.'

He pushes through a small crowd of youngsters and Charles follows him up some steps and through an open door. In an office to their right two young women work at desks, both on telephone calls. Gold pops his head through the door. One of the women, still talking, beckons him over urgently and points to a document on her desk. Gold shakes his head and holds up his hand with his fingers splayed, indicating that he wants five of something. She nods and continues her conversation. Gold whispers hoarsely across the room to the other woman.

'When you're finished, pop to the Gioconda and get us three coffees?' He turns to Charles. 'White okay for you?'

'Yes, thanks,' replies Charles.

The woman, still speaking, gives him a thumbs up.

Gold returns to the hallway and leads Charles up a flight of narrow stairs.

'Are these all you?' Charles asks, pointing to the photographs lining the staircase.

'In my former life.'

At the first-floor landing Charles pauses to look at a framed theatre bill for City Varieties Musical, Leeds. 'You headlined at City Varieties?'

'I did.'

'And you gave it up for management?' asks Charles, surprised.

'I saw the writing on the wall. Variety was finished. And it was time to leave Manchester.'

There is something about Gold's tone which suggests a story behind that last comment, and Charles files it away for further exploration in due course.

Piano music bursts from an open door to their right. Someone appears to be learning or writing a new song. The music continues for a few bars and then the player pauses and repeats the phrase with slight differences. Gold pauses to listen. After a moment he leans into the room and laughs. The music stops and an affronted voice says, 'What?'

Gold shakes his head. 'That'll never pass the old grey whistle test,' he says, teasing, 'not in a million.'

Charles looks over Gold's shoulder. A young man wearing glasses sits at an upright piano, sheet music propped before him and a pencil clamped between his teeth.

He removes the pencil. 'Not finished yet,' he says. 'You don't mind, do you, Bobby? I'd half an hour to kill before meeting Bernie.'

'You carry on, mate. How's the album selling?' The pianist doesn't answer but pulls a face. 'It'll happen,' says Gold cheerfully.

The musician tucks the pencil behind his ear and resumes playing. Gold beckons Charles on and they continue upwards.

'What was that about a test?' asks Charles as he follows.

Gold looks round in surprise. 'Never heard of the old grey whistle test?' he asks.

'Nope.'

Gold speaks as he climbs. 'Fifty years ago this street was all music publishers — sheet music, not records. Writers would come in and play their new song. If the old doorman could whistle it afterwards, the publisher would pay a fiver for the rights and the song would be theirs. A lot of the songwriters lived like that, hand to mouth. The publisher would get his pluggers onto it — bribe band leaders to play it, publicise it with gimmicks and so on — and hope to sell the sheet music in the thousands. And it all started with the old grey whistle test. It still happens, but that part of the business has almost gone.'

'Why?'

'Records.'

Charles nods. 'Who was the bloke playing?'

'Reg? He used to do deliveries for Mills Music down the street, and several of the publishers let him use their pianos during his lunch break. But he's got a recording contract now. I missed a trick there. Nice lad, though.'

They reach the next landing. Again a room opens off it to their right. In this one are two men, each with a desk, and a wall of filing cabinets. Charles sees that the top of the cabinets are stacked high with boxes of singles, all in their sleeves. Gold enters the room and closes the door on Charles. Charles watches through the window as Gold approaches one of the men. He appears to have been waiting because he stands immediately and dons his jacket. He looks like he is about to go on holiday. His desk has been cleared and there's a small suitcase by its side. Gold takes an envelope from his pocket and hands it to the man, who slips it inside his jacket. A short conversation occurs before Gold returns to Charles.

'My pluggers,' he explains. 'Nick's about to go out on the road. Come on.'

'What's a plugger?' asks Charles, as he follows Gold up the final flight.

Gold comes to a halt and turns to face Charles. 'Did you see the boxes of records downstairs? The ones labelled "Johnny Blaise"?'

'Yes. It's your stock, right?'

'No, not really. In fact we've been trying something new, selling forty-fives and merchandise at concerts, but by and large I don't sell records. That's not my job. No, my job is to promote them, and the music charts are all-important in that. If a song's in the charts, it gets played on the radio. If not...' He shrugs.

'So?'

'So the pluggers go into the record shops and buy the records we want in the charts.'

Charles frowns. 'How is that possible? There are hundreds, no, *thousands* of record shops. You'd need an army of pluggers.'

Gold taps his nose confidentially. 'Not if you know which ones are used in the sampling, you don't.'

'You do realise that's dishonest, don't you?' says Charles.

'I don't think it is. I had a lawyer look into it for me. In any case, everyone does it, all the labels. I just do it better.'

Gold sets off again and Charles follows, filing away for further consideration his client's insouciant attitude towards dishonesty.

The top floor of the building houses Gold's office. Waiting for them inside is Mr Serban, the solicitor.

'Sorry to keep you, Victor,' says Gold, taking off his jacket and slinging it over the back of his chair. He indicates another chair to Charles. 'Take a seat.'

'How did it go?' asks the solicitor.

Charles sits down and gives him a quick summary. 'So,' he concludes, 'I'm not sure what's happened on the police side of the fence but, fortunately, we have a little more time.'

'What do you recommend?' asks Serban.

'Firstly, we need to do some digging into somebody called Frankie Perry. His was the only name revealed by Quigley.'

'I know who he is,' says Gold. 'He's one of the people behind Celeb Security. He doesn't actually do much of the work, although he has filled in a couple of times when one of his guys hasn't been available. I've only spoken to him briefly when he's been on duty.'

The woman from downstairs knocks on the door and enters immediately with a tray of drinks. She distributes them and leaves without speaking.

Charles takes out his notebook. 'Did you say that you were recommended Celeb Security through the police?' he asks.

'Yes.'

'Who, specifically?'

Gold ponders. 'Can't remember. I phoned the local police station, they put me onto someone and he put me onto someone else. It was a Met detective who'd worked with private security firms in the past.'

'Did he give you a list of firms, or just suggest Celeb Security?'

'He said Celeb Security were the best, and a lot of visiting musicians use them. I called them and Perry came round to Kingston Grange to see what was required. He put together a proposal for a certain number of staff, we haggled a bit over price, and it was agreed.'

Charles turns to Serban. 'I think we need to look into this chap. If drugs and underage girls were getting into Kingston Grange without Mr Gold's knowledge, Perry's the obvious person to speak to. Either he was permitting it, or one of his staff was. So we'll also need a full list of the men on the rota. See if any of them have criminal records, particularly supplying drugs. I'd recommend instructing a private detective.'

'I don't know any private detectives,' says Serban, 'especially down here.'

'I can recommend someone cheap but very good,' offers Charles. 'He's only been doing it for a few months, but he's an ex-criminal himself and he has a way of getting information without resorting to the tactics required by some of his competitors.'

Serban makes a note. 'Okay.'

'Now,' continues Charles, addressing Gold, 'you said something on the way up about it being time to leave Manchester. Anything I should know?'

'Meaning?'

'Well, do you have a police record, for example?'

'I've never been convicted of an offence, if that's what you mean,' replies Gold. 'But…'

'But?'

'Let's just say I pissed a few people off, including the police. It was almost a closed shop on the circuit up there. If you didn't have a London agent, you couldn't get in. And on top of that, I was foreign.'

'You said "including the police"?'

'Yes. There were a couple of punch-ups. Once with a stage manager who took against me. Nothing serious. I was blacklisted by that theatre and the police gave me a warning.'

Charles records this information in his notebook. 'This needs to go into Mr Gold's statement please, Mr Serban, with the names of the people involved. Maybe someone with a grudge has been talking to the police. Maybe a Manchester copper is now working down here. Now, what about the staff at Kingston Grange? Does the property come with a housekeeper, cleaners, a cook maybe?'

'I've got someone who keeps an eye on things for me. She cleans up, empties the bins and ashtrays and so on,' replies Gold. 'Johnny or Wyatt tell the cook what food they want and the same woman does the shopping for them. I've employed her for a couple of years, and she's reliable. We offer a cook with the house, but not many of the groups want sit-down meals so she's not there most of the time.'

'We'll need to take a statement from the housekeeper,' says Charles to Serban. The solicitor makes notes. 'Maybe the cook too. We need to know if they've seen drugs or girls coming in and, if so, who's been permitting entry. In particular, we need to find out if they saw anything unusual on the day Christine Bailey died.' He addresses Gold again. 'This alleged party.'

'Yes?'

'It followed the concert at the Astoria, Finsbury Park, so that's presumably where Christine met whoever got her into Kingston Grange. Did you go to the gig?'

'Yes.'

'Did you see the girl?'

'There were hundreds of girls! They were outside, at the stage door, crowding the stage, everywhere.'

'How did the group travel there?' asks Charles.

'In buses. We have two.'

'And did you travel with them?'

'No. I went in the limo earlier that afternoon to sort out some details. But I came back on one of the buses.'

'Why?' asks Charles.

'It was a disaster. There were technical problems from the start, even during the soundcheck. Then the main board blew shortly after the concert started, and the place went dark. There was nothing we could do. So we finished early and because Stan, my driver, wasn't due for another couple of hours, I went back to Kingston Grange on one of the buses.'

'Who drives the buses?'

'They've got a guy who's a driver and roadie in the US, but he doesn't like driving on the wrong side of the road, so I've provided them with two.'

'Good. We'll need their names too.'

'Why?' asks Gold.

'Because Christine Bailey must've got back to Kingston somehow, and if she'd been picked up by someone at the concert, going with him on the coach would be the obvious method. So one of your drivers might have noticed her, and if she was with anyone in particular. Did you see her?'

Gold shakes his head. 'Not to my knowledge. I wasn't paying much attention. The group were rowing amongst themselves and I was trying to keep order. There might have been a couple of other people on the bus I didn't recognise, but I think I would've noticed a fifteen-year-old girl.'

Charles records all this in his notebook and then looks up. 'Okay. Lastly, there's the pathology evidence.'

'What about it?' asks Gold. 'Won't we get the full report from the doctor, the … er … pathologist?'

'We should do, yes, eventually. The question is, are we happy with it? We all thought it was going to be a straightforward drugs overdose case, right? That's what the coroner thought too. But the bruises on Christine's arms raise all sorts of questions. Don't we want to at least investigate that aspect further?'

'Won't that be expensive?'

'About a hundred guineas, I imagine. Perhaps a little more.'

'On top of which we've got quite a list of witnesses,' comments Serban, 'and a private detective. I'm sure Mr Gold will need some idea of total cost.'

'You're damn right I do,' affirms Gold vehemently.

'Usually the largest component of pre-trial costs are the solicitor's charges. I presume you apply an hourly rate for investigation, taking statements, preparing instructions to counsel and so on? So it's whatever you charge Mr Gold on an hourly basis.'

'Don't you worry about that, Mr Holborne,' says Gold. 'Victor and I will discuss that.'

'Okay. So far as my costs are concerned, you need to speak to my senior clerk, Barbara. I guess she'll charge for my time today on an hourly basis, or perhaps simply roll up the attendance at the police station with this conference in a single fee. You won't need to instruct me again until the evidence starts coming in, or perhaps until you're arrested. On that, Mr Serban could write a letter witnessed by your lawyers and addressed to the investigating officers, making it clear that you will not be answering any questions at all when interviewed. It's not a perfect solution, as they can simply ignore the letter and give perjured evidence at trial that you changed your mind, but it's better than nothing if you're worried about costs. Or take Mr Serban with you and he can act simply as a witness to your silence, if that's cheaper. You'll probably need further advice on evidence at some point, and depending on the state of that evidence, a fee for the committal hearing if there is one. But in the usual case, the bulk of counsel's costs are incurred at trial.'

'How much?' asks Gold.

For the first time Charles wonders why Gold is so worried about expenditure. He is promoting one of the biggest up-and-coming rock stars from the US. Blaise is halfway through the tour, having played a dozen UK venues to sell-out crowds. The revenue from ticket sales and merchandise should already be pouring in. On the other hand, Charles considers, he knows people who nurture lifelong financial anxiety, no matter how rich they become, and very often it's those who started with nothing.

'There will be a brief fee,' he explains, 'which covers all the preparation and the first day of trial. Then there are refreshers, a lower daily figure for each subsequent day in court. Of course, you don't have to use me. There are other, cheaper counsel, although they'll probably have less experience than me. Hourly rates tend to go up with experience and reputation. I have both. Personally, there's no limit to what I'd invest to prevent being wrongly convicted of murder, but it's your call.'

Charles screws the top on his fountain pen and stands. 'I think that's all you need from me for the moment. I'll leave you to discuss how you want to play this. If you want me involved, let Barbara know.'

# CHAPTER SEVEN

DCI Quigley has spent a frustrating afternoon. He currently sits alone in a small room on the top floor of New Scotland Yard. The room, once an office, is generally unused. It has a superb view over the Thames and the Palace of Westminster, but rainwater has been leaking from a defect in the roof for years and its former occupant eventually gave up on the pervasive smell of mould and decayed timber and moved downstairs into the open-plan office. Since then, furniture that was unused or unwanted by the hundreds of police officers and support staff in the building has gradually accumulated in the unused room.

Then, purely by chance, Quigley discovered that it still contained a working telephone and, astonishingly, it was an outside line. Calls made to and from that telephone did not have to be routed through the Scotland Yard exchange. He immediately went about securing a key to the door. He discovered a room so stacked with furniture that it resembled a small depository, and the smell was so overpowering it was impossible to spend more than a few minutes inside without needing fresh air. These factors made the room perfect for his requirements.

Several times each week, having made sure he is not being observed, Quigley slips away from his desk and heads to the top floor, avoiding use of the lifts. There he can lock himself in and sit, invisible and unheard from the corridor outside, behind a wall of furniture, and make the phone calls that produce the bulk of his income.

The party that Quigley urgently needs to contact has been unavailable for most of the afternoon. The sepulchral DCI has spent the last several hours retracing his steps up and down the dozen flights of stairs between his office and this room, to no avail. On each occasion he has placed the call, waited impatiently, only to be told that it was not possible to connect him and he should try again later.

This, he has decided, will have to be the last attempt of the day.

'DS Feder, please,' he says, when the phone is picked up at the other end. As before, he adopts a London accent. It's not a very good imitation, but will be enough to fool the Yorkshire swedes. 'I ain't giving me name,' he says when asked. 'I'm one of his narks 'n' I got urgent information for him.'

He waits. He hears a series of clicks on the line and then, miraculously, he recognises the voice at the other end.

'Guv? It's Fed.'

'Thank fuck! What the hell's happening? I've been trying to reach you since yesterday!'

'It's been complicated. You want the short version or the long version?'

'Short version.'

'They got caught.'

'I'd guessed that. Are they still being held?'

'They let the Irishman go. He was driving. He gave them a story about coming across an open door and going in to investigate. He wasn't wearing gloves or balaclava, and they've not turned up any of his prints. When he gave a false name and it came up clean, they had nothing on him. But they've still got Perry.'

'Jesus! Is he talking?'

'So far, not a word. But they did find a couple of half-prints near the till. I don't know what the silly bugger was doing messing with the till, as there was nothing in it and I told him over and over "Just the gear", but he obviously didn't listen. Maybe he couldn't get it open with gloves on.'

'What about the skeleton keys?'

'We were lucky. The Irishman was bright enough to hide them just as the locals arrived and went back to get them afterwards. I've got them now.'

'That's a relief. But what about Perry?'

'I'm working on it. I've told them he is an informant in Operation Coathanger —' Quigley utters a short bark of laughter — 'yeah, I thought that was funny too. So I said we needed him back in the Smoke, without being charged. They're not having it. The officer who made the arrest is uniformed, an Inspector Critchlow. Perry'd more or less finished when Critchlow and the other officers stumbled across the van. It was loaded to the roof, and they've gone all starry-eyed over the value. Twenty trouser suits, fifty skirts, over a hundred jumpers, dresses, coats, scarves, lingerie and so on. They put the value at two grand, so it's a big deal for them. You know what these bumpkins are like, they don't catch proper villains. So this is the biggest collar the swedes've had all year, and it's a big deal.'

'We need Perry back, and we need him clean. It's holding everything up.'

'I get it, guv, but I'm only a DS and they ain't listening. You know what they're like with Met officers. I think you're going to have to pull bigger strings.'

Quigley pauses to consider this suggestion. 'Are you at the Town Hall?'

'Yeah, Leeds City Police HQ.'

'Good. There might be someone. See if you can find a DI Lambert. He's from up there originally, but there's a bit more about him than most of his colleagues. I knew him at No. 6 Regional Crime Squad.'

'Will do. If I find him, what shall I say?'

'I'll deal with it. Tell him I want a private word, and see if you can get his home number. If he's reluctant, meet him and get him to a phone box. You can call me at home from there, and put him on.'

'Will do.'

'But make it quick, Fed. I want to arrest Gold tonight if possible, tomorrow at the latest.'

'What about the van driver, Emmerson?'

'He's non-urgent. We'll work out how to get him out once Perry is sorted.'

'Okay, guv. Understood.'

# CHAPTER EIGHT

Charles stands on the Pelican Stairs, leaning on the railings and staring out over the River Thames. He draws a deep breath, savouring the old melange of odours: salt water, fish and sewage. Herring gulls swoop and screech above him and he hears, carried on the breeze from far away to the east, the sound of a ship's horn.

He rarely comes to Wapping nowadays. He is very conscious of the fact that the people he knew here would now be suspicious of him. They would see a middle-aged, middle-class member of the Establishment; a successful barrister with a posh accent and a posh Georgian house in an up-and-coming area on the edge of Clerkenwell; someone who didn't belong here. Thirty years ago, give or take a few months, he was a different person: a cocky Cockney teenage lighterman working the Thames, often under a hail of Luftwaffe bombs — someone who, if he survived, imagined a successful boxing career. He is still that person, but sometimes Charles has difficulty charting the metamorphosis of that boy into this forty-four-year-old barrister. How did it happen?

He loves his present life, his career, the financial security and, especially, his partner and daughter. He recognises how far he has come. He is particularly proud of the fact that, despite the rampant anti-Semitism and class prejudice he faced when starting at the Bar; despite the damage caused by his early association with East End criminals; despite even the hold the Kray twins had over him, he has managed to rise to the point where he has a genuine shout at taking silk — becoming Queen's Counsel — in the forthcoming April round.

Nonetheless, he finds himself coming to Wapping every now and then to remind himself who he *really* is. It helps restore his balance. There is even a part of him, still unarticulated, that worries that his success is only due, in some odd way, to his betrayal of his class, his religion and his ancient culture. That, he knows, is his mother talking. Millie Horowitz's dementia has robbed her of her ability to criticise him — she is almost completely helpless, incapable of speech or self-care — but her voice is still there in his head or, as he sometimes likes to imagine, perched on his shoulder like a malignant sprite, reminding him constantly how he has let everyone down. In Millie's eyes, he is a failure and a traitor to his family, to his people and, most of all, to her. As Charles once said to Sally, he could have been Prime Minister and he would still, in his mother's eyes, have failed her. He changed his name; he married out; he abandoned his faith.

The sun is dipping towards the water in the west and it's becoming chilly. Charles takes a few last deep breaths, turns, climbs the stairs and enters the back door of the Prospect of Whitby. During the war, this pub was his local, where he was introduced to beer, darts and pub skittles by his lightermen uncles and cousin. All dead now.

The hostelry, however, lives on, having stood here beside the lapping water of London's great river for almost half a millennium, the oldest waterside tavern in the world. It has been the haunt of smugglers, footpads and thieves, and the hiding place of centuries of contraband. It has changed little since Charles was a regular in the 1940s. It still disdains hot meals, slot machines and jukeboxes and, despite an increasing number of tourists drawn by the pub's rich history as a villains' pub and the Execution Dock beside it, it still remains somewhere for local working men to gather, to drink good beer and to bemoan their fates.

Charles orders a pint of mild and takes it to a quiet corner table.

Fifteen minutes later a tall man enters the pub via the front door. He has light brown hair swept back from a wide brow and wears highly polished brown brogues and a tailored suit. Charles raises a hand to attract his attention. The man points to the bar to indicate that he will first get himself a drink. After a minute he brings it over and sits opposite Charles.

'All right, Charles?' he asks.

'I'm fine, thank you, Billy.'

'Hope you don't mind slumming it,' says the other, supping his beer.

'No, I'm pleased you suggested it, actually. I like coming here once in a while. Is everything all right?'

Like Charles, Billy Munday got tangled up with the Kray twins and is now trying to go straight. It was Charles who recommended Munday's current line of work as a private detective. He is an attractive man, both in his looks and his personality. He was once employed by the Krays as an enforcer, and Charles has no doubt that he is capable of violence when necessary, but there is something about the big man's manner which persuades people to trust and talk to him. Since Charles first used him on a case earlier in the year, he has begun to develop a reputation as a reliable and discreet investigator.

'I wanted a word about that case you passed me, for Mr Gold.'

'I've not heard anything about it since I did the police station interview.'

Munday nods, as if expecting that information. 'Thought as much. That's answered one of my questions.'

'Mr Gold's been arrested now, hasn't he? I saw it on the news.'

'Arrested and charged with murder. The Filth raided his office in Denmark Street and his home. Took every bit of paper they could find. Even took his wife and kids in for questioning, and the youngest is only twelve.'

'They took the children?'

Charles has heard of CID officers in the Met doing this when trying to put pressure on someone to confess, but only ever in the context of known criminal families where everyone from the elderly grandparents down to the adolescents is guilty of something. It's very surprising for them to take in children from the family of a businessman who, hitherto, has no criminal record.

'Are they okay?' asks Charles.

'They were released after a few hours. Pretty shaken up, I'd say. They're a nice family, Charles. She's just a housewife. She looks after the kids and a couple of others lodging there, musicians down on their luck. And the kids are normal schoolchildren.'

'Has Mr Serban instructed counsel?'

'I'd hoped you were going to say you had the brief, but if it's not you, I think the answer's going to be no. Listen to this. Following your advice, Mr Serban asked me to look into Frankie Perry. Perry's from Peckham, and although it's not my manor I've got a couple of contacts down there, including one at the local nick. He point-blank refused to talk to me.'

'That wouldn't be surprising, would it? Coppers not talking to you?'

'Actually, in this case it would. I've known him since I was underage, and he's usually perfectly fine, 'specially now I'm straight. But soon as I mentioned Perry's name, he clammed up. I couldn't even persuade him to get me a CRO check, which he's always done before. His colleague said, and I quote, "Perry's as clean as a whistle, and always will be."'

'What does that mean?'

'I don't know, but they were both laughing as he said it. Anyway, I gave up on the police and asked about locally. On the face of it Perry's a quiet, unassuming bloke who minds his own business. Not flash, small house in Caulfield Road, and a six-year-old motor. The security job doesn't seem to make much money. I checked it out at Companies House and it's not a company at all.'

'So, a partnership, perhaps, or a sole tradership,' comments Charles. 'No obligation to file returns.'

'You'd know better than me. So I'm trying to find out how he makes a living. People say he's a bloke who can get you stuff. One tells me he has contacts on a couple of market stalls, but I saw some of the fashion gear he's supplied, and it's high-end, designer label goods. The real McCoy. You never get that at low-end markets like Berwick Street and Roman Road. Also, I've been cultivating someone who works at the Land Registry, and they tell me he bought the house outright — no mortgage.'

'Now *that's* a useful contact,' says Charles admiringly. 'Those records are only available to an owner or mortgagee. Very clever. I wouldn't have thought of that.'

Munday colours at the praise. 'Yeah, thanks. You gotta think around problems, right? Anyway, he lives more comfortably than is immediately obvious, and I can't work out how.'

'Does it matter? I was hoping you'd discover a lengthy criminal record, him or his employees, ideally involving drugs. If they're all clean and if it's Gold's word against theirs, Gold's in trouble.'

'There's still the cash lifestyle.'

'Not enough. Lots of people live on the black. No income tax, no purchase tax. London juries wouldn't care about that.'

'All I can say is, there's definitely something not right about him. Someone's supplying him with furs and posh frocks, and I'd bet a pound to a penny they're not legit.'

'Have you managed to trace any of the other security people?'

'I spoke to Mrs Gonzales, the housekeeper. Seems a nice woman, and straight. She gave me a few first names and descriptions, but that's all. She didn't know surnames, and the security guys were casuals. Taken on as and when needed, and paid in cash. Not the sort of people to hang about when things get tasty.'

'Like the possible murder of a fifteen-year-old.'

'Exactly. None of the blokes working now at Kingston Grange were there in July. Looks to me like Perry has swapped out anyone who might've seen something. I'm telling you, Charles, this doesn't feel right.'

'Have you told all this to Serban?'

'I've given him detailed reports. Far as I can see, he does nothing with them. He's a lovely bloke, but I'm not sure he knows what he's doing.'

Charles shrugs. 'Billy, if you're giving him the information but he's not using it, there's nothing more you can do. Just like if he chooses not to instruct counsel.'

There is a shout from one of the barmen. 'Is there a Charles Holborne here?' Charles and Munday look over. The man is holding aloft a telephone receiver. 'Charles Holborne?' he calls again.

Charles frowns, apologises to Munday and goes to the bar. 'It's your missus,' says the barman, offering the handset. 'Says it's an emergency.'

# CHAPTER NINE

Charles starts pulling off his suit jacket as he enters the lift of Sunshine Court. The floor in the care home to which he is ascending, named "Remembrance", is kept at a swelteringly hot seventy-five degrees Fahrenheit, and within five minutes of entering he is usually sweating.

The lift stops and he waits patiently for the doors, always slow to move but today snail-like. They finally open, admitting the familiar waft of disinfectant and stale cooking smells. Charles rushes across the communal lounge towards his parents' suite. Sally is waiting for him, pacing outside his parents' door. Part of Charles's brain wonders, distractedly, who is caring for Leia. Sally sees his approach and strides towards him.

'The doctor is with her now. It looks like she's had a stroke. David and Sonia are on their way.'

Charles nods. 'Can I go in?'

'Give it a minute, yeah? Your dad's in there with her.'

'When did it happen?' he asks.

'They don't know exactly. She was put to bed at six-thirty, and your father stayed up chatting in the lounge. About an hour later he asked one of the carers to fetch him something from their room, and she found your mother on the floor by the bed.'

'Have you seen her yourself?'

'Yes, when I first arrived. Charlie…' She tails off and puts a gentle hand on his arm.

'Yeah?'

'I don't think it looks too good.'

'Okay.' He looks around and sits in the nearest chair. Sally follows him and takes the adjoining one. 'How did you find me?' he asks.

She smiles. 'I know when you're having one of your identity crises. You usually end up somewhere in the East End. The Prospect was the first place I tried.'

'Identity crises?' he replies quizzically.

'You know what I mean. Feeling you don't belong anywhere. And, more recently, feeling old.'

Charles doesn't answer.

They wait. After a while Sally goes to the kitchen and makes them both a mug of tea. Finally the door to the suite opens and the dementia care team leader, Leanne, scans the room, looking for them. She walks over, followed by a woman in her middle years — the doctor, presumes Charles. At the same moment the lift door opens again and Charles's brother and sister-in-law step out. Charles waves, beckoning them urgently.

'Are you the next of kin?' the doctor asks Charles.

'I'm Mrs Horowitz's son. This is my brother,' says Charles, indicating David as he arrives by their side. 'Our father is the next of kin.'

'All right. I've explained this to him, but I'm not sure he took it all in. I'm sorry to say your mother appears to have had a very severe stroke, I suspect to her brain stem. She's suffering from what is called decerebrate posturing, which simply means that her arms and legs are extended, fixed and very stiff. Her pupils are not responsive, her blood pressure is low and her breathing is shallow and irregular.'

'Is she aware of what's happening?' asks David.

'No,' replies the doctor. 'She's unconscious.'

'Can anything be done?' asks Charles, already knowing the answer.

The doctor shakes her head. 'There are some tests that could be carried out to confirm the area of the stroke and its severity, but they are invasive and unpleasant and, I'm afraid to say, unlikely to affect the outcome.'

'What about blood thinners?' asks David. 'Isn't that what you give to stroke patients?'

'In less serious cases, yes. But I'm afraid your mother was on the floor in her room, having almost certainly suffered a stroke, for a good while. I say that without any criticism. Leanne tells me she's never fallen out of bed before or got up once she's settled. I've checked, and there's nothing to suggest she fell trying to get out of bed, no obvious broken bones, bruising or abrasions. I'd say she got out of bed safely and suffered the stroke as she walked to the door. I think it unlikely that her condition has been adversely affected by any delay in discovering her.'

*She's quick to acquit the care home of any blame,* Charles notes. He guesses that Leanne made sure to tell the doctor what he does for a living.

'I'm sorry to say,' she continues, 'I'd be very surprised if Mrs Horowitz were to survive for long. There's no realistic prospect of recovery from a stroke of this magnitude. Now, if you want me to, I will call an ambulance and have her taken to hospital to conduct scans, but there's little we could do except monitor her. On the other hand she could remain here, somewhere familiar to her, surrounded by her family. Have you discussed how you would want to approach treatment in these circumstances?'

'What do you mean?' asks Sonia.

'Some families want us to do everything possible to prolong life, even with patients like Mrs Horowitz who suffer from advanced dementia. Others prefer to keep their loved ones comfortable, but allow nature to take its course.'

David and Charles look at one another. They have not had this discussion. Charles answers. 'I don't know if my father has thought about it. Did you discuss it with him?'

'Very briefly. He said he wants to talk to you both first.'

'Can we do that now?' asks Charles.

'Yes, of course. If you decide you want to keep your mother comfortable, I'll be able to prescribe some drugs and we should be able to get them here later tonight. Leanne has my telephone number —' she addresses the carer — 'and you can phone me at any time. Otherwise, she can call an ambulance for you.'

'Thank you, Doctor,' says Charles.

The family enters the suite. Charles's father Harry is sitting in a chair at Millie's bedside. The bed has been lowered so that he and his wife are on the same level. He is leaning over her bed, holding one of her hands in his and at the same time stroking her thin white hair. Millie is tucked up in bed with the sheets pulled up to her neck. Her eyes are closed and although she is pale, she looks peaceful.

'Dad?' says David.

Harry Horowitz turns to his sons. He too suffered a stroke a couple of years back but, other than some minor residual weakness on one side, he has made a good physical recovery. He can now walk with a stick or a frame, although he still uses a wheelchair for longer journeys. There is no reason for him to be housed in "Remembrance" with the dementia patients, except for the fact that nothing would ever persuade him to leave his wife's side.

There are tears in Harry's eyes, but he seems very calm.

'Hello, boys. I'm glad you're both here. You too, Sonia and Sally.'

The new arrivals all kiss Harry, one after another.

'Get some chairs,' instructs Harry. 'You can bring a couple from the dining area.'

Sonia and Sally do as they are instructed and sit a little distance from the bed. The brothers take seats on either side of their father.

'Did the doctor tell you how serious it was?' asks Charles.

'She did.'

'And the options? Take her to hospital or remain here?' says David.

Harry nods. 'I'll hear what you have to say, boys, but I've considered this eventuality for some time, and believe I know what your mother would prefer. And before you say anything, Charles, I don't want you thinking about legal action against Sunshine, okay? It's no one's fault that your mother wasn't found for a while.'

Charles raises his hands in protest. 'Hadn't crossed my mind,' he lies.

'Good.'

Harry falls silent and returns to stroking Millie's hair.

'Well, Dad?' prompts Charles.

Harry draws a deep breath. 'I think if your mother were able to tell us now, she'd say she doesn't want any further treatment. She's a very proud woman, and she'd hate what she's become, to what she's been reduced. And I feel the same way.'

Charles nods. He agrees. Until she was robbed of her mind and her personality, Millie Horowitz was indeed a proud woman. Always perfectly turned out (often in clothing she made herself; she was a dress-maker and milliner all her working life), she had a very sharp mind and an even sharper tongue. She ruled the Horowitz household, and everyone in the community knew it. Charles rebelled against it, Harry accepted it for a quiet life, and David, the youngest, simply kept his head down. Charles knows that if his mother were aware of the effect of her dementia, she would rather die than be an object of pity. Her loss of dignity; her need for assistance in feeding and toileting; the loss of her incisive intelligence and her sense of humour — these things would have made her life a torment.

'Well?' asks Harry of his sons, not taking his eyes from the woman in the bed, his wife of almost half a century.

'It's your choice, Dad,' says Charles. 'But, for what it's worth, I agree with you  Her quality of life was very poor even before this. If she survives this, it'll be worse still. Much worse.'

'But,' intervenes David, 'she does have some quality of life. I believe she still enjoys seeing us and her grandchildren.'

Charles turns to his younger brother with some surprise. 'How can you know that, Davie? She's unresponsive most of the time.'

'But not all the time. There are still moments when I think she recognises us.'

'When was the last time she spoke?' demands Charles.

'I can't remember…'

'I can. It was March this year. It's been a full six months since there's been the slightest flicker. At least with me. And I always knew it would be like that. I'd know when that last spark was extinguished, because she'd forget to hate me.'

Both Harry and David protest at this.

'She never hated you,' says Harry sadly.

'She did, Dad. I know it's painful for you to hear, but she *told me* she hated me, on that last occasion. And let's face it, it's hardly a surprise, is it? It's been obvious to everyone in the family since, well, forever.'

'This is the very reason you should have no say in this decision,' says David, bitterly. 'Your relationship with her is too complicated.'

'Boys —' starts Harry.

'What are you saying, David? That I want our mother to be dead? How can you say something like that?'

'Boys!' shouts Harry. 'Enough!'

His sons obey and fall silent.

'Charles: if your mother told you that she hated you, and if you're sure she was in her right mind when she said it, then I believe you. But I don't believe she's felt like that for a long time. I spent twenty-four hours of every day with her since we moved here, and even when she couldn't speak, I knew her moods. Don't ask me how, I just did. If you love someone for fifty years like I love your mother, you can tell these things. And when you came here, feeding and changing her, showing her so much kindness despite everything ... I know she loved you. You've been a *mensch* to her, and I truly believe the two of you managed to put your troubles behind you. And David: I'm sure you didn't mean to suggest that Charles would be happier with your mother dead. But that's how it sounded, and you owe him an apology.'

David hangs his blond head. After a moment he looks up and Charles sees tears in his eyes too. 'I'm sorry, Charles,' he says with sincerity. 'I didn't mean it to sound like that. I'm just upset.'

Charles smiles and pats his brother's slender hand. 'Forget it. We're all upset.'

'So, David,' continues Harry, 'do you have anything you want to say about the decision we have to make this evening?'

David considers for a moment and then shakes his head. 'No. Let's leave it in the hands of God,' he says. Considering David's strong faith, this is exactly the response that Charles should have predicted.

'Then we're agreed. The doctor mentioned telephoning her to get some drugs up here. Would you mind telling Leanne what we propose and asking her to call the GP?'

'I'll go,' says Charles, rising.

Sally follows Charles out.

'Charlie?' she calls quietly after him. He turns. 'I phoned Maria and she dropped everything to come round and sit with Leia, but she has a concert in Birmingham tomorrow, so she needs to leave as soon as possible. I should get back.'

'Sure.' Maria Hudson, Charles's former pupil barrister and lodger at Wren Street, is now a highly respected jazz pianist.

'Will you stay?'

'Yes. I want to support Dad.'

'All right. Are you in court tomorrow? Do you need me to call Barbara?'

'No, it's just paperwork.'

'Righto. And I guess we'd better postpone the wedding.'

Charles approaches her and holds her gently. 'Let's discuss that later.'

'But isn't there some rule in Jewish culture that prevents there being a wedding shortly after a bereavement?' she asks. 'Should she, well…'

'Should she die. Yes. You're not supposed to marry during the *shiva* period, that's seven days, or during the thirty days after the funeral. I think there's also some rule about not getting married for a period of twelve months if the deceased was your parent, but I'm no expert, so I'd have to check with

David or Dad. In any case, I don't believe in any of it, so…'
He shrugs.

'I know you don't, but they do,' she says, pointing back to
Millie and Harry's suite, 'and the last thing we want is to offend
your father and brother over the timing of our marriage, on
top of everything else.'

Sally is referring to the fact that she is not Jewish and that
their wedding will not be a religious one. Many in Charles's
wider family will disapprove of his marrying out of the Jewish
faith, and for a second time.

'On the other hand,' points out Charles, 'it was Mum who
was the greatest obstacle. And I'm not prepared to wait
another year, whatever my relatives might say about it.
Anyway, let's discuss this further when … when we know if
she's going to recover.'

Millie Horowitz passes away in the early hours of the following
morning, her husband and sons by her bedside. Charles and
David remain with Harry until daylight starts creeping around
the curtains, but when he announces that he wants to sleep for
a while, he sends them back to their respective homes. David
has offered to take charge of the arrangements. Millie will be
collected by the funeral directors later that morning and
they've agreed that, if the cemetery and rabbi can
accommodate them, they will aim to hold the funeral on Friday
of that week. *Halacha*, Jewish law, requires it to take place as
soon as possible after death. It is one of the few parts of the
Bible that Charles remembers: *You shall surely bury him on the
same day*, according to Deuteronomy.

The night staff wheel Millie's bed into a separate room. As
Charles heads towards the lift he passes the door and, on
impulse, enters. He has not been in this room before. He

realises that, with such an aged and frail population, many care homes must have a room designated for such circumstances. It's a pleasant space, with the appearance of having been decorated more recently than the rest of the care home — or perhaps it has been used less — and a small perfumed candle has been left burning on a nightstand. It casts a soft glow over the bed.

Someone has pulled the sheet over Millie's face. Charles advances towards her and lowers it. She looks exactly as she did when Harry was holding her hand before her death.

Charles stands at the bedside, looking down on his mother's face for the last time. It is difficult to recognise the upright, iron-haired, fierce woman with whom he battled the whole of his life. In her last few years Millie lost all her teeth. Her cheeks sunk, her hair whitened and thinned so you could see her mottled scalp and, despite the best efforts of her carers and family members, she lost weight. She changed so much that, had Charles been looking at her for the first time in a couple of years, he wouldn't have known her.

He tries to identify the feeling she generates in him. They fought so bitterly, and for so many years. Charles was never going to be the firstborn son that Millie demanded, and she was never able to reconcile herself to it. Like a terrier with an old rag, she worried at it, and at him, constantly, succeeding only in driving him further away. Nonetheless, Charles never turned his back on her completely. He came back, again and again, only to be criticised afresh. In her last vulnerable years he saw it as his duty to care for and support her exactly as if they had enjoyed a close, loving relationship, and he did it with an open heart. These things are among the foremost reasons why Sally respects and loves Charles so much. The inconstancy of his mother's affection left him scarred and permanently troubled but, right at the base of Charles's personality, Sally has located a deep well of kindness.

Looking down at Millie now, Charles feels as if the referee has rung the final bell on a long and painful boxing match. The last couple of rounds were characterised by few blows, merely an exhausted clinch, but Charles recognises that Harry was right; there was love, and acceptance, at the end.

'Bye, Mum,' says Charles as he replaces the sheet.

He takes a couple of steps towards the door and then, suddenly, uninvited and unexpectedly, another Jewish custom pops into his head. It is usually part of the ritual washing of a body before burial and is something Charles has never seen in person, but he must have heard of it via one of his Orthodox relations, and it suddenly seems appropriate, here and now. So he turns and addresses his mother.

'I ask forgiveness, at this time, for any harm or discomfort I caused you during your life,' he says formally. He waits in the silence for a few seconds. He is not sure why, but the moment feels important, solemn.

Charles describes himself as an agnostic atheist; he does not believe in God or in a life after death but, in the absence of any compelling evidence one way or the other, acknowledges that he might be wrong. Accordingly, he doesn't think his mother can hear him.

On the other hand, just in case, he'd prefer her to start eternity at peace with him.

# CHAPTER TEN

By the time Charles reaches Wren Street it is broad daylight and well into rush hour. Greta is in the kitchen preparing breakfast for Leia, and Sally is upstairs getting dressed. Charles goes straight up to see her.

'Well?' asks Sally.

'She died at around three this morning,' says Charles simply.

'Oh, Charlie, I'm so sorry!' replies Sally, approaching and putting her arms around him.

They hug in silence for a few moments.

'Are you okay?' she asks into his chest.

'I'm fine.'

'And your dad?'

'He was sleeping when I left. He's all right at the moment. I think he's going to be very lonely, despite the fact that Mum's not been much company for the last year or so.'

'Will he go back home now? He's so much better, I reckon he could probably cope at home with a bit of support.'

Charles sighs. 'I don't know. We haven't discussed it. It's just as well the sale fell through, so he still has that option. But I'm not sure it'll feel like home to him after all these months, especially with Mum gone.'

Charles disengages and flops onto their bed.

'Can you take the day off?' asks Sally. Charles shakes his head. 'Then why don't you at least get a few hours' sleep? Greta's taking Leia out this morning anyway, so the house will be quiet.'

'No, I don't think so. I'm wide awake and I'll be better getting lost in some work. To be honest with you, Sal, part of me is relieved. This was bound to happen sooner or later, and at least they've both been spared months of suffering and deterioration. If I get into Chambers now, I can do a few hours. I'm meeting David at Sunshine Court this afternoon to be with Dad and talk through the arrangements.'

'Okay. Do you want me to wait for you? We can walk in together.'

Charles sits up. 'I need a shower and change of clothes. Can you wait that long?'

'Yes. As soon as I've finished dressing, I'll put some coffee on.'

'Thanks, sweetheart.'

Charles and Sally arrive at Temple Bar within five minutes of their usual time. They kiss and part, Sally entering the Temple from Middle Temple Lane and Charles from Serjeants' Inn.

Charles runs up the Dickensian staircase, creating puffs of wood dust as his fifteen stones land on every second tread. Considering he has not slept at all, he feels pretty sharp. Like most barristers, he is used to working overnight on briefs delivered at the last minute. If tiredness hits him at all, it will be in the middle of the afternoon.

Despite the fact that it is only a few minutes after eight, the clerks' room is bustling. Barbara looks up from her desk where she has been opening the post.

'Good morning, sir. There is an urgent set of instructions here for you from Berkeley, English and Co.'

'Who?' asks Charles, not recognising the name.

'Mr Serban, the solicitor from Manchester. The alleged overdose.'

'Oh,' exclaims Charles. 'Trial brief?'

'Looks like it. They've left it late, because it's listed in just over two weeks. So, urgent conference tomorrow morning.'

'Would it be all right if I take it straight away, please, Barbara? I'll need to start on it now. I'm only in for this morning. And I probably won't be available at all on Friday.'

'I think you'll find that you're in court on Friday morning, sir,' she reminds him sternly in her Edinburgh accent.

'Yes, I'm sorry about that. But my mother died last night and the funeral's likely to be on Friday.'

Charles's announcement causes the clerks' room to fall silent.

'I'm so sorry to hear that,' says Barbara, her tone softening considerably. 'Should you be here at all, sir?' she asks.

'I'm fine, thank you. It was very sudden, but she's been suffering from dementia for some time, so perhaps it's for the best.'

Barbara hands Charles the brief. 'I'll bring you up a cup of coffee,' she says gently.

'Thank you. If you've time, you can keep them coming. I've not been to bed.'

Charles takes the instructions up to his office and begins reading.

### BRIEF TO COUNSEL

### THE QUEEN
*– v –*
### BOBBY GOLD

*Enclosures:*
*1. Indictment*
*2. Police statement of Eileen Fairfax*
*3. Police statement of Sarah Bruce*

4. *Police statement of Maria Theresa Gonzales*

5. *Police statement of Dr Neville Durden, GP*

6. *Police statement of Francis Perry*

7. *Statement of Detective Chief Inspector Quigley*

8. *Statement of Detective Inspector Pilcher*

9. *Police statement of Eamon O'Keefe*

10. *Report of Wilfred Spurling, Chartered Accountant*

11. *Report of Dr Benson, Home Office Forensic Pathologist*

12. *Report of Professor Sir Beverly Lymme, Home Office Forensic Pathologist (to follow)*

13. *Proof of evidence of Bobby Gold (to follow)*

14. *Proof of evidence of Stanley Crispie*

*Counsel is instructed on behalf of Mr Bobby Gold. Since counsel's last involvement, Mr Gold has been charged with the murder of Christine Bailey (see enclosure 1). Count 2 is an alternative count of manslaughter. Count 3 alleges the unlawful supply of heroin contrary to Section 5 of the Dangerous Drugs Act 1951 and the Dangerous Drugs Regulations 1953.*

*Mr Gold's application for bail was refused both before the Magistrates' Court and a High Court judge, and he is presently on remand at Brixton Prison. He was committed following a non-contested committal hearing under Section 1 of the Criminal Justice Act 1967 to stand trial at the Old Bailey on a date to be fixed.*

*The Crown's case is that Mr Gold procured or permitted Christine Bailey's entry to Kingston Grange by one or more of the group members. There she was given alcohol and drugs and engaged in sexual acts. The statement of Francis Perry alleges that he previously saw Mr Gold taking delivery of drugs on several occasions from a man who frequently hangs around backstage at Mr Gold's concerts. It will be noted that the Crown are calling no evidence that Mr Gold specifically facilitated the supply of the drugs used on this occasion. Mr Perry also alleges that our client has on several occasions allowed what he calls "groupies" back to the group's accommodation for the entertainment of the musicians.*

*The most significant part of Mr Perry's evidence is to the effect that he claims to have been at Kingston Grange when the after-concert party occurred. He saw several groupies, one of whom he identifies as Christine Bailey, drunk or under the influence of drugs. A number of the musicians and young women went for a swim in the swimming pool and Mr Perry watched them for a while but then returned to the lounge where he fell asleep on one of the couches. He claims to have woken up later. He went into the hallway and looked up and saw Mr Gold coming out of one of the bedrooms. Mr Gold descended the stairs and walked directly out of the house. Mr Perry says he ran upstairs and saw Miss Bailey lying in a corner of the bedroom, naked, with a hypodermic syringe hanging out of her arm. That is the closest the Crown come to placing Mr Gold in the vicinity of the deceased. The Crown's case appears to be based on the inference to be drawn from our client having allegedly lied about permitting underage girls and drugs to be allowed into the property, and about whether he was there at the relevant time. Counsel will note that Mrs Gonzales also says that she was the first to discover Miss Bailey's body. Instructing Solicitors suspect that this apparent inconsistency may be explained by one of them finding the body and leaving the room to seek help, during which time the other arrived.*

*The man or men with whom Miss Bailey is alleged to have had sexual intercourse have not been identified, but the implication from the Crown's case is that Mr Gold believed it to be Mr Blaise. Whether or not Mr Blaise did in fact have sexual intercourse with the young woman is presently unclear as, surprisingly, the Crown's evidence does not include anything from Mr Blaise or any of the musicians. Instructing Solicitors have requested facilities for interviewing them, which requests have to date been ignored. Instructing Solicitors are of the opinion that Mr Blaise is anxious to protect his reputation and has effectively "thrown Mr Gold to the wolves".*

*Mr Gold was interviewed following his arrest by DCI Quigley in the presence of Mr Serban of those instructing. The police were handed the letter recommended by counsel, saying that Mr Gold had been advised not to answer any questions. DCI Quigley's statement confirms that Mr Gold replied "No comment" to every question. It appears from the Chief Inspector's questions that the Crown believe that Mr Gold's motive for the murder was to cover up both his supply of drugs which were used by the minor, and the fact that Miss Bailey was raped. As Counsel appreciates, in law Miss Bailey was too young to have given consent and therefore if intercourse occurred, with Mr Blaise or anyone else, it amounted to statutory (or actual) rape. The Crown have obtained evidence from a Mr Spurling, an accountant, who has analysed Gold Management's books and bank statements. Mr Spurling concludes that if for any reason the tour did not proceed to the European leg, Mr Gold's business would be bankrupt.*

*It seems to those instructing that if Mr Gold was seeking to avoid the bad publicity generated by drug-taking and sexual intercourse with an underage girl, killing her was an unlikely strategy. No doubt Counsel will want to explore this in conference with Mr Gold.*

*Counsel will remember that when Mr Gold was first interviewed, DCI Quigley suggested the possibility that the heroin was administered by a third party. No evidence has been served to support any such suggestion. Mr Gold's fingerprints were taken, but Instructing Solicitors assume from the absence of any evidence served by the Crown that no match could be made with the room in which the deceased was found, or the syringe itself. We are therefore hopeful that DCI Quigley's suggestion is not being pursued.*

*Counsel will note the statements obtained by the Crown from Miss Bailey's mother, GP and her year head at school (see enclosures 1, 5 and 4 respectively). All three paint the picture of a successful, hard-working student who, although a bit of a handful, gave no suggestion at all of being involved with drugs, or indeed significant alcohol consumption. It does seem unlikely that such a girl would voluntarily inject or accept an injection of heroin.*

*Counsel will note the statement from Mr Eamon O'Keefe (see enclosure 9), the former front of house manager at the Liverpool Empire Theatre, who claims to have had an altercation with Mr Gold regarding his supply of drugs to another performer in 1958. The police have confirmed that as a result of this altercation, Mr Gold was convicted of common assault. No conviction was recorded regarding drugs. Counsel will remember Mr Gold's instructions that he had never before been convicted of any offence. No doubt Counsel will want to speak to him concerning this inconsistency in his account.*

*Finally, those instructing have asked Professor Sir Beverly Lymme, a pathologist on the Home Office list, to critique the evidence of Dr Benson. No doubt Counsel has heard of the professor, who is one of the leading pathologists in the country. Full instructions have been sent to him but he is extremely busy and, despite reminders, we have yet to receive his preliminary report. Instructing Solicitors will continue to chase.*

*Counsel should not hesitate to contact those instructing if he has any queries. A conference has been arranged for 10 am tomorrow morning at Brixton Prison, for which Mr Serban will travel to London.*

*Berkeley, English & Co.*


*Pretty good Instructions*, thinks Charles, *especially from a solicitor with little experience in the field.* He glances over at the old wooden clock on his wall. He has less than three hours to read and assimilate all of this evidence before leaving for Sunshine Court.

His first thought is: *Where are the statements from the people staying at Kingston Grange?*

Given the circumstances of Christine Bailey's death, they should have been the first to be interviewed, both about what happened that night and Gold Management's general attitude to the group's use of drugs and groupies. He makes a note to get Serban to ask the Crown to confirm in writing that all statements taken by the police have been disclosed. The prosecution is required to reveal any material that might assist the defence or undermine its own case, but the rule is not enshrined in law and the obligation is frequently ignored. Even when Charles has unequivocally proven at trial that the Crown have wrongly characterised unserved evidence as irrelevant, judges rarely take any action beyond gentle chiding of prosecution counsel.

He continues by making notes on the charges in the indictment. The prosecution has been clever. Gold faces a "ladder" of charges, starting with the supply of heroin, for which he could receive a period of imprisonment of up to ten years. If they can additionally prove that this heroin was administered to Christine Bailey and she died as a result, they will be more than halfway to proving manslaughter, for which Gold could go to prison for life, although a sentence of somewhere between ten and fifteen years would be more likely. If they manage to go all the way and prove that Gold actually administered the heroin, he will be convicted of murder. Again, life imprisonment and, most probably, exactly that.

Charles turns to the most important statement, that of Frankie Perry.

# CHAPTER ELEVEN

*Statement of Francis Perry*
*Occupation: Clothing Wholesaler*
*Address: 175 Commercial Road, London EC1*

*This statement is true to the best of my knowledge and belief, and I make it knowing that, if it is tendered in evidence, I shall be liable to prosecution if I wilfully state in it anything which I know to be false or do not believe to be true.*

*Signed: Francis Perry*

I am a clothing wholesaler, supplying clothing to dealers to sell at the London street markets. I have my own business. My brother-in-law, Derek Emmerson, runs a security company known as Celeb Security. He specialises in supplying security staff to pop groups and other celebrities when they are in the UK. His company is very successful and he is very busy. Paperwork is not his strong suit and so he sometimes asks me to assist him with his accounts, putting together shift rotas and company policies, etc. In that capacity I visited Kingston Grange, a large property rented by Gold Management and Talent Ltd, in advance of the visit of the pop group, Johnny Blaise and the Hellraisers. Mr Gold was the tour promoter and organiser. Derek asked me to go and find out exactly what Mr Gold wanted, and I reported back to him to enable him to put together a quotation.

More rarely, usually when he has been let down by someone, Derek also asks me to assist by being part of the actual security team. I am not really built for such work but when he has a low-risk job and needs my assistance I try to help out.

In early July this year one of his regular security team suffered an injury and Derek asked if I would fill in. I agreed. I was therefore part of the security team that travelled with Johnny Blaise and the Hellraisers to the Liverpool Empire Theatre. Our job was to ensure the group were not hassled on their way to and from the bus, and to prevent fans without tickets from getting into the venue. I was backstage before the concert started and saw Mr Gold meet another man. There was something about the way they were speaking that made me suspicious. Mr Gold took the man into a quiet corner and I saw him accept a package from him. Gold reached into his jacket pocket and handed over an envelope. I did wonder at the time if he was paying for drugs. Both men were acting furtively, looking over their shoulders and whispering.

A few days later the group were playing at the King's Hall in Stoke-on-Trent, and I was again part of the security team. This time I was on the stage door. The concert had already started when the man I had seen with Mr Gold on the previous occasion came up to me and asked to be allowed in. I had instructions not to allow anyone through the door, but he told me that Bobby was waiting for him and he had something very important for the group. Because I had seen him speaking to Mr Gold on the previous occasion I thought it would be okay to let him in, as the two men obviously knew one another, so I let him pass.

I have been asked about the night of the group's London concert at the Astoria Theatre. There were technical problems from the start and eventually all the power failed, so it ended early. We left the venue by nine and were back at Kingston Grange where the group were staying before ten. I went with them on one of the two group buses. Several of the musicians were on the same bus, although I didn't pay attention to which ones. However, I did notice that two or three young women who I assumed to be fans were allowed onto the bus. Mr Gold was not with us.

When we arrived at Kingston Grange, the musicians and the girls went inside. I helped unload the equipment and Mr Gold was definitely there at that time as I saw him through the window. He was in the Grange's kitchen and appeared to be having a heated discussion with Johnny Blaise and his brother Wyatt.

My shift ended at midnight. One of the musicians asked if I wanted to have a drink before I left, and I agreed. I sat with everyone else in the Blue Room. There was music playing and a number of the group members were drinking and smoking with the girls. There were three or four groupies there, two of whom I recognised from previous occasions. One was cuddling up to the Hellraisers' keyboard player. They eventually went off on their own. Another I recognised as a regular from other post-concert parties. I have been shown photographs of Christine Bailey and I can confirm that she was definitely there that evening. She was laughing and dancing and having a good time. I can't say if she was with anyone in particular. She seemed to me to be drunk or under the influence of drugs. Some of the group went for a swim in the swimming pool at the back of the property, including Christine. I went out with them. They all stripped off and jumped in the water. I watched for a while but then returned to the Blue Room. The music was off and there were only three or four people there by then, and a couple of them were asleep on the couches. It was late and I had had quite a bit to drink so I put my head down. I fell asleep on the couch.

I woke up some time later. I looked at my watch and it said a few minutes to four. The room was dark and silent. I was walking across the downstairs hall when I saw Mr Gold running down the stairs from the bedrooms. He ran straight to the front door and out onto the drive, leaving the front door open. I don't think he saw me. I could tell from his face that he was in a panic.

A moment later I heard shouting from upstairs. I guessed something bad must have happened so I ran up to investigate. I found the girl lying in a corner of one of the bedrooms with a syringe in her arm. She was naked. Her eyes were wide open. I called out to Mr Gold to stop him but heard the sound of his car starting up and going down the gravel drive. I left the room and was met on the landing by the housekeeper, Mrs Gonzales, and

*Johnny Blaise. The housekeeper told me she had discovered the girl a few minutes earlier and had gone to wake Mr Blaise. Everyone else in the house seemed to be asleep.*

*I can definitely say that Mr Gold permitted drugs to be used on the premises and appeared to me to be the person who supplied them to the group. He also seemed relaxed about groupies travelling on the tour buses and entering Kingston Grange for the entertainment of the musicians. I witnessed some pretty wild parties on occasion at Kingston Grange, with drugtaking and a lot of sex in almost all the rooms.*

*Signed: Francis Perry*

Charles puts the statement down on his desk. Perry's evidence is going to be critical. If the jury believe that Gold bought drugs for the musicians and allowed them to be administered to a fifteen-year-old girl, he's in trouble.

# CHAPTER TWELVE

Charles and Sally are having breakfast. As usual for a weekday, Sally is having hers at a run. While Charles sits at the kitchen table, drinks coffee and listens with one ear to *Today* on Radio 4, Sally is grabbing interrupted mouthfuls of tea and the occasional bite of toast while giving instructions for the day to Greta, gathering the papers she brought home the previous night, repacking her bag, and running to and from the bathroom as she applies her makeup.

Charles knows that she prefers to be left to it in the mornings. His offers of help are appreciated but, usually, rejected. It's as if she has a list of things she has to do, in a strict order, and she needs to do them herself before crossing each one off mentally. It is only when they leave the house that she relaxes.

They finally close the front door and head towards Gray's Inn Road. Charles is due at Brixton Prison, but has time to check his post in Chambers before going south of the river. Usually this is the moment when Sally would start chatting, telling Charles what her day will entail, discussing one of her guvnor's cases or sharing chambers gossip. However, this morning she is uncharacteristically silent, her brow furrowed in thought.

'Something up?' Charles asks eventually, as they turn south.

'No, not really.'

'This is about the funeral, right? I've told you, it's not a big deal.'

'That's easy for you to say. For me it is a big deal, and it will be for most of your extended family. Your dad's a sweetie, and you know I love David and Sonia, but I'll be on display for your aunts and uncles, cousins, the whole Jewish community. You won't be able to hear the vicar — rabbi, sorry — for all the whispering. *"There's that shiksa, the tart living in sin with Charles."'*

'I'll be there,' he says reassuringly. 'No one'll say anything.'

'Not to your face, maybe. But they'll all talk about me, and point. And in fact you won't be there, will you? Sonia tells me that men and women are segregated.'

'But it's a small place. And at the graveside you'll be a couple of feet from me. I promise you, it'll be fine. My family are not mean, except my mother. And she won't say a word.'

Sally doesn't laugh.

They cross Holborn at the traffic lights. They have cut through Staple Inn Buildings and turned left onto Chancery Lane before Sally speaks again.

'I know your family aren't mean. They're lovely, but they are exclusionary,' she says. 'Most of them don't associate with non-Jews and they're suspicious of outsiders. And they most certainly don't approve of elder sons of the Horowitz dynasty marrying out. I need you to understand, Charlie, this is going to be hard for me.'

'I do understand.'

'And telling me it'll all be okay doesn't help. It minimises how I'm feeling. I think Sonia gets it better than you, and she's the perfect Jewish wife.'

'Have you discussed your worries with her?'

'Yes. And she's supportive, as always. She's promised to stay with me throughout and make sure I don't put my foot in it.'

Charles makes a mental note to thank his sister-in-law. David married Sonia a few years ago, and although Charles was uncertain of her at the outset — she came from an even more orthodox family than the Horowitzes — he now has huge affection for her. She's kind, generous and surprisingly open-minded considering her narrow upbringing and very limited exposure to people outside of the Jewish community.

'It's just a funeral, Sal, with the service in Hebrew. I've been to Christian funerals and it's pretty much the same. Prayers, coffin, fill in the grave, more prayers.'

She turns to look at him as she walks. She loves this man more than she has ever loved anyone, and there is not a scintilla of doubt in her mind about spending the rest of her life with him. He is handsome, intelligent, generous and sometimes very funny. But sometimes she despairs at the lack of understanding, the want of subtlety, when it comes to putting himself in others' shoes. He is not selfish and he is rarely unkind, but he is himself unusually robust, and where people's sensibilities are concerned he can be a bull in a china shop — completely oblivious to the finer feelings being trampled around him.

Yellow London brick is ubiquitous throughout the capital and its hinterlands. From the perimeter walls and cell blocks making up HM Prison Brixton, to the impoverished south London housing estates whose former occupants now reside there, to the bijou, wisteria-garlanded squares of Islington — the same brick can be found in each.

Perhaps that is why Brixton Prison always reminds Charles of a housing complex. Or, he thinks, a factory, because looming before him is the largest crime-factory in the south of England. These doors admit callow young men who were insufficiently skilled to evade arrest. Some months or years later they are shown out of the same doors, declared rehabilitated, but in fact better-skilled in their criminal enterprise of choice than when they entered. In addition, they will have gained unofficial qualifications in such subsidiary subjects as drug-trafficking, safe-breaking, forgery and long-firm fraud. Charles jokes that HM Prison Service offers the best professional development courses available in England. As a member of the society upon whom these improved criminals prey, Charles thinks it a scandal that half of those released will re-offend — usually with more serious offences — within a year. Rehabilitation? It's a joke.

As a member of the Bar, on the other hand, he is more sanguine. Like every criminal barrister he knows, Charles's early practice was built upon repeat offenders such as these, their families and their friends. Indeed, had it not been for a couple of villainous clans in south London on whom Charles relied almost exclusively in his first two years, his career would probably have failed.

Charles presents his visiting order, his Bar Council certification and his letter of Instruction from Serban, and ducks under the door. He is pointed towards another door, where he will be searched. He waits in a short queue, watching as the lawyers in front of him are processed. He attends prisons with as few personal possessions as possible to oil the wheels of the system. Accordingly, he carries his brief under his arm and not in a briefcase; before leaving home he emptied all his pockets of extraneous items; and he carries no law books.

By the time he is beckoned forward by a prison guard in uniform, he has emptied his pockets ready to place his loose change and pens in the stainless steel bowl offered to him. He empties onto the table the two packets of cigarettes he carries (universal prison currency, whether his client smokes or not) to prove that the packets contain no contraband, and he fans out his case papers to demonstrate they've not been hollowed out to accommodate a weapon. Having been told he may move to the next stage he stands, as directed, with his legs apart to permit a strange man to feel up the inside of his thighs, and watches as another tests his jacket collar and cuffs for rigid objects, such as concealed razor blades.

Ten minutes later he is allowed to enter the cacophonous visiting area. He gives his documents to another prison officer who also examines them again, and is finally directed to a table at which the solicitor, Mr Serban, is waiting.

The large room echoes with noise. Other prisoners, at tables no more than a couple of feet from where Charles sits, are meeting family and friends. A few are talking to lawyers. One of the problems faced by barristers when visiting incarcerated clients at Brixton Prison is the absence of a dedicated area for legal meetings. Barristers have to take instructions surrounded by prisoners, their wives and families, with prison officers patrolling the aisles between the tables. It is impossible to have a confidential conversation, and more than once Charles has had experience of overheard information being sold on, including by corrupt prison officers. It was well known that the Kray twins had officers on the take in most of the London prisons.

'Good morning,' says Charles, sitting next to the solicitor. 'Been here long?'

'About forty minutes,' replies the other. 'The train timetable from Manchester didn't work out well, so I decided to get here early. Also, I wasn't sure exactly where to go or what the procedure would be once I arrived, so I thought I should leave extra time. I'm so sorry to hear about your mother.' Charles looks at him questioningly. 'Your clerk mentioned it when we were looking for dates to fix this conference, that's all.'

'I see. Thank you. I've read the new papers.'

'I'm sorry it's all last-minute,' says Serban. 'I've had trouble getting Bobby to take this seriously. He was still insisting that it's all a mistake.'

'I'd have imagined being charged with murder would've focused his mind somewhat,' says Charles wryly.

'I think that, subconsciously, he was refusing to engage with it. Despite all his bluster, he's terrified of the police.'

'Because of what happened to him in Romania.'

'Exactly.'

'And now?' asks Charles.

'Now he's seen the prosecution evidence,' replies Serban grimly, 'he's certain he's the victim of a police conspiracy. He's even asked if the Met could've been coerced by the Securitate, or working with them.'

'The Met need no coercion, believe me. As for working with foreign intelligence, I think that's a tad unlikely. This smells to me like common or garden corruption. Any news from our pathologist, Professor Lymme?'

Serban shakes his head. 'I spoke again to his secretary, yesterday. She promises this week. But she said that last week, too.'

'Okay. Keep chasing, please. I'm not expecting any surprises, but you never know.'

The two men wait for ten minutes before Gold is shown in. He weaves his way past tables and children towards his legal team. He wears a pair of slacks and a crew-necked jumper, is close-shaven and, to Charles's surprise, looks relaxed.

'Hello, Victor, Mr Holborne,' he says. He takes a seat and places a bundle of papers on the table.

'How are you?' asks Charles.

Gold pulls a face. 'Not too bad, all considered. The food's better than it was in the Army, and my young cellmate doesn't snore, so could be worse.'

'Army?' asks Charles, curious.

'Of course. I was twenty when Romania joined the Axis powers and I was conscripted.'

'So you fought for the Nazis?' asks Charles, trying to keep his voice level but aware of a lurch in his stomach.

Gold looks embarrassed. 'For two years, until 1944. Then Romania switched sides, and I fought with the Russians for the Allies. You hadn't realised?'

Charles shakes his head. 'Never occurred to me. I suppose it should have.'

Their table becomes an island of prickly silence in the noisy room.

'Does this make a difference?' asks Gold eventually.

Charles looks up. 'To your case? No. I'm obliged to represent you whether I want to or not. It's called the "cab-rank rule".'

'But you don't want to anymore?' presses Gold.

'I didn't say that.'

'But you'd rather not?'

'I didn't say that either. But I've never met a Nazi before,' says Charles, staring into the other man's eyes. 'You know my family background, don't you?'

Gold leans forward and lowers his voice. 'Yes, Victor told me. But I'm not a Nazi, Mr Holborne. I was conscripted, as I said. I had nothing to do with your people, and to the best of my knowledge my unit did no damage to them. And I try to judge every individual I meet on their merits, and how they treat me. I'm sure you do the same, right?' he adds, and Charles recognises the challenge.

'I try to.'

'Well, then?'

'If you're happy for me to proceed, let's get to it. I'm duty-bound to do the best I can for you, and I'll continue to do that. I like to think ... well, I hope I would do the same even if you were a Nazi. Or a Soviet Communist.'

'Well, I'm neither, and I never have been. Like you, I'm an ordinary guy who got caught up in a war started by governments, and who chose to chance it and get out of Romania as soon as he could.'

'All right then. Let's start. Are you having any trouble here?' asks Charles.

'What, from other inmates?' Gold laughs briefly. 'A couple of likely lads tried it once. They won't do it again. I can look after myself.'

'I'm pleased to hear it. Now, have you looked at the prosecution statements?' asks Charles, nodding towards the documents.

'Yes. Victor asked me to mark them up. What I agreed with, what I didn't, any comments, and so on.'

'Good,' replies Charles, realising that although Victor Serban might lack experience in criminal cases, he is clearly competent. The skills he has acquired in contentious civil work appear to be transferable.

Charles picks up the well-thumbed bundle of prosecution witness statements and scans the first couple of pages.

'Yes, I think I can read your writing. If you don't mind, I'll take these back with me to go through them carefully. We don't have long and there's a lot to get through. So perhaps I can just fire questions at you. Will that be all right?'

'Sure.'

Charles pulls out a document from his Instructions. 'Let's start with Frankie Perry.'

'Simple,' says Gold, jabbing a thick forefinger at the document in Charles's hand. 'It's a pack of lies. As I told you before, I've never really spoken to him. He's only worked a couple of shifts since Johnny Blaise arrived. He's not the "security" type, know what I mean? He's skinny, got something wrong with his back or shoulder and can't even look you in the eye when you talk to him. A strong wind'd blow him over! As for seeing me taking a delivery of drugs, utter nonsense. I told you, I won't tolerate drugs, especially at the concerts.'

'Ever had any beef with him?' asks Charles.

'Beef? Like an argument?'

'Yes.'

'Never.'

'So our case has to be that he's making this up. Why would he do that?'

Gold shrugs. 'That's what you're here for.'

'No, Mr Gold, I'm here to represent you. I'll do the best I can to discredit the evidence produced by the Crown, but I'm not a magician. I can only work with what you give me, or what we can discover. Barristers work with evidence.'

'Then I can't tell you. I never had any problem with him; I barely know the man. Why he'd say all this is beyond me.'

Charles turns to the solicitor. 'I understand you instructed Billy Munday on my recommendation?'

'I did, but he wasn't able to find much. We can't even get a criminal record number for a list of previous convictions, but it doesn't appear he has any. Although Mr Munday remains very suspicious of him. Something about his lifestyle not matching his earnings.'

'We have to dig deeper,' says Charles. 'I know you're worried about the cost of all this, Mr Gold, but Perry is the key. He's preparing to perjure himself to get you — a virtual stranger — convicted of murder, and we absolutely have to find out why. I recommend we ask Munday to follow him for a few days. And to do it properly, he needs at least one other investigator, ideally two or three. I won't pretend; it will be expensive.'

Gold shakes his head sorrowfully. 'I understand. But I'm skint.'

'Not according to your accounts, you aren't. Companies House shows that Gold Management made a very healthy profit last year.'

'That was last year. Believe me, my bank accounts are empty.' He pauses. 'How much do you think Munday will need?'

'I don't know, but it won't be less than five hundred.'

Gold turns to his cousin. 'Victor, if I write a letter for you to give to Mickey, will you deliver it by hand?'

'Of course.'

'I'll get the money,' says Gold to Charles.

'We'll need to go back to the accounts in a moment, but let's continue with the eyewitnesses. Tell me about Mrs Gonzales, the housekeeper at Kingston Grange. She apparently found Christine Bailey's body.'

'Maria? She's lovely. I got her through an agency. She was working for this Libyan millionaire in Mayfair, but she wasn't happy and was looking to move. She's been with me for a couple of years.'

'She says she saw Christine Bailey at the house that evening.'

Gold shrugs. 'No doubt she did.'

'And she saw you.'

'Yes. I've never denied I was there earlier. When we got back from the Astoria, Maria was running round wringing out

118

towels and emptying buckets. One of those idiots left a bath tap on. Maria found water pouring down the stairs. When I got back I pitched in with a mop. The bathroom was all right, but the carpets outside were saturated and there was some staining downstairs where water had come through from above. Then I made some notes for the insurers. In fact, I asked the group's photographer to take some pictures for me, which he did. I did all I could, and said I was going. Maria said she'd get the last bus.'

'Is Mrs Gonzales likely to be a sympathetic witness?'

'Yes, I think so. We got on very well. She introduced me to her boys.' He grins. 'They want to be musicians.'

'And is she reliable? She doesn't provide you with an alibi but she is quite helpful. The last time she saw you at the house seems to have been well before midnight.'

'I don't know what you mean by reliable, but she's very sensible and competent. I think she'll give evidence well. But she's being called by the prosecution, isn't she?'

'Yes,' replies Charles, 'which allows us to cross-examine her.' Charles pauses to look at his notes. 'Mr Serban's got a statement from your driver, Stanley Crispie.'

'Yes?'

'Who confirms that you left the property at around half ten.'

'Exactly.'

'He drove you in the limousine?'

'Yes. I'd told Stan I wouldn't need him at Finsbury Park until midnight, so he'd taken the car and gone home. When everything went tits up at the Astoria, I decided to go back to Kingston Grange with the boys.'

'Why? You live in Brixton, don't you? The bus could've dropped you off on its way.'

'Yes, but there were things to sort out. Glyn, that's the front of house sound engineer, said the problem was caused by the Astoria's technicians, and they were blaming him. I'd already shelled out a couple of hundred on refunds, and I needed to get to the bottom of it.'

'Right. So you get to the property and discover the flood. What time did you call Stan to collect you?'

'Within a couple of minutes of arriving. I wanted him there, ready to go, as soon as I was able to leave.'

'Do you think there would be witnesses to his arrival and departure?'

'Sure, at the gates. But will any of the security team help me, if their boss is sticking the knife in? There's the group members, I suppose, but whether they'd have been paying attention or were sober enough to remember...' He shakes his head doubtfully.

'Okay, we'll make enquiries. Worst case: Stan's our only witness to the time you left. How long have you known him?'

'Twenty years, but I've only employed him in the last six months. I had another driver but I didn't like him. Bit of a boy racer, which you can't do in a limo. I'd met Stan on a couple of occasions when I was on the boards myself. He's always been on the fringes of theatre work. He was an assistant stage manager and did a bit of acting up north. When I heard he'd given up and was driving for a living, I asked him if he'd like to work for me full-time, and he agreed.'

'Does he have a police record?'

'You'd need to ask him, but I think there is something. He grew up on a rough estate in Toxteth.'

'And what sort of bloke is he?'

'He's all right. Divorced, two grown-up girls, steady sort of chap in his mid-fifties. When I put him on a salary he moved down here willingly enough. Said he'd give the Smoke a try, and he's made a success of it. He makes friends easily, and people like him. He was a pretty good actor; tells a good story.'

'Sounds promising, except for the trouble with the police. Mr Serban, can you get details from him?'

'Certainly.'

Charles checks his notes, ticks off subject headings and comes to the next point. 'Now, the accounts. This Mr Spurling, the accountant instructed by the prosecution, says you're in financial trouble, and if the Johnny Blaise tour collapses, you'll go bust. This, they say, provides motive. You needed to hush up everything around Christine Bailey to protect Blaise's reputation and the tour.'

'I'm good with numbers, and I've a good memory. On the back of Spurling's statement I've made detailed notes, with figures,' replies Gold, tapping the bundle of prosecution statements. 'I've already explained, the US label would only let Blaise come over if I paid their end upfront. No one's done this sort of European tour before and they weren't prepared to take risks. So, yes, I'm stretched, but the UK leg will put me back in the black. Ninety per cent of the expenses for the European dates have been paid and I've plenty of stock.'

'Stock?'

'I showed you the singles, and we're trying out other stuff, like T-shirts. The tour's all about promoting the album generally, but in particular the singles. The European leg of the tour is all profit. These sorts of ups and downs aren't unusual in the business. It's always high risk, especially when introducing a group to a new market.'

Charles turns over the prosecution bundle and looks for Spurling's report. The back of the first page is covered in notes and what look like summarised accounts. Charles skim-reads, and is impressed. He will need time to go through it — he wonders if he might ask his accountant brother to have a quick look — but to have been able to remember the figures sufficiently well to produce this rebuttal from a prison cell is impressive. And Gold speaks with absolute confidence. Charles feels his doubts about his client dissipating slightly.

'We might need to instruct our own accountant to give evidence, ideally someone who's been in the business,' he says. 'Maybe your accountant can recommend someone?'

'Why don't we use him?'

'Because he's your accountant. It has to be somebody independent.'

'I think he'll be able to recommend someone, then.'

'What's the answer to the Crown's point? If all the profit depended on the European leg to come, you couldn't risk the tour collapsing, so you'd do anything to bury damaging publicity. Even if you didn't intend to kill Christine, perhaps you were trying to get her to be quiet? Perhaps she'd woken up, only to find she'd been raped? Or perhaps she was calling out for help? I'm sure you'll be cross-examined on the basis that, if you didn't kill her deliberately, you did something which led inadvertently to her death.'

'Nothing like that happened, certainly not while I was there,' replies Gold adamantly. 'I had no interaction with the girl at all. Anyway, how does killing her and then running out of the property cover it up? It makes no sense.'

'Maybe, as Perry suggests, you were panicking.'

'Total nonsense. I don't panic. Not in my nature.'

Charles smiles. It is difficult not to be impressed by this man's confidence. He checks the time again. There is one remaining aspect of the evidence that has to be addressed.

'The police have dug up this guy, Eamon O'Keefe.'

'Yeah, I remember him. He was front of house manager at the Liverpool Empire.'

'Yes. He says in 1958 you were on the bill, waiting in the wings and about to go on, and he saw you having a fight with a drug dealer.'

'That's what I've been saying. I can't stand them. But he wasn't just a drug dealer. His name was Lawrence Geddes. Everyone called him "Gettit Geddes". In the forties and fifties he was a black-market racketeer. Food, booze, nylons, whatever it was, he could get it. Hard times for most people, still rationing, but the top billers on the circuit earned good money, so there was always a ready market at the big theatres. After the ban was lifted and American entertainers started coming over, he began selling marijuana too, especially to the jazz men. And that's what took off.'

'What was the row about? I don't doubt the prosecution will say you were having an argument with your dealer.'

'Oh, it was nothing, really. He'd been pestering one of the girls in the chorus, so when I saw him, I told him to piss off. It escalated from there.'

'He says you were convicted of common assault, which is what led to you being banned from performing at the Empire.'

'Possibly I was definitely banned after that, which is one of the reasons I decided to change direction.'

'But when we last met, you told me you had no criminal convictions,' points out Charles.

Gold raises his hands in supplication. 'Sorry. I forgot. It was just a scrap, no big deal.'

'Any other convictions you might have forgotten?' asks Charles.

'Not that I recall.'

Charles turns to Serban. 'Have we asked for the client's CRO?'

'No. Sorry. I assumed they'd serve it without being asked.'

'Best to ask. We need to get ahead of anything there may be, and not be responding at trial.' He addresses his client. 'Time's almost up. Any questions for me?'

Gold considers. 'No, I don't think so.'

'Okay. We have seven working days before trial. I'll try to visit again after we've taken these investigations a bit further, all right, but I can't guarantee it. Your case will be fully prepared, I promise, but my mother just died, the funeral is tomorrow, and believe it or not, I'm supposed to be getting married in just over a fortnight.'

'Sorry to hear that,' says Gold. Charles isn't sure if Gold is referring to the funeral or the wedding.

Gold seems to have something further to say. Charles waits. 'Look,' he says eventually, 'is there any possibility the Met are doing this because they've been asked to by the Romanian security services?'

'Mr Serban mentioned this worry to me. I think it's very unlikely. Why would they want to, anyway?'

'To get me deported back to Romania, maybe?'

'But what for?' asks Charles. 'I can see they might want to prevent people from leaving, but what's the point of bringing you back? It's not as if you're important politically, right?'

'No, not really.'

'If you were a spy, part of the opposition or even perhaps a journalist, I could imagine they might want you back for some sort of show trial, but you're just one of thousands of people who got out, now making a life in another country. No. The motive for this is closer to home. We need to focus on Perry and the police.'

# CHAPTER THIRTEEN

It is a Jewish custom for the men of the family to help fill the deceased's grave. All males over the age of thirteen queue to file past the hole, waiting for a spade to be passed to them so they can throw a shovel-full of soil onto the coffin. In some less orthodox families, women are also permitted to take part. Whenever Charles attends Willesden Jewish Cemetery for a funeral or stone-setting (the event a year later to erect the headstone) it seems to be raining. He invariably returns home, shoes heavy with thick, clinging London clay and trousers that require dry-cleaning.

Yet here he is, at his mother's funeral, and, bizarrely, the weather is exceptionally lovely. The air seems clearer than usual, the streets shine with the residue of overnight rain as if given a special wash for the day, and the green and orange foliage of the trees appears unusually vibrant. It is sufficiently warm to force mourners to carry their overcoats and raincoats over their arms, which involves a lot of passing of clothing before the deployment of spades. To Charles the anomaly seems significant, although he could not easily explain why. Perhaps because, to him, Millie is associated with tears and unhappiness, so the skies should be dark and the mourners cold, wet and miserable.

Charles and David stand on either side of their father. Harry insisted that he could walk to the graveside, which he did slowly with his sons' support, Charles with an arm around his waist and David, who is taller, with an arm around his shoulder. Prayers have already been said in the prayer hall — the black and white floor tiles always remind Charles of a chessboard; the deceased, checkmated at the last — and at the graveside. Harry has wept quietly on a few occasions, particularly after the rabbi and a lifelong family friend each spoke movingly about Millie's life. David and others have also been affected at various times.

Charles's eyes have remained dry, providing yet another reason for folk to scrutinise him with sidelong glances or even, in a couple of cases, to stare at him with frank hostility. The boy who turned his back on his religion, his family and his community; the undergraduate who hid his Jewishness behind an Anglicised name and married out without a word to his family; the man whose hoity-toity wife was murdered; the man now living in sin with another *shiksa* and their bastard; and now, finally, the *mamzer* who couldn't shed a single tear for that poor, dear woman, his mother. He can almost hear the scandalised verdict: *Poor Millie! Better off dead than to have a son like that.*

Sally, who knows Charles better than anyone in the world, often says that he never deals with his "stuff". The conflicts and pain he carries are crated up and stored away in some secret psychic warehouse, ostensibly to be examined and resolved at some future date but, in reality, nailed shut and never addressed. She's right, he knows. But half that warehouse is taken up with crates labelled "Millie Horowitz" and although they managed a degree of reconciliation in the last few years, the pain Millie and Charles inflicted on each other is too big, too fresh, to be explored. Certainly not now; probably not ever.

So while Charles is sorry his mother has died, his sorrow is principally for Harry, who must now start a life without the woman he adored for over half a century.

Charles lifts his eyes to the opposite side of the grave. Sonia and Sally stand side-by-side, their arms linked. To Charles's surprise he sees Sally raising a handkerchief to dab at her eyes. Their gazes meet, and Sally half-smiles and shrugs lightly as if to say she doesn't know why she should be so affected, but she nonetheless is.

The funeral service concludes with the close family reciting Kaddish, the ancient Aramaic prayer for the dead and, although Charles doesn't believe in it at all, he nonetheless feels the hairs on the back of his neck rising and a constriction forming in his throat. It's powerful magic, and he is not immune to it.

Prayers completed, people start to drift away from the graveside, walking in small groups back to the prayer hall where, also in accordance with Jewish custom, they will wash their hands at the tap. It takes nearly half an hour for everyone to disperse. Harry, Charles and David wait in line to kiss the mourners' cheeks or shake their hands, and to be wished, once again, a long life. Then everyone piles into cars and heads back to Sunshine Court, where hot drinks and snacks await them. David and Sonia offered to host both the after-funeral gathering and the more formal, religious *shiva* at their home. Unlike Wren Street, their house is kosher and therefore acceptable to all who would attend. However, in the end, the decision was taken to use the large private rooms at Sunshine so that if Harry felt fatigued he could rest in his room. Furthermore, using the private function room meant that the female members of close family could go to the cemetery, rather than waiting with prepared sandwiches and pots of tea. That function could be delegated to Sunshine's staff.

It proves a wise decision. By early afternoon Harry announces that he needs to lie down, and he is taken to his room. He sleeps for several hours, waking just in time to wash his face and greet those attending the *shiva*. Almost two hundred people arrive and all the windows have to be opened because the room is hotter than ever. A young rabbi unknown to Charles leads the prayers, men to the fore, women at the back, all clutching a thin black prayer book as they recite in Hebrew and English. There are people from the Horowitzes' current synagogue in north London and their old one in the heart of the East End; relatives and lifelong friends; business acquaintances of half a century or more; and, the largest contingent, friends and acquaintances from Mile End. It is, as everyone comments, a wonderful turnout for someone of Millie's age, whose generation have already started dying off. It demonstrates the extent to which Millie was loved by those who knew her.

After prayers are completed and female members of the family prepare to circulate the packed room with cups of tea and bridge rolls, Charles sits with his father and brother on low chairs to accept the condolences of the attendees. In a lull between well-wishers, Harry turns to Charles.

'Your wedding,' he says.

'Don't worry about it, Dad. We're going to cancel. We can do it next spring, perhaps.'

'No,' says Harry firmly. 'I think you should go ahead.'

'It's all right, really. Sally and I have discussed it, and she understands.'

'And that's to her credit, but she's not Jewish and these rules don't apply to her. And, let's face it, son, they've barely applied to you either, not since you were bar mitzvah. The one person who might've been upset, if she'd been able to think about it, is your mother. And … she's no longer here to be upset.'

Charles turns to face his father. 'You don't have to say all this, Dad.'

'I know I don't. But Sally's been waiting a long time for you to realise what the rest of us did years ago.'

'Which is?'

David, listening at his father's other shoulder, leans forward and addresses Charles. 'That she's the right girl for you, and you need to make an honest woman of her.'

Charles smiles. 'That's a very old-fashioned attitude,' he chides.

'Charles,' says Harry, 'I promise you, I shan't be in the least upset if you get married at the end of this month as planned. It was always your mother who felt so strongly about these rules. Whereas, for me —' he lifts his hands in a typical Jewish gesture — 'they're more ... *guidelines*. I don't want you to use your mother's death as an excuse to put off what you should have done a long time ago, do you understand?'

'I wouldn't do that. I've made a commitment and I will honour it.'

'Good,' says Harry with an air of finality. 'I look forward to seeing you married at the end of the month.'

# CHAPTER FOURTEEN

The Golden Lion pub in Peckham was once a quiet neighbourhood boozer in an unexceptional working-class area of south London. Three generations of the same family held the licence, and for decades the pub peacefully and uneventfully served the households in the surrounding suburban streets.

However, over recent years the "Lion" as it was known locally began to acquire a reputation as a "villains' pub". As it became popular with shady men doing deals in corners and hard men fighting over territory and betrayals, the locals drifted away. The licensee, an astute middle-aged woman and a publican since her twenties, was faced with a simple choice: complain and be shut down, or acquiesce and keep her head down and her business afloat. She decided on the latter. Since then she has taken great pains to see nothing, hear nothing, and say nothing.

It is a minute or two after five-thirty and the pub has just opened. Detective Inspector Pilcher, DCI Quigley's right-hand man, is one of only two customers in the entire place and the other is in the public bar. Sunlight streams through the glazed door and windows.

The shaft of sunlight from the saloon door is dimmed as someone approaches it, and Pilcher looks up. The door opens. A skinny, shambling man wearing workman's overalls and a paint-stained cap pauses briefly on the threshold. He scans the room. Pilcher closes the newspaper he was reading. The newcomer sees him in the corner and enters fully, allowing the door to close behind him. He approaches Pilcher's table with a curious sideways gait as if, although proceeding forwards, he has spent so much of his life looking over his shoulder that his spine has become permanently twisted.

'Sorry I'm late,' he says. 'I was working —' he indicates his overalls — 'and thought we'd said tomorrow.'

The detective scans the room. The man who served his pint has disappeared and he and the twisted man are the only two people in the bar. He nonetheless lowers his voice before he speaks.

'Sit down.'

'Can I get myself a pint?' asks the newcomer.

'No. You won't have time to drink it. Sit down and shut up.'

Pilcher is a different prospect to his master. Younger, less cadaverous and better dressed, he is shorter but powerfully built, with a swarthy complexion and such dark brown eyes they appear almost black. The twisted man knows that he is no less dangerous than DCI Quigley, albeit in a more obvious, more immediate way. He complies with the instruction.

Pilcher slides his hand across the table. The other looks down and sees, hidden in the policeman's fist, the glint of metal.

'You're lucky we got these back,' says Pilcher. 'In fact you're lucky, period. You've no idea of the effort required to winkle you out of that one. Boss had to call in a lot of favours.'

'Yeah, sorry 'bout that, Mr Pilcher. Guess I'm not always lucky.'

'Two grand down the toilet. Well,' urges the detective, 'take 'em.'

The twisted man's hand flashes out and slips the offering into his pocket. 'What about Derek?'

'Don't worry about him. He'll be fine. Wheels are in motion.'

'Righto,' says the man after a pause. 'I'm getting it in the neck from the family. Got another one for me?' he says, indicating with a slight movement of his arm the skeleton keys he has just pocketed.

'Yes, but there'll be a short delay.'

'Righto. Wanna tell me where? Always takes a day or two to get me alibi in place.'

'No, Frankie, I don't want to tell you yet. To be honest, I had to persuade Mr Quigley you're still up for it. He wonders if you're still any use to us. You *are* still up for it, I suppose?' There is sarcasm and a threat in the question.

'If you've got a job for me, Mr Pilcher, I'll take it. It's not like I have a choice.'

'That's right, and don't you forget that. I've got enough on you to earn you fifteen now, and that's after parole. And it goes up with every job.'

'Mr Pilcher, Mr Pilcher,' whines the other plaintively, 'you ain't got no need to threaten me. I know the score, don't I? You've made it clear enough ever since we started.'

'Just a timely reminder, Frankie.'

Perhaps it's the pleasant afternoon sunshine slanting in through the window, or perhaps it's the beer, but to Perry, despite the aggressive language, the detective seems relaxed.

The balance of power between the two men is such that the DI would never believe Francis Perry capable of cheating him. Perry has spent years cultivating Quigley and Pilcher's impression of him as a scared weasel: good at what he does, but a coward. Perry's walk, his voice, even his clothes, have been painstakingly curated to create the impression that he never will, never *could*, be a threat to his police controllers.

'As for the next shop,' says Pilcher, lifting his drink, 'you needn't worry. It's London. Furs, this time. You'll need to take

132

someone with you again as there's too much for one man to load quickly.'

'Will Derek be available by then?' asks Perry.

'Probably, but we'd prefer you to take the Irishman. Seems he can handle himself all right.'

'Yeah, he's got his wits about him, that one.'

'Good. I'll set it up.'

Perry pauses, expecting further instructions.

'Well, what're you waiting for?' asks Pilcher. 'Fuck off.'

# CHAPTER FIFTEEN

It is the Monday after the funeral, and Charles is walking home, crossing High Holborn at its junction with Chancery Lane, when he notices a headline on the front of the news vendor's corner stall. He stops, gives the man sixpence and is handed a folded copy of the *London Evening Standard*. He opens it and reads as he continues towards Gray's Inn Road.

His stride slows briefly as his eye is caught by the now-infamous photograph of the naked Woodstock festivalgoer among outraged Bethel shoppers. He grins at her pretty backside and insouciant over-the-shoulder smile, and turns to the article that initially attracted his attention. It is headlined "Johnny Blaise tour to proceed" and, under a subtitle reading *"Tour manager awaiting murder trial at Old Bailey"*, it continues:

*Johnny Blaise and the Hellraisers today announced that despite the charges of murder faced by their tour manager and British representative, Bobby Gold, they will complete their planned concerts in England and continue with their European tour. Mr Gold was charged in relation to the death of a fan at the group's accommodation in Kingston upon Thames in July. Since then long queues have been seen outside record stores and theatre box offices as fans demand to know if the remaining dates of the tour would be honoured...*

The next section deals with the background of Johnny Blaise and the Hellraisers, their reputation as "the wild men of rock" and their phenomenal success in the US. Charles skims the rest of the article until he reaches the final paragraph, which recites a press release issued by the group. It is phrased as if the words came from Johnny Blaise himself.

*I and all the members of the Hellraisers have been deeply saddened by the death of the young woman, Christine Bailey, and our sympathies and condolences go to her family. Johnny Blaise and the Hellraisers, their management and record label, are unable for legal reasons to comment on the ongoing investigation or prosecution of Mr Gold. However, having co-operated fully with the Metropolitan Police investigation into Miss Bailey's death, we're informed we have no evidence to assist in that enquiry and are not required to remain in England for the trial. Although the circumstances are very sad, we cannot disappoint the thousands of fans who have already purchased tickets, and consider it our responsibility to honour our contractual obligations by continuing with the tour as planned.*

Charles looks for the author of the press release: WCA Records, the group's American label. *They must have taken over management of the tour*, he thinks.

He folds the newspaper and continues northwards on Gray's Inn Road, deep in thought.

'I'm home!' he calls from the hallway.

'We're up here,' replies Sally from somewhere above him.

Charles drops his things and goes directly to the bathroom on the first floor. Leia is in the bath playing with her ducks and Sally is on the floor beside her. Charles kisses both of them, takes off his jacket and kneels next to Sally.

'No Greta?' he asks.

'I told her to get off. I was at my desk just after seven this morning, didn't stop for lunch, and by half five I'd had enough. Andrea's very good and I can trust her to finish off the diary.'

'Andrea?'

'New administrator.'

'Administrator? You mean junior clerk.'

'No, I don't. Times have changed. She's in her thirties, is very experienced and has a degree. "Junior clerk" is a patronising label. And probably sexist.' She pauses. 'So, how was your day?'

Charles smiles. In fact he doesn't disagree with Sally. He is often irked when referred to as "junior counsel" which, notwithstanding years of experience, he will be for the rest of his career, unless and until he takes silk. Nonetheless, he allows himself to be led into less dangerous waters.

'Not too bad,' he replies.

'Anything from Sean?'

Charles shakes his head. 'No.'

'We're running out of time, Charles.'

'I know. I thought I'd give him till mid-week, Wednesday say, and if I've still heard nothing, I'll ask David.'

'Good. Thank you.'

'How's the catering going?' he asks. 'I'm sorry I haven't time to help.'

'It's fine. I'm enjoying it and, let's face it, entertaining's not your strong suit. Mum and me sisters are coming for Sunday tea and final decisions.'

'Really? Wouldn't it be easier for you to go to Romford?'

'Yes, but they want to see the house. Mum's only been here once and needs to understand the layout so we can plan how to use the rooms.'

'It's only forty people. We've had that many here before,' he points out.

'Yes, but in the summer, when we could use the garden. We have to assume it'll be raining, and no one's going outside to a muddy garden in their best frocks. And quite a few people won't be able to manage the stairs to the kitchen. Don't worry about it, Charlie, it's all under control. What've you got there?' She nods in the direction of the newspaper Charles carried into the bathroom. 'If that's important you'd better move it. It's getting wet.'

Charles picks up the paper and hands it to her. It's open at the right page. 'I wanted to show you. I think we're in trouble on the Gold case.' He points to the relevant article. 'Here, I'll take over.'

They swap places and he positions himself with a hand close to Leia's back. She is able to support herself in the bath, but she so loves the water that she gets overexcited when splashing, and sometimes tips backwards unpredictably. He gives Sally a few moments to read the article.

'They're throwing Bobby Gold under the bus,' he says.

'You can understand it from Blaise's perspective, though,' says Sally. 'If he's got no evidence to give, why cancel the tour? Gold would have to reimburse all the people who've bought tickets. So it's in Gold's interests to proceed, too.'

'Maybe. But I can't work out why Johnny Blaise and his entourage are refusing to speak to Serban. Blaise may have nothing to help the prosecution, but he might have something which could help Gold. Yet he's going out of his way to hide behind his lawyers and the US label. I don't know. It feels pretty unchristian to me.'

'Is he Christian?'

'Supposed to be.'

'What do you know about him?'

'That's one of the problems. Almost nothing. We've got the bland biography put out by the label, just a couple of lines.'

'It's a pity you haven't got someone like Billy Munday working in America,' comments Sally.

'Yes, it is.' Charles frowns.

'What?' asks Sally.

'Just had a thought. Do you remember that lawyer we met when the American Bar Association came over?' Sally shakes her head. 'Young guy, suntan, good-looking, Somebody Somebody the third?'

'No, don't think so.'

'Yes, you do,' insists Charles, grinning. 'Claimed he drafted Dionne Warwick's contract with Scepter Records. You remember. He couldn't take his eyes off you.'

Sally blushes. 'Oh, him. Yes.' She grins at the memory. 'Spencer Wainwright the third.'

'That's it! Spencer Wainwright the third. Entertainment law specialist. *"I spent the weekend on Dean Martin's yacht,"'* mimics Charles, with an attempt at an American accent.

Sally laughs. 'It was Peter Lawford's yacht.'

'Same difference. If I could get contact details for him, would you be prepared to drop him a line or, better still, call him?'

'Oh, Charlie, no! I met the geezer once and he was a total prick.'

'You didn't think so that evening,' teases Charles. 'I recall you danced with him more than once.'

'I was being polite.'

'Yeah, course you were. But he was very taken with you, wasn't he? Invited you to visit him in New York.'

'He invited both of us, actually.'

'Yeah, so you say. But, Sally, I'm serious. Would you do it, please? If not for Gold, then for me?'

Sally sighs. 'What do you want me to say?'

'Tell him I need some information about Johnny Blaise, background, family history and so on. If he really knows everyone in the business, he's bound to know more than the PR output.'

Sally nods reluctantly. 'Okay, but it might have to wait a day or two. My head's too full.'

'The trial starts next week,' he points out.

She sighs again, this time with obvious irritation. 'All right,' she replies. 'Get his firm's number.'

Charles bends and kisses his fiancée's cheek. 'Thank you. You're wonderful.'

Sally doesn't answer. Instead she stands and addresses Leia. 'Come on, madam, that's enough splashing for one evening. Grab the towel, will you, Charles?'

Charles sits on the lavatory lid with the bath towel spread across his knees and Sally places their pink, wriggling daughter in his lap. He wraps her up warmly.

They work together efficiently, drying Leia, pinning her clean terry towel nappy in place, and getting her into her nightclothes. Until recently the child wore a nightdress, but Sally is trying her in something new, what is being called a sleepsuit, and Leia hasn't yet got the hang of making her limbs go floppy to be inserted into the soft cotton arms and legs.

Charles lifts her, now fully dressed, by the armpits, and bounces her on the bath mat.

'Spencer Wainwright the third! Spencer Wainwright the third!' he says, bouncing the child in time with his words.

Leia squeals with enjoyment.

Sally stands, shaking her head and smiling despite herself. 'You'll get her overexcited,' she says.

'What, like her mother? Spencer Wainwright the third!'

Sally swipes his arm.

# CHAPTER SIXTEEN

Billy Munday is bored. He has been bored for all of the last seven hours. His two colleagues, one positioned at each end of Caulfield Road, are bored too.

The team of four (only three today; Colin called in sick) have been monitoring Frankie Perry for days. They have absolutely nothing to show for it. The man appears to live an entirely dull life.

They've followed him on multiple occasions, to the supermarket, to the launderette, the chippie, to watch Millwall Football Club being thumped four-nil by Blackburn Rovers, and to an address a few streets away where he appears to be giving a neighbour a hand cleaning out the gutters. He always seems to wear the same clothes — grey slacks, plaid shirt, paint-splattered decorator's cap, grubby anorak and a Millwall FC scarf — and there is a pervasive sense of misery about him. He drives his old Mark 1 Ford Cortina consistently at five miles per hour under the speed limit, which makes even short journeys interminable and increases the difficulty of following him without being spotted. When on foot, his demeanour and gait suggest someone suffering from depression. He trudges, rather than walks, head hung, shoulders drooped and with a curious twist to his spine as if leading with one shoulder. At the end of the previous day's shift, Munday pronounced Perry the most uninteresting person on whom he had ever had to conduct surveillance. Indeed, so unutterably dull did Perry's life appear that Munday was increasingly convinced that he must be hiding something. Surely *nobody* could really lead the life being portrayed? At least, not without feeling suicidal.

It is now dusk and the streets, which filled up an hour or two ago with people returning to their homes from work, are emptying. Kitchens are being illuminated as evening meals are cooked; televisions are being switched on; teenagers are flicking on bedroom lights before closing curtains and reluctantly starting homework.

Munday's stomach grumbles. He opens his glove compartment, but his emergency supplies have been consumed. The crisp packets, chocolate bar wrappers and apple cores have been collected and are now in a cardboard box in the boot, awaiting disposal. He looks at his watch. Still an hour to go before being relieved by the night team. He toys with the idea of standing them down. It's embarrassing; this week's invoice to Mr Serban is going to be huge, with nothing to show for it

A figure emerges from the alleyway between Perry's house and the identical one next door. Munday looks diagonally across the road, checks the figure and dismisses it. It's a man, but he is taller and younger than Perry and distinctly better dressed, wearing a suit, a dark raincoat and a stylish fedora hat. Then Munday remembers the couple next door to Perry and his wife: both elderly, the man requiring a walking stick. So, this person doesn't appear to belong in either household, yet there is no other entrance to the alley. The passageway simply connects the pavement to the two side doors facing each other at the far end. Curiosity aroused, Munday lifts his binoculars from the passenger seat and focuses them.

He just has time to train on the stranger's face before the man turns swiftly to his right and walks away from Munday's position, but it's enough. It's him! Munday picks up his walkie-talkie and presses the call button.

'Units One and Two, this is Control.'

'Come in, Control.'

'It's him! The guy walking towards you, Unit One. Blue suit and fedora.'

'No, Control, it's not him. Two tall, for a start. Over.'

'I'm telling you it is him. He's just standing up straight! Look carefully. Over.'

Pause.

'Control, Unit Two. You're right! It *is* him. Talk about a bloody transformation! Orders, Control, over?'

'I'm going on foot,' replies Munday. 'Ed, wait till he disappears round the corner and follow in the van. Michael, stay put in case we lose him and he comes back. Out.'

'Roger that. Out.'

Munday leaps out of his car, locks the door and follows on foot. Perry is now seventy or eighty yards ahead of him on the opposite side of the road. It is sufficiently dark, and the street so crowded with parked vehicles, that the detective is not worried about being identified, but he takes care to leave a constant distance between himself and the man striding purposefully towards the corner. The transformation really is extraordinary. Perry's length of stride, his energy and his appearance together have the effect of reducing his apparent age by over a decade. Munday would have placed Perry in his late forties, perhaps early fifties; now he looks little older than Munday himself, thirty-four.

He allows Perry to turn the corner so he is hidden behind the flank of the end property, and runs with as light footsteps as possible up to the junction. He looks right just in time to see Perry inserting a key into the front door of another house. Munday hears a vehicle approaching from behind, turns and sees Ed approaching in the van. He signals urgently for his colleague to slow, which he does. Perry enters the house quickly and shuts the door behind him.

*What the…?*

Munday is still on the pavement, wondering what to do next when he hears the sound of an electric motor. The rollup door of the garage to the property which Perry has just entered begins to move. Munday barely has time to duck back around the corner before the headlights of a vehicle emerge. It's a brand-new Triumph TR6 in bright red, a playboy's car and, rarely seen on the roads of England, a left-hand drive.

The shiny vehicle rolls onto the road as the automatic doors clatter closed behind it. Fortunately for Munday, Perry turns the wheel in the opposite direction. Munday jogs back, opens the passenger door of the waiting van and jumps in.

'Follow him! I'll try Michael before we're out of range.'

By the time the van has reached the end of the road, the TR6 has accelerated into the evening traffic. Munday and the van driver look left and right.

'Can you see him?' demands Munday urgently. 'I can't see him!'

'No. Which way do you want me to go?'

'Try left Dressed like that, he's probably heading up West.'

The van turns into the traffic, its driver doing his best to overtake slower-moving vehicles ahead of them. But they are too late. Perry and his flash sports car are nowhere to be seen.

# CHAPTER SEVENTEEN

Leia has had her last feed of the night and, although it's still quite early, Charles and Sally are on their way to bed. Sally is exhausted. Charles is optimistic, and about to be disappointed.

He is turning off the kitchen lights when the phone rings. He picks up.

'Terminus 1525,' he says.

'Charles, it's Billy. I hope it's not too late but I've got something I think you'll want to see immediately.'

'What is it?'

'Can I show you?'

Charles hesitates. 'We're trying to get an early night. Sally's already gone up.'

'I'm in a call box by King's Cross. I can be with you in two minutes. It won't take a second.'

'Okay, come round. I'll put the kettle on.'

'Don't worry about that,' says Munday, and the line goes dead.

Charles replaces the receiver and runs up to the top of the house. Sally is just coming out of Leia's bedroom.

'Fast asleep,' she says. 'Was that the phone?'

'It was Billy Munday. He's coming over. Says he has something urgent to show me, but it won't take more than a minute or two.'

Sally sighs. 'I knew it was too good to be true, in bed by nine-thirty.'

Charles hears a car pulling up outside. 'That must be him. I won't be long.'

He runs downstairs in time to see Billy's bulk looming through the stained-glass panels of the front door. He unlocks the door and opens it.

'Come in,' he says, standing back.

'No, thanks, you're all right.'

'Okay. What's this about?'

'Frankie Perry. Been leading us a merry dance. Tuesday we discovered he's got another house round the corner from the first. In one he dresses and lives like a slob, and in the other he's got a brand-new sports car and designer suits. It's like he's got a double life.'

'Sure it was him?'

'Absolutely certain. I'm telling you, he looked totally different from the way we've seen him till now. Younger, too. Like a split personality, or something. He's definitely got money, and judging from what we saw, tons of it. We lost him. I had the new guy in the GPO van, and it doesn't move fast. But we got these yesterday, and a picture's worth a thousand words — ain't that what they say?'

Munday holds out a brown A4 envelope. Charles takes it and clicks on the hall light so he can see clearly. Out slides a sheaf of large glossy black and white photographs. He peers at the first. It shows the frontage of a restaurant, tables visible through plate-glass windows.

'I know where this is,' he says. 'That's the steakhouse at Piccadilly Circus.'

'It is. That's what they call an establishing shot. Now look at the rest.'

Charles turns to the next photo. Four men can be seen at a table. The shot's been taken from the side and behind them, so the two closest to the camera can't be identified from the back of their heads. However, one of the two facing the camera is known to Charles.

'Bill Moody,' says Charles, pointing at a middle-aged man with an upturned, waxed, RAF-style moustache.

'Correct. Detective Chief Superintendent Bill Moody.'

Like every barrister, solicitor and police officer working in London, Charles knows Moody only too well: the head of the Obscene Publications Squad. His team, known on the street as "the Dirty Squad", was created to crack down on the two principal pornographers and strip-club owners in the capital, Jimmy Humphreys and Bernie Silver. Instead it is widely rumoured that they took a five-figure bribe from Humphreys and Silver, together with a slice off the top of the profits, to look the other way.

'And sitting next to him…?' asks Charles.

'Don't you recognise him? That's Commander Kenneth Drury, head of the Sweeney.'

'Okay,' says Charles, 'so we have corrupt cops having a meal at a steakhouse. Even bent coppers have to eat.'

He looks up, waiting for the punchline. Munday indicates the next photograph. This one must have been taken from the opposite side of the table, as now the two police officers are viewed from behind.

'Getting that was tricky. Michael pretended to be a waiter,' says Munday with some satisfaction.

Charles immediately recognises Frankie Perry sitting opposite Moody. He is wearing the old anorak Charles saw in Munday's previous reports but has removed his workman's cap, which lies on the table by his elbow. He is holding a glass of beer, but alone of the four men does not appear to have been invited to eat. He is looking up deferentially, almost obsequiously, at the two police officers opposite him. Charles is reminded of Uriah Heep from *David Copperfield*.

'Any idea who that fourth bloke is?' asks Munday.

Charles continues to study Perry for a moment longer. Then his eyes scan right and land on the final man in the group. He gasps.

'What?' asks Munday.

It takes Charles a moment to get his tongue to work. 'Yes, I know him. His hair's longer than I've seen it before, but that, Billy, is a chap who used to be my closest friend. That's Detective Sergeant Sean Sloane.'

The steps leading up to Sloane and Irenna's flat are, for once, deserted, but the main front door is, as always, open to Charles's shove.

He climbs silently to their landing. This time he doesn't bother knocking on the door. Instead he slips two of the photographs taken by Munday and his team underneath it, quietly retraces his steps and returns home.

Sally, who has given up any hope of an early night, is reading at the kitchen table in her dressing gown, a mug of Horlicks by her elbow. She looks up as Charles comes down the stairs.

'Well?' she asks.

'I'd give it thirty minutes. They might have been in bed.'

'Lucky them,' replies Sally.

In fact it is only five minutes later that the telephone rings again. Charles looks at Sally and picks up.

'Charles?' says Sloane.

'Yes?'

'It's me, Sean We need to talk.'

147

'Really? I've been trying to get you for weeks. Then I pop a candid camera pic under your door and, all of a sudden, we need to talk? What about?'

'Don't play games, Charles. This is too important and too dangerous. I need to talk to you before you do any damage.'

The intensity of Sloane's voice gives Charles pause. He relents. 'Okay, talk.'

'No,' replies the Irishman swiftly. 'Not by phone. I can be there in less than half an hour. Will you still be up?'

Charles puts a hand over the mouthpiece and whispers, 'He wants to come over.'

'Now?' asks Sally quietly. Charles nods. 'Sure.'

'Yes, all right,' replies Charles into the receiver. 'But Sally's here.'

'That's fine. I trust her. See you soon.'

Just over twenty minutes later the doorbell rings and Charles climbs the stairs from the kitchen to answer it. To his surprise, on the stone steps are both Sloane and his fiancée, Dr Irenna Alexandrova.

'Irenna wanted to come,' says Sloane. Charles frowns. 'It's not a bad idea,' adds Sloane opaquely. He looks around nervously at the deserted street. 'Can we come in?'

Charles opens the door wider and allows them to enter. Irenna kisses him on the cheek as she passes and their eyes lock. She appears to be trying to communicate something to him, but he's unable to decipher the glance.

'Go down to the kitchen,' says Charles, closing the door, and he follows them down.

'Irenna,' says Sally, approaching her. The two women hug warmly. 'The kettle's on. Tea? Coffee? Or there's beer in the fridge.'

'Too late for alcohol,' answers Irenna in her South African accent, 'but tea would be lovely.'

'Sit down then,' says Sally, indicating the cleared table and taking out a teapot and cups from the cabinet.

The two visitors each take a seat. Sloane throws Charles's photos onto the table. Charles studies the man who saved his life seven years earlier. Sloane, usually conservatively and smartly dressed, wears jeans, T-shirt and a leather jacket. His light brown hair is long, almost reaching his collar, and he hasn't shaved for days. The Irishman was always strikingly handsome, tall and lean with a triangular face and laughing blue eyes, but now there is something roguish about his appearance. *Like a rock star*, thinks Charles. *It suits him.*

Charles pulls out a seat, and waits. Sloane is studying the table. 'Well?' says Charles. 'You wanted this meeting.'

'Charles,' reproves Sally gently. 'Give him a chance.'

Sloane looks up. 'I did. Just trying to find the right place to start.'

'You might struggle with that,' says Charles, cynically. 'All those years insisting how much you hated the corruption all around you. The hypocrisy —'

'Charlie!' snaps Sally.

Charles raises his hands. 'Okay, okay. I'll stay *schtum.*'

'I know how it looks,' starts Sloane. 'I'm working undercover.'

'Heard that before,' comments Charles. 'Standard excuse of coppers caught out.'

'Give me a moment, Charles, please. Have you ever heard of "the Team"?'

Charles, still angry, stares at Sloane for a moment but then shakes his head.

'They're a team within a team in the Met,' continues Sloane. 'Invitation only. They sell licences to commit crime. So, once you're a licensee and you get arrested, you call your handler and he gets you released.'

'How?'

'It depends where. If it's within the Met, evidence is usually "lost", either by your handler or, if you've been arrested in a different division, via a call to a similarly-minded officer. If there's no one amenable in that division, the word is given to the chief inspector or superintendent of the nick: the man arrested is an important informant, and has to be released.'

'What's in it for Team members?' asks Sally, placing a tray on the table.

Sloane turns to her to answer. 'A percentage of anything the licensee makes. Usually half but sometimes more. Sometimes it's everything.'

'What's the point of having a licence, then?' asks Charles. 'If you're taking all the risk and keeping nothing?'

'It's not always nothing, and the risk is reduced by the protection you're given. But they leave you enough to make a living, often a very good living. And then there's the blackmail. For every job the licensee commits, the deeper in he gets, and the more evidence the police have for blackmail. If a member of the Team is short of money, or simply fancies buying his wife a birthday necklace, he'll put pressure on one of the licensees. Fifty quid here, two hundred there, or else. The senior members of the Team are making a fortune.'

'So, you're a member of the Team, yes?' asks Charles.

'Not quite. I'm on probation. But, yes, I've been working me way in.'

'And you're going to take them down, are you?' asks Charles sceptically. 'Drury, Moody and all the others?'

'I'm not working alone, Charles. As you very well know, the Met has no internal investigation department. Complaints against officers are investigated by their own mates. That's the law. And this sort of graft's been going on for generations. So much so, it's part of everyday routine. If you were to ask Drury, he'd probably say he has no choice but to befriend certain criminals so they trust him and give him information. And that involves occasional back-scratching.'

'And backhanders,' adds Charles.

'Yes, that too.'

'But Frankie Perry's a low-life,' points out Charles. 'What information does he have?' He deliberately does not mention that Perry has two homes and an expensive sportscar. He will play his cards carefully until he has heard Sloane out.

The Irishman shakes his head firmly. 'That's where you're wrong. We think he's been making a lot of money, although we can't prove it yet.' He pauses and takes a deep breath. 'Now I'm going to tell you something that is highly confidential, okay? If you talk about this to anyone, Charles, you could put my life at risk. Understand?' Charles nods. 'Sally?' he asks.

Sally, having handed out cups of tea, sits opposite Sean. 'Of course. You're safe here, Sean. We love you, Charlie and I. We'd never say or do anything to put you in danger.'

Sloane smiles and briefly grips Sally's hand. 'Okay. Have either of you heard of Operation Coathanger?'

'No,' replies Charles. Sally shakes her head.

'Somehow the Team have got skeleton keys for some of the biggest wholesalers and retailers of high-end fashion clothing. Stores and warehouses all over England. They've been leasing them to the highest bidders.'

'Perry?' asks Charles.

'One of the most successful. He's been responsible for half a dozen of the biggest burglaries in the last two years. Hundreds of thousands of pounds. Coathanger is the name of the operation to close them down. It's led by a chief inspector called Olney. He's from Bedfordshire, so outside the Met. Unfortunately his new number two is a DI called Robson, and it looks like he might be dirty.'

'So, you're working with Olney?'

'He recruited me, but I'm not working with him directly. This again is completely confidential, okay? I'm only telling you because I can't risk you blowing my cover. Olney is one of a handful of senior officers who are determined to fight back. They're not all working together. It's a loose arrangement. They're all at risk, and no one knows who to trust. Perry isn't only involved in stealing clothing. He has a side-hustle.'

'Security.'

'You know about that? Okay. The two men running Perry are called Quigley and Pilcher, both bent as a nine-bob note.'

'And both involved in the case against my client, Bobby Gold.'

'That's right. Pilcher is in the Drugs Squad, and when he heard about Perry and his brother-in-law's business he spotted an opportunity. He's been taking seized drugs from the police property store, fiddling the chain of custody documents and using Perry to sell the drugs to pop and rock stars and their friends. And we're not just talking a little grass.'

Charles sits back in his seat. He nods, a slow smile spreading across his face. 'Now, *that* makes sense.'

'I've been sent on a couple of the burglaries,' continues Sloane, 'both with Perry.'

Charles sits forward again. 'You've taken part in burglaries?' he asks, astonished. 'Isn't that entrapment?'

'That's bollocks, as you know full well! They set the whole thing up, and I was simply ordered by Pilcher to ride shotgun. But we're not talking about that. One job went wrong and I got Perry out of a bind, so he now trusts me. So he invited me to work on security at Kingston Grange, and I've seen what's going on.'

'But that's fantastic!' says Charles, excitedly. 'You can give evidence for Gold!'

'No, I can't.'

'Did you see Gold supplying drugs or allowing them into the property?' demands Charles.

'No. That was Perry, on Pilcher's orders.'

'Then you *can* give evidence!'

'No, I can't. We're only just beginning to make progress with the investigation. It's too soon. As for the drugs at Kingston Grange, at present it's my word against Perry's. And even if I were to be believed, it would jeopardise the entire investigation. There are much bigger fish to fry — as your photos prove. And it's not just the investigation that would be at risk. There's also the small matter of me life.'

'But Gold is innocent.'

'I can't say whether he's innocent or not. He's charged with murder as well as supplying drugs.'

'But the Crown's case is that he supplied the drugs and killed the girl to hide the fact. If he knew nothing about the drugs, he'll be acquitted.'

'I'm sorry, Charles. I can't do it.'

Charles sits back in his chair, shaking his head. 'And you're okay with allowing an innocent man to go to prison for life when your evidence could stop it?'

Irenna intervenes. 'Of course he's not okay with it! But he'd be hanging himself out there, alone. Surely you see how dangerous that would be?'

'Remember Cremin,' reminds Sally softly.

Bruce Cremin was a Met police inspector who tried to blow the whistle on his corrupt colleagues a year earlier. He and his family were threatened, he was beaten up and he was eventually found by his teenage daughter, hanging by a curtain cord from his loft hatch. The coroner found suicide on what most in the legal profession thought was very insecure evidence. Many still believe he was murdered by his own team.

'Of course,' says Charles softly. 'But, Sean, I'm going to have to cross-examine Perry at trial. I have no choice. I understand your difficulties, but my duty is to do everything I can for Gold. Surely that's going to put your cover at risk anyway?'

Sean and Irenna look at one another. 'We've talked about this,' says Irenna. 'If you start asking questions of Perry, suggesting he allowed drugs in, he's going to know it was Sean who grassed him. The whole thing will unravel.'

There is silence in the room. Charles pushes back from the table, stands and starts pacing. He has always thought best on his feet. Some of his most successful cross-examinations and submissions have been developed walking round and round this very kitchen table.

The others watch him, sipping their drinks. He stops. 'Do you think you could get me an interview with Perry?' he asks.

'I don't know,' replies the Irishman. 'I doubt it, without some pressure.'

'Let me think,' says Charles. He pauses. 'What if you told him you've heard he's about to be subpoenaed, but you might be able to prevent it, *if* he agrees to speak to me off the record?'

'What's your plan, Charlie?' asks Sally.

'Perry might not be essential if we can move higher up the food chain. I need to get some evidence on Quigley and Pilcher.' He addresses Sloane again. 'Do you think you could persuade him?'

Sloane considers the question for a moment. 'Maybe. He thinks I'm part of the Team, so he won't trust me easily. But I can try.'

'And if that doesn't work, I'll show you where his money is.'

# CHAPTER EIGHTEEN

It is the early hours of Sunday morning, and Francis Perry is on his way home. He has spent an extremely pleasant evening in the company of a very attractive young woman, a German art historian working at the Victoria and Albert Museum. He managed to obtain two of the hottest tickets in London, front row circle seats for *Hair*, followed by after-show oysters at J. Sheekey's and dancing at Annabel's. It took Perry four years of careful cultivation and bribery to secure membership of the prestigious nightclub, and this was a rare opportunity to make use of it. He hoped the young lady concerned might be impressed by dancing shoulder to shoulder with royalty and celebrities, but she appeared frustratingly immune. The evening ended on a Mayfair pavement earlier than he would have liked, with *'Gute Nacht'* and a chaste kiss on the cheek, followed by her departure in a taxi.

Slightly disappointed, but looking forward to the next occasion, Perry returned to his car and drove south.

His TR6 now cruises slowly through Peckham, his head moving from side to side as he scans the dark streets for movement. There are no pedestrians and few moving cars. He's pleased to note that the GPO van parked at the end of his road has gone. It has been there on and off for the last few days and was beginning to worry him.

He circles the block twice and only when entirely satisfied that his destination is not being watched does he turn onto the driveway and open the electric roller door. He inches carefully into the garage, and the door descends behind him.

Fifteen minutes later he emerges from the property's side door, a changed man. His suit and polished brogues have been replaced by his customary baggy workman's trousers, anorak and paint-stained cap. He slides out of the alleyway between the two houses, limping slightly and his back twisted. His entire being radiates defeat and depression. He plods slowly down the road, turns the corner and heads towards his other front door.

He has sometimes wondered if it is necessary to persist with the impersonation even in these circumstances, at night, on deserted suburban streets, and for such a short walk between his two front doors. But his perfectionism will not permit him to let the mask slip. This is only one of several personae he has adopted over the course of his criminal career, and he enjoys the challenge of inhabiting characters as different as possible from his own. Indeed, over the years he has assumed so many different personalities, he would now struggle to say who he genuinely was. An occupational hazard of being a professional con-man, he guesses.

On this occasion he is vindicated because there, sitting outside his other home, is a vehicle he recognises: the unmarked Mark II Ford Cortina used by DCI Quigley. Perry has been expecting this visit, although he hoped it might not come until the morning, when he was completely sober and rested.

He pauses on the pavement, still some forty yards from the rear of the police car, wondering if he could simply return quietly to the other house. But Quigley might have seen him in the rear-view mirror. Perry composes himself, takes a deep breath and approaches the car. He bends down to look in the passenger window. Quigley sits in the driver's seat, alone, his head back and his eyes closed. Perry knocks gently on the window.

The policeman opens his eyes and looks over. He immediately opens the driver's door and steps out.

'Inside,' he says peremptorily, pointing at Perry's front door.

Perry limps up the garden path and opens up, flicking on the hall light switch. He stands back to let the police officer precede him into the house.

A combined kitchen/living room opens off the hall and Quigley steps inside. His nose wrinkles.

'Jesus, Frankie, this place stinks.'

Perry turns on a light to reveal a room cluttered with old newspapers, overflowing ashtrays, plates of congealed leftovers and empty beer bottles.

'Sorry, Mr Quigley,' says Perry, scuttling to pick up enough detritus from an armchair to allow Quigley to sit down. 'I weren't expecting visitors.'

'How can you live like this, man?' says Quigley, not expecting an answer.

He inspects the armchair recently cleared for him and, apparently satisfied, lowers himself into it. His sharply pressed suit trousers are creased from sitting in the car, but with his neatly knotted necktie and polished shoes he looks as out of place as a rag-and-bone man at a debutante's ball. Perry perches on the arm of the couch opposite and throws his anorak on top of the rubbish that fills the seating space.

'Now, do you mind telling me where you've been? We've been calling for days and DI Pilcher has been round twice.'

Perry hangs his head. 'I got ... I got ...' he mumbles.

'Speak up, man!'

'Sorry,' says Perry, 'I got problems.'

'What do you mean, problems?'

A sob seems to catch in Perry's chest. 'It's the wife.'

Quigley looks surprised. 'You have a wife?'

'I did. Well, I suppose I still do, technically,' replies Perry, and Quigley can see tears filling his eyes. 'We're separated.'

'You're not making yourself clear.'

'The chap I took on that job up north, Derek, well, he's me brother-in-law.'

'The warehouse in Yorkshire?'

'Yeah, that one. And Derek got nicked, remember?'

'Yes, I do.'

'And you couldn't do nothing about it. So 'e's facing a stretch and the wife is up in arms. She 'n' the whole family.' Now Perry is crying in earnest, tears running down his sallow cheeks. 'I was 'oping we'd patch things up, but now she says she's divorcing me.'

'We're working on that. The case'll never go to court, trust me. The evidence will disappear. Derek'll be fine.'

Quigley watches the wretched man cry for a few moments. He stands, goes to the kitchen, casts about for something absorbent, and returns with a tolerably clean dishcloth. 'Here,' he says. 'For God's sake, pull yourself together.'

Perry takes the dishcloth and to Quigley's disgust, blows his nose wetly on it. 'Sorry, Mr Quigley,' he mumbles.

'I'm sorry to hear about your personal misfortunes, but that doesn't explain where you've been. We needed you for a job.'

'I went to Norfolk. That's where she is, see? To persuade her to come back.'

Quigley gestures at the room. 'An invitation which, I guess, she declined.'

'Eh?' replies Perry blankly. 'So, I gotta go to court now. Something called the PDA? You ever heard of the PDA, Mr Quigley?'

'Probate, Divorce and Admiralty Division, on the Strand. But you'll be available next Saturday night? We can't afford to put this off another week.'

Perry raises his pathetic face. 'I guess so. Is that the London job? The one Mr Pilcher mentioned?'

'Yes. It's in the West End, and you're going to need at least two people with you. We'll supply the Irishman, so find another. Pilcher'll call tomorrow, so stay by the phone.' He stands to leave, and looks around himself again. 'And, really, Perry, you should clean this place up. Have you no self-respect?'

Perry nods, sniffs noisily but then reconsiders. 'Not really, no. But I'll give it a go, Mr Quigley, promise.'

He shows the Detective Chief Inspector out and then returns to his living room. He watches Quigley drive away. His tears have ceased and he permits himself a small smile.

# CHAPTER NINETEEN

Charles and Sean Sloane sit opposite one another in the conference room. Every now and then one of them looks at his watch.

Frankie Perry is late, if he is coming at all.

They are in the Royal Courts of Justice on the Strand, the seat of the Probate, Divorce and Admiralty Division of the High Court. It is a small room but immensely tall, its walls punctuated only by a small window. Charles wonders how, if ever, the window is cleaned, because it must be eighteen feet above floor level. Other than a small table and four chairs, the room is entirely bare: stone walls, stone floor, stone vaulted ceiling. Every now and then they hear litigants, their solicitors and counsel, hurry past the door on their way to or from their hearings, talking furiously under their breath. Once or twice the conference door has opened suddenly and a harassed lawyer has stuck his or her head in, hoping to use the room, only for them to sigh, disappointed, and scurry off to try elsewhere. The building housing the Royal Courts of Justice on the Strand is a folly, built at the end of the nineteenth century to resemble a fairytale castle. It is a quirky and magnificent building, with spacious marble halls, statues and great original oil paintings; but George Edmund Street, its architect, cannot have taken soundings from the barristers who were to use it, for it is equipped with far too few conference rooms. There is always a scrum to find one available, and Charles had to arrive very early to secure his.

Finally, half an hour after the appointed time, there is a light tap on the door and Charles rises to open it. Standing before him is the man he has seen in various guises in the photographs, Francis Perry. Perry wears an ordinary suit, a white shirt and tie and carries a leather briefcase. The suit is well cut but not ostentatious. He could easily pass for one of the solicitors or barristers with business in the building.

'Mr Holborne?' he asks.

'Yes. Come in.'

Perry enters, sees Sloane and nods a greeting. Charles closes the door behind him and sits. Perry places his briefcase on the floor and, to Charles's surprise, walks slowly around the seated men, looking carefully at their clothing. He crouches, looks under the table, and feels around its edges.

'Don't fret,' says Charles, watching him. 'There's no recording equipment. And neither of us have brought bags or coats, as requested.'

'I need to frisk you,' says Perry.

Charles raises his eyebrows at Sloane, who shrugs. They both stand and allow themselves to be frisked. Apparently satisfied, Perry pulls out one of the available seats and sits at the table.

'Sorry I'm late,' he says. 'I thought for a while I was being followed and I had to mess about a little on the Tube.'

Charles is good with accents and can usually place speakers' cities or counties of origin pretty accurately; with Londoners, he can often name the borough. But Perry's accent is curiously non-specific although, notes Charles, his words are precisely articulated.

*Rather like one of those embarrassingly fluent foreigners*, he thinks. *Scandinavian, or, maybe, German.*

'But you've let it be known that you've got a hearing concerning your divorce at the court here, haven't you?' asks Charles.

'I have. That was a good idea, by the way. But I wasn't taking any chances.'

It was Charles's strategy to pretend that Perry had an early hearing in a contested divorce. In cases requiring confidentiality the court may be persuaded to list only with initials, for example "P v P". In that way, he hoped, this meeting would remain secret from anyone who might be following either Perry or Sloane. No one would blink an eye at discovering Charles having a pre-hearing conference at the RCJ. It's commonplace.

'So,' says Perry, 'you're going to subpoena me to give evidence for your Mr Gold, is that right?'

'If you won't help us voluntarily, I am,' replies Charles. 'Or, rather, the solicitors will.'

'What do you think I can say that will help your client?' asks Perry, coming straight to the point.

*He's clever*, Charles reminds himself, *and this is going to be delicate.*

'I think you can tell the court when he left Kingston Grange that night. Not what's in your statement, but the truth. I think you can also say that, whoever allowed Christine Bailey and the drugs that killed her into the house, it was not Bobby Gold.'

Perry shakes his head. 'I've already given my statement to the police. That's what I'm going to say in court, if the prosecution calls me.'

He looks over at Sloane, who has not spoken yet, frowning slightly. Charles senses him reevaluating the detective sergeant.

'Everyone in this room knows that your statement is a pack of lies, and was probably dictated to you by either Quigley or Pilcher,' says Charles. Perry's face is impassive and gives nothing away. 'We also know that you have been recruited by them to carry out numerous burglaries for which they've provided skeleton keys.'

Perry's expression still does not change, but Charles detects a fractional involuntary flick of his eyes towards Sloane.

*He can't work out why Sloane would have divulged that information,* thinks Charles, *especially to me. You can't trust anyone these days, can you, Frankie? Time for the stick.*

Charles leans forward on the table, closing the distance between himself and the other man. He locks eyes with him. 'Look, you're essential to the Crown's case. I can't see any way they could convict Gold without you. And I have no choice but to cross-examine you. We know about your new TR6; we know about your two properties in Peckham.'

He watches Perry carefully as he says this. The man's expression remains the same, but Charles would bet that this comes as a shock.

'Yes, we know about the second house. My guess is, there's more than two, and we're going to keep digging. On top of that, we can prove you were involved in half a dozen burglaries. It's all going to come out at trial, surely you can see that?'

'What do you want from me?' asks Perry.

'I want to know why Quigley and Pilcher have required you to make a statement dobbing my client in, when we both know he's innocent.'

Perry returns Charles's gaze without speaking. Then: 'I'm not sure I'm comfortable speaking while Sean's here.'

'You're worried he's going to report what you say to Quigley and Pilcher, right?' says Charles. 'On the other hand, he arranged this meeting. Quigley and Pilcher are the engine of this prosecution against Bobby Gold, while I represent the defence. There's your problem: who's side is he on?'

Perry does not answer.

'This meeting never occurred,' says Sloane. 'You can speak openly to Mr Holborne.'

Perry smiles sceptically and spreads his hands in a gesture that means *Yes, but how can I believe that?*

'What do you suppose your bosses would do if they knew I'd put you in touch with the defence team?' says Sloane. 'I'm taking a huge risk here, Frankie.'

'I see that,' replies Perry. 'And I can't work out why.'

Sloane smiles, but offers no further information.

'I don't have much to do with Derek's company,' says Perry, 'but I was on site the evening that girl died and, I suppose, nominally in charge of the security team. Let's assume for a moment — just playing around, right? — that I could give you a little further detail, some … *refinement* of the evidence contained in my police statement. And you start asking questions in court based on that information, questions that, for the sake of argument, might embarrass certain police officers. Those police officers are bound to guess where the information came from. That wouldn't be very conducive to my continued health, would it? It's one thing coughing to involvement in some burglaries. This is murder. And there's nothing a barrister such as yourself can do to protect me from any repercussions.'

Sloane replies. 'There are other factors at play, which you know nothing about. This is a lot bigger than you giving perjured evidence over that girl's death.'

Perry shakes his head, smiling. 'I think you're bluffing. You can't prove I had anything to do with burglaries without admitting that Sean went with me. And you're not going to do that.'

Charles looks at Sloane. The next move is his, and even now Charles is not sure he's prepared to make it.

'My admitting that I was on that burglary with you will not have the outcome you might imagine,' says Sloane. 'My involvement is more complicated than that. I can't give you details. But in case this reassures you: I don't only report to Quigley and Pilcher.'

Charles watches as Perry digests that information. 'You're telling me you're working undercover. What, for another part of the Met?' Sloane doesn't respond. 'That's not much reassurance, Sean. Even if you're not part of the Team, I don't know who you *are* working with, and you want me to admit to burglaries which will get me a long prison term.'

'Let me put a scenario to you, okay, Frankie?' says Sloane. 'Let's assume for a moment that you're one of the lucky licensees, given a free hand by the Team to commit crimes, as long as they get a proportion of the profits. Sometimes all of the profits.'

'I don't know what you're talking about.'

'Of course you don't. But let's imagine you do. Let's also assume that, whether you want to or not, you have to carry on doing as they tell you. If you don't play ball, they have enough on you now to send you away for a very long stretch. With every job, that stretch gets longer, you're getting in deeper, and now you're up to your ears. Every time Quigley or Pilcher wants a holiday, fancies a night out with the missus, he only has to ask you. You're better than a bank, aren't you, Frankie? I'm prepared to bet that, at the start, you received some pretty hefty deposits, but since then the rate of return has dropped. Now you're being asked to pay out far more than is coming in.' He pauses to watch Perry's expression. 'With me so far?'

'Go on,' replies Perry.

'Quigley and Pilcher, and you, have been under surveillance for some time. And I can tell you that, so far as their little business is concerned, the writing's on the wall. When that business comes a cropper, which it will, and quite soon, it won't only be its directors who find themselves in prison.'

'Unless, perhaps,' intervenes Charles, 'instead of being a willing associate you were a mere pawn. An unwilling employee.'

'Yes, thank you,' says Sloane. 'The way I see it, Frankie, you have three choices. You can walk out of here now, ignore the offer we're going to make, and take your chances with Quigley and Pilcher. That's your first choice. Secondly, I suppose, you could pack a bag and run for it. You'd get rid of your sports car within a couple of hours, I guess, but that wouldn't raise much for a lifetime on the run, and it takes a while to sell semi-detached properties in Peckham. Maybe you have liquid assets, false passports, escape plans and so on, maybe not. Your third choice is to talk to us. The bankers call it "hedging", like an insurance policy. Quigley and Pilcher are going to be prosecuted, it's just a matter of time, and your evidence could be crucial. It could well buy you immunity or, at least, a reduced sentence.'

The room falls silent. Eventually Perry looks up. 'So, what you're saying is, if I tell the whole story, about how I was forced to commit some *alleged* burglaries, and what I know about the night the girl died, you'll get me immunity?'

'I can't promise immunity,' replies Sloane. 'I'm only a DS, and that's well above my pay grade. But I promise I will push for it as hard as I can.'

Perry closes his eyes and lowers his head, deep in thought. 'What if you were to ask for something in writing from a senior officer offering me immunity?'

Sloane answers immediately. 'No. No one's going on the record at this stage. Our enquiries are continuing on several fronts, but we're not ready to go public. As soon as we do, the rest of the Met'll close ranks.'

'That's what I guessed. What do you think are the chances, then? If I give you the evidence you're looking for — and I'm not saying I can, even if I'm willing — how confident are you that the offer you're making will be honoured?'

'There's a range of possibilities. If you help us now, I can guarantee it will reduce any potential sentence. As for complete immunity, that'll depend on what offences are revealed. Where you were blackmailed by corrupt police officers into committing crimes, you'll be able to raise entrapment as a defence. Wouldn't you agree, Charles?'

'Definitely. Although, to be fair to Mr Perry, entrapment is not a complete defence in English law. The court has to take it into account, but where police officers, for example, obtain skeleton keys to shop or warehouse premises, and blackmail an individual into using them so the police can make a corrupt profit from burglary, well, in my experience that would be a plain abuse of process, and no judge would allow it to go to a jury.'

'Do you understand that?' asks Sloane. Perry nods. 'Obviously, it'll be different for anything you've done on your own account, in other words not forced by Quigley and Pilcher. If you reveal such offences, it'll all depend on their seriousness.'

Perry closes his eyes again. Charles is impressed by him; he thinks clearly, even when under immense pressure.

'Can I have some time to think?' he asks eventually.

'How much time?' asks Charles.

'Is there anywhere here I can get a cup of coffee?' asks Perry.

'Yes. If you go down to the main hall on the ground floor, at the back, in other words walking away from the Strand doors towards Carey Street, there's a cafeteria. It's quite new, and not at all bad.'

Perry rises. 'Thank you. I'll be back in fifteen minutes.' He reaches to take his briefcase from the floor.

'No. Leave it,' says Charles. He smiles. 'We need you to come back with an answer, whatever that answer may be, and not just disappear.'

Perry hesitates. Charles watches as he considers whether he is prepared to depart without his briefcase or, perhaps, whether an insistence that he retain it will suggest that he is indeed planning to run. After a moment he withdraws his hand.

'Won't be long,' he says, and he leaves the room, closing the door behind him.

Charles and Sloane listen to his fading footsteps on the flagstones outside. Then Sloane reaches for the briefcase and opens it. He smiles and without disturbing the contents, shows them to Charles. The briefcase is empty except for a small Philips tape recorder, its red recording light illuminated.

'And all the time, he was recording us,' says Sloane.

Charles reaches in and takes out the recorder. The wheels turning the cassette tape are still rotating. He presses the "Stop" button, removes the cassette, places it in his pocket, and presses "Record" again.

'I don't think it'll work without a cassette in there,' says Sloane quietly.

He's right; the button won't depress. Charles opens the machine again and inspects the interior. He puts it down on the table, tears a corner off his blue counsel's notebook and rolls the cardboard into a little tube. Locating the lever that should be held down by a cassette, he jams the tube into the tray and, this time, the "Record" button clicks into place and the red light illuminates again. Charles looks up and winks at Sloane before putting the cassette recorder back in the briefcase, and the briefcase into its former position on the floor.

'What do you reckon?' asks Sloane, indicating the door.

'My money's on him coming back. He's no fool, and he must realise the game's up, or will be soon. He needs to start making new friends.'

'Unless he does have escape plans,' points out the Irishman.

'Yes, in which case he'll be of no use to either prosecution or defence. So, from Gold's perspective, that would be a good result.'

'Not from mine,' says Sloane drily.

'I know, and I'm as keen as you are to see an end to Met corruption. Let's keep our fingers crossed.'

Just under fifteen minutes later, the door opens quietly and Perry re-enters the room. He closes the door and resumes his seat.

'Okay,' he says heavily. 'I'm prepared to speak to you. But I want you to understand that I've committed no offences except when forced to by DCI Quigley and DI Pilcher. I'll answer your questions about them, and I'll tell you what I can about Kingston Grange, timings and so on. But don't expect too much on that subject, because I can't help about the girl's death. I don't know what happened. And for God's sake, don't tell Quigley or Pilcher, or I'm a dead man.'

'You needn't worry about that,' says Sloane. 'The last thing we'd do is tip them off. If you give evidence they were behind the burglaries, they'll be arrested.'

'I thought you said the people above you aren't ready to take action yet?'

'You giving evidence against Quigley and Pilcher will change all that,' replies Sloane.

'All right. I'm trusting you to uphold your end of the bargain, okay?'

'You have my word, Frankie,' replies Sloane. 'I'll do everything I can, and I know my superiors will be of the same mind.'

'Right.' He draws a deep breath. 'Fire away, then.'

Charles turns his notebook over, takes out his fountain pen and unscrews the top.

'You're going to take handwritten notes?' asks Perry of Charles.

'Yes.'

'That'll take hours, and I have a busy morning.' He reaches down to the briefcase, opens it and takes out the cassette recorder. He grins roguishly. 'This'll speed things up.'

Charles smiles in his turn. 'Yes, it will, thank you. In which case, we'll also need this,' he says, taking the cassette tape from his pocket and putting it on the table next to the recorder.

# CHAPTER TWENTY

*Draft witness statement of Francis Perry*
*Occupation: Garment Wholesaler*
*Address: 202 Choumert Road, Peckham, SE15*

*I presently work mainly as a clothing wholesaler, supplying clothing to dealers to sell at the London street markets.*

*In 1963 I was out of work. A friend put me in touch with a man who had several stalls in the London markets and I got temporary work with him selling direct to members of the public. I realised that I could make a living selling clothing to the stall holders and so I borrowed some money and bought a job lot of unsold stock from the previous season that was no longer wanted by the major retailers and resold it at a good profit. That was the beginning of my current business.*

*In 1965 I was approached by two police officers. One of them was DI Pilcher (although he was only a detective sergeant at the time). He wanted to supply me with some fashion items. He gave me a story about how he acquired them, but I didn't believe him and I refused.*

*Over Christmas 1965 my premises were burgled and I called the police. DI Pilcher was the officer who attended. On going through the stock I realised that it included half a dozen fur coats about which I knew nothing. I had never sold fur items and I had no idea how they came to be there. They were worth over £1,000. DI Pilcher told me they were stolen, and that he was going to arrest me for handling stolen goods. He claimed I would receive a prison sentence. It was obvious to me that the burglary had been staged to plant them in my warehouse.*

*DI Pilcher said that if I agreed to sell his goods with my wholesale clothing and pay him fifty per cent of the prices I received, he would "lose"* the evidence about the fur coats. I was very reluctant, but I felt I had no choice.

Over the next few months DI Pilcher would bring clothing to me in his car and I would move it into my warehouse, price it up, and sell it with my other clothing lines. Sometimes it was of sufficiently high quality that it could be sold through normal retail channels but usually it was sold through the market stalls. Pilcher used to come round once a month to collect his money, for which I would have to give a full account.

Then he began simply demanding money from me. He said I had been handling thousands of pounds worth of stolen goods and he had enough evidence against me to send me to prison for a long time. I had no choice but to pay up. It started with small sums of money, like £20 or £30, but once he told me he wanted to take his wife to Paris for their anniversary and demanded £100. Sometimes I'd refuse or ask him to try someone else, but Pilcher told me that prosecution was not the only thing I had to worry about. He said he knew where I lived. He didn't spell out what would happen to me, but I believed he was prepared to use violence. He often used to tell me of people he had arrested and who had confessed after, in his words, being "spoken to sternly" in the cells, and when he said this he always used to show me his knuckles, which were bruised and scraped. I took him to mean that he had beaten the suspect up, and I was afraid of him. I always had to pay.

On one occasion Pilcher approached me with a large box of cigarettes. It contained about eight cartons, so eighty packs. He told me they had been stolen, and he wanted me to leave the box in the storeroom of a local corner shop. I knew the owner, and Pilcher wanted leverage over him. At first I refused, but after he threatened me I agreed to do it. I subsequently learned that the shop owner had started paying sums of money to Pilcher, presumably to avoid being charged with handling the stolen cigarettes.

I kept a secret ledger of every date on which Pilcher delivered goods, the specific items, how much I sold them for, and how much I paid him. I produce that ledger marked FP1. I kept a separate record which simply showed what I had sold on his behalf, and that record I used to give him so he could calculate what he believed I owed him. He always destroyed it before he left my warehouse.

At the beginning of 1967 there was a two-month gap when Pilcher didn't come round with clothing. I hoped that he had decided to work with someone else. Then, one evening, he approached me in my local. He said that his contact was now serving a period of imprisonment and that his source of supply had dried up. He told me he might be able to get access to some skeleton keys for a number of fashion outlets, and that he wanted me to break into some premises and steal luxury clothing. I had never done anything like that before and I refused. I told him I wasn't cut out for that work. As always, he threatened me with prosecution for handling stolen goods and told me that no one would believe me if I said it had been he who supplied them to me. I still refused and I left the pub.

A couple of weeks later he arrived at my home with another man who he introduced as DCI Quigley. That was the first time I had confirmation that Pilcher was working with other police officers. Quigley was his boss. He said he had reviewed the evidence and thought that I was looking at ten years because of the value of the goods I'd sold for them. He said he would go out of his way to make sure the court gave me the maximum possible sentence unless I agreed to undertake the burglaries. I said I had no skill at burgling, but they wouldn't listen. They wanted me to burgle a warehouse in Birmingham which stored the new spring season clothes for Marks & Spencer, John Lewis and other large stores. Quigley said he would provide me with assistance. He said something like: "You don't think you're the only licensee, do you?" That was the first time I heard myself referred to as a licensee and I didn't understand it. He explained they had a number of people like me who had a licence to commit crime on the basis that the Team received their share. He said he would put me in touch with a couple of others.

I only met the other men involved on the day of the job. I never knew their real names and they said they didn't want to know mine, but one had a licence to drive an HGV and the other was a professional burglar with expertise in alarm systems. I opened the warehouse locks and the alarms man disabled the alarm. Then we spent all night clearing the warehouse. There was so much clothing we had to leave some behind, and when we got back to my warehouse there was insufficient space for all the clothes we'd taken. They were expensive high-end ladies' fashion items, dresses, blouses, skirts, coats and all accessories, all in multiple sizes. There was so much that I didn't think I could get rid of it all through my contacts at the markets, but when Mr Quigley came to look at it the following morning he said not to worry. He went with the HGV driver and took the excess somewhere else, I assumed to a different outlet.

I mentioned at the beginning of this statement that my main job was as a clothing wholesaler. However, for the last eighteen months I have also been assisting my brother-in-law, Derek Emmerson, in his business. His firm, Celeb Security, provides security to celebrities, actors and pop groups, and one of his clients is Gold Management and Talent Ltd, run by Bobby Gold.

In July Mr Pilcher got very keen for me to do some shifts at Kingston Grange, where Johnny Blaise and the Hellraisers were staying. At that stage I didn't know what Pilcher was up to, but I guessed he had an ulterior motive. Pilcher wanted to know when I was doing a shift so he could arrange for a man called "Fed" to come to the property. I was to let Fed in and out without recording his presence. I wasn't told what he was there for, but more than once I saw him selling drugs to a roadie everyone called "Chug". I never spoke to Fed and I don't know his real name. He was about five foot nine, of stocky build, in his twenties, and had fair hair. I once saw him wearing polished black leather shoes with his jeans, which I thought odd for a drug dealer, and that plus his rather "square" haircut made me suspect he was a police officer.

I have been asked if Mr Gold knew of these transactions. While working at the property Mr Gold spoke to me on several occasions. Because he knew I was Derek's brother-in-law, he treated me as if I were

175

part of the management rather than just another security guard, and I came to know him reasonably well. He always insisted that it was important not to let any of the fans in because, he said, they tended to cause trouble with the group members. He was also adamant that the security team were to do all they could to keep drugs off the premises. We weren't expected to search the musicians or crew, but the security team travelled with them to gigs and rehearsals, and were constantly told to be on the lookout for people approaching any of the entourage in case they were trying to sell drugs. From my experience it's part of the business that when famous groups go on tour, they are a magnet for drug dealers and girls. On a couple of occasions I saw Mr Gold arguing with men at gigs and at the property gates because he suspected them of trying to sell drugs to a member of the crew. Once he intercepted a man who had bribed his way past the gates and it came to blows. Mr Gold knocked the man down and actually dragged him out again.

I now turn to the events leading up to the death of Christine Bailey. On the evening of 19th July Johnny Blaise and the Hellraisers had a concert at the Astoria Theatre, in north London. I was doing a night shift at Kingston Grange that evening. The nightshift ran from 10 p.m. until 6 a.m. the following morning. On the days when the group had a gig, we had fewer people on duty at Kingston Grange as the fans tended to follow the group rather than remain outside their accommodation. When I started my shift there were only a few fans hanging about the gates, and the house was empty except for the housekeeper.

The two buses returned about the same time as I started, much earlier than expected. I understood there was some technical problem at the venue. I helped unload some of the gear from the buses and heard the group members and crew complaining about something going wrong. Unusually, Mr Gold returned to Kingston Grange with the group and the crew on one of the buses. When I was helping carry gear inside I saw that water had run down the stairs from somewhere above, and he started helping the housekeeper to mop up.

I have been asked if there was a party at the house that evening. I wouldn't describe it as a party. About half the group members and crew were in the main lounge, playing music and drinking, and some went for a swim later that night as it was very hot. There were a couple of groupies around but I don't remember seeing Christine Bailey at that stage. I can say for certain that she did not try to get past the gates while I was on duty.

After he had finished helping the housekeeper, Mr Gold was picked up by his driver and left in the limousine by about 10.30. I was back on the gates, and I was responsible for logging in and out all vehicles. I specifically remember the white limousine leaving. I don't know what happened to the entry/exit logs, but I haven't seen them since that night.

At some point later that night I was in the main kitchen having a break and a cup of tea. The downstairs of the house was more or less deserted. It was around three a.m.

I heard talking upstairs and went to investigate. Wyatt Blaise was speaking quietly on the phone in the library. That's what we called a room on the first floor lined with bookcases. He was in boxer shorts but wore nothing else. He beckoned me in and said there had been an accident and he'd called the police. He handed the phone to me. DCI Quigley was on the line. Quigley told me to go back to the gates, make sure all other security staff were sent home immediately, and wait in the sentry box for him to arrive. No one else was to enter until then.

About forty minutes later Quigley arrived and I let him in. He told me to follow him to the house and then stand at the front door and let no one in. I was there for a long time, almost an hour, but then Quigley came down and handed me a holdall. He told me to go outside and wait for Pilcher, who was on his way, and to give the holdall to him. He told me not to look inside.

I did as I was told. I waited for about twenty minutes and began to wonder what was in the bag. I looked inside and saw a very large sum of money, more cash than I'd ever seen in one place before. No one passed me

177

*or spoke to me, except Vinnie, the photographer hired by Mr Gold for the tour. He was on his way home. He asked me what was going on and I said I didn't know. Eventually Pilcher arrived and I handed the bag to him.*

*Some days later I was arrested by Pilcher and taken to a police station. Once we were on our own in an interview room, he produced a typewritten statement and told me I had to sign it if I wanted to stay out of prison. That's the statement the Crown have served in the prosecution against Mr Gold. The information in it about seeing Mr Gold receiving a package at the Liverpool Empire Theatre, and allowing someone through the stage door at Stoke-on-Trent, is completely made up. I have never been to either city in my life. Nonetheless, I signed the statement. Everything I said about Mr Gold that night is untrue. As I have said before, he'd gone by 10.30 p.m.*

*Since then the two policemen had been on at me to do another burglary, but I have been making excuses. I want to make it clear that none of the burglaries to which I have referred above were planned by me and I did not want to take part in any of them. I was being blackmailed by two corrupt police officers and I did it only because they threatened to send me to prison on false evidence, originally relating to the fur coats "found" in my warehouse.*

Charles drops the typewritten statement on his desk and leans back in his seat, satisfied. He looks over at Peter Bateman, his former pupil with whom he now shares a room, who is still reading the same document.

'What do you reckon?' he asks.

Bateman looks up. 'It's a shame he can't be more specific about the time. Everyone else places the discovery of the body at almost four a.m., and he puts it before then. Otherwise, though, I think it covers everything. It makes this case a pretty simple calculation. If he says *this* —' he points at the document — 'and not what's in his first statement, we win.'

'I agree. I'm going to call Serban and make sure he's got Perry's signature — you'll note these copies aren't signed — but other than that, I don't think we could be in any better position.'

'Roll on Monday,' says Bateman.

# PART TWO

# CHAPTER TWENTY-ONE

Charles and Bateman wait outside the door leading down to the Old Bailey cells. They have arrived early for a pre-trial conference with Bobby Gold and the Great Hall is relatively quiet. Bateman is fully robed; Charles is not. He hates wearing his horsehair wig, and only ever dons it at the last moment.

Gold, ever-worried about the cost of his defence, initially resisted the suggestion that a junior barrister be instructed with Charles. If, he said, Charles was as good as he claimed, why did he need another barrister sitting behind him earning a hundred and fifty guineas for the first day and twenty-five guineas per diem thereafter just to take notes? Surely Serban or one of his clerks could do that more cheaply?

Charles pointed out that this was a murder trial; even clients on legal aid were entitled to leader and junior, and in fact by instructing a senior junior (Charles), Gold was saving himself the vast costs of a QC. More importantly, however, Charles pointed out that the prosecution team would include a QC, a junior barrister, probably two solicitors, and the weight of the entire Metropolitan Police force which, as Gold already knew to his cost, was largely corrupt and wholly bent on having him convicted. While it was true that if all went well Bateman would not be required to do much more than take notes and assist in directing strategy, if the Crown started playing dirty, producing new evidence, new witnesses and so on, having another barrister to share the load would be vital.

Gold eventually agreed, and this will be the first time Bateman has met him.

The two barristers are great friends, and have worked together successfully in the past. Many solicitors instructing Chambers regard them as the "dream team", which has led to some resentment by other less-favoured members of Chambers. Charles and Bateman share an eye for strategy and method, both being prepared to take calculated risks when necessary, and they are both very successful before juries, able, in their different ways, to win their trust. The two men also share a sense of humour and an irreverence which has more than once caused them to suppress giggles, even in court.

Beyond that, it is difficult to imagine two more different men. While Charles grew up in the impoverished East End of London and had to pull himself up by his bootstraps following a "good war" and then a scholarship to Cambridge, Bateman is the grandson of minor aristocracy whose ranks include Cabinet ministers and High Court judges. He followed the conventional course for entrants to the Bar — public school, Oxford University and, courtesy of family connections, a more or less guaranteed tenancy in the Temple following qualification. Charles has never enquired as to the younger man's means but knows that he is, by any normal standards, extremely wealthy. By way of recognition of his call to the Bar, his family bought him, outright, a large apartment in Mayfair so he would always have accommodation close to the Temple. Bateman gives away little of his private life but, sharing a room with him, Charles has picked up quite enough to know that the tall, handsome young man's love life has hitherto been characterised by a series of short-lived relationships with debutantes. Opera, ballet, Ascot, trendy clubs and late-night dancing feature large. Charles has had to bite his tongue when Bateman complains, as he does every now and then, of the flightiness of the young women who feature in his life. The remedy, Charles thinks, lies in Bateman's own hands; he needs to look for a little less excitement and a little more "heft" in his girlfriends. But then, as Charles sometimes reminds himself, it wasn't until he was almost forty that the penny dropped for him.

The wicket in the door opens and Charles gives their names to the gaoler. The wicket closes again and the door is opened to admit them. They wait while it is re-locked and follow the gaoler down the stone steps to a desk where they give their names again to allow the man to record them.

'Your instructing solicitor is already here,' says the gaoler.

'Thank you,' replies Charles.

'This place always makes me hungry,' says Bateman quietly.

'Me too. It's the bacon.'

Outside of the inmates and the lawyers who visit them, the quality of the kitchens serving the cells in the Old Bailey is a well-kept secret. Here may be obtained the best bacon sandwiches — indeed, some inmates say the best fried breakfasts — in the capital. The barristers working at the Bailey are usually oblivious to the minor functionaries of the law, those invisible people oiling the wheels of criminal justice. Charles is an exception. He knows these people, the ushers, the clerks, the librarians and the kitchen staff. He and they are often on first-name terms and, although he is no longer quite "one of them", they know he shared their struggles to escape rationing, bomb sites and prejudice in the East End; he too had to fight his way out. It is this mutual recognition which allows Charles every now and then to schmooze an additional Old Bailey breakfast to be eaten with his clients.

Unfortunately he has never met this gaoler before, and they will have to go without. The man points to a cell along the corridor and precedes them to unlock the door.

Sitting on a wooden bench set into the tiled wall is Bobby Gold. An empty plate on the small table bears testament to the fact that he has already finished his breakfast, although he still holds a tin mug of tea. Sitting at the table, notebook and pen at the ready, is the solicitor and Gold's cousin, Victor Serban.

'Ring the bell when you're finished, gents,' instructs the gaoler, and he locks Charles and Bateman in.

Serban introduces Gold and Bateman, and the lawyers take seats around the table. Gold remains on the wooden bench, curiously distant from his legal team and what is happening to him.

'Well?' he asks. 'Perry?'

'I spoke to him last night,' says the solicitor. 'He says he's still coming.'

'But we can't guarantee it?'

'No,' answers Charles. 'Quigley's so confident that Perry is bought and paid for, they haven't bothered to subpoena him.'

'But then,' adds Bateman, 'we've seen a side of Perry they haven't. They think he's a worm, whereas we know otherwise.'

'So why don't we subpoena him then?' asks Gold. 'He's as vital to us as he is to them. More so.'

'Mr Holborne's explained this, Bobby,' says Serban. 'If we issue a subpoena against him, they'll be told, and realise his importance to us. They'll know we've turned him. So we keep our heads down.'

Gold nods unenthusiastically.

'Okay,' says Charles brightly. 'I've spoken to the staff upstairs at the public gallery and they know your wife is coming. They'll make sure she finds a seat.'

Charles expected this good news to lift Gold's spirits — the promoter hasn't seen his wife or children for six weeks while on remand — but the usually bumptious little man still seems completely deflated.

'Mr Gold?' prompts Charles.

'Why?' he asks, still staring fixedly at the bench on which he sits.

'Why what?'

'Why are those coppers framing me? Why me?'

'We discussed this when I last saw you,' replies Charles gently. 'It has to be because they're protecting someone else.'

'Who?'

Bateman answers. 'We don't know. Perhaps Perry, because he's so useful to them; perhaps this guy Chug; perhaps themselves. But, Mr Gold, it doesn't matter. We just have to raise a reasonable doubt that it wasn't you, and you have to be acquitted.'

'But Mickey's going to hear all this, right? How I pimped for those musicians, got drugs in, caused that girl's death?'

Charles and Bateman share a glance. 'You asked us to get her here. So, yes, she's going to hear all that evidence. But she knows it's a pack of lies.'

'And I'll remind her at the lunch adjournment,' adds Serban. 'Okay?'

'I suppose so,' responds Gold, unconvinced.

'If you'd prefer her not to be here, just tell me and I'll explain it to her,' says the solicitor.

Gold shakes his head. 'No, I really want to see her. I'm just … frightened.'

'Of course you are,' says Charles kindly, 'but, frankly, I prefer that to your previous overconfidence. It's going to be okay. Now, we haven't long and there are a couple of other things to go through.'

Charles spends a few minutes reminding Gold of the instructions he has already been given. Any comments on the prosecution evidence should be written in the notebook Serban has left with him. Under no circumstances should he become emotional, even when he hears lies given against him. When he comes to give evidence he must listen carefully to the questions, and answer as shortly and concisely as he can, offering no extraneous detail. If Charles wants more, he will ask. He should direct his answers to the judge, whom he addresses as "my Lord", and he must watch the judge's pen to make sure he's keeping up with Gold's answers.

Within a further ten minutes the conference is concluded and the lawyers are escorted out.

'I've got a couple of calls to make,' says Serban, 'if you don't need me.'

'No, you go ahead. I'm going to pop up to the public gallery and make sure Mrs Gold got in,' replies Charles. 'Peter, I'll see you in the Bar Mess.'

'Righto. Tea or coffee?'

'Tea, please.'

Charles crosses the Great Hall, now full of lawyers, policemen and members of the public, and follows the queue of hopeful onlookers to the public gallery. At the head of the queue he finds an usher.

'I'm just trying to discover if my client's wife managed to get in,' he says to the man.

'Would that be a Mrs Gold, sir?'

'Yes, that's right.'

'Yes, she's at the front, down there,' says the usher, pointing. 'Wearing the pink hat, on the end of the row.'

'Thank you.'

Charles eases his way past the people taking their seats and walks down the steps to the brass railing.

'Mrs Gold?'

'Yes?'

Charles extends his hand. 'I'm Charles Holborne, your husband's barrister.'

'Hello,' she replies. 'How is he?'

Charles crouches so he can speak quietly to the woman. He is surprised by how young she looks. He knows from his client that the couple have two daughters, one of whom is a teenager, and he imagined a housewife approaching middle age. Mrs Gold is round-faced and apparently several years younger than her husband, with sparkling dark eyes and dark hair cut in a fringe. She reminds Charles a little of Marianne Faithfull.

'He's all right,' says Charles. 'Obviously, he's worried about the outcome, but I think he's more worried that you're going to think badly of him. The Crown are going to say some pretty awful things.'

'Tell him not to worry, would you? I know my husband, and he's a good man. Convicted or acquitted, I know he's not capable of doing what they're saying.'

She speaks perfect English, albeit with an accent.

'I will tell him. Did Mr Serban ask you to bring a pad or notebook?' She replies by indicating what looks like a small flower-patterned diary on her lap. 'Good. It's very unlikely anything'll come up, but just in case you think of anything or have any comment on the evidence, something you think I need to know, jot it down, and I'll see you at lunchtime. Okay?'

'Yes.' She lifts both hands with fingers crossed.

'Amen to that,' replies Charles, standing and retracing his steps.

On his way up to the Bar Mess he puts his head into Court 2 where the trial is listed and gives his and Bateman's names to the clerk, asking her to inform prosecution counsel where they can be found.

'Any sign of the prosecutors?' asks Charles as he joins Bateman at a window table in the Bar Mess.

'No one's identified themselves.'

Charles frowns as he picks up his tea. The defence has had no contact whatsoever from the prosecution, which is unusual. Especially in a "big case" such as this, as a matter of common courtesy counsel for the Crown will usually get in touch with counsel for the defence in the days prior to trial, to touch base, make sure both sides are ready and, most often, to sound out the defence about the possibility of a plea.

*Perhaps they've appointed someone late or there's been a change of counsel*, he thinks.

He looks over his notes as he drinks. The Mess gradually empties as barristers head downstairs to their courts and eventually Charles and Bateman follow suit.

They enter the courtroom and walk down the slope towards counsels' benches. They are amongst the last to arrive. The public gallery above them is now full, as are the journalist's benches. Charles looks up and nods towards Mrs Gold.

Already in position, standing behind a lectern and a tall pile of documents is the barrister whom Charles supposes is leading for the Crown. Charles slides in the opposite end of the bench immediately behind his. The man is leaning over, talking confidentially to his junior. He stands up, turns to the two defence barristers, and Charles's heart sinks.

Charles whispers to Bateman. 'Shit! It's Lindsay Cartledge.'

Bateman leans forward and whispers in turn. 'Who?'

'He's from One Pump Court, third floor set. He's arrogant and rude, thinks he's God's gift to the law.'

'Is he?'

'He's no fool, but he acts as if he's the possessor of the greatest intellect at the Bar, and everyone else is a dullard.'

Bateman smiles. 'Sure it's not that chip on your shoulder, Charles? You do find offence pretty much everywhere.'

Charles sighs, irritated. 'If, which is not admitted, I do take offence at the anti-Semitism and class prejudice I endure in this bloody profession on a daily basis, that has nothing to do with this wanker!'

The swearing takes Bateman by surprise. 'Hey, calm down, son. Only teasing,' he says, affecting a Cockney accent.

Bateman's delivery and use of the word "son" — which he has picked up from Charles — are his way of placating his friend. Charles draws a deep breath to calm himself.

'Yeah, sorry,' he says. 'But, honestly, this chap is as difficult as they come, and my religious heritage makes it worse still. He's awful to everyone, including judges, but since he got silk last year he's been unbearable.'

Bateman looks over at the QC in the prosecution benches. 'How old is he?'

'One year ahead of me.'

'So, not that brilliant then, or he'd have been in silk years ago.'

Charles nods.

Cartledge turns to them. 'It's Holborne, isn't it?' he asks superciliously.

'It is.'

'And your junior?'

'Peter Bateman,' offers Bateman.

Cartledge makes a note of the names. Without turning round, indicating the barrister behind him, he says, 'Jennifer Cole.'

Bateman smiles. 'Hi, Jenny.' He addresses Charles. 'Jenny and I were in the same Bar Finals year.' He drops his voice. 'And she's a complete sweetie.'

'Ready for arraignment?'

It is Cartledge who has spoken, but he does so without looking up from the notes on his lectern or addressing anyone in particular. Charles ignores him.

'Holborne,' snaps Cartledge, looking across the bench this time, with a scowl. 'Did you not hear me?'

'Sorry, Lindsay, I didn't realise you were addressing me. Yes, dear chap, we are indeed ready for arraignment.'

Out of the corner of his eye Charles sees Jennifer Cole bow her head to hide her smile.

'Excuse me, gentlemen,' says a voice. Charles turns. The black-robed associate has descended from her seat below the judge and is addressing them. 'This is still a trial, is it?'

'Yes,' confirms Charles.

'In that case I'll bring in the judge,' she says.

She climbs the stairs to the door in the panelling behind the judge's seat which leads to the Judges' Corridor, opens it and disappears. She reappears a few seconds later with the judge's red book and pens and lays them out on the desk. She returns to the half-open door, knocks twice on it, and calls, 'Silence in court! All rise!'

There is a low rumble of thunder as over one hundred people rise from wooden seats. His Honour Judge Pullman enters court.

Charles has had run-ins with Pullman several times over the years. A dyed-in-the-wool prosecutor when at the Bar, Pullman is a famously prosecution-minded judge. He is also famously short-tempered, especially with inexperienced advocates who beat about the bush or ask the same question more than once. The nadir of Charles's relationship with him was when he accused the judge, with good reason and to his face, of anti-Semitism. Since then the two have come to a sort of understanding; even, perhaps, mutual respect.

Charles had understood Pullman to have been ill; "cancer", reported the grapevine. That wouldn't have been surprising, as the man smokes forty cigarettes a day and frequently rises during trials to sate his addiction. Charles has not seen him for a couple of months. His initial thought that, perhaps, the old boy might have had successful treatment is instantly dashed when he sees his face. It is grey and has lost much of its covering of flesh. He looks little more than a skeleton. Nonetheless, he bows to the barristers and, as he takes his seat, speaks to Charles.

'A pleasure to see you once again in my court, Mr Holborne.'

'The pleasure is mine, my Lord.'

'What is your time estimate?' asks Pullman.

'The listing's for eight days, but I think we'll beat that. Day six for speeches and summing up and perhaps a seventh for jury deliberations.'

'Very well,' says Pullman. He smiles, his gaunt face making his teeth look even more like those of a shark. 'If you're right, I should still be breathing.'

It's an attempt at humour and the barristers smile, but Charles does wonder how many cases the judge has left in him.

*Perhaps this is where he's happiest*, thinks Charles, trying to remember if Pullman is married and has a family.

By the time Charles focuses on the court again, Bobby Gold has been brought up from the cells and is standing at the request of the associate.

'Robert Gold?' she asks.

'Well, actually it's just Bobby, not Robert,' answers Gold.

The associate turns to the judge. 'The indictment, my Lord, says "Robert".'

'Leave to amend granted,' replies Pullman, anticipating the application.

The associate starts again. 'Bobby Gold, you're charged on this indictment containing three counts. The first alleges murder contrary to common law in that on the twentieth of July 1969, in the county of Surrey, you did murder one Christine Bailey. How do you plead?'

'Not guilty.'

'The second count is of manslaughter. You are charged that on the twentieth of July 1969, in the county of Surrey, you unlawfully killed Christine Bailey. How do you plead?'

'Not guilty.'

'Finally, you are charged that, between the first and twentieth days of July 1969, you did unlawfully supply heroin contrary to Section 5 of the Dangerous Drugs Act 1951 and the Dangerous Drugs Regulations 1953. How do you plead?'

'Not guilty.'

'My Lord, may the prisoner be seated?' asks the associate.

'Yes. Bring in the jury in waiting.'

Charles and Bateman have discussed their tactics relating to jury make-up. They will challenge men of the cloth, anyone suspected of having such strong views against sex and drug-taking that they might not give the defence a fair hearing, and any jurors who, judging from their age, might have teenage children. Essentially, they will aim for as young a jury panel as they can get.

Half an hour later, in a game of tit-for-tat, Charles and Cartledge have challenged or asked to stand by all but two of the jurors called to take the oath. The potential jury panel is running thin and the judge's mood has moved from amusement to irritation to suppressed fury. He finally loses it when Cartledge again asks a woman in her thirties to stand by.

'Mr Cartledge, Mr Holborne, stand up please.' The barristers rise. 'I don't know what you two are playing at, but this is becoming ridiculous, and if this case has to be adjourned because you're unhappy with every juror in waiting, I'm going to be extremely displeased with you. I thought I'd made it clear that time is pressing. Now, I'm going to rise for two minutes and not a moment longer, and I expect you two to go outside, discuss this, and come back with some sensible agreement that will allow us to get on with the case. Do I make myself clear?'

'Yes, my Lord,' reply both barristers simultaneously.

'I hope so.' Pullman nods at the associate, who stands and calls, 'All rise!' as the judge sweeps out, his hands already feeling in his jacket pocket for his cigarettes.

Three minutes later the judge re-enters court wreathed in cigarette smoke. Before everyone has even taken their seats he says, 'Well?'

Cartledge replies. 'If the associate continues calling jurors, I can assure your Lordship that everything will proceed smoothly.'

'Let's see, shall we?' replies the judge.

The associate calls the rest of the jurors in waiting and administers the oath to each without objection from any quarter. The result is a jury of six men and six women of an average age, estimates Charles, of perhaps forty. Not ideal, but not disastrous. Apparently Cartledge is of the same view, which makes Charles wonder if it was worth all the fuss. The prosecutor rises again.

'With my Lord's leave?'

'Certainly, Mr Cartledge.'

The QC turns to the jury. 'Ladies and gentlemen, I appear on behalf of the Crown in this case. I lead Miss Cole, who sits behind me. The prisoner is represented by Mr Holborne, who sits nearest to you and, behind him, Mr Bateman.

'My purpose in speaking to you now is to give you an outline of the case so you will understand it when the evidence is called. What I say is not evidence, and if anything I say conflicts with what you hear from the witness box, or what is read to you as agreed evidence, you will ignore that part of my opening. The prisoner is charged with murder and, as an alternative, with manslaughter. He is also charged with supplying drugs to the musicians and technicians staying at Kingston Grange. The Crown ask you to consider murder first and then, if you cannot agree on a verdict on that count, or you are minded to find him not guilty of murder, you should consider manslaughter. Murder is the unlawful killing of another human being with malice aforethought, which means intending to kill or to do serious bodily harm. In these circumstances, manslaughter means that the prisoner did not intend to kill or cause serious harm, but caused death through his reckless or negligent behaviour. His Lordship will give you further directions on the law after the evidence is complete, and I will have something further to say on it as well.'

Charles notes the repeated reference to Mr Gold as "the prisoner". It says something about Cartledge, who clearly prefers the old-fashioned and more brutal appellation. In Charles's experience, most barristers now prefer the term "defendant"; some even give the unconvicted man in the dock the temporary benefit of the doubt, by calling him, more respectfully, "Mr".

'Finally, the prisoner faces a count of unlawfully supplying heroin. The Crown invite you to consider that charge only once you have considered the two more serious charges and only if you are minded to find the prisoner not guilty of both of them. The learned judge and I will address you as to the legal requirements of this last charge later if necessary.

'This case has received a great deal of press attention, but you must put whatever you may have read or heard out of your minds. You must make your decision entirely on the evidence you hear in this court.

'Christine Bailey was a fifteen-year-old schoolgirl who had been allowed by her mother to visit her older sister in London for the weekend. You will hear from her mother, from a teacher at her school and from the family doctor, all of whom will tell you that she was not at all a "wild child", but a hard-working, intelligent and sensible girl who passed the eleven-plus exam and got a place at her local grammar school, through sheer hard work. She did not smoke, she did not drink, and she had absolutely no connection with drugs. She was also, and I'm sorry it is necessary for me to emphasise this, a virgin with no sexual experience at all. In other words an innocent and naïve young girl who, but for her brutal and squalid death at the hands of that man —' he jabs his finger towards Gold in the dock — 'was destined to live a happy and fulfilling life.'

Charles notes Cartledge's florid and emotive language with distaste. It's a cheap trick, designed to appeal to the jurors' emotions and not to their intellects. But he can see from the expressions on the faces of the jurors, particularly the women, that it's working.

'The two sisters intended to go to a rock concert at the Astoria Theatre, Finsbury Park, where a group known as Johnny Blaise and the Hellraisers were headlining. Ominously, by the time the concert finished, the two sisters had become separated and the younger, Christine, left with the group and its crew on one of the tour buses. The buses returned to where Mr Blaise and his entourage were staying, a large property known as Kingston Grange just outside Kingston upon Thames in Surrey. It was in Kingston Grange that Christine was killed.

'You'll be hearing from two witnesses who saw her there with the musicians. The first was one of the people in charge of the security team whose job was to man the gates and prevent unauthorised access by fans, journalists and others. He saw her in the lounge of the property with Mr Blaise and the other musicians and describes her as laughing, dancing and having a good time. He formed the opinion that she was either drunk or under the influence of drugs. The second witness was the housekeeper of Kingston Grange, a Mrs Gonzales. She will tell you that Christine Bailey looked very young to her and she remembered actually thinking that she was relieved she didn't have daughters of her own.

'Now, the prisoner's name is Bobby Gold. He is the managing director of Gold Management and Talent Ltd, and he was the group's UK promoter and tour organiser. He was responsible for every aspect of their stay here, providing accommodation, food and transport and arranging the concert tour in this country and in Europe. He rented Kingston Grange for the use of the group and its crew. He also hired all the staff, including Mrs Gonzales and the security team. We will call evidence to prove that the prisoner was seen on numerous occasions before these events buying drugs for the use of his client musicians and hangers-on. He was also seen to encourage young women — you may have heard the expression "groupies" — to enter Kingston Grange to cater to the sexual appetites of the musicians. In that respect, we say he was no more or less than a pimp.'

Charles looks at the jury and sees several of them turn to fix their eyes on Gold in the dock.

'The concert at the Astoria ended early, due to some technical problem. The Crown will prove that once back at Kingston Grange, a pretty wild party started, with alcohol, drugs, loud music and dancing. To give you a flavour of the degeneracy of this gathering, men and women were jumping naked and cavorting in the swimming pool. After the party, Christine, this innocent young girl, was found dead, curled up in the corner of a bedroom. She was wearing no clothes, someone had had sex with her, and there was a hypodermic syringe containing heroin hanging out of her arm.

'The police have been unable to find witnesses to what happened to Christine between the last time she was seen dancing and when she was found in that terrible state. However —' and Cartledge turns to point aggressively at Gold again — 'that man, with absolutely no care for Christine at all, allowed her to be brought into the house and used as a plaything by a member or members of the group. Like an object. That man —' and again he points hard at Gold — 'created the atmosphere where it was perfectly normal for hard drugs like heroin to be used there. And, says the Crown, that man —' another jab with his forefinger — 'either himself supplied or allowed into the property the heroin that was injected into Christine's body.'

Cartledge pauses and looks down at his notes, and Charles realises suddenly that the other barrister is acting, pretending that he's struggling to control his emotions.

After a moment he looks up and continues. 'The police have never been able to discover who raped Christine or injected her. I say "raped" because one thing is absolutely certain: she was below the age of consent. The law says she was too young to agree to having her virginity torn from her, even if she might have, at that moment, perhaps under the influence of alcohol and drugs, appeared to agree to the act. So, whoever had sex with her certainly committed rape. And, we say, can it really be suggested that a young, naïve, innocent fifteen-year-old girl such as Christine Bailey would willingly have injected herself with heroin, the most hard-line drug available even to habitual users? No. Inconceivable. We will invite you to the inference that that is so unlikely as to have been impossible.'

Cartledge drops his voice and leans forward, as if disclosing an important secret to the jury. 'You will hear evidence from the Home Office pathologist that Christine had tell-tale bruising on both her arms which prove that she was held down forcibly before her death. We say that evidence will drive you to the conclusion that, without any doubt at all, she was held down and injected against her will.'

He pauses, scanning the ranks of jurors.

'The house was awakened after the discovery of Christine's body, but just before that, just before the alarm was raised, the prisoner was seen running out of the bedroom where Christine was found. He was seen. He appeared to be in a panic and he ran straight down the staircase and out of the front door, disappearing from the house. We say that is very strange behaviour for an innocent man. An innocent man would have stayed, raised the alarm, and assisted the police to find out

what had happened. Not this prisoner. He ran for it. So —'
and here Cartledge ticks off the high points of his case on his
fingers — 'he had motive, he had access to means, he was the
last person to see Christine Bailey alive, and his actions
thereafter suggest guilt, not innocence.

'The police were called in the shape of Detective Chief
Inspector Quigley and Detective Inspector Pilcher, both highly
experienced and in the case of Quigley, decorated, officers.
You will hear from them concerning their investigations and
their interviews with the prisoner. After his arrest all his books
and accounts were seized. You are going to hear evidence from
Mr Wilfred Spuring, a chartered accountant experienced in
forensic analysis of accounts. He will tell you that the
prisoner's business was on a knife-edge. He had sunk all his
assets into the success of the Johnny Blaise European tour, and
if for any reason the tour failed, he would have been ruined.
He will also tell you that there was cash missing from the
business. You needn't concern yourself with how or why, or
indeed who might have taken that cash. The Crown only raises
that to demonstrate how essential it was for the prisoner to
ensure this tour went forward.

'Now the Crown does not have to prove any particular
motive to you. If at the end of the evidence you are sure that
the prisoner killed Christine Bailey, the fact that you cannot
fathom his motives is neither here nor there. However, imagine
yourself in his position: you have supplied drugs and underage
girls for the use of your celebrity musician clients. You
discover that one of those girls, a mere child, has been raped.
If the girl wakes up and points the finger at one of the
musicians, the tour is over and you are financially ruined. How
can you take that risk? Much easier, you may think, to make
sure the girl does not wake up. Much easier to take some of the

drugs lying around in this … this … den of iniquity, inject her and leave no witness.'

Bateman leans forward and tugs on Charles's gown. 'Jesus!' he whispers. 'Don't you think he's overdoing the emotive language?'

Charles whispers back. 'He has to, because some of the links in the evidence are tenuous, certainly on the murder charge. But look at them —' he nods at the jury — 'they're lapping it up.'

Cartledge is continuing. 'As in all prosecutions the Crown brings the case and the Crown has to prove it. If you are anything less than sure on any of the charges, you must acquit the prisoner of that charge.' He turns to the judge. 'Unless there is anything, my Lord…?' Pullman shakes his head. 'Then I shall call the first witness. Eileen Fairfax, please.'

# CHAPTER TWENTY-TWO

'Call Eileen Fairfax!'

The door at the back of the court opens and Christine Bailey's mother enters. She wears a brown raincoat and carries a brown leather handbag over her forearm. Charles recognises her from the inquest but he hadn't remembered, or perhaps noted, how small she is. She is pointed by the usher towards the witness box and walks tentatively down the slope, her eyes darting left and right. She looks like a frightened mouse.

She halts in the well of the court, unsure where to go next. The associate, already standing with the oath card in her hand, points to the witness box and Mrs Fairfax steps up. The rail comes up to the woman's chest and Charles realises that were she to get permission to sit during her evidence, she might disappear from view altogether.

She is given the oath card and a Bible and she reads the words on the card, her voice inaudible beyond the closest benches.

'Mrs Fairfax,' says the judge, 'you will need to raise your voice, I'm afraid. I could hear you give the oath, and perhaps the barristers did too, but I doubt anyone else in court heard you.'

He looks at the jury, most of whom shake their heads.

Cartledge identifies her and her relationship to Christine Bailey, and then leads her through evidence very similar to that which she gave at the coroner's court. She answers simply and in the same dignified way as she did earlier, silent tears seeping from her eyes. When Cartledge has photographs of Christine distributed around the court, Mrs Fairfax has to pause in her answers to collect herself, and Charles notes that one of the female members of the jury is also weeping quietly. Her evidence in chief only lasts a few minutes. Charles rises. He knows he has to use even greater care than he did before the coroner.

'Do you remember me, Mrs Fairfax? We met at the coroner's court, if you recall.'

'Yes, I remember you,' she says, sniffing and drying her eyes with a handkerchief.

'Please accept from me that I am genuinely sorry you've had to relive these events by giving evidence here. No one would wish to cause you even greater pain than you've already suffered.' She nods. 'So I'll be as quick as possible in asking my few questions. If you need me to stop at any point, please just say so.' She nods again. 'I think you gave evidence at the coroner's court that Christine was a big fan of Johnny Blaise and the Hellraisers. Her bedroom was plastered with posters of him and his group.'

'Yes, that's right.'

'Her older sister, Karen, was eighteen at the time, was she not?'

'Yes.'

'The two sisters looked much alike, didn't they?'

'Well, Chrissie was three years younger...' Her voice tails off.

'But they were enough alike that she could have passed as Karen. Is that accurate?' asks Charles.

'Yes, I suppose so.'

'They went to the concert together.'

'Yes.'

'But we know that at the end of that night Christine was found to be in possession of her older sister's identification. The authorities were at first misled as to her identity and age.'

'Yes.'

'So, Christine was pretending to be eighteen that night.'

'I don't know.'

'Why else would she have pretended to be her older sister?'

Mrs Fairfax shrugs but does not reply. Charles has no need to press the issue; the point has been made.

'After the concert, which we are told ended early, she and Karen split up. Karen didn't go to Kingston Grange, did she?'

'No.'

Cartledge jumps up. 'I object, my Lord. Hearsay. Mrs Fairfax wasn't there and cannot know, except via what someone else has told her.'

Pullman answers. 'Is it really an issue, Mr Cartledge? No doubt either you or Mr Holborne could call the sister with a resultant waste of court time, but none of the evidence suggests she was present. Is your case to the contrary?'

'No, my Lord, but the rules of evidence —'

'Let's just move on, shall we? Mr Holborne, ask your next question.'

'Thank you, my Lord. Christine was an independent young woman, was she not?'

'She was fifteen, not a woman.'

'Of course. But fifteen can be a difficult age, can't it? Intelligent and confident fifteen-year-olds are forever pushing the bounds of their independence, aren't they? They think they're grown-up when, in fact, they are not.'

'I suppose so. But Chrissie wasn't a particularly difficult fifteen-year-old. She worked hard at school and enjoyed being with her friends.'

'So, you'd say there was no greater conflict between you and her than might be expected with any independent-minded teenager taking her first adult steps? Would that be a fair way of putting it?'

'Yes, that would be fair.'

'Sometimes she would do things of which you disapproved.'

'No, I don't think so.'

'Well, you see, the Crown have put all of Christine's school records in the court bundle. It does seem that on occasion you were called into school because she'd been sent to the year head, yes? Once, I think, to the headmaster.'

Mrs Fairfax answers with a hint of defiance. 'She wasn't a difficult girl,' she repeats. 'If she thought something, she'd say it, and that teacher was being unreasonable. Chrissie was confident, that's all.'

'Yes, I understand. She trusted her own judgement.'

'Exactly.'

'So, if she found herself invited to a party by Johnny Blaise, of whom she was an ardent fan, she might well go. She'd trust her own judgement.'

'Yes, but she was naïve. It would never occur to her that someone would … take advantage of her.'

'No, I understand that. What happened to her later that night was awful. My questions focus on the choices she made which persuaded her to go to Kingston Grange in the first place.'

Charles turns to Bateman, who shakes his head slightly. He has no further questions to suggest.

'Thank you, Mrs Fairfax,' says Charles, sitting down.

'Does my Lord have any questions?' asks Cartledge.

'No, thank you.'

'Then I call Sarah Bruce.'

Sarah Bruce's name is called by the usher, and after a moment a tall, thin woman in her mid-forties appears at the door and walks purposefully towards the witness box. She has frizzy hair tied back off her face and wears glasses. She takes the oath in a clear voice heard throughout the court.

*Teachers, actors and barristers*, thinks Charles. *We all learn how to project.*

Cartledge identifies her as a physics and chemistry teacher, who did not actually teach Christine but was her year tutor.

'What is the role of a year tutor?' he asks.

'We're responsible for taking morning registration, but our duties are principally pastoral. To make sure the students are all right, to spot any problems that might be occurring at home, things like that.'

'And Christine was in your year group prior to her death?'

'She was.'

'What sort of student was she?'

'We're a grammar school and, unlike Christine, most of the pupils are from middle-class families. It took her a while to settle and find a group of friends. But after that she became very popular both with staff and her peers. She had a mischievous sense of humour which I, for one, found delightful. I would say she was one of our most successful students, destined to do well. She worked hard and took her studies seriously. She was very bright, one of only a small handful who sat and passed two O-levels a year early. She was also fully involved in school life, playing for her year teams in hockey and netball, and she regularly attended the chess club. She also sang in the school choir. She was particularly interested in music and told me she wished to take the subject at A-level.'

'Do you have any difficult pupils at your school?' asks the QC.

'Of course. Show me the school that hasn't. Some boys are involved in gangs, and in one or two cases we've had to suspend them. Last year we expelled two boys for selling cannabis on school premises, which was unusual. But Christine had nothing to do with any of these pupils. She was on a much more successful trajectory.'

'We know that following her death, toxicological tests revealed that she had drunk alcohol to excess and had taken heroin. Is that consistent with the student you knew?'

The teacher shakes her head firmly. 'Absolutely not. I find the suggestion difficult to credit. If it's true, it would have been completely out of character.'

'Thank you. Please remain there. There may be further questions for you.'

Charles rises. 'You found Christine's sense of humour delightful?'

'Yes.'

'But some staff reacted differently to it.'

Miss Bruce thinks carefully before answering. 'I think it often depends on your experience and confidence as a teacher. Some, and I count myself among them, don't find it difficult to maintain order, even with boisterous pupils. I wouldn't describe Christine as boisterous, but she had a strong sense of humour and occasionally she would misjudge when it was appropriate to be funny. I remember a couple of occasions when she would say something and the class would fall about laughing, and I would have to restore order again. I can understand if less experienced teachers might struggle with that.'

'Do you think that might be why she ended up in confrontations with a couple of the teachers, resulting in her being reported?'

'I do. I should emphasise that it was never serious. Christine was never sanctioned. She had an ebullient personality and it would have been difficult, not to mention a great shame, to suppress her —' she pauses while finding the right word — 'exuberance.' Miss Bruce is silent for a moment. 'She was her own person, and mature for her years. I shall miss her very much.'

'Thank you, Miss Bruce,' says Charles, sitting.

Cartledge rises and raises his eyebrows towards the bench. 'My Lord?' he asks.

'No questions, thank you.'

'Then I call Dr Neville Durden. Page nineteen of your Lordship's bundle.'

Charles addresses the judge. 'We have already indicated to the Crown that Dr Durden's evidence is not contested.'

'Mr Cartledge? Why are we wasting the time of a busy GP by dragging him to court?'

'I apologise, my Lord, but I was unaware of that fact. It appears there's been a breakdown in communication. However, Dr Durden is here now, so I will take his evidence swiftly.'

The witness is called and a balding, bespectacled man in his sixties enters court. He wears a tweed three-piece suit and carries a file under his arm. He strides to the witness box and takes the oath without being prompted.

'Dr Durden, I believe you are the family doctor for the Bailey/Fairfax family?' asks Cartledge.

'I am. Mrs Fairfax, formerly Mrs Bailey, and her two daughters have been patients of mine for many years. In the case of Karen and Christine, since they were born. When Mrs Bailey married Mr Fairfax and he moved into the Bailey household, he also became a patient at the practice, although he was registered with my partner, Dr Tyburn.'

'You have been asked, have you not, to look through Christine Bailey's medical records to see if there were any potential signs of drug-taking.'

'I have. As you can see, her records were not extensive. She enjoyed good health and came to the surgery infrequently. The records relate mainly to her childhood vaccinations and other minor illnesses.'

'In the three years prior to her death, how many times was Christine seen at the surgery? Other than for vaccinations.'

'Only once. That was in May this year when she suffered a flare-up of eczema, to which she was prone when under stress. She was revising for her O-level exams and was rather anxious. On examination, I found some minor flaking and reddening of the skin on the inside of her elbows and behind her ears, and I prescribed some cream for it. It was very minor.'

'And on that or any other occasion, did you see any signs of drug-taking?'

'None at all. Unfortunately, I do have several patients who are addicted to alcohol or drugs and I know the signs to watch out for. There was absolutely nothing like that in Christine's case. In fact, on that occasion in May I examined her skin carefully, and would certainly have noted signs of hypodermic needle administration.'

'Do you have any specific recollection regarding Christine's attitude to needles?'

'I do, yes. I know that she was very frightened of hypodermic needles. Ours is a small practice and we don't have a nurse, so my partner and I are responsible for administering the vaccinations. Mrs Fairfax would often cancel the appointment at the last minute because she couldn't get Christine to attend voluntarily and, often, when she did finally persuade her, the girl was extremely nervous. On one occasion she fainted as soon as she saw the syringe.'

'Thank you. Lastly, did Christine or her mother ever approach you for contraceptive advice, for Christine, that is?'

'No. There was no evidence in her medical records to suggest she was sexually active.'

'Thank you. I don't think the Defence wishes to ask you anything…' Cartledge looks across at Charles, who shakes his head. 'My Lord?'

'No, thank you,' says Pullman. 'I apologise, Dr Durden, that you've been brought here. It was unnecessary and a waste of your time.'

'That's perfectly all right, my Lord,' says the doctor, stepping out of the witness box.

'Maria Theresa Gonzales, please,' says Cartledge.

The door opens and Mrs Gonzales enters court. She is a striking woman, perhaps in her early forties, with long, thick black hair brushed back from her forehead. She wears a tight-fitting tulip skirt in dark blue and a matching jacket with puffy sleeves over a white blouse. The blouse leaves rather more cleavage on display than Charles would have advised had she been his witness.

Charles turns and raises his eyebrows at Bateman. 'That's the most glamorous housekeeper I've ever seen,' he whispers. Bateman grins.

She gives the oath and Cartledge asks for her name and address. She replies in perfect English but with a slight accent, Spanish perhaps, thinks Charles — maybe South American.

'You are employed, I believe, by Gold Management and Talent Ltd?' asks Cartledge.

'Yes, that is right. I have worked for the company for two years.'

'In what capacity?'

'I am a housekeeper.'

'Who employed you at Gold Management and Talent Ltd?'

'Mr Gold.'

'What are your duties?' asks Cartledge.

'I work at various properties, but mainly Kingston Grange. My job is to support the guests staying at the house, who are usually pop stars. I order the food and drink they need, keep the place clean and report to Mr Gold. I am his "eyes and ears" on the ground.'

'Does Mr Gold employ other staff at Kingston Grange?'

'There's a part-time gardener but he's employed by the owners of the property, which is an investment company. Mr Gold employs a chef who comes to the property once a day to find out if the residents want any formal meals to be prepared, for example for dinner parties or meetings. If they do then I liaise with her to get the appropriate ingredients in, and she plans the meal and arrives in time to cook it. She does not return to the property on days when no meals are required. If residents require snacks, such as sandwiches, I am expected to do that.'

'Thank you. Were you working at the property when the rock group Johnny Blaise and the Hellraisers took up residence?'

'Yes. I was there throughout until they went to Berlin, where they were staying next.'

'And were you on duty on the night of the nineteenth to the twentieth of July of this year?'

'I was.'

'During the group's tenure, did you ever see young fans on the premises?'

'I can't tell you how young they were, but sometimes there were women with them.'

'Where did these women come from?'

'I'm sorry, I don't understand your question.'

'Well, were they permanent members of the entourage?'

'Oh, no. After the concert sometimes the group would return on the tour buses with young women. On one occasion I remember a girl being allowed in at the main gates, but she might have been a reporter there for an interview.'

'I see. Did you ever see drugs being taken at Kingston Grange?'

'On a few occasions I saw and smelt cannabis being smoked, and I mentioned it to Mr Gold. I have never seen hard drugs being taken, pills or injections or anything of that sort.'

'So you witnessed criminal behaviour on the premises?'

'I don't know if it's criminal or not. I'm not involved with that sort of thing. I saw, and smelt, funny-smelling cigarettes, that's all.'

'Do you remember the evening of the nineteenth of July of this year?'

'Yes. It was unusual because they came back much earlier than expected. They normally don't return until well after midnight, by which time I've finished for the day.'

'Is there any other reason why you specifically remember that night?'

'Yes. There was a flood.'

'A flood?'

'Yes. Someone left a bath tap running upstairs in one of the master suites. When I arrived I realised that the carpet in the corridor outside was saturated, and then I saw water running down the stairs. I went into the bedroom to find the bath overflowing. That's why I was still there, cleaning up, when the group returned.'

'Can you estimate the time when the group returned?'

'Around ten. I wasn't paying close attention to the time.'

Cartledge slows the pace of his questions, watching the judge's hand as it makes a verbatim note in his red book. It is what Charles himself would do, as he approaches the critical evidence.

'Did you actually see the group return?' asks Cartledge after a moment.

'I heard the first bus pull up on the drive, and I looked out of the window because I was surprised. I was still in the bedroom suite.'

'Did you notice anything in particular?' asks Cartledge.

'Yes. They were in a temper, some of them arguing amongst themselves. I got the impression that something had gone wrong at the concert.'

'And did you see anyone other than the group getting off the bus?'

'There were a few young people I didn't recognise, some men, some women. And Mr Gold.'

'So Mr Gold was on the tour bus?'

'Yes. He doesn't usually come back with the group, and if he does, he's in the limousine.'

'So you are sure that he was at the property from some time after ten o'clock?'

'I am.'

'Have you been shown photographs of any of the other people on the tour bus, not members of the group or its crew?'

'The police showed me some photographs,' she says.

'And was Christine Bailey amongst them?'

'Yes.'

Cartledge pauses in his questions to consult his notes and Charles has an opportunity to evaluate Mrs Gonzales as a witness. She answers questions simply and straightforwardly, without any hesitation, and she is making a good impression on the jury.

Cartledge looks up and resumes. 'Were you aware of what was occurring downstairs while you were cleaning up the water?'

'I wasn't paying much attention, but there was music playing. At one point I had to go down and check the Blue Room —'

'Blue Room?' interrupts the QC.

'It's what they call the large lounge. There are several reception rooms and the Blue Room is the largest. That's where the musicians and crew tend to congregate in the evenings when they're not giving a concert.'

'Thank you. Please continue.'

'Water was dripping from above, and I wanted to check the downstairs rooms, so I went round all of them, including the Blue Room. There was a sort of party in progress.'

'Can you give any more detail?'

Mrs Gonzales shrugs. 'Not really. They were drinking, a couple were smoking, and they were mostly sitting on the couches. There was one girl dancing, but no one was paying much attention.'

'Was that Christine Bailey?'

'No. She was sitting on a couch next to Mr Blaise.'

'Was she drinking or smoking?'

'She had a glass in her hand. I didn't notice if she was smoking. I don't think so.'

'Did she seem intoxicated?'

'I didn't notice any signs of her being drunk. I'm not sure how people act when they're on drugs, so I can't answer about that. I didn't look at her for long. I just noticed that she was someone new in the household. Mr Blaise had his arm around her shoulder, and she looked happy.'

'What was Mr Gold doing?'

'He was helping me clear up the water, emptying buckets, opening bedroom windows, that sort of thing. It was a very warm night, so we hoped if we opened the windows we could dry off the soft furnishings. He was also taking notes of water damage and of items that might have to be thrown out. For the owners of the property, I assumed, or perhaps their insurers.'

'Thank you. What time did you leave the property?'

'The last bus is at quarter past midnight, and I was rushing to get that.'

'Did you do anything in particular before leaving?'

'Yes. I ran upstairs to close some of the windows. I was worried that the weather forecast said thunderstorms overnight.'

'Did you see anything when you went back upstairs?'

'Yes. The bedroom suite where the flood had occurred, the one where the carpet was wettest, its door was now locked. I could hear voices and laughter from behind the door.'

'How many voices?'

'I can't tell you. At least three. Two men, maybe more, and definitely one woman.'

'What did you do?'

'I knocked on the door several times, but either they didn't hear me or they ignored me. I was worried about catching my bus, so I shouted through the door that they should make sure the windows were shut before they went to bed.'

'Did you get a reply?'

'No. I don't know if they heard me. But I had to go, so I ran down the stairs to get the bus.'

*He is good*, concedes Charles.

Examination-in-chief is a frequently undervalued art. It looks so simple to ask questions, the answers to which are contained in a written statement in front of the advocate. But counsel may not ask leading questions, questions that actually suggest the answers sought; queries must be designed to elicit the desired response, and it requires skill to examine your own witness and bring out their story naturally, emphasising exactly the points that require underlining but without seeming to manipulate or make it too obvious. It must look unconstructed, when in fact it is being constructed very carefully.

'How far is the bus stop from Kingston Grange?' asks Cartledge.

'About two hundred yards. But it takes time to get from the house to the gates and sign out.'

'Did you catch your bus?'

'No. I just missed it.'

'So, what did you do?'

'I decided to walk back to the Grange and make a phone call from there. I hoped that my husband might come to collect me. I used the telephone in the staff kitchen, but he didn't pick up.' Mrs Gonzales smiles. 'He's a very heavy sleeper. So I decided to stay there. There's a small bedroom at the back of the house for the staff, in emergencies, and I'd used it once or twice before. I had no night things, so I simply took off my shoes and lay on the bed.'

'Did you sleep?'

'Yes, I did. It had been a long day and I guess I was tired.'

'What time did you wake?'

'Two minutes to four.'

'That's a very specific time, Mrs Gonzales. How can you be so precise?'

'Because I was woken by a loud noise. I was startled. For a moment I didn't remember where I was. And I looked at the time. It was two minutes to four.'

'What did you do?'

'Well, the house seemed quiet, but a noise had woken me and I was responsible for the house. I'd heard some horseplay around the swimming pool after I went to bed, and I was worried. So I put my shoes on and went out into the hallway.'

'What did you find?'

'The door to the room where the flood had occurred, the one I couldn't get into before, was open. And all the lights were on.'

'Can you describe what you saw?'

Mrs Gonzales closes her eyes, as if casting herself back to that moment. 'The bed had been slept in, or at least used, and there was a smell of cannabis in the room. At first I thought the room was empty, but then…'

For the first time the elegant woman pauses in her delivery and looks troubled. Her eyes lose their focus on the QC and the court around her, and Charles realises that she has travelled back in time to that awful moment.

'Then?' prompts Cartledge.

'I … I saw bare feet. On the floor, sticking out from behind the bed. I … I know it sounds strange, because she could have been asleep, but somehow I knew immediately that something terrible had happened.'

'What did you find?'

'I went round the bed. The carpet was quite squelchy there, from the water, you see? And I saw that it was the young girl.'

'Can you describe her for us?'

Mrs Gonzales looks down and draws a deep breath. She swallows hard. 'She was sort of half-propped against the corner of the room, where the two walls meet. Her eyes were open, but I knew straightaway that she was dead. She was naked, and there was a syringe sticking out of her arm.'

As she answers, Mrs Gonzales's voice drops and everyone leans forward to hear her. The stillness in the court is so intense, it feels to Charles as if it might snap.

'What did you do?' asks Cartledge quietly, careful not to dispel the tension.

'It was an awful shock, seeing her like that. I think I screamed. Then Wyatt Blaise came in. Maybe I'd woken him, I don't know. He told me to go back to bed and said he'd call Mr Gold and the police.'

'Did you do that? Go back to bed?'

She shakes her head, her black hair moving like a sleek curtain around her shoulders. 'No. I was too shocked, too awake. My hands were shaking. So I woke up Johnny Blaise and then went downstairs to make myself a cup of tea.'

'Last question, Mrs Gonzales. Can you place the last time at which you saw Mr Gold at the property that evening?'

'The last time I actually saw him, because I was speaking to him, was sometime before eleven p.m.'

'Did you see him leave?'

'No.'

'Was his limousine there when you ran to the gates to get the last bus just after midnight?'

'I believe so. It's a long white car, and it stands out.'

'Thank you. Please remain there.'

Charles rises to cross-examine.

# CHAPTER TWENTY-THREE

'Mrs Gonzales. A few minutes ago you said that on the occasions when you saw and smelt cannabis being smoked, you would mention it to Mr Gold.'

'That's right.'

'Why did you do that?'

'Because Mr Gold hates drugs on the premises. It's impossible to control completely — the musicians are adults, right? So we can't go searching them like policemen — and I understand he has to be ... how would you say? Yes, diplomatic. He refers to them as "the talent" and he can't afford to upset them. But he does everything possible to keep drugs out.'

'Could you give us some examples of how he does that?' asks Charles.

'The security guys on the gates have strict instructions about it. I've seen them refuse entry where they've suspected the purpose of the visit was to supply drugs.'

'Anything else? Other examples?'

Mrs Gonzales thinks for a moment. 'Yes. I remember there was an incident a few months ago, with a different group, when Mr Gold caught a guy doing a deal with one of the group's roadies. I don't know how, but he'd got into the garden at the back of the house, by the greenhouses. Mr Gold saw him from the window. He raced downstairs and out the back door. There was a big argument. We were all watching from the house.'

'What happened?'

'Mr Gold confronted him. He snatched something out of his hand and there was a fight. I was amazed. Mr Gold isn't very tall, but he more or less carried the guy to the gates and threw him out.'

Charles hesitates before moving to his next subject. He felt confident asking Mrs Gonzales questions about drugs on the premises because of her answers to Cartledge, but he only has Gold's evidence of the manager's attitude to groupies. It's dangerous to launch into a series of questions blind, trusting only what your client has told you. All too often, and for all sorts of reasons, clients lie. Nonetheless, he decides to take the chance.

'Did Mr Gold ever talk to you about groupies or young women entering the Grange?'

'Yes. Several times. He said they were even more trouble than the drugs.'

'So he tried to keep fans, especially young women, out of the property?'

'Yes. Always. Whenever a new member of staff joined us, for example on the security team, or gardeners, even the handyman — and he was actually employed by the landlords — everyone got the same speech about it.'

Charles glances at the jury and notes with satisfaction that two of them are taking notes of the housekeeper's evidence.

'Thank you, Mrs Gonzales. I have one other issue I need to explore with you, please. You say you think that Mr Gold's limousine was there when you ran to get your bus.'

'Yes.'

'Now, what time do you usually leave the property?'

'On a night when the house is empty because they're out at a concert, or perhaps in the West End at a club or restaurant, I usually leave by six p.m. There's nothing left for me to do. On the other hand, if they're at home I have to stay later in case they need something. In those cases my shift ends at eleven.'

'Do you have a bus that you aim for on days when the group are "at home"?'

'Yes. There's one at just after eleven.'

'So you would've taken that bus on many occasions?'

'Yes, many.'

'And I think you've already told us that, usually, Mr Gold's limousine and his driver are there to take him home from Kingston Grange.'

'That's right. It was unusual for him to come back on the tour bus, but I assumed it was because there'd been problems at the venue.'

'So, on the occasions you would take the eleven o'clock bus from two hundred yards outside Kingston Grange, I guess you would be leaving the property at about ten to eleven?'

'That's about right, yes.'

'Thank you. In the two years you've been working for Mr Gold, how often would you have seen his limousine parked in the driveway of Kingston Grange, waiting to take him home, when you were leaving at ten fifty to catch the eleven o'clock bus?'

'I don't know, but many times. Stan, his chauffeur, always parks in the same place, and I have to walk past him to go through the gates. So … seventy or eighty occasions maybe?' she hazards.

'Thank you. Would I be right to suggest that on this occasion, when you ran out of Kingston Grange, desperate to catch the last bus at quarter past midnight, you were in a bit of a panic?'

'Not a panic, but I was anxious. I really didn't want to miss that bus.'

'Did you speak to the security men at the gates?'

She smiles. 'No. I just ran through, and I shouted "Please sign me out!" and kept running.'

'Yes, I see. Now, you told Mr Cartledge that on this occasion, when you left over an hour later than usual, at a run for the last bus, you believe you saw the limousine in its usual place.'

'Yes.'

Charles pauses for a moment, locks eyes with the witness and smiles. He is about to challenge her, but he cannot afford to get her back up.

'Mrs Gonzales, I'd like to ask you to think back very carefully to that night. Is it possible that, because you saw Mr Gold's limousine in that same position on so many occasions when you left at ten fifty, you may be mistaken about seeing it as you left around midnight on this particular occasion?' Mrs Gonzales looks at Charles, frowning. He clarifies his question. 'I want to know if it's possible you confused this occasion, when you were paying less attention because you were in such a rush, with all the previous occasions.'

She looks at him, and nods slowly. 'I understand what you are asking. It's possible, but I don't think so.'

'Okay,' says Charles. 'Let's park that for a second. Did you actually see the last bus heading off into the distance?'

'I did. I missed it by seconds.'

'Did any other vehicles pass you in those seconds?'

'No. It was late and the roads round there are very quiet.'

'So, after you miss the bus, you turn round and retrace your steps to the Grange.'

'Exactly.'

'And you go back through the gates, and walk back to the house.'

'Yes.'

'You would have walked right past where Mr Gold's limousine was usually parked on your return. So, did you see it on your way back into the house?'

Now Mrs Gonzales pauses and frowns again. She shakes her head. 'You know, I can't remember.'

'You can't remember if it was there?'

'No.'

'But you told us no other vehicles passed you while you were running to the bus stop.'

'That's right. I'm sure no other vehicles left the Grange while I was outside. You can hear the gates moving, and there's a yellow flashing light when they're opening. I'm sure I would have heard and seen that. And, in any case, the limousine would have gone past me.'

'And it didn't.'

'No. I'm certain of that.'

'So, Mrs Gonzales, I go back to my original question. If you didn't see the limousine as you walked back into the house, and you walked right past where it would have been parked, this big, long, white limousine with a chauffeur waiting patiently in the driver's seat, is it possible that it wasn't there as you ran out in such a hurry? In such a hurry you didn't even have time to sign yourself out at the gates?'

There is another long pause before she answers. 'I think, perhaps, that *is* possible. I'd seen it there on so many occasions in the past but … maybe I was mistaken after all.'

'So, it is possible that by the time you left the property at a few minutes prior to twelve fifteen, Mr Gold had already departed.'

'Yes, I think that's right. I'm sorry.'

'No need to apologise, Mrs Gonzales. Thank you for answering my question so carefully.'

Charles turns to Bateman, busy scribbling to keep up with the evidence. He raises his eyebrows to ask if his junior can think of anything else. Bateman grins and raises a thumb. He mouths the words 'Well done!' and Charles sits down.

Cartledge rises. 'Mrs Gonzales, you gave your statement to the police the day after this event, did you not?'

'Yes. They wanted me to give a statement that night, but I was too tired and too upset. So they agreed I would give it the following morning.'

'Do you think your memory of the events would have been fresher the morning immediately after they occurred, or now, months later?'

'The morning after, I guess.'

'Exactly so. And the morning after, you told DCI Quigley that you thought Mr Gold's car was still there when you left Kingston Grange just after midnight.'

'But I think he —' Mrs Gonzales nods towards Charles — 'makes a good point. I don't remember seeing it on my way back. And I did say only that I *believed* it was there on the way out, not that I was sure. In fact, I said I wasn't absolutely sure, and the more I think about it the less sure I am.'

'Why is that?'

'Well, I like Stan, the driver. He's a nice man, and very patient. He waits for hours outside in that car. So sometimes, when I have a moment, I take him a cuppa, and I always say hello or goodnight as I go past. But I'm almost certain I didn't do either that night. Which makes me think he must already have left.'

Charles locks across at his opponent, who is evidently weighing up whether pressing the issue further will recover the

223

position for the Crown or make things worse. After a few seconds' silence, he turns to the judge. 'Does my Lord have any questions of this witness?'

'No, thank you.' Pullman turns to Mrs Gonzales. 'Thank you for coming, Mrs Gonzales. You are free to go or to stay, as you wish.'

She nods at the judge and steps down out of the witness box.

'The Crown's next witness is Mr Francis Perry, my Lord, page twenty-six in the bundle,' says Cartledge.

The door at the back of the court opens and Charles hears Francis Perry's name called. He and Bateman turn to watch the door, both curious as to the version of Perry that will emerge: the shambling crook-backed loser in paint-splattered cap and overalls, or the slick man about town, sports-car driver and frequenter of Annabel's nightclub.

Perry's name is called again. Everyone in the courtroom waits, eyes on the door. The black-gowned usher reappears. 'The witness does not answer, my Lord.'

'Mr Cartledge?' asks Pullman.

Charles looks up at his opponent. Cartledge is a good poker player, but even his impassive face betrays some surprise.

'Would your Lordship be kind enough to give the Crown a five-minute adjournment? So I can make enquiries?'

The judge smiles and immediately pats his jacket pocket for his cigarettes. 'Three minutes, Mr Cartledge, and no more.' He turns to the jury. 'Not enough time for refreshments, I'm afraid, but long enough to stretch your legs. The prisoner may remain in the dock.'

The judge is already disappearing through the door behind him before the associate has time to call, 'All rise!'

Cartledge turns to talk to his team, but as he does so he catches Charles's eye. He leans towards Charles. 'If I discover you're behind this, Holborne, there's going to be serious trouble,' he threatens, voice lowered.

'You have my word, Cartledge,' replies Charles, 'I know nothing about why your witness isn't here.'

'The word of a member of your race is worthless to me!' spits Cartledge, before wheeling round and striding towards the court doors, his minions following in his wake.

Charles shakes his head briefly, beckons to Bateman to follow him, and strides to the dock. He addresses Gold in a whisper. 'I think Perry's done a runner.'

# CHAPTER TWENTY-FOUR

Lindsay Cartledge QC remains standing after the rest of the court has settled. Five minutes have elapsed since the judge gave him permission to locate his missing witness. Normally, as a matter of courtesy, prosecution counsel would keep defence counsel informed as to whether the witness had been found or, if not, whether there was some issue, such as ill-health, preventing his attendance. In this case, in his usual arrogant manner, Lindsay has offered Charles and Bateman nothing.

From the corner of his eye Charles sees Gold waving, trying to attract his attention, but the judge has already entered. Charles flaps his hand behind him to Bateman and points to the dock. Bateman nods and slips out from his bench to find out what Gold wants.

'Yes, Mr Cartledge?' asks the judge.

'Enquiries have been made, my Lord, but unfortunately we have not been able to locate Mr Perry. All I can tell your Lordship is that he was a perfectly willing witness, who has throughout assisted the police. He was spoken to last night by the officer in the case, DCI Quigley, and confirmed that he would be here. Calls have been made to his home and his place of work, but there's no reply at either. I'm afraid therefore I cannot explain his non-attendance. Perhaps he's been taken ill or has had travel problems.'

'What's your position, then? Have we other witnesses we can get on with?'

'I'm sorry to say, we have not. As you will see from Mr Perry's statement, he's an extremely important witness for the

Crown and we anticipated his evidence lasting at least a day. We didn't want to waste other witnesses' time by calling them today when they were very unlikely to be reached. I regret I have no choice but to seek an adjournment until tomorrow when, hopefully, we will know more.'

Pullman draws a deep breath, clearly irritated. 'Mr Holborne?'

Charles rises just as Bateman is resuming his seat behind him. He turns with raised eyebrows towards his junior.

'Important, but it'll wait,' whispers the younger man.

Charles faces the judge. 'This is most unfortunate, my Lord, but if my learned friend has not had the foresight to have other witnesses waiting, I'm not sure what we can do.'

The judge nods. 'Unfortunately, I agree. Very well. I shall want to hear why the witness hasn't arrived and I should warn you, Mr Cartledge, I'm reserving my position on the wasted costs of this afternoon. Members of the jury, it looks as if we have gone as far as we can today. I'm going to adjourn until the morning. I propose starting at ten rather than at ten-thirty tomorrow to try to make up some time. We may also have a rather abbreviated luncheon adjournment tomorrow. Would that inconvenience any of you?'

He waits until he has received negative shakes of the head from most of the jury members.

'Thank you. Now, I'm going to give you a warning which will apply to the rest of the case. Please do not speak about this case or the evidence you've heard outside of the jury room. Firstly, we have barely started and it's far too early to draw any conclusions. Secondly, and more importantly, your friends and family are sure to ask you questions about the case. The danger is they will then offer an opinion or say something which might affect your decision. It is critically important that the decision comes from you twelve alone. So it is best all round if you don't discuss the case until it's over, you understand? Thank you. Mr Holborne, I assume there is no application for bail? No, I didn't think so. Ten o'clock tomorrow then, please.'

'All rise!'

The judge sweeps out of court and the buzz of conversation erupts. Charles turns and leans in to speak to Bateman.

'I think you need to hear this from Gold directly,' says Bateman quietly. 'Shall we go down to the cells?'

'Yes.'

Ten minutes later Charles, Bateman and Mr Serban, their instructing solicitor, are once again sitting with their client in the tiny conference room in the bowels of the building. It has a new, sour, sweaty smell.

'Tell him what you saw,' says Bateman to Gold.

'When you went out of court, when the prosecution were looking for Perry, one of the people from their team was looking through your papers.'

'What?' exclaims Charles. 'Are you sure? That'd be grounds for striking off!'

It is commonplace for barristers to leave their papers on their benches during adjournments, sometimes overnight. Particularly in a document-heavy case where the papers might fill several boxes, it's impractical to keep carting them backwards and forwards from the Temple to court twice a day. It is an unwritten rule that no barrister ever looks at the papers of his opponent, no matter how tempting it might be. The Bar is so cloistered, so select, that everybody knows everybody else. The vast majority of the country's three thousand barristers practise, cheek by jowl, within the tiny enclave of the Temple and the two other Inns, Gray's and Lincoln. Those practising in crime, perhaps five hundred in total, are gathered together in a mere score of sets. Barristers routinely find themselves against members of their own chambers, even, sometimes, their roommates. The profession is so close-knit that any hint of impropriety is the subject of gossip within hours. Reputations and careers can be lost in an instant.

'Tell me exactly what you saw,' says Charles.

'Okay,' replies Gold. He thinks for a moment and then starts. 'There's a guy who's been sitting behind the junior barrister for the Crown, since we started. He's wearing a dark blue suit and has fair hair.'

'A lawyer?' asks Bateman. 'Or a clerk, perhaps from the prosecution solicitors?'

'Possibly, but … I don't think so. As you were leaving court just now, DI Pilcher came down the aisle and had a quiet word with the bloke. There was something about the way they were talking … I don't know.'

'What?' presses Charles.

'Well, if Pilcher was talking to one of the lawyers, I imagine he'd have a certain amount of respect for him, but it looked the other way round. It was as if the bloke was reporting to Pilcher. He spoke very quickly, whispering in his ear, and then Pilcher said something to him and the other guy, who was younger, was nodding, as if he were receiving orders.'

'So, a copper, then?' asks Charles.

'Could be. Yes.'

'What exactly happened during the adjournment?'

'I saw the guy with the fair hair go into the bench where you'd been sitting,' says Gold to Charles.

'And?'

'He looked around, but there was no one looking at him.'

'Were the prosecution barristers there?'

'No. As soon as the judge went out, they raced out of court.'

'Looking for Perry,' adds Bateman. 'And we'd gone out too.'

'Yes. So, he had his back to me, and it was very quick. But he made a movement with his hand, and seemed to fan out your documents on the bench.'

'Did he pick them up? Did he read anything?'

Gold shakes his head. 'I couldn't see. He was only standing in your place for maybe five or six seconds. But he looked as if he was reading from something on your bench. Then he saw the usher approaching — she had a fresh carafe of water in her hand — and he straightened the papers again and moved away quickly.'

Bateman and Charles look intently at one another. 'What do you think?' asks Bateman.

'There are only two things in our papers which we've got and they haven't. Mr Gold's defence statement —'

'And Perry's.'

'Exactly.'

Charles addresses Gold. 'So, later, when court rose for the day, and Pilcher came down the aisle to talk to this bloke, was it your impression that the man was reporting what he read?'

'I may be misinterpreting it completely but, yes, that's what I thought.'

There is a long silence in the room.

'How serious is this, Mr Holborne?' asks Serban finally.

'If it could be proved, it's a serious contempt of court and imprisonable. If a barrister did it, he'd be struck off. I'm not much concerned about them seeing our client's statement. That's just an expansion of his denials to the police already, so no surprises. But if he saw Perry's statement to us, that's a different matter. That could put Perry in danger.'

'But if he's already done a runner...' says Bateman.

'Maybe that's why,' postulates Charles. Bateman looks puzzled, and Charles explains. 'It's taking a hell of a risk to read the other side's papers in a bustling courtroom. Even if no one's paying attention, it just takes someone to turn round, and you're caught red-handed. I know we're dealing with corrupt coppers, but it would take something big, something important, to chance your arm like that. If they already suspected that we turned Perry, they might be prepared to take the risk to get confirmation.'

Bateman nods. 'What do you think we should do? Tell the judge?'

Charles shakes his head. 'I need to think about it. From Mr Gold's perspective, if Perry's done a runner, that's pretty much the end of the case. I'd like to expose these coppers as much as anyone, you know that, but our first duty is to our client. Without Perry, they might even throw their hand in, so I'd be inclined to let matters take their course. And I'm not sure we can predict where it will go if we do raise it with the judge. Firstly, he may simply not believe Bobby at all, and then the whole thing gets diverted into allegation and counter-allegation.'

'Other people might have seen him,' suggests Serban.

'That's true, but they wouldn't have thought anything of it and, anyway, what do we do? Corral the entire public gallery, all the journalists, over a hundred people, and interview them all? No. I can't see that working. And there's another factor to consider.'

'Which is?' asks Bateman.

'We give away the element of surprise. We know they've been looking at our evidence, but they don't know we know.'

'How does that help?' asks Gold.

'I'm not sure yet,' replies Charles. 'Maybe not at all. Like I said, I'd like time to think about it. For the moment, I suggest we do nothing. We'll regroup tomorrow morning before court sits and discuss it further, yeah?' He looks round the table. Everyone nods. 'In the meantime, we need to get Billy Munday down to Peckham as soon as possible.'

# CHAPTER TWENTY-FIVE

Charles is waiting in Sean Sloane's former bedsit in the gloom. There is no carpet on the floorboards and the room contains only two pieces of furniture, a stained and stripped mattress on a sagging bed frame, and an old dining room chair. He chose the chair.

The room is on the top floor of a tall, run-down Georgian property in Powis Square, literally round the corner from Colville Terrace. Irenna, then Sloane's hospital doctor, found it for the Irishman when he threw himself on her mercy, homeless, still battered from the effects of a severe beating and reeling with concussion. So fast did their romance take off in the following days, he barely occupied the room. Within a week he had moved into her larger and much more comfortable bedsit, where they've been living as a couple for the last four years. For appearances' sake, until they are married, Sloane has retained this room in Powis Square. Unmarried police officers are supposed to live in the section house or, when that's full, with landladies whose rooms are on the Metropolitan Police's approved list. Sloane's superiors are relaxed about his living in unregulated premises; they are unaware he is living with Irenna.

Charles was let in by the son of Kholwa, the woman who has the lease of the top half of the house. Although Sloane and Irenna are the only white people living in the locality, they are well known and liked, Irenna because of her life dedicated to advocacy for the Black community and Sloane because, despite his occupation, Irenna vouches for him. The Irishman informed Charles that he was expected and that no one would mention his visit. He told him, however, to park some distance away and to approach on foot.

Charles has now been waiting for forty minutes. He has not illuminated the lights. He listens to the muffled sounds of the lives being lived below and next door. He can hear, seeping through the thin partition from the adjoining bedsit, the sound of Creedence Clearwater Revival's 'Bad Moon Rising', currently at number one in the charts. He likes the song.

Also drifting into the room is a melange of cooking aromas from around the world. Kholwa, whose apartment is directly below, comes from Northern Rhodesia; Charles has also met the Sudanese family in the other attic room and a West Indian couple on the floor below. His stomach, empty since breakfast, grumbles loudly in response.

Eventually he hears light footsteps on the staircase below him. They continue towards the door, which opens. Sloane stands on the threshold, letting in light from the hall behind him. Charles's chair is in a corner, and it takes the Irishman a moment to scan the room and see him. He steps in and shuts the door behind him quietly.

'Sorry to have kept you. I don't think I'm being followed, but I needed to make sure.'

'No worries,' replies Charles.

Sloane crosses the dark room in a couple of strides and sits on the bed. The springs creak loudly and he drops several inches. 'Jesus!' he swears gently. 'I don't know how I ever slept on this.'

'You didn't, as far as I recall. Certainly not for more than a couple of nights.'

'True. Okay, do you want to start?'

'Sure. Have you been in touch with Perry in the last thirty-six hours?' he asks.

'No. I take my orders from Quigley and I'm not supposed to have any contact with Perry other than through him or Pilcher.'

'I didn't think so. I'll lead with the headline: it looks like Perry's done a runner.'

'Fuck. Are you sure?'

'He didn't turn up today, which clearly took the prosecution by surprise. Apparently he assured both them and us as late as yesterday afternoon that he'd be there, but he didn't show and there's no sign of him at either of his houses or his warehouse.'

'Have you been down to look?'

'Billy Munday has. He's looked in the windows of both properties in Peckham. The one known to Quigley and Pilcher looks exactly as it did before, a total tip, so it's difficult to tell. But the other one, the one round the corner, seems to have been cleared. Billy says there was a high-end TV and hi-fi in the front room, and they're gone. There was also a coffee machine in the kitchen, and he can't see that either. I didn't want him breaking in, but from what he's seen, I think Perry's taken everything of value and cleared out.'

Sloane does not respond. Charles allows him some time to process the new development.

'He was my connection with Quigley and Pilcher,' says Sloane eventually. 'That's months of undercover work wasted.'

'But surely now you've proven yourself to them, they'll continue to make use of you?'

Charles can see Sloane shaking his head in the darkness. 'It's not as simple as that. Maybe, maybe not. They're obsessive about keeping outsiders at a distance. Half the Met is on the take, but "the Team" is very selective. You might be used for a job, like I was, but still kept at arm's length. Paid on a job-by-job basis but never allowed into the inner circle.' He draws a deep breath. 'But from your perspective, it's a win, right?'

'Looks like it. Especially after the housekeeper's evidence.'

'Oh?'

'Yes. Don't worry about that. The question is, what are you going to do?'

'Speak to Chief Inspector Olney, I suppose, and give him the bad news.'

'Sean, I've been thinking. Surely this would still be a good time for him to go public. I can't believe his only line of investigation has been through Perry and Operation Coathanger. If Perry's only one of numerous licence-holders, surely there are other avenues?'

'I can't tell you. Not because I don't want to, but because Olney is as secretive as Quigley. It's a bit like Nipper Read's investigation last year. Read drew on a handful of honest coppers he knew he could rely on, just like Olney's doing now, but Read's investigation was authorised by Assistant Commissioner Brodie, right from the top. Olney and the others are doing this off the books.'

Charles feels guilty. He knows the risk to which his friend is exposed and he shares his aim of trying to clean up the Met. He went into the law because he wanted to do some good, without realising that he was jumping into a fast-flowing river of corruption. He's been swimming against the tide ever since. And now, by putting Perry under pressure to give evidence for Gold, he's scared off a witness who could have brought down two of the most corrupt coppers in the capital.

'I'm really sorry, Sean. You predicted this, and I didn't listen.'

'You never do, Charlie, but on this occasion I don't blame you. You're representing an innocent man framed by the Team. You had no choice.'

'Listen, I don't think the Crown are going to throw their hand in straightaway. Cartledge is too arrogant to believe he can't still beat me. I think he'll play for time, call other witnesses, and see if Perry can be traced. From Quigley's perspective, Frankie Perry's a loser, without resources, and should be easy to find. Cartledge only has a few witnesses to play with, and my guess is he'll call Quigley to waste some time. Once he goes into the witness box I can have a shot at him. I can put to him the stuff Perry told us. I know most of it won't stick; he'll just deny it and I can't produce anyone or anything to prove him a liar. But some *might* stick. And if your Chief Inspector Olney can give me anything, any other evidence of Quigley's criminality, I can do it.'

'Even if it relates to other cases, other investigations?'

'Of course. Cross-examination is "at-large" and I'm entitled to attack Quigley's credibility. If you can get the ammunition from Olney, I can fire it.'

'I'm not sure.'

'I'm happy to speak to Olney myself, if you think that'll help.'

Sloane laughs briefly. 'That man doesn't tell his left hand what his right hand is doing. No, that won't work. But … okay … I'll talk to him.'

'Tonight? It has to be tonight, Sean. We might get one shot at this tomorrow, while Cartledge plays for time. By the end of the day he'll have run out of other witnesses and I'll be making a submission of no case to answer.'

'Understood. If I can get hold of him, can I ring you? It could be late.'

'Absolutely. Doesn't matter what time. But get back to me tonight if you can '

# CHAPTER TWENTY-SIX

Charles finds Billy Munday waiting for him as he enters the main doors of the Old Bailey. Munday waits patiently while Charles goes through security, then hurries over, taking Charles by the arm and dragging him into a corner.

Munday leans close and whispers. 'Perry was seen by one of his neighbours driving off in his sports car, the boot and backseat loaded with suitcases. I couldn't get hold of flight manifests, but I thought that, with a loaded car, he'd probably aim for the ferry anyway. We've struck lucky. I'd sent Michael down to Dover, just in case, and he saw Perry driving onto a ferry, headed to Ostend.'

'Belgium?' whispers Charles, surprised. 'How sure was Michael of the ID?'

'Absolutely sure. It's a conspicuous vehicle, and he got pretty close.'

Charles pats the big man's forearm. 'Well done, Billy. Perry's definitely not coming.'

'One other thing,' adds Munday, looking a bit sheepish. 'I've not told you this before, so I'm sorry. But the TR6 was a left-hand drive.'

Charles looks up, his eyes alight with interest. 'Curious. That suggests a more significant continental connection.'

'Yeah, I realise that now. I just thought it was him being flash. Y'know, the continental playboy, right? But Michael said it's now got foreign plates.'

Charles whistles softly. 'Did he get the number?'

Munday takes a notebook from his jacket pocket and leafs through half a dozen pages of smudgy pencil notes. ''Fraid not.

But he gave me a description. Yes, here. Black background and white letters. And a sort of shield on the left.'

'Swiss.'

'Swiss?'

'Definitely. They're the only country in Europe with plates that colour. And the shield's not a shield. It's a canton coat of arms.'

'How do you know all this?' asks Munday, impressed.

Charles shrugs. 'I'm a magpie. I collect all sorts of odd facts. And vehicle registration in Switzerland requires residence. Perry — or whoever he really is — is Swiss!'

'Unless that plate's also false,' says Munday.

Charles considers the point. 'Yes, true. But I'd bet one hundred pounds that he has another identity — probably with a criminal record — somewhere in Europe. Maybe even a family. Well, interesting, but no help to us either way. Was there any police presence at Dover?'

Munday shakes his head. 'Michael reckons only the usual, and they looked relaxed, which makes sense. With Quigley and Pilcher working off the books, they could hardly put Perry's name on a stop list, not without drawing attention to themselves.'

Charles nods. 'All right, thank you.'

'I've got a few other things to check out,' says Munday, 'but I'll be in touch.'

He pushes his way past the incoming tide back out onto the pavement.

Charles shoulders his way through the scrum in the robing room towards the circular dressing table where Bateman is changing. There are thirty or forty male barristers jostling for position at the table, all trying to get robed at the same time. Robing involves removing their ties and day collars and replacing them with stiff, starched wing collars; fastening the replacements to their tunic shirts with hinged brass and mother-of-pearl studs, front and back; tying band strings round their necks; donning black gowns with ridiculously voluminous sleeves that snag on door handles and regularly sweep carafes of water off court benches; and, finally, assessing the smell and cleanliness of their greasy horsehair wigs before perching them on their heads. A few who are not keen on detachable day collars are pulling off their shirts and hurriedly redressing. Charles is once again bemused by the silliness of it all. He wears a wig that was fashionable in the days of Charles II and a black gown which signifies that, inexplicably, barristers remain in mourning for a queen who died over two and a half centuries ago. "Tradition," say his colleagues; "bonkers," replies Charles.

'I've news,' Charles whispers excitedly to Bateman.

'What's that, then?'

Charles leans in close to him. He can't see Cartledge or anyone from the QC's chambers, but he won't take chances. 'Firstly, Perry's definitely done a bunk. Last seen heading towards Belgium. Secondly, remember I told you about the undercover operation against the Team?'

'Your mate, yes? The Irish DS from West Hendon?'

'No longer at West Hendon but, yes, that's the guy. He's persuaded the officer running the operation to go public on their investigation.'

Bateman stops fiddling with the strings of his bands and focuses properly on Charles. 'And it'll really damage Quigley and Pilcher?'

'He says it will. He'll say they blackmailed Perry into allowing drugs into Kingston Grange — drugs stolen from the police property store — and into giving evidence against our client. Plus there's the Operation Coathanger burglaries.'

'Who is it?'

'A DCI called Olney. He can get here tomorrow.'

'Tomorrow?' answers Bateman. 'It's Saturday tomorrow.'

'Yes, sorry, Monday then.'

'Surely, if they've lost Perry, we can finish this off today?' says Bateman, doubtfully.

Charles grins. 'We could, but why hurry?'

Now Bateman peers suspiciously at Charles. He drops his voice even further. 'Now, wait a minute, Charles. No Perry, no case; they're dead in the water. Even if Cartledge tries to stall, by the end of today the judge won't wear it. If Cartledge doesn't throw his hand in then, we've got to make a submission of no case. Agreed? Our first duty is to Gold, and that's to get him acquitted. We can't deliberately prolong this thing in the hope of busting a couple of corrupt coppers.'

'In principle, I agree. But if it's a case of stringing it out over the weekend to get Olney here, surely that's worth it?'

Bateman shakes his head firmly. 'No. Sorry, Charles, I know how strongly you feel about this, but we can't take chances with our client's liberty. Who knows what Quigley might manufacture given a weekend to think about it? If I was leading you, I'd be asking the judge to get Cartledge to show his cards *now*. Do they know where Perry is? If not, the court should assume he's not coming and Cartledge needs to consider his position. And if he won't, we make the submission.'

Charles steps back and starts unpacking his robes. He knows Bateman's right. They can't play fast and loose with Gold's liberty. He'll want to be acquitted and get out of prison as soon as possible.

*Or would he?*

'Okay,' says Charles. 'Let's ask Mr Gold if he's prepared to take the risk and face another forty-eight hours in prison to get *real* justice — not just an acquittal, but the scalps of the two men who framed him. Will you run with me on this?'

Bateman considers, then nods. 'Yes. On the condition that we explain the risks fully and without reservation to him. He has to be in possession of all the facts.'

'Agreed.'


The door clangs shut behind the barristers. Gold appears to sense something is up, as he puts his tin mug down on the table and looks up expectantly.

'What?' he says.

He waits, frowning, as Charles and Bateman lock eyes with each other.

'What's going on?'

Bateman shrugs reluctantly, indicating that Charles may speak first.

'Okay,' says Charles, taking a seat. 'As you know, we had a pretty good day yesterday. Mrs Gonzales was very helpful and Frankie Perry didn't turn up.'

'Which is good news for me, right?'

'Right. And it gets better. The investigator's been down to Peckham — that's where Perry lives — and it's pretty clear he's done a bunk. We don't think he's coming at all.'

Gold's eyes open wide as he absorbs this news. 'That's it, isn't it? Didn't you tell me that without Perry they don't have enough?'

'Yes, I did —' starts Charles, but Gold half-stands and interrupts him.

'That's fantastic news! You can make — what did you call it? A submission? Is that right? A submission of no case to answer?'

'Yes, we can. Please sit down for a moment. It's a bit more complicated than that.'

Gold looks from one barrister to the other. Bateman avoids his eyes. He slowly resumes his seat. 'Well?' he asks.

'I can indeed make a submission of no case to answer. The Crown's case isn't finished, but this judge is no fool and he knows that, without Perry, the prosecution is bound to fail.'

'So make the submission!' insists Gold.

'I can. I will, if those are your instructions. But if I do, and you're acquitted, it will let Quigley and Pilcher off the hook.'

'So?'

'So, they framed you! For murder. These men are completely corrupt and utterly arrogant. They think they can do whatever they like with the law, with the evidence. They were perfectly happy to see you, an innocent man, spend the rest of your days in prison to protect their business interests.'

'Yes, I know.'

'Well, don't you want to see them brought to justice? Wouldn't you love to see them inside for what they've done to you?'

'Of course I would, but what can I do? I just manage pop groups.'

Charles leans forward. 'That's the thing. Now, you've got to keep this to yourself, okay? We've been told that there's an investigation into them by other, honest, coppers. It's all been under the radar. But one of the officers involved in it has promised to come to court on Monday and provide us with the evidence.'

'What evidence?' asks Gold.

'The drugs that have been getting into Kingston Grange come from the police property store,' explains Charles. 'Pilcher is a member of the Drugs Squad. He's been stealing seized street drugs. And there's other stuff — burglaries, blackmail and so on.'

Charles has been aware for several seconds that Peter Bateman's foot is tapping insistently. The other barrister's impatience to speak finally overcomes him.

'The point is, Mr Gold, we have an opportunity to make a submission of no case today,' he says, looking directly at their client and ignoring Charles. 'If it's successful, you'll be out this afternoon. It'll all be over. Charles wants to keep the case going until Monday when this officer turns up, so he can attack Quigley and Pilcher in the witness box. I think that's a mistake.'

'Why?' asks Gold.

Charles answers. 'It means another two days in custody —'

Bateman interrupts. 'And it allows Quigley an opportunity to regroup.'

'But what can he do?'

Bateman raises his hands. 'We don't know! Maybe he'll locate Perry. Or maybe he'll simply manufacture some new evidence. He's as bent as a nine-bob note! He wouldn't think twice about it. His career's on the line. And his own liberty.'

Gold looks from Charles to Bateman and back again. 'So, let me understand this: you two don't agree, is that it?' He points at Bateman. 'You want to bring the trial to an end now, if possible.' He turns to direct his finger towards Charles. 'But you want to wait until Monday when this straight copper turns up with the evidence to screw Quigley and Pilcher.'

'Yes,' affirms Charles. 'Exactly. Peter's worried about the risk, and I can't pretend there isn't one. Quigley's a snake, and he's cornered. On the other hand, if you can hold your nerve, we have an opportunity to bring him down.'

Gold leans back in his seat. 'I see.'

The two barristers watch his internal debate. The silence in the tiny room lengthens.

'I hate policemen like those two,' he says after a while. 'We had plenty of them in Oradea.' He sees Charles's uncomprehending frown. 'The city in Romania where I grew up. You're right; it's their arrogance, their sense of superiority.'

'Exactly,' agrees Charles intensely. 'They treat ordinary people like objects. To them, you're a means to an end, that's all.'

'Charles,' warns Bateman softly.

Charles sits back and his shoulders slump. 'Yes. Sorry. It's just that it makes me very angry. But Peter's right. I'm not the one facing life imprisonment. You have to make up your own mind, Bobby.'

'Do you need an answer immediately?' asks Gold.

'No, not this instant,' replies Charles. 'Cartledge will probably want to call the chap from the Liverpool Empire first, and then there's the police evidence. But that won't take long. I'm sure Peter would say that the longer we leave it, the greater the risk that Quigley will come up with something.'

'Do you think you could get permission for Mickey to come down here?'

Charles shakes his head. 'I'm sorry, but that won't be allowed. Why?'

'I'd like to discuss it with her, that's all. Could you explain the situation to her? I trust her judgement. I'll do whatever she says.'

# CHAPTER TWENTY-SEVEN

The two barristers leave the cells and climb the steps back up to the Great Hall.

'I wasn't expecting that,' comments Bateman.

'What?'

'Gold. He portrays himself as this sharp businessman, the rock executive, all hustle-hustle ... and he wants his wife's advice!'

Charles smiles to himself, imagining how he would react in Gold's situation. A few years ago he might have shared Bateman's surprise. Now, a little older and wiser, he'd certainly want to discuss it with Sally before making a decision.

'I get it,' he says. 'He and Mickey are a team. And the decision will affect all of them. There's two children, remember?' He points to a woman leaving the public canteen. 'There she is.'

'That's Mrs Gold?' asks Bateman out of the corner of his mouth. 'Not what I expected at all. She looks too young.'

'Good morning, Mrs Gold,' says Charles, intercepting her.

'Oh, hello. I'm on my way to the public gallery,' she says. 'The girls are waiting.'

'We need a moment with you, please,' says Charles. 'This is Bobby's junior barrister, Peter Bateman.'

The woman looks from one lawyer to the other and her tentative smile fades. 'Has something happened?'

'Shall we sit down for a moment?' asks Charles, indicating the canteen behind her.

Mrs Gold frowns, nods and leads the way back to her table, where she removes her coat and folds it neatly on her lap.

Charles realises that she's filling time to steel herself for whatever is about to be said.

She looks up. 'Okay, I'm ready.'

Charles quietly repeats the explanation given a few moments ago to her husband.

'He wants to know what you think before making a decision,' concludes Bateman.

'You said if he is found guilty, he will go to prison for a long time,' she says.

'Yes,' affirms Charles. 'Anywhere from ten years to life, depending on the verdict.'

'So everything will end. The girls won't see him again.'

'Not outside prison, no. Not for a very long time.'

'And the business will collapse, yes?'

'If there's only Bobby running it … I would guess so,' answers Charles.

'So we lose the house too.' She smiles grimly. 'A big gamble then.'

'Very big,' says Bateman. 'That's why I think it's too high a risk, and you should let us make the submission as soon as possible.'

Mrs Gold turns to Charles. 'But you, you would take this chance, yes? Perhaps because you have seen injustice, I think?'

'Forget what I would do, Mrs Gold. It's not my life we're playing with here. You're right to focus on the family, the home and the business, because if we get this wrong, it will spell the end of your present life. Yours, Bobby's and the girls'.'

She closes her eyes, and Charles notes her long, dark eyelashes. She appears strangely calm.

'We still have family in Romania,' she says finally. 'Maybe you know what it's like there. The Securitate has the country by the throat. People are arrested and sent to court on made-up charges. I don't mean important people, politicians, but ordinary people, like my sister's husband. He was arrested two years ago. There was a feud with their neighbours and they informed on him. We're still trying to find out if he's alive. People just disappear.'

Bateman looks at his watch and raises his eyebrows at Charles. They only have a couple of minutes. Charles nods.

'This is why we left. We aren't political people, Mr Holborne. We simply wanted to live our lives in a free country.'

'Mrs Gold,' intervenes Bateman gently, 'I'm afraid we don't have much time.'

'This man, Quigley, and his friend … they would do well in Romania. It has been a shock to discover that here, in England, the same thing happens.'

Bateman opens his mouth to speak further but Charles holds up a hand to stop him.

'Do you think Bobby is the only one?' asks Mrs Gold. 'The only one that these policemen are … I don't know the word.'

'Framing? No. We think he's one of several, perhaps one of many.'

'To lose Bobby and everything we've built here would be a disaster,' says Mrs Gold. She looks into Charles's eyes. 'But I think, if there is a chance that Bobby could have these two policemen sent to jail, he should take it. Whatever the risk. Tell him I will accept whatever decision he makes, but if he lets this chance go and looks only to his own skin, I think he will regret it. We can't do anything about the Securitate, but we can do something about these two.'

'Are you sure?' asks Bateman.

'Yes,' replies Mrs Gold in a firm voice. 'I trust you. Both of you. You'll do your best. And maybe we are worrying over nothing.'

Charles rises and the others follow suit. 'Very well. I'll tell Bobby what you said, and let him make up his own mind. Now, we'd better get going.'

They part in the Great Hall, Mrs Gold hurrying off to the public gallery and the barristers climbing the carpeted stairs to court.

'She's an impressive woman, don't you think?' says Charles.

'Yes,' agrees Bateman. 'I really hope they don't come to regret it.' His tone makes plain that he thinks they're making a mistake.

Bateman pushes open the double swing doors and they enter court. Gold has already been brought up from the cells and is awaiting them in the dock. They go directly to him and Charles relays Mickey's opinion.

'Good,' whispers Gold. 'I'm prepared to take the chance, but I needed Mickey to say she agreed. I wouldn't do it otherwise. So, what now?'

'Cartledge will delay,' replies Charles. 'We're sure Perry won't be found, but I don't think they know it yet. They'll be looking for him. Cartledge will worry that as soon as he closes his case, I'll be on my feet making the submission. So he'll string it out to give the police the weekend, either to find Perry or come up with something else.'

Charles is interrupted by the associate calling for silence.

The jury files in, followed shortly by the judge. Charles notes that he has a little more colour in his face than on the previous day. *Glad to be back in the saddle, perhaps*, thinks Charles. He tries to imagine what it must be like, forcing yourself to carry on working with a diagnosis of imminent terminal cancer. He would want to spend those precious last weeks with Sally, Leia and the rest of his family. But if he had no one, he can see why being at work, in a profession where you have a semblance of control and where you've been at the top of your game for decades, would feel appropriate; to go out doing the thing that has given you the most satisfaction in your life.

'Are we ready, gentlemen?' asks Pullman.

Cartledge stands. 'We are, thank you, my Lord. I call Dr Benson.'

The pathologist enters and Charles recognises him from the coroner's court. He is wearing the same three-piece suit and gold-rimmed glasses, but his dark blue bow tie has been replaced by Paisley green which clashes with his tweed.

'Were you expecting him next?' whispers Bateman from behind Charles.

'No.' He turns to Serban, who is sitting next to Bateman. 'Nothing from our chap yet?'

The solicitor shakes his head and stands immediately. 'I'll chase again.' He hurries out of court.

While Charles digs deep into his papers for the notes he took at the coroner's court, Dr Benson takes the oath and Cartledge establishes his identity and qualifications.

The QC proceeds to take the pathologist through his report, line by interminable line. The detail he requires of Benson in establishing the deceased's state of undress and the fact she engaged in sex shortly before her death seems to Charles to be prurient and unnecessary, but he doesn't object and Pullman allows the evidence without raising an eyebrow.

It takes Cartledge over an hour to reach the findings regarding alcohol and heroin metabolites, by which time it is obvious (to the defence at least) that he's on a deliberate go-slow. Leaving the bruising to the deceased's arms until the end as his *pièce de résistance*, it takes him a further forty minutes to deal with the other physical findings. This is an even more obvious play for time, because everyone knows that Benson found nothing of note; all Christine's organs were meticulously removed, weighed, sliced and diced, and revealed nothing unusual.

Finally Cartledge turns to the fingerprint injuries on the deceased's arms. Benson again produces his little sketches, which are handed to the judge, the jury and the advocates.

There is a noise at the back of the court as a door bangs open. Charles looks up to see Serban scurrying down the slope towards him, holding a document in his hand. He comes directly to Charles and whispers to him.

'Our professor's report! Hot off the press, and still unsigned, but that's what he's going to say.'

Charles nods his thanks and takes the document. It has been typed, and is headed "Draft Report of Professor Sir Beverly Lymme, Home Office Forensic Pathologist."

It comprises a single paragraph:

*I have read and considered the report of Dr Benson and conducted my own post-mortem examination of the deceased, Christine Bailey. There are no points of disagreement. I support all of Dr Benson's conclusions.*

Charles turns in his seat. 'This is it?' he asks, astonished.

Serban nods. He leans forwards and whispers, 'One hundred guineas, for two and a half lines. Bobby's going to be furious!'

Pullman is speaking. 'Mr Holborne, I'm addressing you.'

Charles rises, realising that Cartledge has finished with Benson and has resumed his seat.

'I'm sorry, my Lord. We have just received further evidence, which I was considering.'

'And I was asking you, Mr Holborne, if you have any questions for this witness.'

Charles pauses before answering. 'The document we have just received, my Lord, is from the pathologist instructed on behalf of the defence. I apologise that it only just arrived, but on reviewing it…' He shrugs. 'We have no questions of Dr Benson.'

Pullman frowns. 'Are you telling me, Mr Holborne, we have wasted nearly two hours going through Dr Benson's evidence in detail when it is, apparently, agreed?'

'I'm very sorry, my Lord, but that is the case. We have been chasing this report for weeks. I can only apologise to the court.'

Charles catches sight of Cartledge from the corner of his eye, and sees the man smirking.

*That smug bastard has managed to shift the blame for wasting two hours onto me!*

'Very well,' says Pullman. 'I have no questions of the witness. Dr Benson, thank you very much for your time.'

Benson collects his papers and scurries out of court.

'Eamon O'Keefe, please,' says Cartledge.

O'Keefe's name is called and after a moment a tall man appears with wisps of hair combed horizontally across a largely bald pate. He lopes to the witness box and recites the oath in a strong Liverpudlian accent.

'Your name and occupation, please?' asks Cartledge.

'Eamon O'Keefe and I am presently unemployed.'

'Were you employed between 1950 and 1959?'

'Yes, at that time I was the front of house manager at the Liverpool Empire Theatre.'

'What were your duties at that time?'

'We had a team for all front of house duties so, for example, guiding people to their seats, selling ice creams and programmes, manning the doors, bar staff and security. All that. I was in charge of the team.'

'What sort of performances were held at the Liverpool Empire?' asks Cartledge.

'Everything. Opera and ballet, touring productions from London's West End, variety shows. We had world-famous acts all the time, like Bobby Darin and Judy Garland.'

'Do you know the prisoner?'

Cartledge points to Gold in the dock and O'Keefe looks across. 'I recognise him. It's almost ten years since I last saw him, but I recognise him.'

'In what context?'

'His name's Bobby Gold. When I knew him he was in variety on the northern circuit. He appeared a few times at the Empire. What we used to call a "song and dance man". He also did jokes and impressions.'

'Did you have any particular dealings with him?'

'Yes, in 1959, I think it was. The Empire tended to attract some unsavoury types. During and after the war it was often black-market dealers trying to sell their stuff to people who had money, like the performers, directors and better-heeled patrons. They were a nuisance. They tended to gather outside and pester people in the queues and at the stage door. After the war, when the ban on US jazz and other artists was lifted, we started to notice some of these people trying to sell drugs, especially to the artists. Very often they were happy to buy them, which made it difficult to keep them out. Sometimes they forced or bribed their way into the artists' changing rooms. Some carried knives — I even heard talk about a gun, once — and the security team at the theatre was no match for them, so we often called in the police.'

Charles jumps up. 'My Lord, my learned friend hasn't established any connection between any of this and Mr Gold. At present this evidence seems more prejudicial than probative.'

'Mr Cartledge?' asks Pullman.

'Just getting to it, my Lord. Mr O'Keefe, was Mr Gold involved in any way?'

'Yes. He was on the bill for a variety show. This was the 1958/9 season. During the interval, before he was on, I was backstage and saw a man I recognised as a drug dealer. We'd had to chuck him out more than once before. Mr Gold was in the wings, made up and in costume, as he was the first to go on after the interval. He was having an almighty row with the dealer. There was a third man present trying to separate them. It turned into a fight with blows traded. A few minutes earlier I'd been speaking to a police officer outside the front foyer and I ran to get him. The drug dealer and Mr Gold were arrested and Gold was unable to perform that evening. After that, the theatre banned him altogether.'

'Was that the end of your involvement?'

'I was asked to give evidence at the Magistrates' Court, but I was eventually stood down. I understood he pleaded guilty, but I don't know for sure.'

'Yes, thank you, Mr O'Keefe.'

Charles rises. 'Now, Mr O'Keefe, you're not telling us you ever saw Mr Gold buying drugs, are you?'

'No. I never saw him buy drugs. It was the fighting, and his attitude, that got him banned.'

'On the contrary, I think you're telling us you saw him fighting with the man you thought was a drug dealer.'

'Yes.'

'Did you ever find out why he was fighting with the drug dealer?'

'No, I didn't. Gold was a difficult customer, and I'd learned to keep clear of him. That's why I called the police rather than intervene myself.'

'He was the sort of man who stood up for his rights, wasn't he? If he thought he was being treated unfairly. For example, by the theatre.'

'He was a stroppy bugger. Excuse me, your worship,' he says, addressing Pullman. 'A perpetual agitator, you might say.'

'You mean he stood up for his rights, and for those of others, isn't that so?'

'That's not how I'd put it. He led a walkout of the chorus girls once!' replies O'Keefe, apparently still outraged. 'He had no idea of how things should be done, and rubbed everyone up the wrong way.'

'But not the chorus girls, apparently,' says Charles, smiling. O'Keefe doesn't answer. 'Yes, thank you, Mr O'Keefe.'

Cartledge has no re-examination and the judge no questions, and O'Keefe leaves the witness box. Charles looks down the list of prosecution witnesses. There is only Wilfred Spurling, the accountant, to go before Cartledge has no choice but to call the police officers. If that happens before Sloane's DCI Olney arrives, the chance of nailing Quigley and Pilcher will be lost.

# CHAPTER TWENTY-EIGHT

'Mr Wilfred Spurling, please,' says Cartledge.

A man enters and walks towards the witness box carrying two large files under his arm. He does not look like any accountant Charles has ever seen. He is in his mid to late forties and has long floppy hair that almost reaches his shoulders, and although he wears a suit, it is electric blue in colour and covers a flower-patterned shirt open at the man's suntanned neck, where there is a necklace or choker with a dangling golden pentangle. As he walks past the end of Charles's bench, Charles notes that he is wearing brown leather cowboy boots.

His appearance is so surprising that there is a momentary pause as the usher, about to step forward and offer the man the Bible and the oath card, hesitates, and looks towards the judge for guidance.

'You are Mr Wilfred Spurling, FCA, chartered accountant?' asks Pullman for confirmation.

'Indeed I am. Wilfred Edward Spurling, Fellow of the Institute of Chartered Accountants, and the senior partner of Spurling and Blackthorne. The firm has been in existence for ninety-four years and was founded by my grandfather. I have personally been in practice for twenty-one years.'

'Yes, well, please step up and take the oath, Mr Spurling,' says the judge.

Spurling rests the two files on the edge of the witness box and takes the oath in a cut-glass accent.

'Mr Spurling,' starts Cartledge, 'please could you give us your name and professional address again, for the record?' Spurling does so. 'And perhaps you would summarise your professional qualifications and experience?'

'Certainly. Before the war I took a First in Economics from the London School of Economics. After I was demobbed from the Royal Navy I started work at my grandfather's firm as an articled clerk. I passed my final professional exams for the Institute of Chartered Accountants in 1950 and was invited to apply for Fellowship status in 1959, which was granted. I have spent the whole of my professional life at Spurling and Blackthorne, specialising in the accounts of people in the entertainment business.'

'What sort of clients do you have?'

'Some music publishers and promoters, a couple of companies who press vinyl records, but principally pop groups and individual artists,' replies Spurling with a trace of pride in his voice. 'Some very famous ones, actually.'

*Which presumably explains the flamboyant clothing,* thinks Charles.

'Thank you. Now, following a raid on the offices of Gold Management and Talent Ltd, all its working documents and accounts were seized and you were asked to look at them. What exactly were you requested to do?'

'I was asked to give a snapshot of the current state of the finances of the company. A little like an audit, although I was asked to focus on the current financial year which has not yet ended.'

'Perhaps you could summarise your findings for us?'

'Certainly. The company has been running for just over a decade and has been in profit throughout. Over the last few years the expenditure of the company has increased sharply, which I suspect coincides with the new direction it took.'

'New direction?' asks Cartledge.

'Yes. Before then it had managed individual artists and a few rock and pop groups. Then it began promoting tours, which has been an increasing part of its business and of its revenues for the last four years.'

'When you say "tours", do you include tours such as that of Johnny Blaise and the Hellraisers?'

'Yes, although that specific tour falls within the current accounting period, and the company's most recent accounts don't have to be filed until next April.'

Cartledge pauses. Charles understands why the QC is hesitating. Spurling's evidence proceeds, over many pages, to give an extremely detailed breakdown of the company's balance sheet. Running through it will take some time, and Cartledge has a motive to plough through it in detail. It would fritter away a further hour, perhaps more; it would certainly take them past lunchtime, which would give him an opportunity to talk to Quigley for an update on the whereabouts of Frankie Perry. On the other hand, this evidence is very detailed and highly technical, and Charles knows the jury will be lost within a few questions. In the end Cartledge resolves the conflict by opting for simplicity.

'Is the company solvent?' he asks.

'That's not an easy question to answer, because before a company can be insolvent it has to be unable to pay its debts, and for all I know Gold Management and Talent Ltd could access a line of credit from its bankers. But subject to finding additional funding, in my opinion the continued survival of the company is dependent on the Johnny Blaise and the Hellraisers tour proceeding uninterrupted. The company has had to front all the expenses, which are very considerable. The business plan shows that, including the receipts from merchandise at concerts, the UK leg should result in the project breaking even, but all the company's profits this year depend on the European dates.'

'So if, for any reason, the pop group was unable to continue with the tour...?'

'Then Gold Management and Talent Ltd would be in serious financial trouble,' finishes the accountant.

'Thank you. Please remain there.'

Cartledge resumes his seat and Charles rises.

'Just one point of clarification, I think, Mr Spurling,' he says. 'Your conclusion that the company might be in serious financial trouble has two important caveats, doesn't it? The first is that it is not yet the end of the accounting year, and so predictions of whether or not the company will break even are premature. Right?'

'Yes, that's right.'

'And the second caveat is that you have no idea what further lending the company might be able to secure.'

'Yes, that's also right.'

'And we're not just referring to banks, are we? There are plenty of other big players in this field, for example American promoters and record companies, who might be disposed to lend the company money or, perhaps, enter into more complex financial arrangements, such as a buyout or a joint venture?'

'That would always be possible, yes. But there is one other matter which I take into account in predicting difficulties for the company.'

'Yes?' asks Charles, looking at his notes for the next witness, and satisfied that he has nullified the accountant's evidence.

'It's to do with merchandise sales at concerts. I found a surprising inconsistency between the year in progress and previous years. The sale of merchandise at concerts is a relatively new phenomenon, but revenues have been increasing over the last few years. I produced draft accounts for the first eight months of this year from the original documents seized from the company, and it seems that the proportion of revenue from merchandise at concerts has dropped significantly, despite more concerts and higher-profile bands. And it's all cash takings. I couldn't see where it's gone.'

Charles's heart sinks. He wasn't paying attention. He should have slammed the door on any further comment from the accountant. 'There is an issue of law on which I need to address your Lordship,' he says to the judge.

'Yes, I thought there might be, Mr Holborne. You've only yourself to blame. You asked for that by opening the door.'

'It doesn't matter who opened the door, my Lord, the witness isn't permitted to go through it.'

Pullman turns to prosecution counsel. Charles flicks a glance to his left and sees another smug grin on the QC's face.

'Mr Cartledge,' says the judge, 'I will hear argument on the point in the absence of the jury if you wish, but if this witness is heading where I think he is —'

'No, my Lord, I'm not going to pursue the point. I'm entirely happy to leave the evidence as it is. The prisoner will have an opportunity to explain where the cash takings have gone, if he is so minded, when he gives evidence.'

This is Cartledge putting Gold under pressure to go into the witness box, an issue on which no final decision has yet been taken. Nonetheless, the danger has been headed off for the present.

Pullman addresses Charles, a small smile curling his grey lips. 'Anything further for Mr Spurling?'

'No, thank you, my Lord.'

'Very well. We'll rise now and take the next witness at ten past two.' He indicates the court clock, which shows a time of five past one. Judges jealously guard their sixty-five-minute lunch adjournments.

'All rise!'

The defence team are again down in the cells, firing questions at Gold as he wolfs down his lunch — beef stew and mashed potato.

'But then how do you explain it?' persists Charles, referring to the missing cash.

Gold is focusing on his food and shrugs, his mouth full. 'There's probably someone skimming,' he says. 'Happens all the time.'

'Have you taken on someone new this year?' asks Serban. 'Someone you don't trust?'

Gold clears the last fork-full of mash and gravy from his plate and swallows. 'I'd need the sheets from each concert, to see who was on the stalls. Have you got them?'

'No,' replies Charles, 'but surely you'd remember if you'd taken on a new member of staff?'

Gold shakes his head dismissively. 'I've got more to worry about than T-shirt sales. There's always an element of wastage when taking cash from crowds of fans. It's easy to make mistakes and we often use casuals.'

'What's the usual procedure for collecting the cash and handing it over?'

'The team leader gives it to Stan, and he gives it to me.'

'Who is the team leader, and how long have they been with you?' asks Bateman.

'His name is Adam Downey, and he's been with me for years.'

'Stan, then?'

'No, never. He's as honest as the day is long,' asserts Gold.

'And extremely loyal,' adds Serban.

Charles sits back and puts his pen down. 'Then, what? How do we explain this? We have to have an explanation, or the jury will suspect you're embezzling money from the business. That's not a good look, regardless of what counts you face on the indictment.'

They persist for another ten minutes but Gold has nothing further to offer, and the lawyers give up. They leave the cells and head for their own lunches.

'Well?' asks Bateman as they climb the stairs to the Bar Mess. 'What do you think?'

'I think that, for the first time since we met him, Bobby Gold just lied to us,' replies Charles.

'I agree, but does it matter? He's charged with murder and drugs offences, not fiddling his tax.'

'Yes, but he'll either be forced to lie about it in the witness box, and you can be sure Cartledge will make a big deal of it, or Pullman will have to give him a warning about self-incrimination which, if he follows, will look every bit as bad.'

# CHAPTER TWENTY-NINE

It is ten past two, and the court is assembling. Cartledge comes down the aisle, surrounded by his usual team of acolytes. He is laughing and in good spirits.

*Still crowing about Spurling's last contribution,* thinks Charles sourly. *Now the jury think Gold's dodgy with his company's money, and we have no good explanation.*

'All rise!' calls the usher.

'No jury,' comments Bateman from behind Charles, and for the first time Charles realises that the jury has not been brought in.

'He's up to something,' says Charles out of the side of his mouth in reply, nodding towards Cartledge.

Everyone stands for the judge to enter and the court settles.

Cartledge rises. 'My Lord, I have asked for the jury to be kept out for the moment as I have an issue of law to raise.'

'Yes, Mr Cartledge?'

'Since yesterday, enquiries have been progressing regarding the failure of Mr Francis Perry to attend court. It appears that he has fled. The police have been to his address in Peckham and made enquiries. It's thought that he may already be out of the country.'

Charles permits himself a small moment of satisfaction. Thanks to Billy Munday, for once, they've been a step ahead of the prosecution.

'And your application, Mr Cartledge?'

'May I hand up to your Lordship a Notice of Additional Evidence together with the statement of a Mr Derek Emmerson? I have copies for my learned friends.'

The usher distributes copies around court. Charles looks over his shoulder to his client in the dock. Gold looks bemused. He shakes his head. He has no more idea of what is occurring than does his legal team. Cartledge has resumed speaking.

'You will remember, my Lord, that Mr Perry is one of the guiding hands behind Celeb Security. He was supposed to give evidence of certain security matters at Kingston Grange and the relaxed attitude to the admission of young women and drugs. Mr Emmerson is, or perhaps was, Mr Perry's business partner. If anything, he has greater experience of actually working at the property than Mr Perry. Overnight, when it became clear that the Crown were not going to be able to produce Mr Perry to give evidence, further enquiries were made of Mr Emmerson who, it transpires, is capable of giving almost identical evidence to that of his partner, had Mr Perry not been persuaded otherwise.' He turns to stare pointedly at Charles.

Charles leaps to his feet. 'That's outrageous! Is Mr Cartledge implying that the defence had something to do with Mr Perry disappearing? Unless he withdraws that accusation —'

'Calm down, Mr Holborne! He was not accusing you of anything, were you, Mr Cartledge?'

A couple of seconds elapse before Cartledge answers. 'If that was the impression I gave, I apologise. I have no evidence to prove that Mr Holborne or any member of the defence team put pressure on Mr Perry.'

'Very well —' starts the judge.

'That's not sufficient, my Lord,' interrupts Charles. 'Whether Mr Cartledge has evidence or not, he still implied that we've been up to no good. Your Lordship knows me well, and knows that I would never —'

'*Du calme*, Mr Holborne, *du calme*. You may lower your handbag. You too, Mr Cartledge. We have no jury, so these histrionics are quite unnecessary. Mr Cartledge, your application, I assume, is to call Mr Emmerson in place of Mr Perry, is that right?'

'It is, my Lord. The court will appreciate how important Mr Perry was to the Crown's case. Whatever may lie behind his disappearance, it leaves the Crown in a difficult position. I submit we should not have to throw the towel in, if an alternative witness exists whose evidence covers the same ground. I would not oppose an adjournment for Mr Holborne to take instructions, but he shouldn't need more than a few minutes to discuss this development with his client. It is, after all, the same evidence. So his cross-examination's already prepared.'

'Mr Holborne?' says Pullman, turning to Charles.

'It's not as simple as that, my Lord. What if Emmerson has a long string of convictions for dishonesty? I'd be able to cross-examine on that, but we have had no opportunity —'

Cartledge jumps up and interrupts. 'Emmerson is of good character. No criminal record at all.'

The judge raises his eyebrows at Charles. 'Any other objections, then, Mr Holborne?'

Charles turns to Bateman and whispers, 'I can't think of anything, can you?'

Bateman glares at Charles. 'No. And this is your fault, Charles. If this evidence goes in, we're screwed on a submission. Frankly, we're screwed, period!' he hisses.

Charles turns back to the judge. 'I will need some time with my client,' he says. 'My learned friend may assert that the evidence of Mr Perry and Mr Emmerson is identical, but I must be allowed time to compare the two carefully, and take instructions on any subtle differences.'

'I agree,' says Pullman.

'May we have until Monday morning, please, my Lord?'

'No, Mr Holborne, you may have half an hour. If, after that, you can persuade me that you cannot proceed for some reason or other — and at present I can't see any possible difficulty — I will hear you again. We'll reconvene at two forty-five.'

Charles and the defence team once again face Gold over the table in the Old Bailey's cells.

'Well,' says Charles, looking up from the Notice of Additional Evidence, 'it's bad, but it's not as bad as it could be. But Emmerson does assert that you were relaxed about girls and drugs being allowed in, and he claims he's seen you paying for drugs from various dealers.'

'What, that nonsense about the Liverpool Empire?' asks Gold.

'No, obviously, he can't say he was there. But other times, at Kingston Grange, when he was on duty.'

'Jesus Christ,' whispers Gold. 'They've got to him — they must have.'

'It's not over yet, Bobby,' says Charles, in what he hopes is a reassuring tone. 'Let's just think this through. Perry says his police statement was made up by Quigley and he was being blackmailed into giving evidence. The same has to be true of Emmerson. They must have something on him. I wonder...'

'What?' asks Bateman brusquely. He is still angry.

'Well, I wonder if Emmerson's name's come up anywhere in Olney's investigations.'

'And how are we to find out in the next twenty-five minutes?' points out Bateman.

Charles sits up and looks at his watch. He stands and addresses Bateman. 'If I'm not back when we're called in, cross-examine on the basis of what Perry put in his statement to us, okay?'

'Where are you going?' asks Bateman, alarmed.

'To get hold of Sean.'

Charles signs out and is allowed out of the cells. He pauses in the Great Hall, considering whether to run up to the Bar Mess. A phone is provided for the use of barristers, but he's likely to be overheard. Further, the subterfuge he has in mind involves the risk that the number for the Old Bailey switchboard would be recognised. He checks furiously in his pocket, finds some change and races out onto Old Bailey, looking left and right for a phone. Then he remembers: there used to be a public phone box down the cobbled lane beside the Magpie and Stump, the pub otherwise known in the legal profession as Courtroom Number Ten. It acquired its nickname due to its proximity to the Old Bailey and its popularity with lawyers and observers of legal proceedings for the last three centuries. Before the Bailey was built, this was the site of Newgate Prison, and the first floor of the Magpie and Stump was a favoured spot for fans of hangings.

As usual when the weather is fine, a large crowd of lawyers has gathered outside on the pavement, glasses in hand, enjoying the autumn sunshine.

Charles dodges a couple of taxis and, still wearing his robes, runs across the road, through the crowd and into the lane. It is gloomy here, the sky a narrow strip of blue, and it's cold. He shivers. His footsteps slow as he comes round the slight bend in the alley and sees the red box. A nameless dread creeps over him. His legs suddenly feel as if they have lead weights attached. He comes to a halt five yards from the red door.

Something is compressing his chest, bands of steel squeezing so tightly he thinks his heart might burst.

He can't go any closer. He can't enter that telephone box. He can't.

*Is this a heart attack?*

And then he remembers.

It was in this very phone box that he almost died five years ago, stabbed on the orders of Ronnie Kray.

*How could I have forgotten? Could I really have blotted it out all this time, that terrifying brush of Death's wings?*

Charles takes a deep breath and forces his reluctant legs to carry him the final distance. He reaches out to grab the door handle but, again, stops.

*Idiot! Get a grip!*

He yanks open the door and steps inside. The reek of urine hits him — the place is still used by drunks as an emergency urinal — and in that second he is thrown violently back in time as the memory of the attack floods through him like a tidal wave. He is there again, searching desperately for Sally, whose life is in danger. The assassin is behind him, this very second, lashing out with his knife, and Charles actually feels a sharp pain in his kidney, a ghost memory of the blade skidding off his leather belt and entering his flesh. His heart is thundering and he pants, his respiratory rate having doubled in an instant. He is convinced, he *knows*, that if he looks round he will see his attacker again, lunging at him, aiming to finish him off. He forces himself to turn. The alley is empty.

He reaches into his pocket with a trembling hand, finds some change and dials.

He waits, his heart still pounding and sweat trickling down his forehead, for the telephone to be picked up at the other end.

'Finchley Memorial Hospital,' says a female voice.

Charles presses coins into the slot. 'Please can you page Dr Irenna Alexandrova?' he gasps. 'It's a family emergency!'

'Who can I say is calling?'

'Sean ... Sean Sloane ... her fiancé.'

'Please hold.'

The line goes dead. Charles turns his back to the apparatus and looks back up the alley. It's still deserted. If he cranes his neck he can just see the bustle of taxis and other vehicles passing on Old Bailey at the end of the passageway. There is something reassuring about the quotidian city traffic and he feels the panic recede a notch. He wills himself to take deep breaths.

He waits for a minute, then another, then a third. He inserts more coins. Finally the line comes alive again. 'Hello?' says a voice.

'Irenna?'

'No, it's the operator. A call has gone out for her, but she hasn't responded. It's possible she's at lunch. Would you like to leave a message, or try again later?'

Charles curses silently. He has no idea where Sloane might be and he dare not risk leaving a message at the police station.

'No, thank you —' he says, about to hang up, when the operator interrupts.

'Hang on, caller, I think we've found her.'

Relief washing through him, Charles waits and finally hears Irenna's clipped South African voice.

'Sean? What's happened?'

'Irenna, it's not Sean, it's me, Charles. Sorry for the deception.'

'Jesus, you scared me to death, Charles! So, no emergency?'

'Yes, there is, but it doesn't involve you or Sean's family. I'm having a panic attack. I'm in the call box where I was stabbed a few years ago. But that's not it. Sorry, I'm wittering. Listen: I absolutely have to get hold of Sean, right now. I've got less than ten minutes. It's about the work he's been doing, and I daren't ring the police station. But I thought maybe you could.'

'He's never there when I call,' replies Irenna.

'No, but there'll be people who can contact him. I haven't time to explain but can you do this for me? I need you to ring, sound desperate, tell them there's a family emergency in Ireland, get them to tell him, and have him call you back immediately. But, and this is important, don't give him your number at the hospital, give him the number of this call box. Do you understand?'

'Yes. Hang on … okay, give me the number.'

Charles does so.

'If he isn't able to call in the next seven minutes or so, I'll have to leave.'

'Okay. I'll do my best.'

# CHAPTER THIRTY

Fifteen minutes later Charles barges into the courtroom and runs towards the bench. Everyone has assembled and the associate is standing in the aisle waiting for him.

'You're ten minutes late and the judge is livid,' she says. 'Are you ready?'

'Yes.'

'Sure? With all due respect, Mr Holborne, you don't look it.'

Charles wipes the sweat streaming from his forehead, stands stock still, closes his eyes and takes two very deep breaths, which he releases slowly. 'I'm fine,' he says, opening his eyes.

'Okay. I'll bring the judge in. Prepare for a rocket.'

'All rise!'

Pullman sweeps into court, glaring at Charles. Charles decides to take the initiative. Even before the judge has sat down fully, he starts.

'I offer my apologies to your Lordship and the court. I had to use a telephone to contact a potential witness urgently, and I found myself in the call box where I was the victim of an assassination attempt a few years ago. Your Lordship may remember the circumstances?'

Pullman, about to unleash his annoyance on Charles, stops. Everyone in the Temple knows of the murder attempt. Indeed, it was the matron of the Old Bailey, Mrs Hamlin, who discovered Charles lying on the cobbles, close to unconsciousness and bleeding out. She saved his life that day.

'I'm afraid,' continues Charles, 'I was … well … overcome. I suffered a flashback — it's the first time it's ever happened — and it took me a few minutes to recover.'

Pullman peers hard at Charles's sweaty face and elevated colour, and eventually nods. 'Are you well enough to continue?'

'I think so, my Lord. My learned friend will be calling his next witness, and sitting quietly while he does so will allow me a few more moments.'

'Very well. Mr Cartledge, your next witness, please.'

Bateman leans forward and whispers in Charles's ear as he sits down. 'You're completely bloody shameless!' he says, without a trace of humour.

Charles half-turns in his seat. 'No, it's true. I did suffer a flashback. I'll tell you about it later.'

'Derek Emmerson, please,' calls Cartledge.

'And?' hisses Bateman, wanting news, but Charles has no time to respond. He gives an optimistic thumbs-up and swivels to face front.

Emmerson's name is called, there is a bang at the back of the court as a door is thrown open and a man enters. He strides towards the witness box. He is tall and sturdy, with a shaved head, a thick muscular neck and the flattened cauliflower ears of a rugby player or former wrestler. Charles can well believe he used to be a bouncer.

Emmerson takes the oath in a surprisingly quiet voice and stands in the witness box looking around, as if waiting for something to happen. When Cartledge addresses him he looks surprised.

'Are you Derek Emmerson?'

'Yeah.'

'Please would you give the court your full name and address.'

Emmerson does so.

'What is your occupation?'

'I run a firm called Celeb Security which provides the security for concert venues. I have about twenty staff on permanent contracts and another twenty casuals who work on a regular basis. Built from nothing.' Everyone hears the man's pride in his achievement.

'Thank you. Do you know the prisoner?'

Emmerson looks over at the dock. 'Bobby Gold? Yeah, I know him.'

'How did you come to meet him for the first time?'

'He got in touch with me. Said I'd been recommended. He was planning a major European tour by an American musician called Johnny Blaise and his group. He wanted security. I was rushed off me feet at the time so I asked Frankie Perry to meet him at the property where the group would be staying to discuss his requirements.'

'Is Mr Ferry one of your employees?' asks Cartledge.

'Nah, he's me brother-in-law. But he's also in business, and sometimes when I'm rushed he helps me out. And I trust him, particularly with paperwork and scheduling stuff.'

'Does he ever do the actual security work for you?'

Emmerson grins. 'On the odd occasion, when it's soft. He's not what you'd call a hardman.'

'Once the group were in residence at Kingston Grange, did you ever go to that property?'

'Yeah, every now and then, just to check everything was hunky-dory.'

'Did you meet Mr Gold?'

'A few times.'

'From what you saw of him there, would you be able to give us an impression of his attitude to groupies?'

Until now Emmerson has answered the questions easily, confidently, but there is a minute hesitation before he responds to Cartledge's query.

'Yeah, he seemed okay,' he says vaguely.

'What do you mean by "okay"?'

Emmerson shrugs. 'Just okay. He didn't seem to have a problem with it.'

'So you saw him on the premises when there were young women around?'

'Probably.'

'Yes or no, Mr Emmerson? Did you see young women around or not?'

'Yeah, I expect I did. I weren't paying much attention.'

'Did Mr Gold ever eject such young ladies from the premises in your presence?'

'No, I can't say as I saw that.'

'Thank you. What about drugs?'

'What about 'em?' asks Emmerson.

Charles looks up at the judge and then across at the jury. If Emmerson's task is to replicate Perry's false evidence, this is an odd performance. He must know what he's expected to say, but he seems strangely reluctant to say it. At that moment the only person in the courtroom who understands why, is Charles. His foot starts tapping with impatience for his turn.

'Did you ever see drugs on the premises?' persists Cartledge.

'Of course. They're always smoking wacky baccy, ain't they? They're in the music business.' He shrugs.

'What about hard drugs?'

'I wouldn't know about that. They're not going to shoot up in front of me, are they? Wouldn't be surprising if hard drugs were used every now and then, but you don't advertise that sort of thing. You'd slope off to a bedroom, or somewhere quiet, wouldn't you?'

Cartledge's fixed smile remains in place, but Charles can see his frustration building. 'What was Mr Gold's attitude to drugs? From what you saw yourself,' asks the QC.

'I never discussed it with 'im.'

'But from what you saw, would he have known that musicians or their entourage were using drugs?'

'He couldn't have missed it. When they were there, the place stank of dope. I never saw him complain, if that's what you're asking.'

'But you never saw hard drugs being handed over, sold, or used?'

'Not that I recall.'

Cartledge gives up this avenue of enquiry and begins another. 'Do you remember the night of the nineteenth of July of this year?'

'The Astoria concert, yeah?'

'That's right.'

'I remember. Something went wrong at the venue, and I got a call from one of my chaps saying they were having trouble. Bunch of fans got on stage, and some backstage, demanding their money back. There was a bit of a ruckus.'

Emmerson now seems back on track and is answering smoothly again.

'What did you do?'

'Well, it was nothing to do with us, really, or the group. They should've been told to speak to the management at the venue, but matters got out of hand, punches thrown. They wanted reinforcements, but there wasn't anyone, 'cept me. As I live in Highgate, only a few minutes away, I went down myself.'

'And what happened?'

'It was a song and dance over nothing. By the time I got there, most of the fans had dispersed and the team had everything under control.'

'What did you do next?'

'I don't rightly recall.'

'Did you go home?'

'Yeah, course.'

'Straight away?'

There is another pause before Emmerson answers. 'No. I went back with them to Kingston Grange.'

'Why?'

'Don't really remember. Maybe I was worried about there being problems with the fans there. That was probably it.'

'Was there?'

'Nah, it was all quiet.'

'Did you see the prisoner at Kingston Grange that evening?'

Another short hesitation. *As if he's struggling to remember what he's been told to say*, thinks Charles.

'Yeah, he was there.'

'Thank you. And this is very important, please, Mr Emmerson: when was the last time you saw Mr Gold at Kingston Grange that night?'

Emmerson looks down but his answer is clear. 'Early hours of the morning. Maybe around two.'

'Two?' asks Cartledge, as if expecting a different answer.

'Around then.'

Charles tenses his legs, ready to jump up and object if Cartledge presses further. You can't cross-examine your own witness. Except in very narrow circumstances, where a witness is declared hostile, you are bound by their answers. Cartledge has now twice received the answer of two in the morning or around that time, and further enquiry will take him over the line. Even this answer potentially makes Gold a liar for saying he left at around ten-thirty, but it's certainly better than four a.m., the time in Perry's police statement.

Charles waits, but Cartledge knows the danger and sits down quietly. Charles stands. 'Mr Emmerson, you are married to Mr Perry's sister, is that right?'

'It is.'

Charles pauses and lobs his first grenade. 'Your wife and her brother, Mr Perry, have fallen out over the last few months, isn't that right?'

'They ain't been talking, but that's nothing unusual in a family.'

'And the reason they aren't talking, is because you were pressured to assist Mr Perry in doing something which got you into trouble with the police. Your wife warned you against it, but you did it anyway, and you were arrested. That's right, isn't it?'

Emmerson stares at Charles, his mouth slightly open. Several different and competing emotions pass across his face, like clouds scudding across an undulating landscape. At first he looks simply surprised; then a half-smile plays upon his thick lips; then he frowns. He looks down at the top of the witness box, chewing his lip, apparently undecided about how to answer.

'Did the police tell you that, if you gave evidence in the way they directed, your nights spent in the cells at Leeds would never come to light?'

Cartledge rises. 'I fail to see the relevance of this, my Lord.'

Charles is about to respond when the judge holds up his hand. 'The Crown rely on Mr Emmerson to prove the defendant permitted underage girls and drugs onto the premises for the entertainment of the musicians, isn't that right?'

'Yes, my Lord, but —'

'Credibility, Mr Cartledge. The jury are entitled to know the character of the man making the allegation. You may continue, Mr Holborne.'

'Thank you, my Lord. I understand your difficulties in answering, Mr Emmerson. You've been made promises which the police can't keep. No, don't look at Mr Cartledge. He can't help you, and Mr Quigley and Mr Pilcher aren't in court. You have a choice: you can continue to give the perjured evidence the police have put in your mouth, in the full knowledge that your part in this burglary is no longer a secret, or you can tell us the truth and get the monkeys off your back.'

Pullman leans forward. 'I'm sorry, Mr Holborne, but I may have been too hasty in my ruling. I'm starting to agree with Mr Cartledge: what's the relevance of this? It no longer sounds as if you are cross-examining on credibility. Or is there some other more extensive allegation?'

'My Lord,' responds Charles, pointing across at Emmerson, 'I think we're about to hear the answer to that question.'

'I never wanted to do it!' says Emmerson energetically. 'I had no choice.'

'Never wanted to do what?' asks Charles.

'That burglary.'

The judge intervenes. 'Mr Emmerson, you are not on trial here, and you cannot be forced to answer any questions that incriminate you, do you understand? I'm not sure I follow what's going on, but no one, including Mr Holborne, can force you to admit to a criminal offence.'

''E ain't forcing me! I want to tell the truth! But that Quigley told me if I did, he'd make sure I went inside.'

'Start at the beginning, Mr Emmerson, yes?' suggests Charles.

Emmerson takes a deep breath. 'Right. That detective chief inspector — Quigley, he's called — and his sidekick, DI Pilcher, have been blackmailing Frankie for years.'

Cartledge is on his feet objecting instantly, but Emmerson keeps talking, raising his voice with each phrase to be heard over the QC.

'Mr Emmerson —' starts the judge.

'Planting stuff on him, threatening to take 'im to court, and all to force him to go thieving for them!'

Pullman eventually manages to stem his flow. 'Mr Emmerson! Mr Cartledge is trying to object and I need you to stop for a moment so I can hear him.'

'Yeah, sorry, but it makes my blood boil! Why d'ya think Frankie did a runner? He was caught between the devil and the deep blue sea!'

Pullman addresses Cartledge. 'Your objection is that this is all hearsay, I take it?'

'Indeed, my Lord.'

Pullman turns to Emmerson. 'Mr Emmerson, you can only tell us what you know yourself. You can't tell us what one person may or may not have done to another unless you were actually there. Do you understand?'

'But I *was* actually there. Pilcher told Frankie he had to do a certain burglary up north, big clothing warehouse, only it's so big he had to take someone along. So Frankie begged me to go. I kept on saying no till I got a visit from Pilcher, who said I had no choice. If I didn't do it, Frankie and I were both going inside. So I did it, and we got caught.'

'So,' clarifies Pullman, 'you claim that Mr Perry begged you to go on a burglary set up by DI Pilcher, and DI Pilcher himself threatened you with prison if you didn't, is that right?'

'Exactly. And we got caught,' he repeats.

'You got caught?' asks Pullman.

'Yeah! You can check it yourself if you don't believe me. We was in the Leeds City Police station. Course, they pulled strings for Frankie and got 'im out after a few hours, 'cos he was so important to them, but I was banged up for days!'

'And have you been charged with burglary?'

'Well, someone "lost" the papers and I got out eventually, but the wife's still hopping mad. We're barely talking, and she won't speak to Frankie at all, she's so furious with 'im.'

Charles starts to ask another question, but Pullman puts up his hand to stop him. Charles watches his pen until his note catches up with the evidence and then starts again.

'What about your evidence today?' asks Charles. 'Did Mr Quigley or Mr Pilcher have anything to do with that?'

'Well, with Frankie in the wind, they was stuffed. He was s'posed to say that that bloke there —' he points to Gold — 'was letting groupies and drugs in, and he was there at four in the morning the night the girl died, seen running from her bedroom. But, like I said, Frankie's on his toes, so Quigley turns up at my gaff, mob-handed, and tells me I have to say it!' His outrage is plain for everyone to see. 'I mean, I know coppers and I know some of 'em are bent, but this is … next level! This Quigley said unless I gave the evidence, all the papers from the burglary would turn up again, and I'd do time.'

'So what you're saying is that DCI Quigley told you that if you gave false evidence to get Mr Gold convicted, he'd lose the papers permanently?'

Emmerson jabs his stubby finger at Charles in affirmation. 'Got it in one.' He turns to the judge in supplication. 'I mean, your honour, I've never been in trouble with the law, right? Despite me job, which can get a bit tasty every now and then,

I've always kept me nose clean. It's how I was brought up. And then this all happens, and I'm up to me neck in it!'

'So, Mr Emmerson, why are you telling the truth now?' asks Charles.

''Cos you already know about the burglary! Quigley ain't keeping it a secret, is he? It's out in the open, so I don't see we have a deal anymore.' He turns to the judge again. 'I'm really sorry, your honour, I would never've done that burglary if it hadn't been for them threats. Go all the way up North to nick some dresses? You gotta be joking! I gotta business to run.'

Charles sees a few members of the jury hiding smiles behind their hands. 'So, Mr Emmerson, let's hear the truth now, yes? Do you know if Mr Gold allowed underage girls and drugs onto the premises?'

'I've no idea. I only met the bloke once or twice, and he seemed okay. I mean, there were girls there, yeah, but I don't know who let them in or how old they were. And they were smoking dope too, but again I can't tell you how the drugs got there.'

'What about Mr Gold being there that night?'

'Nah. I was on the same coach as him coming back from the Astoria, and we both left Kingston at the same time, around ten-thirty. I know 'cos I got stuck behind the white limo checking out at the gates.'

'And that's the truth, is it, Mr Emmerson?'

Emmerson nods his head vigorously. 'On me life.'

'Thank you.'

*Get out of that!* thinks Charles. He turns towards the dock as he sits and winks at Gold. Then, unable to resist temptation, he leans backwards and whispers to Bateman, 'Even better than having Perry, wouldn't you say?'

Cartledge rises. 'The Crown applies to treat the witness as hostile, my Lord,' says the QC. 'You've seen his statement attached to the Notice of Additional Evidence, and it gives entirely contradictory evidence to what he's just said. I therefore ask permission to cross-examine him.'

'I don't think I've ever seen a clearer case — have you, Mr Holborne? You can't possibly object. Permission granted,' rules Pullman.

'Mr Emmerson, please look at this statement,' continues Cartledge. He hands a copy of Emmerson's police statement to the usher and she walks it round to him. 'Do you see your signature at the bottom?'

'Yeah, that's me signature.'

'And do you see your signature at the top, just after the declaration which says that you make the statement believing it to be true and that if you say anything in it which is false or which you do not believe to be true, you face prosecution?'

'I see it.'

'So, either you are lying in your evidence today or you were lying in your statement.'

'Well, the statement ain't true, but I don't see how you can say I was lying when it's not my statement. I never wrote it. Quigley or Pilcher or one of their mates wrote it, and Quigley told me I had to sign it, and come here to say what was in it. Or else.'

'When you wrote your signature, you knew what you were signing was false?'

'Only because I was threatened.'

'And I think you've just admitted to carrying out a burglary, from a warehouse somewhere in the north?'

'Like I said, only 'cos I was threatened. And Frankie was.'

'How much was stolen in that burglary?' asks Cartledge.

'I don't know. A lot. It wouldn't all fit in the van.'

'Would you disagree with me if I told you the value of the stolen clothing came to about ten thousand pounds?' asks Cartledge, reading from a document.

'No, that wouldn't surprise me.'

'And what was your cut?'

Now Emmerson looks uncomfortable. 'I got two hundred pounds. For me time and the petrol,' he insists. 'I should've been working that night, so I reckoned it was fair, for the loss of income.'

'So you went on a burglary, from which you profited to the extent of two hundred pounds.'

'But I've explained. I only did it 'cos we were threatened. And Quigley and Pilcher kept almost all the profits, thousands.'

'Let's come to that. Do you know anything about Detective Chief Inspector Quigley?'

'Only that he's a right bastard. Sorry, your honour.'

'DCI Quigley is a war hero, did you know that? Decorated twice. And he's one of the most successful thief-catchers in the Met.'

'Don't mean he ain't bent.'

'The outlandish suggestion that he was forcing you to commit a crime and taking the proceeds is, I suggest, a complete fabrication, designed to get yourself out of trouble.'

'No. It's the truth. I've just admitted burglary! How's that getting me out of trouble?'

'So, on the one hand, we have an admitted burglar, one who also admits he lied in his police statement, and on the other hand we have a twice-decorated, highly respected police officer with a sparkling record of fighting crime. Would you like to tell the jury why they should believe you and not Mr Quigley?'

Emmerson turns to face the jury and shrugs. 'I'm telling the truth. He ain't. That's all I can say.'

Cartledge sits down without, for once, asking the judge if he has any questions. Pullman apparently has none because he says, 'Mr Emmerson, you are free to leave. Next witness, Mr Cartledge?'

'Yes, my Lord. I call Detective Chief Inspector Quigley.'

# CHAPTER THIRTY-ONE

The funereal policeman enters court. He looks exactly as he did when Charles first met him at the police station: black three-piece suit, deep-sunken eyes and a pale, almost bloodless complexion.

He makes his way to the witness box and, without being prompted, gives the oath and then, turning to the judge, offers his name, rank and professional address.

'DCI Quigley, would you please give us a brief summary of your career to date?' asks Cartledge.

'Certainly. My Lord, I applied to join the Metropolitan Police in 1936 when I was eighteen. I was a uniformed constable when war broke out. I volunteered for the Army and did most of my service in North Africa. I rose through the non-commissioned ranks as a tank commander and in early 1943 I received my commission as a lieutenant in the Royal Tank Regiment. I was then promoted to captain, a battlefield promotion, in charge of four tanks. That was right at the end of the Tunisian campaign. During my service in North Africa, I was awarded both the Military Medal and the Distinguished Conduct Medal.'

Quigley projects his voice well, as might be expected of a man used to command, and he knows to half-turn to the Bench to make sure both judge and jury can hear him clearly. He also prefaces his answers with "My Lord", thus — as is correct — addressing the judge and not the questioner. This is something of which Charles has reminded Bobby Gold, but most inexperienced witnesses forget both judge and jury and direct their answers to whoever is asking the questions.

Charles casts a glance at the jury. They are taking it all in, several making notes, and seem impressed with Quigley's war record. Charles has often wondered when the after-effects of the war will wear off. A quarter of a century later, juries still seem inappropriately swayed by historic bravery on the battlefield, when it has nothing whatever to do with a witness's credibility or honesty in civilian life. Quigley's wartime heroics warrant his honesty or integrity no more than do Charles's own. Nonetheless, thinks Charles, it probably won't change until the current generation are dead and buried.

'What did you do after the war ended?' asks Cartledge.

'My Lord, I went back to the Metropolitan Police, where I've been ever since. I've been promoted gradually to my present rank. Until I was seconded to Scotland Yard, I was the second in charge of No. 6 Regional Crime Squad based in Brighton.'

'Why were you seconded to Scotland Yard?'

'I had significant success in catching a group of crooks who were responsible for a spate of high-value burglaries and robberies. It was felt that my experience might be useful.'

'Thank you. Now I want to ask you briefly about your involvement in this case against Bobby Gold.'

'I am what is known as the "officer in the case", which means that I, and subordinates acting under my direction, collate the evidence, take statements, and put it all before the solicitor instructed by the Met to decide if there's enough evidence to charge.'

'Were you responsible for interviewing the prisoner?'

'I was, my Lord, together with Detective Inspector Pilcher. However, Gold answered "no comment" to all questions put to him, as was his right, so no evidence actually came out of those interviews.'

Charles looks again at the jury. Quigley sounds fair and reasonable, and they seem to be warming to him.

'The witness who gave evidence before you, a man called Derek Emmerson, has made certain allegations against you which I wish to put to you,' says Cartledge.

'Oh yes?' replies Quigley, and the look of surprise on his face seems entirely genuine.

'He said that you and DI Pilcher pressured him into taking part in a burglary of a clothing warehouse by threatening to charge him with criminal offences of which he was innocent. He says he was arrested for that burglary and taken to Leeds police station, and that you were responsible for "losing" the papers so he could be released. What do you say to that?'

'My Lord, as for pressuring him to take part in that burglary, that's complete nonsense. But I do know about the offence, because the Leeds City Police contacted me about it. Shall I explain?'

'Please do,' replies Pullman.

'Mr Emmerson was indeed arrested for a burglary in Leeds, together with a man called Francis Perry, his brother-in-law. Perry is presently on the run from the police, and has been the subject of a major investigation into warehouse burglaries. I was involved in that, at the London end, which is why I was contacted when the Leeds police arrested these men. Now, Perry has his fingers in many dishonest pies, but Mr Emmerson is of good character, and he gave us a story about having been blackmailed into taking part, not by the police, but by his brother-in-law. Knowing Perry, that seemed entirely plausible. Accordingly, Mr Emmerson was invited to give evidence on behalf of the police should a prosecution of Perry go forward, and on that basis he was released.'

'What about the papers he alleged were lost?'

'No papers were lost, but I suppose, in all fairness, he might have misunderstood that.'

'Mr Emmerson says that you threatened him with prosecution if he did not give perjured evidence here today, against Mr Gold.'

'My Lord, that's completely untrue. I'm surprised and, if I admit it to myself, a little disappointed he would make that allegation.' Quigley faces the jury, to make sure they can see him looking disappointed. 'He could've been charged with burglary, but I gave him a break. If he's now making up stories about the police putting him under pressure, that seems to have been a mistake.'

'So, to make it absolutely clear,' says Cartledge, 'to your knowledge, did you or any other officers put Mr Emmerson under pressure to commit offences or give false evidence?'

'Of course not. His story is —' he reaches for the right word — 'fantastical. My Lord, Metropolitan police officers entering into criminal conspiracies with known criminals to commit burglaries? Persuading Leeds City Police to "lose" papers for an arrest they've made? Why on earth would they do that? No, it's all completely implausible. Mr Emmerson's presence on that burglary had nothing whatsoever to do with us, and he made his police statement without any pressure at all. Until this afternoon he seemed perfectly willing to assist the court by telling the truth.'

'Yes,' says Cartledge, 'thank you. My Lord, the Crown ask for permission to put Mr Emmerson's original police statement before the jury, so they can see it for themselves.'

'I object to that course,' says Charles. 'What Mr Emmerson said outside court in that statement, and does not adopt here, is not evidence. It's hearsay.'

'I agree, Mr Holborne. But that doesn't prevent the jury seeing it, does it? Given an appropriate warning by me. They're entitled to see the prior statement for the purpose of assessing Mr Emmerson's credibility. Isn't that right?'

'And that,' intervenes Cartledge, 'is why the Crown want them to see it. They have to decide whether Mr Emmerson or DCI Quigley is telling the truth. The police statement, even though it has not been adopted in his evidence under oath, will help them.'

'I agree,' says Pullman. 'Crown exhibit DQ1. Will you have copies made over the adjournment?'

'Of course,' replies Cartledge. He turns to Quigley. 'Please wait there,' he says, before sitting down.

Charles looks at the court clock. It is still only quarter to four and Pullman is going to want to continue, but the defence have nothing left to ask Quigley. They're out of time.

Charles rises. 'Would your Lordship give me a moment to have a word with my junior, please?' he asks. Pullman appears to be making a note, perhaps correcting something in his red book that is illegible, and nods briefly.

Charles bends to Bateman, who whispers, 'Time's up, Charles. We have to make the submission. Quigley adds nothing of significance, and they're now entirely reliant on inferences to be drawn from Emmerson's evidence, and that's been fatally weakened.'

'I don't know about "fatally",' argues Charles. 'It's all very well telling the jury that Emmerson's police statement is not evidence, but they'll never draw that distinction. They'll all have copies of it, right in front of them, and if they believe what's in the statement, the Crown will have enough, at least to get past half-time.'

'The situation isn't going to improve if we wait, and it might well get worse. You have to make the submission now!' insists Bateman.

Charles frowns, then shakes his head. 'No. The client gave us the weekend and this is still our best chance to shoot Quigley down. We'll wait until Olney arrives with his evidence, if I can persuade the judge. It's Friday afternoon, it's hot … you never know.'

He stands upright and faces the judge.

'My Lord, the defence applies to adjourn now for the afternoon. I will have further questions for the chief inspector, but I'm unable to proceed with them immediately. I appreciate that we will lose approximately twenty-five minutes of court time, but the admission of Mr Emmerson's evidence was sprung on us without any warning. Had the Crown informed us in advance that they were unable to locate Mr Perry and were thinking of substituting Mr Emmerson, we would have had time to prepare. As it is, I have several more questions for DCI Quigley, after which the defence will very likely make a submission at the end of the Crown's case.'

'But, my Lord,' protests Cartledge, 'the evidence for the Crown is essentially complete. Mr Quigley has no further contribution to make. This is one of those rare prosecutions where the case relies entirely on lay, as against police, witnesses. As Mr Quigley has explained, he acted as officer in the case, but he has no substantive evidence to give. On the basis that no questions were asked of him concerning the taking of the witness statements, the Crown can see no purpose in calling Mr Pilcher, and I am ready to close my case now. This is pure Micawberism; Mr Holborne is wasting time in the hope that "something will come up".'

Pullman turns to Charles. 'Well, Mr Holborne? Are you merely hoping that "something will come up", or do you assure me there are specific matters on which you wish to ask this witness further questions?'

'I will have very specific questions of this witness on Monday morning, my Lord.'

Pullman frowns while he considers the position. 'I confess I find it difficult to see what further issues the defence might wish to raise with this witness. Other than concerning Emmerson's evidence, he hasn't been asked anything significant at all. On the other hand, it is true that Mr Emmerson was sprung on them very late in the day. On balance, I am prepared to allow the defence a little time, notwithstanding the fact that we will have to adjourn early this afternoon. Mr Holborne, you will not be allowed any further leeway. If you're not ready on Monday morning, we will move on. And I think we shall start at ten o'clock again, if that's all right with you, members of the jury? Good. Thank you, gentlemen. I will rise until Monday morning at ten o'clock.'

'All rise!'

# CHAPTER THIRTY-TWO

Charles and Bateman have seen Gold in the cells to make sure he is all right and have returned to the robing room. They have changed out of their court gear in silence and Bateman won't meet Charles's eyes. Charles holds open the door to allow the younger man to precede him out of the room, which he does without a word.

They head towards the main doors.

'I'm meeting Sean Sloane at the King Lud,' offers Charles. 'Want to come?'

'What for? This has nothing to do with me or the case. Count me out of your private crusade,' mutters Bateman angrily.

'This could be a once-in-a-lifetime chance to expose an entire generation of corrupt coppers. Don't you want to be part of that?'

'I've already explained. In theory, yes. Not when it puts our client's acquittal at risk.'

Charles shakes his head. Few of the other courts have risen and the route they are taking is relatively quiet, but he can't afford for them to be overheard. When he answers, it is with a low voice.

'Maybe you'd have more fire in your belly if you'd ever been on the receiving end,' he says, not entirely able to keep the bitterness from his voice.

'What the hell do you mean by that?' retorts Bateman angrily. 'I may not have been at this game as long as you, but I've done scores of cases where my client faced corrupt coppers. Bungs, verbals, confessions beaten out of them, planted evidence!

Everything you've faced. And I fight as hard as you do, and get my hands just as dirty.'

'I'm not talking about your clients, Peter. I'm talking about you personally. Sons of Cabinet ministers and nephews of High Court judges don't get bullied, blackmailed and framed and, if they do, they've enough money and family contacts to fight their corner. Try being poor, Jewish, Irish or Black in our fair city,' he says, adding more quietly, 'maybe then you'd understand.'

Bateman halts on the stairs and it takes Charles a few moments to realise that his former pupil is no longer walking with him.

'How dare you —' starts Bateman, but he bites back the rest of his protest as he sees Cartledge ascending the staircase towards them.

'Tactical discussion?' sneers the QC. 'Here,' he says, and he thrusts a document towards Charles. 'That'll give you something to chew on over the weekend.' He leans towards Charles and adds, in a venomous whisper, 'Unless you have religious duties to perform.'

Charles is so stunned at the crude anti-Semitic side-swipe that he actually laughs. He imagines punching the QC in the face, the aristocratic nose suddenly spurting red, the

howl of pain. He pushes the thought out of his head. Assaulting the man would produce short-term pleasure but long-term pain. Instead, he shakes his head and studies the document in his hand.

It's a medical certificate. For a second, all Charles can absorb is that someone has been signed off work for depression and anxiety.

'Who…' he starts. His eyes widen as he realises what he is holding: a medical certificate excusing Detective Chief

Inspector Robert Olney from attending court. He recovers quickly, but knows that he wasn't completely able to disguise his shock. 'And who is DCI Robert Olney?' he asks innocently, handing the document to Bateman.

'Oh, no one, apparently,' replies the QC insouciantly, already moving off towards the top of the staircase. 'So, submissions first thing Monday, yeah?' he throws back over his shoulder, and he laughs.

Bateman descends the three stairs separating him and Charles and returns the document to his leader. 'We've a leaky ship,' he says quietly, the argument forgotten.

'Maybe,' replies Charles, thinking. 'But not necessarily. Anyway, what's it matter now? They're onto us, and there'll be no cavalry on Monday morning. I've pissed off the judge for no good reason, and he's going to have my head.'

Charles turns and hastens down the staircase.

'Hey!' calls Bateman. 'Wait for me!'

The enter the noisy bar of the King Lud on Ludgate Circus. The pub is named after the famed but probably mythical King Lud, who was said by Geoffrey of Monmouth to have founded a pre-Roman city on the site of London and was then buried at Ludgate. The pub has been here since 1870, and for the last several years has been providing alcohol and cheap lunches to office workers. It is not one frequented by the legal profession, which makes it a good place to meet Sloane.

They find him at the back of the bar, keeping his head down but with a clear line of sight to the front doors. It's only five days since Charles last saw his friend, but Sloane's hair is now touching his shoulders. He wears a worn black leather jacket and jeans. He looks up suspiciously as he realises Charles isn't alone.

'Sean, you remember Peter Bateman, my colleague in Chambers? I'm leading him in the Gold case. The two of you have met at Wren Street, more than once, I think.'

'I do remember, yes, but…' He tails off, looking towards Charles for an explanation.

'He knows, Sean. I had to tell him. It meant persuading our client to hold his nerve till Olney turned up.'

The two barristers take seats opposite the tall Irishman. Without saying anything further, Charles slides the medical certificate across the table. 'Handed to us five minutes ago by prosecuting counsel.' he explains.

Sloane studies it. 'Holy Mother of God!' he exclaims quietly. 'They've got to him. Did you —'

'Not a word. We all know how important this is. I don't know how it's got out. Could they have been aware of your surveillance?'

Sloane considers. 'Always possible. But more likely it's someone on Operation Coathanger playing both ends.'

'Why now, though?' asks Charles. 'Seems a bit coincidental. It's one thing for the Team to learn Olney's onto them. The Met leaks like a sieve. But why would Cartledge hand me that unless he knew I was calling Olney as a witness?'

Sloane nods. 'I need to speak to Olney. Is the entire operation blown, or only him? If it's just him, then maybe we're still good.'

'Is that likely, or even possible?' asks Bateman. 'Could they really discover what Olney's up to without knowing he's got accomplices?' he says.

'I'll find out,' says Sloane. 'I know where to find him.' He knocks back the last of his pint and stands. Charles follows suit. 'Where the hell do you think you're going?' demands Sloane.

'I'm coming with you. I'm not ready to give up yet. Maybe there's something I can do to persuade him to go through with it. If not, perhaps he can still give us enough to damage Quigley. It's worth a shot, isn't it?'

Sloane thinks for a moment. 'Sure, why not?' he says, and heads for the door.

Charles pauses to speak to Bateman. 'You head back to Chambers. I'll call with an update over the weekend.' He pauses and then adds, 'And I'm sorry, mate. I lost my temper. What I said ... I didn't mean it.'

Bateman smiles. 'Forget it. You weren't wrong. This is personal for you — and Gold — in a way it's not for me. I should've remembered that.'

Charles nods. 'Okay. I'll call later,' he says, and he rushes off to catch up with Sloane on Fleet Street.

'Where are we going?' he asks.

'Wembley Park.'

'Probably quickest to nip back to Wren Street and collect my car, then.'

Sloane stops. 'You don't mind?'

'Not at all.'

'Okay, let's do that. Thank you.'

Charles raises his hand and flags down a taxi.

'You realise you've not actually confirmed whether you'll be my best man?' says Charles conversationally as the taxi heads up Farringdon Street.

'Is that still on? You've not mentioned it for a while, so I wondered.'

'Course it is.'

'Just checking. You might want to reassure Sally about that. She spoke to Irenna yesterday, and thought you might've forgotten.'

Detective Chief Inspector Robert Olney lives in a quiet residential street in suburban Wembley Park. They've been sitting in Charles's Rover watching Olney's house for an hour. Sloane has twice ordered Charles out of the car and directed him to walk from one end of the street to the other, slowly enough to look in parked car windows, but not so slowly as to attract attention.

'And don't just turn round at the far end,' he directed. 'Turn left, left again, walk up Wembley Park Drive, and come back to the car from the other end, okay?'

Sloane's belief was that, while he would probably be identified by members of the Team, that was less likely in Charles's case, especially without the wig and court robes. Charles pointed out that he was just as likely as Sloane to be recognised, having sat opposite Quigley for an hour at Scotland Yard when he attended Gold's first interview, but he was enjoying himself. He was pleased to be spending time with the Irishman. The weeks during which his friend was uncontactable had saddened him; he feared that, for some reason he couldn't fathom, the friendship had been lost.

'Nothing,' he says, as he gets into the car after his second perambulation. 'Unless they're watching from some upstairs bedroom window, there's no one. And his house isn't directly overlooked anyway. Satisfied?'

Sloane looks at his watch. 'Yup. Let's go,' he says, and he steps out onto the pavement.

The two men walk towards Olney's house. It's a pleasant family home, a small detached villa built in the 1930s, slightly set back from the road, with a neat lawn and flower beds at the front. A path runs down the side of the house into a fenced back garden where the frame of a child's swing can be seen.

Charles makes to go to the front door but Sloane gestures with his head that they should take the path to the back. Charles follows him.

The smell of cooking greets them as they reach the end. They pass a side door and reach what looks like an extension to the original building, a kitchen. Its lights are illuminated. Sloane puts his hand behind him to halt Charles and, leaning close to the wall, peers cautiously in the window. A stout middle-aged woman with short grey hair is washing saucepans in the sink, speaking to someone. The person she is addressing is not visible from Sloane's position. He moves forward very slightly to get a better view. The woman screams and he ducks back.

'Damn!' he says quietly.

Seconds later the door behind them opens and a man comes out, brandishing what looks like a cast-iron skillet.

'What do you want?' he shouts.

'It's me, guv,' says Sloane hurriedly.

'Sloane?'

'Yes. This is Charles Holborne. We need to talk to you.'

The man steps out of the door and takes a few paces towards the road. From the corner of his house he looks both ways before returning. He glares angrily at the intruders.

'We weren't followed, guv. We've been watching for over an hour. It's all quiet.'

Olney takes a deep breath. 'You'd better come in,' he says reluctantly.

They follow him into the house. He leads them away from the kitchen, goes through a door and flicks on the light. They're in a television room furnished with a small couch, two Parker Knoll reclining armchairs and a drinks trolley. It's a comfortable, peaceful room with prints on the walls, family photographs on a small display cabinet and soft cushions in pastel colours. It smells of pipe smoke.

'Who are you again?' demands Olney of Charles.

Charles has an opportunity to study the man for the first time. He's well-built, about Charles's height, and appears to be in his fifties, with short greying hair and a salt-and-pepper moustache. Charles guesses he could still look after himself, but he has deep rings under his dark eyes and the dejected slope of his shoulders suggests exhaustion, perhaps defeat.

Charles offers his hand. 'Charles Holborne, of counsel. I'm a friend of Sean's. I'm also counsel defending Bobby Gold.'

The outstretched hand is ignored. 'Yes, well, you're wasting your time. I can't attend court.'

'What's happened?' asks Sloane.

'They threatened my wife for a start!' replies Olney angrily.

'Who did?'

'One of Quigley's minions. A little shit called Feder, a DS from the Sweeney. She cried for two days.' He pauses and cocks his head, listening. 'And you two have set her off again.'

The door bursts open and a teenage girl in school uniform enters. 'Mum's crying again,' she announces.

'I know, sweetheart. I'll be right there,' replies Olney. The girl doesn't move. 'Please, Susie. Make her a cup of tea and tell her I'll only be a minute. I have to talk to these gentlemen.'

The girl disappears.

'You need to leave,' says Olney to them.

'Chief Inspector,' says Charles, 'Derek Emmerson gave evidence this afternoon about the Leeds burglary. He said Quigley and Pilcher blackmailed him and Perry into doing it. So it's all come out. You're *this* close to getting them! We just need your evidence to clinch it.'

'It's too late.'

'But —' starts Charles.

'You're wasting your breath. I won't be giving evidence.'

'Why not, sir?' asks Sloane.

'I've retired. As of yesterday afternoon.'

'That's no reason —' tries Charles again.

'And my pension's in the balance.'

'I thought you needed another eighteen months,' says Sloane.

'I did, but there's something called pension augmentation. Ken Drury explained it. If I agree to go now, they'll bring forward my pension date and top it up to the full value. If not, I'll be brought up on a disciplinary and he'll make sure I don't see a penny.'

'Ken Drury?' says Charles. 'Head of the Sweeney?'

'Yes,' replies Olney.

The room falls silent for a moment.

'My client's still in Brixton Prison, right now,' says Charles eventually, 'because he wants to see Quigley and Pilcher buried. He's an innocent man, putting his liberty at risk, and he's relying on you.'

Olney turns towards Charles. 'I'm sorry about that, really I am, but it's not my problem. From what I've heard, your chap's going to get off anyway. Now, you need to leave.'

'Is my cover blown?' asks Sloane. 'Do they know I've been working with you?'

'I don't know, Sergeant. They didn't say anything to suggest they knew, but that doesn't mean anything. Do you know DI Benchley?'

'At Savile Row?'

'Yes. He's also been working on Coathanger. Unless they've put the frighteners on him too, he's got part of the file.'

'Can you show me what you've got, sir?' asks Sloane.

'Not anymore Pilcher and Feder were here. I had to give them what I had. Now, I want you to leave. My family's been put through enough.'

'Come on, Sean,' says Charles. 'There's nothing to be gained here.' He turns to address Olney. 'Please apologise to Mrs Olney for us.'

He moves towards the door, but Sloane hangs back. 'I thought you'd be different, sir,' he says sadly.

# CHAPTER THIRTY-THREE

Charles drops Sloane off at Wembley Park tube station.

'Will you go and see this DI Benchley?' he asks as Sloane gets out of the car.

Sloane stands on the pavement, watching but not seeing people coming and going from the underground station. He rests his hand on the roof of the car and leans back in.

'I don't know,' he answers sadly. 'If they can get to a chief inspector, I begin to wonder if I'm wasting my time. And I certainly can't do this on me own.'

'Want to go for a drink and talk it through?' suggests Charles.

'No…' replies Sloane, distracted. 'But, thank you. You've been grand. Your client, too.'

'What are you going to do?' asks Charles, leaning across from the driver's seat.

'Go home, talk it through with Irenna and sleep on it. Even if my cover hasn't been blown, I'm scared of being dragged further into Quigley and Pilcher's little schemes without the cover Olney gave me. And if they think I'm bent, they'll keep asking. On the other hand, if my cover *has* been blown, but I've no support higher up the chain of command, what do I do? I'm not due for a pension anytime soon.'

'I don't know, mate. I wish I could help.'

'Nah, not your fault. I volunteered for this. But I'm no longer sure I'm going to be on the winning side. Mind yourself,' he finishes, and slams the passenger door closed.

Charles watches his friend's dejected form slip into the crowds at the station entrance before he drives off.

He heads for the North Circular and then turns south onto the A5 at Staples Corner. The journey down Edgware Road and around Regent's Park is swift, most of the rush-hour traffic having now dissipated. The journey home takes him thirty minutes.

He is able to park immediately outside the house on Wren Street and runs up the stairs to the front door, preparing his excuses. He and Sally have fallen into the habit of calling one another if either of them is going to be unable to get home in time for Leia's bedtime routine, a part of the day they both treasure. It is now gone seven o'clock, and Charles has missed it, but he had no time to warn Sally.

He opens the door and puts his bags on the floor tiles. Only then does he hear voices from downstairs. One is definitely that of a man, and it's not a voice that Charles recognises.

He heads down to the kitchen and opens the door quietly.

Sitting at the head of the long refectory table is Sally. She's changed out of her work clothes and, whereas on a Friday evening she would normally be in jeans and a jumper — often damp from Leia's bathtime splashing — she looks very smart, as if about to go out. She is wearing a dark blue dress that she reserves for special occasions, and she's refreshed her make-up and pinned back her hair.

The man sitting next to her has moved his chair from the side of the table and sits at its corner, sufficiently close to Sally that their elbows are almost touching. He is a strikingly handsome blond man in his mid-thirties wearing an expensive suit, an expensive haircut and a silken grin: Spencer Wainwright the third.

Sally jumps up, scraping her chair loudly on the oak floorboards and almost knocking over the half-empty glass of wine before her

'Hello, Charles. I didn't hear you come in.'

'Evidently,' replies Charles.

'Do you remember Spencer? He arrived in Chambers just as I was leaving.'

'And followed you home, I see.'

Wainwright replaces his glass on the table — *he's drinking my best single malt*, notes Charles — stands and advances, his hand outstretched. 'It's a great pleasure to see you again, Charles. Sally was kind enough to invite me back here. We've been waiting for you. I've booked a table at Le Gavroche. I hope you'll join us.'

Charles hesitates for a moment and then grips the American's hand. He doesn't remember having shaken Wainwright's hand before and he is surprised both by its size — it's no smaller than Charles's own hands, which are uncommonly large — and the firmness of his grip. He moves with the easy grace of someone who has lived a life of privilege and entitlement, as if he knows he's the top dog in every room he enters.

The lights in the kitchen have been dimmed, but Charles can see enough to evaluate the man's physicality.

*Light heavyweight*, thinks Charles. *I wonder if I could take him?*

'Pleased to meet you again, Spencer. This is a surprise.'

'Sally asked me to do a little research on your behalf, and I was planning a trip to Paris at the end of this month anyway,' he says easily, 'so I thought I'd build in a layover in foggy old London for a night, and deliver in person. I hope that's okay with you?'

'Of course.' Charles points to the glasses. 'What are we celebrating?'

'Don't be peevish, Charles,' chides Sally. 'Spencer's come a long way to give you an extremely useful bit of evidence. You should be thanking him.'

*Trust her, Charles.*

It's a very long time since Charles last heard his dead wife's voice. The Honourable Henrietta Lloyd-Williams haunted him daily for two years following her murder, passing tart commentaries on Charles's diet, clothing, lifestyle and choice of female companions. She left him alone once Charles and Sally became a permanent item, apparently approving of the relationship. Or, looked at another way, Charles's grief loosened its grip and the hallucinations ended. Nonetheless, he could have sworn he heard Henrietta speaking again, her cultured tones behind and to one side of him.

He pauses to reflect.

*This guy's a decade younger than me, has film-star looks and pots of money, and clearly still fancies Sally. So this is jealousy,* he acknowledges, *and maybe a little insecurity. Not feelings with which I am very familiar.*

He smiles. 'You're absolutely right,' he says, unsure if he's answering Henrietta, Sally or both. 'I apologise. It's been a long and very disappointing week, I'm knackered, and I was expecting to crash out in front of the TV. Let me start again. Spencer, I'm very pleased to see you, and I'd be delighted to join you at Le Gavroche for dinner.'

'Good fellow,' says the other, causing Charles to bridle afresh at the condescension. 'Sally, why don't you pour your man a drink, and I'll show him the good news — get work out of the way before we let our hair down?'

'Good idea,' replies Sally, sounding relieved.

She fetches another glass and pours Charles a large whisky. 'I'll drive,' she offers quietly.

At the same time Wainwright goes to the oak dresser and picks up a slim attaché case, monogrammed, Charles notes, in gold leaf. While Charles takes a seat at the table, Wainwright brings it over, sitting next to him. He opens the clasp and lifts out a document, placing it before Charles.

'I think you might find this interesting,' says the American.

Charles stands and strides to the switch for the light fitting over the table. Illumination floods the room. He returns to his seat.

He has before him a single sheet of paper. The text is difficult to read, as it appears to be the product of multiple copying. There is an unfamiliar code number at the top right-hand corner. At the bottom is a page number, suggesting that this sheet has been taken from a longer document or perhaps a report. The text gives details of a man named Mark Robinson, Caucasian, fair hair, date of birth 1st May 1938, height five feet ten inches, weight 169 pounds, no identifying characteristics.

'You've probably not seen something quite like this before, but it's what we call a rap sheet,' explains Wainwright. He points. 'Georgia, see? And note the date, 1959, so you've been lucky.'

'Why's that?'

'Georgia started using Xerox machines in the late fifties. Some states were still on paper records, and I'd never have got my hands on this. The offences are here —' Wainwright's beautifully manicured forefinger appears in Charles's field of view. '*Felony carnal knowledge of a juvenile*,' Wainwright reads aloud.

'What we would call statutory rape. She was fifteen.'

'Yeah. He got three years, suspended for two.'

'Sounds light,' comments Charles.

'No, about right for the times and circumstances. Claimed he was in a relationship with the girl and she was Black. Different attitudes. A generation earlier and he'd never have been prosecuted at all. Less serious than criminal damage to property.'

Having absorbed details of the offence, Charles looks more closely at the photograph of Mark Robinson in the top right-hand corner of the document. There are in fact two images next to each other, one full-face and one in profile, each with a prisoner number below. The copying process was rudimentary and the contrast too high, and Charles doesn't recognise the man.

'Okay, I'll buy. Who is this?' he asks.

'That's Johnny Blaise.'

'Looks nothing like him,' points out Charles.

'Look again,' instructs Wainwright.

Charles studies the photo more closely. He tries to picture the man wearing a long dark stage wig and demonic makeup. He remains unconvinced. He stands and strides across the room to a basket by the fireplace. He takes out an old newspaper, leafs through it, and returns to the table, flattening the wrinkled sheets. At the top of the page is a photograph of Blaise giving a post-concert interview, still in costume. He places it beside the rap sheet and compares them.

'Yes,' he says finally. 'I see it. It's him.' Charles turns the document over. The reverse is blank. 'Anything else?' he asks Wainwright.

'Afraid not. Took a lot of work just to track that down. Not to mention a tidy sum.'

'I'll make sure you're repaid,' assures Charles.

Wainwright waves that aside. 'Forget it. Happy to help. It's not often I get involved in a case like this, so it's been pretty exciting. Sally's been telling me a little about it. I wish I could stay and watch some, but I have to be in Paris tomorrow evening.'

Charles reads the document again from top to bottom. 'I'd love to know when Mark Robinson became Johnny Blaise,' he muses. 'And whether the US label is aware of this.'

'Good questions,' says Wainwright, standing.

'It'd destroy his career, if it came out. Also, I'm wondering if my client knows anything about it.'

'I was thinking that,' says Sally. 'Wouldn't that make the Crown's case on motive even stronger?'

'It would,' confirms Charles.

'Okay, guys,' says Wainwright, draining his glass. 'We need to move soon or we'll lose this table.'

Charles also stands. 'Thank you, Spencer. I really appreciate this,' he says sincerely. He turns to Sally. 'I'm really sorry, Sal —'

'But you're going to have to work this weekend,' she finishes for him.

'Yes. I need an urgent order to get into Brixton Prison.'

'Just remember, Charles, we've nine days,' Sally reminds him. 'So: new suit; transport for the wrinklies; wine to be tasted, paid for and collected from El Vino's; and folding chairs from the loft. And I know there are other items on your list.'

'I know, I know. It'll all get done, I promise.'

'I'm sorry, sir, but that's not going to be possible,' says the prison officer.

The procedure for obtaining an emergency visiting order at a weekend (not, to Charles's knowledge, actually codified in any formal practice document) is to get the trial judge to make an order requiring the governor of the prison to admit the lawyer.

However, that involves locating the judge's home address and telephone number, and such details are not publicly available. This isn't the first time Charles has needed a judge over the weekend, and it infuriates him that one has to rely on personal connections. Is there anyone in Chambers who knows the name and phone number of the judge's clerk? Does anyone have a social relationship with the judge so as to know his home telephone number? Charles has always been excluded from these networks, with the result that, despite his best efforts, his clients sometimes receive a poorer service from the criminal justice system than those whose barristers move in the right circles.

After consideration, he rejected this strategy — too much time, too many steps and too many chances of mishap for his liking. Furthermore, he didn't feel comfortable disturbing Pullman over the weekend, particularly in his state of health. That, Charles felt, was an intrusion too far. Finally, he couldn't risk Pullman refusing him; the famously acerbic judge could easily do that, and there would be no appeal.

So he decided to get dressed in his suit (something he hates doing at weekends), take his credentials and case papers, and present himself at the prison gates. He got through the main doors, but not beyond the first duty guard.

'I appreciate I don't have a visiting order, but the governor can allow me in. Please call him. The prisoner's case is ongoing at the Old Bailey and the judge has specifically given us an adjournment until Monday morning to obtain further evidence.'

'I'm sorry, sir,' repeats the gaoler, although he sounds anything but sorry. He's a florid man with a red complexion and a truculent stare.

'I shall be twenty minutes, half an hour at most.'

'It's not possible. It's the weekend, the visitor centre is deserted, there's no one available to staff it, and the governor isn't here.'

The man extends his arm to start ushering Charles back out of the door. Charles realises that this is not an occasion for charm.

'Okay, but before I go I need your name.'

'No, you don't, sir. Come on now, out you go. If you get a visiting order from your judge, by all means come back.' He grabs Charles's arm, not forcefully, but enough to start turning him around. Charles resists.

'The judge is His Honour Judge Pullman,' he says. 'He's dying of cancer. This is likely to be his last case. The man's very sick, and you're telling me to disturb him on a Saturday morning, so I'll need your name.'

'I'm not giving you my name. You don't need it for a visiting order,' says the officer, but there is now some uncertainty in his voice.

'Very well,' says Charles. 'Monday morning at ten a.m. I shall explain to Judge Pullman that the case has to be adjourned again because you prevented me from taking instructions from my client. I'll tell him that you refused to identify yourself or call the deputy governor to listen to my explanation of the urgency of the situation. And I'll tell him you manhandled me out of the door. You know what'll happen then? The judge will call the governor. He'll go through the shift rotas to find out who was on this door at —' Charles checks his watch — 'five past ten. Then you'll be hauled before him to explain why your refusal, which has cost the administration of criminal justice around a thousand pounds, should be paid for by the Prison Service and not by you, out of your pay.'

Charles has made up the figure, although he has been told by several judges in the past that it costs a fortune to adjourn a criminal trial in mid-flight. Indeed, he has been threatened with having to pay such costs himself.

'I'd be surprised if you still had a job following that interview,' Charles continues. 'But if you're prepared to gamble your career, that's up to you.' He turns and heads for the door.

'Wait,' says the prison guard.

'Yes?' says Charles innocently.

'Wait there.'

The gaoler goes through a door behind his desk and closes it. Charles hears a telephone being picked up, followed by a muffled conversation. Sixty seconds later the officer reappears.

'The deputy governor's on his way down. You can sit there,' says the man, pointing to a bench behind Charles. 'Filthy Jew,' he adds under his breath, loud enough to be heard.

'What did you say?' challenges Charles angrily.

'Nothing, sir. I coughed.'

Charles stares down the guard. He could make a formal complaint, and he wants to do it, but it will be his word against the guard's, it will waste time and it will deflect him from his purpose. For the second time in twenty-four hours, he lets it go.

He takes a seat.

Ten minutes later a slender young man in his late thirties arrives. He shakes Charles's hand and listens carefully while Charles explains.

'I'm sure we can help,' he says finally. He turns to the obstructive gaoler. 'Call the wing and have Gold brought down here. You stay here. I'll get Murray to take Mr Holborne through security and wait while he speaks to his client.'

'Thank you very much,' says Charles.

Thereafter Charles's visit goes through on skates. Within ten minutes he has been searched and his details taken and he's sitting in an echoing and entirely empty visiting area, awaiting Bobby Gold, the first time he has ever been here alone and at a weekend. The silence is odd, and disconcerting.

The door opens and Gold is shown in. A different prison officer addresses Charles. 'Can you give me an estimate of time, please, sir?' he asks. 'We are very thin on the ground today, and it would help if you could keep this meeting short.'

'I reckon twenty minutes, thirty at most,' replies Charles.

'That would be most helpful. Tea?'

Charles raises his eyebrows in surprise. 'If you've time, yes, please. White, no sugar.'

'Same for me, if that's possible,' adds Gold.

The gaoler nods and closes the door, leaving the two men alone. Without saying anything further, Charles takes the rap sheet from out of his blue counsel's notebook and places it in front of Gold. Gold looks at it in silence for a couple of seconds, nods, and sits back in his seat.

'You've seen this before,' says Charles with sudden realisation.

'Yes. That's why the merch takings at the concerts are short. I'm being blackmailed.'

'By whom?'

'Search me. Although after the last few days, I could hazard a guess.'

'You're saying Quigley? Or Pilcher?'

Gold shrugs. 'I think so. Or it could be Perry.'

'I can't see Frankie Perry obtaining a Georgia rap sheet from a decade ago. Anyway, tell me the story,' orders Charles. He is angry at his client for having lied to him.

'I received a copy of that in the post. It arrived at the offices on Tin Pan Alley. There was a demand for money, a typed letter, no signature. I've paid twice, both times leaving the money at a corner shop in Camberwell.'

'And you didn't think to tell me that you knew Johnny Blaise was a rapist? Are you completely insane?'

'You don't understand. It wouldn't just destroy me. The US label would be in trouble as well. Do you have any idea how hard it's been to persuade them to let me promote this tour? Nothing like this has ever been done before! I'm a pioneer. If this works, I'm made for life. If it goes wrong, they'll never trust me with their talent again. It can't get out.'

'And you're prepared to go to prison for something that Blaise did?'

'Didn't you say that I only have to show a reasonable doubt? Can't I do that without pointing the finger at someone else? This trial's about whether I'm guilty, not who actually did it. Or did I misunderstand you?'

'No, you've understood. We do only have to raise a reasonable doubt. But didn't it occur to you that demonstrating who *actually did it* might create that doubt?'

'Of course, but at what cost? Anyway, it doesn't prove what you think it does.'

'What do you mean?' demands Charles. He jabs the rap sheet with his finger. 'That's Johnny Blaise, isn't it?'

'Yeah, I think so, though it's difficult to be sure. The photo's terrible. But that's not what I mean.'

'What, then?'

Gold frowns, hesitating. 'You can't tell anyone what I say, can you?'

'Not without your permission, no. Anything you tell me is covered by legal professional privilege.' Still Gold hesitates. 'What is it?'

'You have to guarantee you'll never mention this to anyone,' insists Gold.

'I can't tell anyone unless you give me permission. You don't need a separate guarantee. But, for what it's worth, I promise. Now, what is it?'

Gold leans forward again, lowering his voice, despite the fact that no one can possibly hear them. 'I don't believe Johnny Blaise was guilty of that rape, whatever it says there, and whatever that Georgia court decided.'

'Why's that?'

'Because Johnny Blaise is gay.'

'What? How do you know?'

'No one knows this, right? Not even the US label.'

'Okay.'

'I caught him. In an … embarrassing situation … with one of the crew.'

Charles frowns. 'Do you mean what I think you mean?'

Gold nods. 'Yes.'

'Are you sure you understood what you saw … accurately?' asks Charles.

'Yes. It wasn't something you could misinterpret. Very definitely not.'

Charles sits back in his seat and considers this new information. 'That doesn't mean he couldn't be into women too, though,' he muses. 'Some people have very … wide-ranging tastes.'

'Of course. I've been in the entertainment business for twenty years. But not in this case. Johnny has female friends, but he's never had a relationship like that with a woman.'

'He might just say that.'

'No. He and this other man have been … friends for years. It's a committed relationship.'

'How do you know?'

'Because I've spoken to Johnny about it. For the first day or two after I stumbled on them, no one said anything. It was embarrassing and I could see he was getting really stressed, worried that I'd go to the newspapers or something. I needed him to trust me if we were going to work together. So I had a private word with him. I told him it didn't bother me, I wasn't going to tell anyone, and that as long as he was more discreet in future, he could trust me to keep his secret. He and Zach, that's the boyfriend, were very grateful. We've become quite good friends, actually. Certainly more than promoter and talent.'

'Then why did you pay the blackmailer? If you don't believe that this —' Charles waves the rap sheet — 'is true?'

'Doesn't matter whether it's true or not. How could I come out and say I know the rap sheet can't be right because Johnny Blaise is a homosexual? It may be legal over here, but it isn't in forty-nine out of fifty US states, and anyway, attitudes haven't changed. His entire career rests on this persona he and the US PR guys have created. If it got out, he'd be finished, the label would lose its most valuable asset, the tour would be off and Gold Management and Talent Ltd would go bust.'

The two men sit in silence for a while.

'Is this why Blaise refused to talk to us?' asks Charles after a moment.

'I couldn't tell you. I've been banged up in here. But probably, yes.'

'Do you think a personal approach from you might help? You said you and he were more than just promoter and talent.'

Gold considers the suggestion. 'Maybe, but how?'

Charles thinks. 'Where is he now? Where's the group?'

'I don't know. If they stuck to my schedule, they're back at Kingston Grange. They've got one more concert, Brussels, on Tuesday, but because there was a four-day gap I thought it would be cheaper to have them come back here for the weekend than stay in a hotel in Paris or Belgium. Also, Johnny wanted to finish recording a couple of tracks. So I didn't book other accommodation. But I don't know if the US label has stuck with that. I've no idea what's going on.'

'Okay,' says Charles, reaching a decision.

He spins his notebook round and slides his pen across the table. 'You're going to write him a letter. I'll dictate. I'm going to try to get into Kingston Grange and talk to him.'

# CHAPTER THIRTY-FOUR

It is Sunday afternoon. Charles and Sloane are once again conducting surveillance in a quiet residential street from Charles's Rover. However, this suburb of London is in a totally different class. The carriageway is twice as broad as that in Wembley, it is lined with tall lime trees, and the properties are widely spaced mansions in large walled grounds.

'No?' queries Charles.

Sloane shakes his head despondently. 'I don't recognise any of them, not one.'

'Well, Plan B, then. It's not as if we didn't predict this.'

'Yeah, I just thought that some of the guys I knew might've been kept on, but they're all new. Different uniforms, too. I guess the US company brought their own people in. You can't blame them.'

'No. Well, come on then,' says Charles.

'Let me do the talking for once, eh, Charlie?'

They get out of the car, Charles locks it, and they walk along the pavement to the main gates of Kingston Grange. The gates are shut. There is a sentry box between the stone gatepost and a tall hedge. Charles notes that the hedge is hawthorn, impossible to get through without serious injury. The sentry box is quite large, with a man sitting by the window doodling on a pad and another sitting behind him, listening to sport on a transistor radio as he idly turns the pages of a newspaper. Charles notes two coaches in a gravelled area of parking inside the gates.

Sloane presents himself at the window.

'Hi,' he says. 'So, nothing's changed, then?'

'Can I help you?' asks the man nearest to him.

'Yes. I was part of the security team here,' replies Sloane, and he shows the man a Celeb Security pass bearing his photograph.

'Yeah? You lot got the sack.'

'Don't know about that,' retorts Sloane. 'With the bosses scarpered or in prison, most of us thought we'd never get paid, so we moved elsewhere.'

'Whatever. What do you want?'

'I've got a message for Johnny Blaise from Bobby Gold, his UK promoter.'

'The one in prison,' says the man, and at the sound of Gold's name, his colleague looks up and starts paying attention.

'Yes. But he still has the contract for the tour, and he needs to get an important message to Mr Blaise about the Brussels concert.' Sloane brandishes an envelope.

'Okay,' says the man, holding out his hand.

'Sorry,' replies Sloane. 'I've got strict instructions to put it into Mr Blaise's hands personally. It's sensitive commercial information, for his eyes only.'

'Well, you can't get in, so what do you want to do about it? There's a post box down the road,' he says, pointing.

'Look, I've sat exactly where you're sitting, and I know you've got a telephone there to ring the house. Please call and tell Mr Blaise that I'm here.'

The two security guards look at each other uncertainly, and eventually the second one picks up the phone and dials. It's picked up at the other end almost immediately.

'There's a guy here at the main gate who says he has a personal letter for Johnny from Bobby Gold.' There is a short delay. 'Hello, Mr Blaise, I'm sorry to disturb you, but there's a chap here who wants to hand you a letter... No, I already asked. He says it's sensitive commercial information and he has to deliver it personally.'

Sloane leans forward. 'Is that Mr Blaise?' The man on the telephone nods. 'Tell him it involves a breach of his contract with Zach, with potentially very expensive consequences.'

The information is relayed.

The man on the telephone wraps up the call and looks up at Sloane. 'Right. He's going for a walk in the garden anyway, and says he'll meet you at the Orangery. You know where that is?'

'I do.'

'Okay,' says the guard by the window. 'You'll need to sign in. You know the drill.'

'My colleague has to come with me,' says Sloane, indicating Charles.

'Why?'

'I told you. Sensitive commercial information. This is my bodyguard.'

The guard leans out of his window and checks out Charles, who wears jogging bottoms, running shoes, and a baggy top which leaves his heavily muscled arms visible. The guard nods.

'Okay. He'll have to sign in too.'

Sloane and Charles each provide false names, the button is pressed, a yellow light on top of the stone pillar starts revolving, and the electronic gates creak into movement accompanied by a beeping noise. Sloane waves his thanks to the two men and leads the way up the gravelled drive.

Halfway towards the mansion, the drive splits in two. The major route leads to the front portico of the house, while the other, smaller and presumably not designed for vehicles, appears to skirt in a wide circle towards the back of the house. Sloane takes the footpath.

The two men pass tennis courts, a miniature putting green and large greenhouses. A gardener can be seen some distance away, pushing a wheelbarrow full of garden refuse. The paths are dotted with benches and pretty wooden arbours providing views over what are enormous grounds. Charles estimates that the house and its gardens must cover three or four acres. It is dusk and away to their right the lights in the house are beginning to be illuminated. The sound of rock music is borne towards them on the still evening air.

The Orangery, when they reach it, is a large timber and glass conservatory-like structure, situated behind the house and down a slope towards a large pond. It is partly hidden from the house by a copse of trees. Soft lighting emanates from its interior.

Sloane opens a door on the long wall of the building and indicates that Charles should follow him.

The Orangery comprises a single large room set up rather like a hotel lounge, with what resembles a dance floor in its centre. Around the periphery are sofas and armchairs set in discrete groups divided from one another by sections of trellis and lush green vegetation. There is an unattended bar in the corner.

'Great place for a party,' comments Charles quietly.

He closes the door and waits behind Sloane.

'Over there,' says the Irishman, nodding to the far corner, where a man sits in an armchair, looking out of the window towards the pond. 'Follow me.'

They walk across the dance floor, their footsteps echoing round the room. The man in the corner stands to greet them.

Charles has seen Johnny Blaise's photograph hundreds of times. It's in newspapers, on television, on billboards and, of course, on his album sleeves, but he has never met the rock star and never seen him without his stage makeup and clothing. The difference between the man before Charles and the posters of the devil-worshipping "Bad Boy of Rock" could not be starker. His hair is light brown and cut conservatively, and he has astonishingly smooth cheeks, like those of a young teenager. There is something soft and unthreatening about him; he's the sort of young man you might bring home to meet your parents.

Blaise wears light blue Levis and a baggy white shirt fastened at the wrists. His complexion is perfect, which is surprising now that Charles knows he is in his thirties and not, as he believed, his early twenties. In fact, now he thinks of it, although the rap sheet has Blaise's age as twenty-two years at the time of the offence, he probably looked sufficiently young then to have been taken for a teenager, little older than the victim.

'Mr Blaise,' says Sloane, 'I worked on security here a couple of times. You may remember me?'

'Yes, I do recognise you. Bobby has sent you with a message? A letter, I understand?'

'He has. He wants me to take your reply.'

Sloane reaches into his pocket and hands over the envelope.

'Okay. Take a seat, then,' says Blaise, and he drops back into his armchair and opens the letter. Charles sees the lined pages torn from his notebook. He watches as Blaise reads. The singer goes through the letter slowly, twice, and then looks up, the sheets still gripped in his fist.

'I can't. I'm really sorry. I like Bobby, a lot, but WCA have made it clear they don't want me mixed up in the prosecution.'

'WCA?' asks Sloane.

'The record label,' clarifies Charles.

321

Charles's speaking attracts Blaise's attention. 'Who are you? I don't remember you.'

'I wasn't a member of the security team. My name's Charles Holborne. I'm Bobby's trial attorney.'

Charles's answer causes Blaise to stand. 'Sorry,' he says swiftly. 'I think you should leave. I've given you my answer. I wish I could help Bobby, but I can't.'

'Before we leave, you might want to have a look at this,' says Charles. He hands Blaise the rap sheet.

The blood suddenly drains from the rock star's face. For a second Charles thinks his legs might give way, but he steps back and almost collapses back into his seat.

'Where did you get this?' he croaks, his eyes closed.

'From a US lawyer,' replies Charles. 'But Bobby has had a copy for some time.'

'He has?' says Blaise, his eyes open again and his expression bewildered.

'He's been a very good friend to you, Mr Blaise,' says Charles. 'Better than you are being to him. Someone's been blackmailing him, and he's been paying the blackmail personally to protect your reputation.'

Blaise passes his hand over his brow which, Charles notes, is now clammy. 'Oh, sweet Jesus!'

'And you know what he said to me this morning? He's prepared to risk prison for something he didn't do. Something you *know* he didn't do.'

Blaise shakes his head as if denying the truth of Charles's words.

Charles decides to change tack. 'Do you know this chap's name?' he asks, pointing at Sloane.

Blaise shakes his head again. 'Sorry, no.'

'This is my best friend, Sean Sloane. He's not a security guard. He is in fact a police officer.' Blaise's eyes are wide open now. 'He's been working undercover, trying to expose the corrupt officers who, I suspect, are at the bottom of all this. His career, and possibly his life, are on the line too. As I think you know, these are dangerous people.'

Blaise draws a deep, ragged breath, his chest shuddering. 'What do you want from me?' he asks, his voice shaking.

'You and I both know that Bobby Gold is innocent. Someone is framing him, and I think you know who, and I think you know why. We want the truth.'

Blaise shakes his head miserably. 'I can't,' he says, his voice so quiet that Charles and Sloane have to lean forward to hear him. 'I can't,' he repeats. 'You don't know what it'll cost.'

'What will it cost?' asks Sloane. Blaise doesn't answer. 'Well?'

Blaise remains silent. Sloane shakes his head. 'I don't know how you can live with your conscience.'

'Okay, Mr Blaise,' says Charles. 'Or should I say Mr Robinson? I didn't want to have to threaten you, but I'm out of time. Unless you tell us, right now, what occurred that night, I'll be giving a copy of that rap sheet to every newspaper editor in London. I have journalist friends who'll make sure it goes all across America too. Where will your career be then?'

'More importantly,' adds Sloane, 'what do you suppose the police will do when they learn you've already been convicted of felony carnal knowledge of a fifteen-year-old juvenile? Bearing in mind the rape and death of a fifteen-year-old English girl here, in a bedroom next to yours? This little cover-up will disintegrate and, faced with the newspaper coverage, they'll have to make a show of investigating. My guess: you'll be joining Bobby Gold in HM Prison Brixton within twenty-four hours.'

'But, I didn't… It wasn't me! You can't think it was me!'

'What are we to think?' demands Charles.

'But … have you read this?' cries Blaise, brandishing the letter.

'I have.'

'Then you know it wasn't me! I'm not … I'm not … that sort of person.'

'Rather like you know it wasn't Bobby,' says Charles.

'An exact parallel, I'd say,' adds Sloane.

Blaise jumps to his feet, and both Charles and Sloane leap from their seats to restrain him, but he isn't running. He takes a few steps towards the darkening window, turns and starts to pace in the centre of the area formed by the group of armchairs and settees.

'Well?' asks Sloane.

Charles and Sloane share a glance. Charles signals for them to wait. He has seen it before in court, the moment when someone realises the game's up. They lose the impetus to continue lying, evading and blaming, the fight deserts them and then, perhaps, the truth emerges.

Blaise continues to pace but now he is panting, his breathing becoming more ragged. Charles notices that his hands are shaking and sweat is oozing from his scalp. He comes to a sudden halt as one of his hands clutches his chest.

He stares at Charles, his eyes wide with fear. 'I feel sick. And my hands are tingling. I think … I think…' he gasps, 'I might be having a coronary!'

Charles grabs him. 'Sit down,' he says, lowering Blaise to the armchair. 'Now breathe!' he orders. 'Slowly. In through the nose … no, more slowly! Listen to me, Johnny. Breathe in through your nose while I count. One … two … three … four. Good. Now out slowly. One … two … three … four … five

… six. Good! Keep doing that. Put your hands on the arms of the chair, that's right, and your feet flat on the ground. Now, as you breathe, feel your hands and feet grounded. You're okay. You're not dying, I promise. Good, keep breathing slowly. You're safe.'

Charles flashes a glance towards Sloane and then resumes counting Blaise's breaths.

It takes a few minutes, but eventually Blaise regains his composure.

'No chest pain?' asks Charles. Blaise shakes his head but maintains concentration over his breathing. 'Good.'

They wait until his face has regained its usual colour.

'Has that happened before?' asks Charles.

'Yes, but not for a while.'

'That was very impressive,' comments Sloane on Charles's treatment.

Charles looks up. 'Histrionic mother,' he explains. He turns to Blaise. 'Surely you see this can't go on. It's over. It's all going to come out in court, tomorrow morning.'

Blaise nods. 'Yes,' he says softly.

'So?' prompts Sloane gently.

'Okay,' says Blaise. 'Okay,' he repeats, a little louder, as if gathering his strength. He looks up at Charles and then at Sloane. 'That isn't me.'

'What isn't?' asks Sloane.

'The photo on that piece of paper from Georgia. It's not me. It's Wyatt.'

'Wyatt?' asks Sloane. 'Your brother?'

Blaise nods. 'We looked a lot alike when we were younger. It says Mark Robinson.'

'So?' asks Charles.

325

'Mark's my brother. My name, my original name, is Ethan Robinson. And I'm afraid that wasn't the only time.'

'Explain,' demands Charles.

Blaise sighs and his eyes fill with tears as he speaks. 'The life story put out by the label is all fiction. Mark and I grew up on a trailer park in Clay County, Georgia. We were abused by our father, physically and sexually, until I couldn't take it anymore. On my eighteenth birthday I ran away. But I had to take Mark with me. I couldn't leave him there, on his own. He was only fifteen and I knew what my father would do to him.'

'If this is true, why didn't you report it to the police?' asks Sloane.

Blaise turns to him. 'You don't know what it's like in a small traditional community. Folk keep their secrets. You don't go to official people like social workers or policemen.'

Sloane and Charles share a glance. Sloane nods. Having grown up in a small farming community in the west of Ireland, he knows exactly what Blaise means. Everyone knew of the local priest's fondness for choirboys. No one said a thing.

Blaise turns to Charles to resume his story. 'I knew we had to get away from Clay County. We drifted around 'til we got to Detroit, earning money through busking. That's where I was discovered, and we became Johnny and Wyatt Blaise. It was like pouring petrol on a fire. Girls were throwing themselves at us. Not just me and Wyatt, but members of the group, the crew, all of us. Like flies to honey.'

'Does Wyatt have a criminal record?' asks Sloane.

Blaise looks shifty. 'I don't know, sir.'

'You don't know?' asks Sloane, sceptically.

'I've paid girls off. Once, God forgive me, I sent roadies round to see the parents, persuade them to keep quiet. The last time scared him, and he promised it'd never happen again. I thought bringing him with me to Europe would help. And I paid for extra security, to keep the fans away.' He shakes his head.

'Which, of course, didn't work because…' says Charles.

'Because of Frankie Perry. I'd put a fox in charge of the hen house. Within a day or two he was allowing girls and drugs in.'

'Mr Blaise, are you telling us that your brother raped and killed Christine Bailey?' asks Sloane.

Blaise looks up, his face racked with torment. 'I don't know! I think so, but I don't know. The first I knew of it was Mrs Gonzales knocking on my bedroom door. Wyatt came out of his room. He wasn't fully with it — it was the middle of the night and we were all a bit groggy — but he said he'd call the police and deal with it. He told me to go back to my room. He knew I wasn't … alone. The whole house was awake, and there was no way of everyone returning to their usual bedrooms without being seen.'

'Where is Wyatt now?' asks Sloane.

Blaise looks tormented and helpless. 'I don't know. He does this sometimes, goes off on his own. He always comes back. Probably in some club in the West End.'

Sloane looks at Charles. 'What are you thinking?' asks Charles.

'He's a murder suspect. I need to make a Police Gazette entry.'

'What's that?' asks Blaise.

Sloane turns to him. 'It's what law enforcement in the States would call an "all-points bulletin", or a wanted report.'

'You can't, Sean!' says Charles, alarmed. 'It'll alert Quigley and Pilcher we're on to them!'

Sloane considers that, tugging at his ear. It's an endearing "tell" with which Charles is now familiar. The Irishman looks up and addresses Blaise. 'If we were to leave a message here for Wyatt, saying you're going to court tomorrow morning, and telling him to come, would he do it?'

Blaise shrugs. 'I guess so.'

'Okay. There's our answer.' He stands and addresses Blaise formally. 'Mr Johnny Blaise, I am arresting you on suspicion of perverting the course of justice.'

Charles interrupts him. 'Hang on, Sean! You can't arrest him! I need him to give evidence.'

'Sorry, Charles, but I've no choice. He's admitted serious offences. But this won't prevent him giving evidence. Mr Blaise, you are not obliged to say anything unless you wish to do so, but anything you say will be taken down and given in evidence against you.'

# PART THREE

# CHAPTER THIRTY-FIVE

Charles walks carefully up the steps of Chambers, a borrowed (and very full) tray from Mick's café in his hands, a blanket clamped under one arm and his robes bag over his other shoulder. It is quarter to eight and he is the first to arrive, as planned.

He bypasses the clerks' room and climbs to his floor. Setting everything down carefully on the dusty timbers, he takes out his keys and unlocks the huge studded outer door. It is immensely heavy and almost three inches thick. He has often wondered about the proportions of oak to black paint, because since the building was constructed in the seventeenth century this door must have been painted and repainted a hundred times. He uses both hands to swing it back until it lies flat against the wall, picks up his burdens, and pushes open the inner door. He strides towards his room and then hesitates. Perhaps he should lock the outer door from the inside? No, he decides, other early birds might arrive soon, so there's no point, and they'd be bound to ask difficult questions about why he locked himself in.

He knocks gently on the door to the room he shares with Peter Bateman. There is a noise from inside, the door opens a fraction and Sean Sloane's face appears in the gap. The Irishman opens the door fully and Charles enters.

'Good morning,' says Charles cheerfully. His nose wrinkles. 'Do you think we could open a window?' he asks, sniffing the musty air.

'Yeah, sorry about that. Don't suppose this place has been used as a bedroom before,' replies Sloane.

Charles grins. 'You'd be surprised. Several marriages have come to grief through the dual-purpose nature of these rooms.'

He places the tray on his desk and looks across to the far corner. Johnny Blaise, lying across two old leather armchairs, is stirring.

'You took the handcuffs off, I see,' comments Charles.

'He gave me his word, and I'm a light sleeper. I couldn't see him climbing out of the window at this height, and you'd locked us in.'

'How are you feeling, Mr Blaise?' asks Charles. 'I've got coffee and hot bacon sandwiches. No bagels, I'm afraid.'

Blaise sits up. 'Call me Johnny,' he growls, his voice full of sleep and his hair on end, and for the first time Charles can imagine him as a rock singer. 'Can I have a coffee, please? Can't function without it.'

'Certainly,' replies Charles. 'It's probably not what you're used to, but there is milk.'

Blaise throws off the overcoat he was using to keep warm and joins Charles at the desk. 'Don't care,' he says, 'as long as it's black and hot.'

Charles hands him a cup. 'Get any sleep?' he asks.

Blaise takes a sip of the steaming coffee before nodding. 'Yeah, not too bad. After years on the road, sleeping on buses, up to eight of us to a hotel room, I can sleep pretty much anywhere. Those chairs are quite comfortable.'

Charles hands a cup to Sloane. 'How about you?'

The Irishman shakes his head. 'Not much. I got the short straw.' He points to the upholstered captain's swivel chair from which Charles works.

'I find that quite comfortable,' says Charles.

'Try sleeping in it.'

Charles grimaces. 'Sorry, mate. Not many options.'

'I wouldn't have slept wherever I was,' mutters Sloane bitterly. 'I'm so far up shit creek without a paddle right now … I can't see any way back.'

Charles puts a reassuring hand on his friend's arm. 'I know you're worried, but —'

'Worried? I'm in flagrant breach of the Judges' Rules!' He starts ticking items off on his fingers. 'I should've taken him to "*the nearest police station without delay*"; charges should've been recorded in the charge book by the duty officer; then there's legal advice, bail … not to mention taking him before a court!'

'I know, I know,' replies Charles, trying to soothe, 'but you're taking him to court this morning, right? And you've twenty-four hours, not including yesterday, which was a Sunday. And how could you take him to a police station when, odds-on, they'd be on the blower to the Team the second your back's turned? If this works, you're going to get a medal.'

'Don't make me laugh,' replies Sloane, shaking his head. 'What I'm going to get, is dismissed.'

He brings the conversation to an end by opening one of the foil parcels on the tray, extracting a steaming bacon sandwich and taking a large bite. He grunts in appreciation. 'Good,' he manages to say, holding up the sandwich.

'You're both still in one piece,' points out Charles, 'and no one's nobbled you. I call that a win.'

'You always have to have the last word, don't you?' accuses Sloane with a full mouth.

'Sorry to interrupt,' says Blaise meekly, 'but where's the restroom?'

'Far end of the corridor,' replies Charles, pointing. 'By the front door.' He raises his eyebrows at Sloane, who puts his half-eaten sandwich down.

'Come on then,' says the policeman, and he escorts Blaise from the room.

Charles cracks open the window and then returns to his robes bag. He unloads onto the desk two new toothbrushes, a tube of toothpaste, a razor and some clean clothes (the last, courtesy of Irenna). Sloane and Blaise return a few minutes later. Sloane hands the American his sandwich, who takes it back to his makeshift bed.

'I've got some stuff here for you. I've also brought a blanket,' says Charles.

'Could have done with that last night,' comments Sloane. 'Bit chilly in here, no heating and no curtains.'

'Yes, sorry about that,' says Charles. 'This is to hide Mr Blaise's identity for as long as possible.'

There's a silence as the other two men imagine Sloane leading Blaise past the crowds of onlookers into the Old Bailey with a blanket over his head.

'Yes,' says Charles, 'it's not ideal, I know, but can either of you think of anything better? I know most of the staff there, but all the entrances are on public thoroughfares, and the queues are usually right round the block anyway. I think we can risk some of the alleyways between the Temple and Ludgate Circus, but after that … anyone who sees us will assume he's just another criminal.'

'He *is* just another criminal,' says Sloane.

'No, he isn't,' corrects Charles. 'He's been arrested on suspicion, but he's not a criminal till he's convicted, is he? And you promised you'd do your best to get him immunity in return for giving evidence against Quigley and Pilcher. You did the same for Perry, and he definitely *is* a criminal.'

'Okay, okay,' concedes Sloane. 'But this is accessory to murder. It's not the same as burglary.'

They finish their breakfasts in silence.

'I'm usually a yoghurt and fruit guy,' says Blaise, licking his fingers, 'but I could get used to that.'

'Brown sauce,' explains Charles. 'The highest expression of British cuisine.'

'I didn't know Mick's did takeaway orders,' says Sloane.

Mick's is a City institution, beloved of lawyers and journalists. In the centre of Fleet Street, and accordingly both on the edge of the Temple and the heart of the newspaper district, the greasy spoon café provides cheap all-day breakfasts to barristers and scribblers and an informal space for gossip between the two professions. The clerks frequently joke that were it not for Mick's, Mr Holborne would probably starve.

'They don't, usually, but I'm one of their best customers. Right, gentlemen. If we want to be at the Old Bailey before the crowds build up, I suggest we get a move on. You can toss a coin for who uses the facilities first.'

While Sloane and Blaise get ready, Charles slips out and runs down to the clerks' room. He unlocks the outside door, enters and sits at Barbara's desk. He picks up her telephone, secures an outside line and dials.

'Morning, Viv, it's Charles. Sorry I woke you last night. Is he there?'

He waits for Billy Munday's wife to fetch the ex-enforcer.

'Morning,' says Munday, sounding as if he's only been awake a short time.

'Hi, Billy. I know it's unlikely, but we're heading off to court so I thought I'd call. Any news?'

'Sorry, Charlie, but there wasn't much I could do last night and I've only been able to make a couple of calls this morning. But I'm on it, I promise.'

'Okay, thanks. I'll be uncontactable 'til lunchtime, so do what you can and if you strike lucky, get to court as soon as possible, yeah?'

'Will do. Good luck.'

'And you, mate.'

They leave Chambers half an hour later. Charles can hear voices in the clerks' room, but no other barrister has yet arrived on his corridor and they manage to get to the ground floor without incident. Then, instead of descending the main stone steps into King's Bench Walk from where they might be seen through the windows of the clerks' room, Charles takes them towards the back of the building and down into the basement. Unknown to most people, including the barristers, clerks and solicitors familiar with the Temple, there is an interlinked series of corridors and passageways that wind underneath the pavement to the far end of King's Bench Row. Charles leads the way.

Where King's Bench Walk meets Tudor Street, they are forced up to the pavement but it's still reasonably early, and they walk almost all the way to Ludgate Circus before Charles addresses them again.

'I think, from here, we'd better use the blanket.' Blaise, handcuffed unobtrusively to Sloane, looks unhappy at the prospect. 'Better than the perp walk you'd be subjected to in the States,' says Charles. Blaise nods reluctantly.

The last leg of the journey takes only seven minutes and goes much more smoothly than Charles might have predicted. A few people on the pavements turn to look at the three of them, Sloane and Charles each to one side of their "hooded" prisoner, but no one speaks or impedes them. Inside, once Sloane reveals his warrant card to the security men and assures them that he has searched Blaise far more thoroughly than they could, he and Blaise are waved through.

A few minutes later Charles leads them into an empty conference room on the first floor, and positions Blaise out of sight. The conference room door is solid timber, but he doesn't want to risk another lawyer barging in to see if the room is available. They'd have difficulty explaining why a world-famous rock star is in there wearing handcuffs.

'Do you need anything?' Charles asks them. Sloane looks at Blaise and they both shake their heads. 'Okay. I'm going to get robed. Stay here, don't let anyone in, and I'll send Serban down to get you at the right moment. That's Gold's solicitor.'

'Good luck,' says Sloane.

'And you. Both of you.'


'All rise!'

It is one minute past ten. The courtroom is packed, expectant, awaiting the anticipated cross-examination of DCI Quigley arising out of Charles's weekend investigations. Quigley has already taken his position in the witness box.

Charles allows the judge to settle before rising.

'Good morning, my Lord. May I thank you again for the time allowed to me before the long adjournment?'

'I hope you used it productively, Mr Holborne. No further adjournments will be allowed to either you or the Crown unless something very exceptional arises.'

'I understand, my Lord.'

Pullman turns to the policeman in the witness box. 'You are still under oath, Chief Inspector.'

'Of course,' replies Quigley, and he turns towards Charles, awaiting the first question.

'Is it right that you and Detective Inspector Pilcher were called to Kingston Grange after Christine Bailey's body was discovered?' asks Charles.

Quigley turns to the judge to give his answer. 'That's right, my Lord, but not at the same time. I arrived about forty-five minutes before DI Pilcher.'

'Why you?'

'I'm sorry, I'm not sure I understand the question.'

'Well, you're not on the murder rotation, are you?'

'No, I'm not, but —'

'You're not in the Flying Squad?'

'No —'

'Nor in the Drugs Squad.'

'No —'

'You're based —'

Cartledge leaps to his feet. 'If my learned friend would allow the witness to finish a sentence, perhaps he'd obtain an answer!' he says angrily.

Pullman addresses Charles with a smile. 'While I applaud the efficiency, Mr Holborne, you do need to allow the witness to answer questions before you leap in with the next.'

'Sorry, my Lord,' replies Charles, full of forensically simulated contrition. He knew very well that he was interrupting Quigley and would soon be reprimanded for it, but he wanted to prevent the policeman from settling.

'Let me try again. Mr Quigley, you are normally based at the regional crime squad in Brighton, but you've been seconded to Scotland Yard because of your expertise in dealing with organised crime, particularly burglaries. Is that correct?'

'Yes, my Lord, that is correct.'

'And you're not on the murder rotation or a member of the Drugs Squad. So can you explain to us, please, why you were called to a death, on the face of it a drugs overdose, at a rock star's party, in Surrey? That's a long way from your area of expertise — burglary — and well off your present patch in London.'

'My Lord,' intervenes Cartledge smoothly, 'my instructions are that DI Pilcher had dealings with the security company beforehand. It was he who recommended Celeb Security for the job. He was called by the people in the house because he was the only police officer with whom they'd had any dealings.'

'Perhaps American musicians don't know about 999 calls,' offers Pullman.

'Precisely, my Lord.'

Charles jumps back in. 'I thank my leaned friend for that evidence, but it doesn't explain, Mr Quigley, why you were there.'

'Actually, Mr Holborne, it does,' answers the policeman. 'DI Pilcher was tied up with another matter, and when he couldn't be interrupted, the duty sergeant called me. I happened to be free, so I attended.'

'I suggest the reason you were there is that you and Pilcher had been selling confiscated drugs to the people at Kingston Grange, drugs stolen from the police property store at Savile Row.'

Quigley looks suitably shocked. He shakes his head slightly in disbelief and then manages to get his tongue working. 'My Lord, that is completely untrue and totally fantastical!' he replies. He turns to look at the jury with a bemused expression and raised eyebrows.

'I further suggest,' continues Charles, 'that, following the discovery of Christine Bailey's body, you were telephoned by a man named Wyatt Blaise, the younger brother of Johnny Blaise, who was part of the entourage.'

'No, my Lord, that is entirely false. I know who counsel is referring to but to the best of my knowledge I have never spoken to the young man and I certainly didn't have a telephone conversation with him that night.'

'I further suggest that on arrival at the property, following a conversation with Johnny Blaise, you offered to cover up the death of Christine Bailey for a payment of two thousand five hundred pounds. That money was given to you by Johnny Blaise and you called DI Pilcher to the property to come and take it away.'

Pullman intervenes, his voice like thunder. 'Mr Holborne! These are outrageous allegations. If your defence consists simply of throwing mud at this officer — whose evidence is frankly peripheral to the case — you are wasting your time, as I shall make crystal clear to the jury. And you'd better have express instructions to make this case plus substantial evidence to back it up, or you're going to find yourself in seriously hot professional water! This court will not tolerate wild attacks by the defence on the credit of a distinguished, decorated officer.'

Charles foresaw this. When at the Bar, Pullman was a dyed-in-the-wool prosecutor. Since he's been on the bench he has seen enough police mendacity to force him to moderate his views slightly, but he is still a prosecutor's judge.

'I assure you, my Lord, I have both instructions and supporting evidence. I shall demonstrate to the jury that these are not wild allegations but, astonishingly, the absolute truth.'

Pullman and Charles lock eyes. 'You'd better answer Mr Holborne's question then, Chief Inspector,' says the judge.

Quigley also stares at Charles for a long moment before turning to Pullman. He composes his face, takes a deep breath as if attempting to control his temper, and finally replies.

'My Lord, these are entirely false allegations. I attended the property as a result of a report of a suspicious death. I secured the room for forensic analysis and called in an FME — that's a police surgeon, my Lord — to certify death. While I was waiting for him, I called Scenes of Crime and informed the coroner's officer. Then I organised uniformed officers to secure the property generally and take details of the potential witnesses. There were a lot of people there and I couldn't do it alone. The only accurate part of what counsel put to me is that DI Pilcher was one of the officers called to the property to assist.'

Having got that answer Charles sits, taking everyone by surprise.

'Is that it?' asks Pullman of Charles. Charles nods. 'Very well. Mr Cartledge?'

The QC rises. 'Difficult to know what to do with that barrage of falsehood, eh, Detective Chief Inspector?'

Charles half-rises to object but Pullman forestalls him. 'Comment, Mr Cartledge. Perfectly reasonable comment, but now's not the time. Save it for your speech, please.'

'My Lord. Very well. Mr Quigley, let me simply ask you this: other than the fact that DI Pilcher was called to the property to be part of the investigating team, is any part of what was just put to you correct?'

'Not a word. Total fabrication.'

'Thank you. Any questions, my Lord?'

'No, thank you.'

'Thank you, Mr Quigley. Detective Inspector Pilcher, please.'

Charles turns to look at his client. Gold smiles tentatively and nods. For the first time, the defence's actual case is starting to emerge.

# CHAPTER THIRTY-SIX

Detective Inspector Pilcher enters court and marches swiftly to the witness box where he is taken through the oath.

Cartledge addresses the judge. 'I propose tendering DI Pilcher for cross-examination.'

'Yes, Mr Cartledge I will give you some leeway on re-examination if necessary. Mr Holborne?'

Charles stands. 'Detective Inspector, you were called to Kingston Grange on the night of Christine Bailey's death, is that right?'

'Yes.'

'Who called you?'

'If you mean called by telephone, I can't tell you. I was interviewing a suspect in a different investigation. When I finished I was given a telephone message from someone at Kingston Grange saying a body had been discovered. The message did not specify who had called the police station. I was told that DCI Quigley had gone to the property, so I followed him.'

'So it wasn't DCI Quigley who called you directly?'

'No, my Lord.'

'I suggest he telephoned you and told you to come and collect two thousand five hundred pounds in cash, which he had negotiated as a bribe.'

Now it is Pilcher's turn to look completely nonplussed, but he is a poorer actor than his superior and, in Charles's eyes at least, it looks overdone. 'A bribe? A bribe for what?'

'The way this works, DI Pilcher, is that I ask the questions and you answer them. It doesn't matter what the bribe might have been for. Did you go to Kingston Grange and take away a holdall containing two thousand five hundred pounds in cash?'

'Absolutely not, my Lord.'

Charles resumes his seat. Instead of rising to re-examine Pilcher, Cartledge scoffs loudly and throws his pen onto his notebook. After a moment he stands. 'That is the case for the Crown, my Lord.'

Charles turns to Bateman. As he does so, he sees movement in the public gallery and he looks up. Mrs Gold is just entering. She is followed by two girls in their early teens. They look immaculate in their school uniforms. They take seats, one on either side of their mother in the front row. Charles nods towards them and whispers to Bateman.

'Mrs Gold's here, with her daughters.'

'Yes. She asked Serban if it would be okay for the girls to come. They want to support their father when he gives evidence. Also, I think she wants them to hear what happened to Christine, as a warning against drug-taking.'

'Fair enough. Not a decision I'd have taken. Anyway, I think we should go for the jugular. Let's call Blaise now and see how we go. Would you mind going to fetch him?'

'Sure,' says Bateman. He stands, bows to the judge, and walks swiftly out of court.

Charles turns to face Pullman. 'My junior is going to fetch our first witness. It shouldn't take more than a minute, but if your Lordship would like to rise for a short period…?'

'Yes, thank you, Mr Holborne. Five minutes, then. The jury may remain in court,' says Pullman, standing and patting his jacket pocket to make sure he has his cigarettes.

'All rise!'

Charles looks behind him. Quigley and Pilcher, having now given evidence, are permitted to stay and they are sitting next to one another on the bench usually reserved for prosecution solicitors. Their heads are together and they are whispering furiously.

*They can't work out what we're up to.*

'All rise!' calls the usher exactly five minutes later, as the judge steps through the panelling behind his tall seat and takes his place.

Although there is no rule of evidence requiring it, conventionally, when a defendant chooses to give evidence, he is the first defence witness to be called. Accordingly, Charles's decision to call someone other than Gold excites some interest amongst those who know that something unusual is occurring. As the door at the back of court opens, everyone in the well of the court turns their heads, curious to know the identity of the first witness.

Peter Bateman enters court. Behind him is Sean Sloane. Quigley and Pilcher spot Sloane immediately and, for a heartbeat, still apparently believing Sloane to be a probationary member of their "Team", Quigley nods to him cautiously. Then Sloane moves through the open doorway and it becomes clear that he is handcuffed to someone, someone wearing a blanket over their head.

Sloane walks down the slope, leading his witness. All heads in the court turn to follow their progress, as if watching a slow-motion tennis shot. Those in the public gallery stand or lean over the rail.

'I call Johnny Blaise!' announces Charles and, with perfect timing, as if it were a moment of practised showmanship, Sloane whips the blanket off Blaise's head and shoulders.

There is an audible gasp. Whispering breaks out instantly and soon becomes talking; talking becomes shouting. A couple of young women in the balcony squeal in excitement and others start applauding. Folding seats bang like a stuttering machine gun as ranks of observers leap up to get a better view. The volume crescendos and in seconds there is complete uproar. The court associate stands and shouts for order. Charles can see her lips moving, but nothing can be heard above the din. The judge realises that her efforts are having no effect and he too stands. His shout is more successful.

'Silence!' he bellows. 'Silence in court! I will have order or the court will be cleared!' The volume level drops, but not completely. 'Unless this din ceases immediately, the rest of this trial will be conducted in camera!'

It takes a few seconds but eventually the residual commotion fades and order is restored. An expectant silence resumes. It crackles with anticipation.

Pullman collapses back into his seat, his pale face glistening with sweat.

'My Lord?' queries the associate in a solicitous voice.

Pullman dismisses her concern with a brusque wave of his hand. He draws a deep breath, looks down and addresses Sloane. 'Identify yourself,' he croaks.

'I am Detective Sergeant Sean Sloane of the Metropolitan Police. This man was arrested late last night, and I have brought him direct from custody.'

'Mr Holborne,' says Pullman, 'is the man in custody your first witness?'

'He is, my Lord.'

'Is he here voluntarily?'

'The fact that he is under arrest and here to give evidence are not unconnected, my Lord, as you will hear. If he is sworn, all will soon become clear.'

Pullman pauses to dab his forehead with a handkerchief. 'Very well. Is it necessary that he remain restrained?' He addresses this last question to Sloane.

Sloane looks at Blaise, who shakes his head slightly. 'Probably not, my Lord,' he answers, and he removes the handcuffs and returns to sit next to Serban.

Blaise steps up into the witness box and is approached by the usher.

'Religion?' he asks.

'Baptist.'

The answer flummoxes the usher, who turns to the judge for guidance.

'In other words, Christian?' says Pullman, leaning over his bench towards Blaise.

'Yes, sir.'

'Give him the New Testament,' orders the judge.

'Please take this in your right hand,' instructs the usher, handing Blaise the Bible, 'and read the words off the card.'

Blaise holds the Bible aloft and in a fervent voice swears to tell the truth, the whole truth and nothing but the truth. He also adds, redundantly according to English procedure: 'So help me God.' He still somehow looks impossibly handsome, despite the fact that he wears clothes from the day before, he hasn't shaved and he has only managed a perfunctory wash in a small lavatory basin. In fact, Charles thinks as he studies the American, he doesn't appear even to have stubble. His baby-smooth skin looks just as it did the previous evening.

'What is your name, please?' starts Charles.

'My real name or my stage name?'

'Both, please.'

'I was born Ethan Dwight Robinson, but for the last ten years or so I have been known professionally as Johnny Blaise.'

The answer causes excitement from some of the women in the gallery.

'Last warning,' says the judge, looking up at the packed balcony. His voice is weaker than before, as if the shouting has left him fatigued. 'If you wish to watch these proceedings, you will remain silent or I will have you removed. Please continue, Mr Holborne.'

'What is your occupation, Mr Blaise?'

'I'm a rock singer, and I lead a group known as the Hellraisers. We're based in America but we're presently on tour. We've one further date before we head home, in Brussels.'

'What's your address in England?'

'We've been staying at a place called Kingston Grange. I think it's in the county of Surrey. I don't know the full address.'

'I think that will suffice, thank you,' says Charles. 'I'd like you to look at the bench there —' Charles points to where Quigley and Pilcher are sitting — 'and tell me if you recognise those two men.'

Charles holds his breath. This is Blaise's first real test. Promising to give evidence, and then doing it in the terms promised, are two different things.

'Mr Quigley and Mr Pilcher? Sure, I recognise them.'

'When was your first contact with them?' asks Charles.

'I met Mr Pilcher at Kingston Grange, a couple of days after we moved in.'

'In what context?'

'Well, a guy called Frankie Perry runs the company that does security for the group here in England, and he knew Mr Pilcher. So Mr Pilcher came to the property. I heard 'em talking about the security and got the impression that Mr

Pilcher had recommended Mr Perry's company to our promoter.'

'Just so the jury understands, by "promoter" do you mean Mr Gold, the defendant?'

'Yes, sir, that's right.'

'So, your understanding was that Mr Gold needed security for the group and DI Pilcher recommended Perry's company.'

'Yes, sir.'

'How many times did you see Mr Pilcher at Kingston Grange?'

'Three times.'

'Did he ever come with another person?'

'Second time I saw him there, he was with a blond guy called Fed. He's also law enforcement. He introduced Fed to me and Perry, and said that Fed would be delivering … certain goods to the house.'

'Goods?'

'Yeah. Drugs. I don't approve of 'em and I don't touch them. But other group members do and he said Fed would be, you know, the courier. He was to be allowed in at the gates without anyone recording his arrival or departure.'

'After that did you see this man, Fed, delivering drugs?'

'Yeah, a few times. Kingston Grange is the base for the whole European tour, 'cept a few nights in hotels on the continent. And we've been recording some tracks there too. We've been there six weeks.'

'If you disagree with drugs, why didn't you stop it?'

'These guys are adults. They know how I feel about it, but it's not my place to tell 'em how to live their lives. Plus I'd lose some great musicians. Everyone in the business does it. Leastways, pretty much everyone.'

'Did you form an opinion as to Mr Gold's attitude to the admission of drugs into the property?'

'Yeah, we spoke about it several times. He hates drugs even more'n me. He knew someone who died, another artiste, from an overdose. He was her manager. You could see it still really affected him.'

'Did you see him take any steps to stop drugs coming into Kingston Grange?'

'Sure. I heard him lecturing the guys on the gates. But Perry's their boss, and if he okayed Fed in and out on the sly, what could Mr Gold do?'

'Thank you. I'm now going to ask you some questions about the death of Christine Bailey. Before I do so, I have a more general question: did you form any opinion of Mr Gold's attitude to groupies being allowed into the property?'

'The whole point of security at Kingston Grange and at gigs is to keep the fans away. We sign autographs and try to be, you know, available, but only in ways we can control. You ever been to one of our concerts?'

'That's a pleasure I have yet to experience.'

'Well, they're insane! These kids are screaming, crying, trying to get on stage. We've had clothes torn off us! They try to get on the buses —'

'Buses?' asks Charles for clarification.

'We have two tour buses. The group is big, for this tour ten pieces, and there's loads of equipment, roadies, crew, lighting and sound technicians. And some of these girls try to get on the buses. We've even found 'em hiding in luggage compartments.' He looks up at the gallery. 'I wouldn't want anyone to think we ain't grateful, 'cos we are. That's how we make a living. But sometimes the attention's too much. Mr Gold understands that, and does what he can to keep fans out, but … it's like the drugs. The group members, the crew and everyone else, they're grown-ups. If they take a fancy to one of the fans and decide to bring her back, there ain't nothing you can do 'bout it.'

'Do you remember the night when Christine Bailey was at the property?'

'I do, but I don't think I was aware of her 'til afterwards.'

Charles halts his flow of questions for a moment to regard Quigley and Pilcher.

The two policemen have their heads down, their elbows on their knees, as if trying to hide behind the barristers and solicitors in front of them, but they are again whispering furiously, and Charles sees Quigley opening a file and leafing through documents. He can guess the first question that will be put to Blaise in cross-examination, and his suspicions are elevated further when he sees a document being handed forward to Cartledge.

Charles watched the singer's struggle with his conscience, and found himself empathising with the American, despite deep disquiet about the way in which he protected Wyatt from the consequences of his actions. Charles asked himself how he would react if he discovered David was a sexual predator. His brother is such an honourable and upright man, Charles struggles to imagine such a scenario, but he hopes he'd have the courage to report him to the police even if that meant, as surely it would, the family being torn apart.

He thinks Blaise was wrong to bribe or frighten vulnerable victims and witnesses into silence, notwithstanding his role as his kid brother's protector. Even if Wyatt was abused by their father, his behaviour cannot be excused. Allowing him to go unpunished led to Christine Bailey's death.

Nonetheless, what the singer is about to say — at least, what he assures Charles and Sloane he *will* say — will end everything. Wyatt's trip to Europe will finish in an English prison, probably for life. Blaise will almost certainly find himself there too as an accessory. The group's success will be over in an instant. To reveal all that, before the media in the witness box of a foreign court, will take courage.

Charles returns his attention to the star, who waits patiently for the next question.

'You told us you've seen Mr Pilcher at Kingson Grange on three occasions. When was the third?' he asks.

'That was the night of the Astoria concert.'

'We've been told there were technical problems at the Astoria, the group returned to Kingston Grange early, and Christine Bailey was one of several girls who accompanied you back. Can you confirm that?'

'Yes, that's right.'

'How did Mr Pilcher come to be at the property, then?'

'I need to take a bit of a runup to that. When we got back, I saw there'd been a flood from one of the bathrooms and for a spell I helped Mr Gold and the housekeeper do some of the clearing up. My brother and some of the others were drinking and playing music in the Blue Room — that's the big lounge room — but I wasn't in the mood, and I went to the studio in the basement. Maybe I saw Miss Bailey before then, maybe I didn't, but I wasn't thinking about it. I spent a little time working on a new song but it wasn't happening, so I said goodnight to Bobby and went to bed. I got woken —'

'Sorry to interrupt, Mr Blaise. You said goodnight to Bobby? Is that Bobby Gold, the man in the dock?'

'Yeah. He was leaving, so I said goodbye.'

'Right. What time was that?'

'Around ten thirty, I guess.'

'Just to make sure there's no confusion over the language, when you say "I guess" does that mean you're not sure of the time?'

'No, I'm sure. He'd been taking notes of where there was water damage and he was heading out the door.'

'Thank you. Please continue.'

'So I went to bed, and was woken just before four a.m.'

Charles looks up to make sure the judge is keeping up with the evidence and waits until he receives a nod to ask his next question.

'Who woke you?'

'Mrs Gonzales. She knocked on my door and told me to come quickly.'

'What did you do?'

'I put on my bathrobe and followed her to one of the other bedrooms, to the left of mine. Then I saw Miss Bailey on the floor…'

Blaise's eyes lose their focus and he looks down. He takes a couple of deep breaths, obviously disturbed by the scene unfolding anew in his head.

'There was a hypodermic hanging out her arm and her eyes were staring … staring.' He shakes his head before looking up again. 'I'll never forget that. It was shocking. Despite our time on the streets, me and Wyatt, believe it or not, that was the first time I ever saw a dead person. She looked so … lonely.'

'What did you do?'

'Well, Wyatt came in with one of the others — Billy Joe, I think. He's our keyboard player. Perry was there as well. I don't know if he came in with Wyatt or if he was there before. Anyway, I was in a bit of a state. I was angry 'cos I thought someone had given drugs to the girl and she was just a kid.'

Charles and the witness are both disturbed by a noise from above them, and they look up simultaneously to the gallery. Sitting only a few feet from Mrs Gold and her daughters are Mrs Fairfax and her elder daughter, Karen. Both Mrs Fairfax and Karen are crying.

Blaise resumes his answer. 'Wyatt told me to go back to my room, said he would call Mr Pilcher. He had the guy's number. So that's what I did.'

'You haven't told us yet how you saw Mr Pilcher at Kingston Grange that night.'

'Yeah, sorry. So, the cops arrived. It seemed like only a few minutes later. First to get there was Mr Quigley, who I'd not seen before. He knocked on my door. He told me Wyatt had killed the girl, and he was facing life imprisonment, but he could make it look like it was someone else.'

'Did he say how?'

Blaise shakes his head. 'No. Just that he could make the problem go away if I paid him two thousand five hundred pounds.'

'Just stop there, Mr Holborne,' orders Pullman. 'It sounds very much as if this witness requires a warning against self-incrimination, don't you think?'

'Yes, my Lord. Now would be a good time.'

The judge turns to Blaise. 'Mr Blaise. You are not on trial here. In our courts you have an absolute right to refuse to answer any question that might incriminate you. Do you understand?'

'Yes, sir, I understand. We have the same rule in the States. Mr Holborne there has already told me. But I have thought about it and prayed on it, and I've decided I need to answer.'

'Have you had legal advice, Mr Blaise?' persists the judge. 'Mr Holborne owes a duty to his client and to the court, but not to you. I think you should speak to an independent solicitor — that's a lawyer — before proceeding further.'

'I can't do that, sir. It's been weighing on my conscience and it's got me in bad with the Lord. I gotta get this off my chest. This is my fault.'

Pullman considers the answer and raises his eyebrows. 'If you're sure…'

'I am, sir.'

'You may proceed, Mr Holborne.'

'Thank you, my Lord. So, Mr Blaise, do you usually have that sort of money lying around in cash?'

'Normally, no. But in a large venue we can take a thousand in merchandise sales — T-shirts, posters and singles.'

'Is that dollars or pounds?' asks Charles.

'Pounds. And here's the thing. Normally the money's taken by Mr Gold, but the night before he didn't come to the concert and he was supposed to collect it from us after the Astoria gig. But, I guess with the flood and everything that went wrong that night, he forgot, because he left without taking the cash with him. So, as it turned out, I had cash from two concerts, enough to pay Mr Quigley.'

'So, did you pay it?'

Blaise hangs his head. 'I'm ashamed to say, I did. I was frightened for Wyatt, and Lord help me, I just grasped at a way out. All that stuff with the drugs … I just thought that was the way things were done over here. You pay the cops.'

'Unfortunately, Mr Blaise, too often that's the way things *are* done around here,' says Charles. He expects a rebuke from the judge or an objection from Cartledge, and is surprised to receive neither. He watches the judge's lips compress in a thin line as he continues his note-taking.

Charles allows the silence to lengthen. It's an incredible story but, looking at the jury, he thinks they believe it. Revealing all this has required Blaise to admit that he is guilty of a serious crime too, and Charles cannot see any motive for him to do so unless it is, genuinely, to tell the truth and salve his conscience.

'You still haven't told us how you came to see DI Pilcher that evening,' points out Charles.

'You're right. Well, it's simple. I gave the holdall with the money to Mr Quigley, and he phoned Mr Pilcher and told him to come get it. Mr Quigley left Perry with the money and told him not to look in the bag. Said just to give it to Mr Pilcher. I was in the Blue Room when Pilcher arrived at the front door. He went up to Perry, said something to him — I didn't hear what it was — took the holdall and left again.'

Again Charles pauses to let the judge catch up in his note-taking.

'So, you paid a two thousand five hundred pound bribe to DCI Quigley to protect your brother and falsely frame Mr Gold for Christine Bailey's murder, and the bribe money was taken away by DI Pilcher?'

Blaise nods sadly. 'Yes, sir. But I didn't know they were going to frame Bobby. I would have said something to them if I'd known that. They just said they'd make the problem go away.' He addresses the judge. 'And, sir, I'm truly ashamed of my part in it.' He pauses, and when he continues speaking, his voice has dropped and it is redolent with sadness. 'I've been looking out for Wyatt since he was fifteen. He ain't had no one but me. I know I shouldn't have done it. It was wrong. But I was scared for him and I didn't think it through. I'm real sorry.'

'Yes, thank you, Mr Blaise. Please remain there. Mr Cartledge, here, will have some further questions for you.'

# CHAPTER THIRTY-SEVEN

As Cartledge rises to cross-examine Blaise, Charles feels a tug on his gown from behind. He turns. Bateman indicates the back of the court. A man has entered and is in whispered conversation with an usher.

'Is that Wyatt?' asks Bateman softly.

Charles frowns. 'Certainly could be. There's definitely a resemblance.'

They keep their eyes on the exchange at the back of the court. The usher points around and shrugs, indicating there are no seats left. The other man nods and slips back outside.

Sloane, sitting next to Bateman, becomes aware of the barristers' conversation.

'Was that the brother?' he asks urgently.

Bateman answers. 'Not sure, possibly.'

Sloane slides immediately out of the bench and hurries up the aisle.

'Please look at this document,' Cartledge is saying to Blaise, and he hands a sheet of paper to the usher for conveyance to the witness box.

Blaise takes the document, examines it briefly and nods.

Cartledge continues. 'In the American criminal justice system, that's called a "rap sheet", is that right?'

Charles leans back to speak again to Bateman. 'No doubt now who the blackmailer is,' he whispers. 'Quigley's had that rap sheet all along.'

Bateman nods.

'It records,' says Cartledge, 'a conviction in Georgia from 1959, does it not?'

'Yes, sir,' replies Blaise.

'Read the text in the box on the right underneath the photograph,' orders Cartledge.

Blaise does so. *'Felony carnal knowledge of a juvenile.'*

'And tell us how old that juvenile was at the time of the offence.'

'It says fifteen years,' replies Blaise, his voice flat and emotionless.

'The man convicted was Mark Robinson: Caucasian, fair hair, date of birth first of May 1938, height five feet ten inches, weight one hundred and sixty-nine pounds, no identifying characteristics. That was you, was it not? You were convicted of the rape of a girl one month younger than Christine Bailey.'

This time there is no outcry, no screaming, no applause, merely profound silence. Charles looks up.

*This is the moment. Will Blaise have the courage?*

The singer swallows. He opens his mouth as if to speak, but for a moment nothing emerges. He takes a deep breath and tries again.

'No, sir.'

'Really?' scoffs Cartledge. 'I shall be re-calling the police officers in this case who believe it was you. In any case, my Lord, I have copies of that document which I would like to have distributed to the jury.'

He hands a sheaf of copies to the usher and slides one halfway towards Charles without looking at him. He waits until the jury members have the document before them.

Charles rises. 'I object to this, my Lord. Mr Blaise may have decided to give evidence which incriminates him in respect of the bribe taken by DCI Quigley —'

Cartledge interrupts. 'Mr Holborne assumes as a fact that Mr Quigley accepted a bribe. It is not. It is utterly repudiated.'

'So what?' replies Charles sharply. 'This witness has given evidence of the bribe and it's for the jury to decide if he's telling the truth. But my learned friend misses the point. Mr Blaise has waived his right to silence in respect of facilitating an alleged bribe. He has not done so in relation to any other offence. And for my learned friend to attempt a dock identification from an extremely poor Xerox copy dating from a decade ago is quite improper, as I'm sure he knows.'

'But, Mr Holborne,' intervenes Pullman, 'the privilege against self-incrimination doesn't apply to an existing conviction, does it? That's a matter of record, and this isn't a dock identification. Mr Cartledge is entitled to ask this witness if that record of conviction refers to him. His answer is important for the jury to judge Mr Blaise's credibility. No, you may proceed Mr Cartledge.'

'Thank you, my Lord. Well, Mr Blaise. You say it was not you. I say it looks very like you.'

'It's not me. I have never been convicted of any offence, in Georgia or anywhere.'

'If it wasn't you, who was it?'

Charles finds himself holding his breath again.

'It's my brother, Wyatt,' says Blaise eventually, his head bowed. 'He was born Mark Robinson. We looked very much alike at that time. Still do.'

'I suggest that's a lie, Mr Blaise. That's you in the photograph, isn't it? And you're lying about DCI Quigley and DI Pilcher. There was no framing, and no bribe. You've made up this entire fiction to protect your promoter.'

Charles turns towards Bateman and raises one eyebrow. He wondered how Cartledge was going to explain why Blaise would walk himself and his brother into serious criminal charges, but this is surely scraping the bottom of the barrel.

Cartledge must have suggested this on instructions from Quigley, who has proof of successful blackmail to back up the assertion. But, surely, no one could possibly believe Blaise would implicate himself and his brother just to exculpate Gold, a business associate who he met for the first time only six weeks earlier? Charles looks across at the jury. Several are frowning, also struggling to credit the QC's assertion.

'You're crazy,' Blaise responds, articulating the disbelief Charles can see on the faces of the jury. 'Mr Gold's a nice guy, but I wouldn't lie on a Bible for him or for anyone. If I thought he killed that girl, I'd be saying so. And sacrificing my own brother to get him off? You're...' He grinds to a halt, racking his brains for a strong enough word. 'Crazy!' he repeats.

'Is that a good time?' asks Pullman of Cartledge. He nods towards the clock. It is a minute to one.

Cartledge is reluctant to stop there, on a high note for the defence, but he has no choice. 'As your Lordship pleases,' he says, biting the words off in frustration.

'Mr Holborne, I note that the police officer who brought Mr Blaise here in custody is no longer in court —'

'I am, my Lord,' comes Sloane's voice. He has just re-entered. 'Mr Blaise remains under arrest and in my custody.'

'Very well. Thank you. Five past two, please.'

'All rise!'

# CHAPTER THIRTY-EIGHT

Sloane takes Blaise into custody again, handcuffs him and escorts him out of court. Charles and Bateman follow closely behind.

He leads them upstairs to the conference room and opens the door. Inside, Wyatt Blaise sits at a table with Victor Serban. A third man is standing behind the door and for a second Charles doesn't recognise him.

'Olney!' he exclaims, astonished. 'What the hell are you doing here?'

'Your chum called me last night and told me what you planned. He persuaded me to give it one last shot. So, did Blaise spill the beans about Quigley and Pilcher?'

'He did, and he came over pretty well. But what about your pension?' asks Charles.

'If this works, the Team'll be finished. Kenneth Drury won't be able to resist the pressure to take action. Which means the pension should be safe. I hope.'

'Is it just the two of you?' asks Bateman.

'No,' replies Sloane shortly.

'What's going on, Johnny?' asks Wyatt.

For the first time Charles sees that Wyatt is handcuffed to the leg of the table.

'It's about the girl who died,' replies Blaise. 'I'm so sorry, Wyatt, but I had to tell them.'

'What?' asks Wyatt, looking from his brother to the police officers and back again. 'What did you tell them?'

'Everything. I'm sorry,' he repeats. 'It couldn't go on. Not murder.'

'What?' says Wyatt again, this time saying the word differently, not with panic but with utter disbelief. 'I didn't kill her! You think I killed her?'

'Give it up, Wyatt,' says his brother. 'Quigley told me.'

'Quigley? That lying piece of shit? How could you believe anything *he* told you? I didn't kill her! I didn't!'

DCI Olney takes charge. 'Sloane, park the older brother there, and keep him quiet. Holborne, I'm going to take a statement from the younger brother. Are you comfortable with my doing it now?'

'I'm not representing him. I'm not instructed to represent either of them.'

'Okay. Why don't you and your colleagues grab something to eat, and leave me and Sloane to get on with it?'

Charles and Bateman look at one another. 'The trouble is, we need to know what he says,' says Bateman.

Charles explains. 'If there's any possibility I'm going to be calling Wyatt in Bobby Gold's trial in an hour's time, I can't do it blind.'

'I'm not concerned about your trial,' replies Olney. 'This man has to be interviewed under caution on the charge of murder.'

'I keep telling you, it wasn't me!' interrupts Wyatt.

'Quiet, you!' orders Olney, pointing at him threateningly. 'You'll get your chance.'

'But, boss,' intervenes Sloane, 'it's the same charge of murder that Gold's presently facing. Gold *is* Charles's client and he has a right to know the evidence, especially if it points to the real killer. And we'd never have got this far without him. There's clear evidence now that Christine Bailey was alive when Gold left the property that night. I don't think he could've killed her. And it's only because Gold's volunteered to remain in custody that we even have a shot at this.'

Olney ponders Sloane's words, but then shakes his head. 'I'm not prepared to interview this man with two barristers and a solicitor present, none of whom are apparently representing him and all of whom have a conflict of interest with him. I dread to think what a decent defence brief could make of that. No. But I'll tell you what, Holborne, I promise to let you see any statement I take before you go back into court. Now, bugger off and let me get on. We've got fifty minutes to ask questions that would usually take hours.'

Charles and Bateman look at one another again, and Charles nods. 'Sean, please bring me a copy of whatever you have no later than five to two, outside court. All right?'

Sloane looks at Olney for approval and receives a short nod. 'Will do.'

The court reconvenes at five minutes past two.

'Any further questions for this witness, Mr Cartledge?' asks Pullman.

Cartledge stands. 'At the appropriate juncture I shall be making an application to recall DCI Quigley and DI Pilcher to rebut these baseless allegations, but I've no further questions of this … pop singer,' he says, his tone scathing.

'Very well. Over to you, Mr Holborne. Any re-examination?'

'No, thank you, my Lord.'

'Well, I have no questions. Let's have the next witness.'

Charles turns and signals towards the back of the court. Movement is visible through the window and the door opens. DCI Olney enters, leading a man in handcuffs. Again, his head and shoulders are covered by the blanket.

Cartledge leaps to his feet. 'My Lord, I protest in the strongest of terms! Mr Holborne is turning this trial into a circus! How many more witnesses are to be dragged to the witness box in handcuffs and incognito?'

'I have no idea, Mr Cartledge,' replies Pullman, with a slight smile. 'But I know of no rule that prevents witnesses being brought to give evidence from custody. It's commonplace. Nor, for that matter, from under a blanket. But that's Mr Holborne for you. Shall we ask him?'

Pullman turns to Charles, and for the first time Charles sees a definite twinkle in the judge's sunken eyes.

*Perhaps even he's beginning to believe the defence case.*

'So, Mr Holborne, who do we have under there this time? Frank Sinatra, maybe?'

A roar of laughter rolls around the court which, oddly, the judge allows without complaint.

Charles detects a definite change of atmosphere. The tension in relation to Bobby Gold's trial seems to have almost dissipated, a change which he hopes is due to the jury having already reached a decision in his favour. Charles casts a glance at Quigley and Pilcher. They are now both sitting upright, alert. DI Pilcher's lips are compressed in a thin, angry line and he is staring with hatred at Olney from under hooded eyes. Quigley's pale face gives nothing away.

DCI Olney is now at the witness box and removes the blanket from the man in his custody.

'And who is this?' asks Pullman.

'I am Detective Chief Inspector Olney, my Lord, and I have arrested this man, whose name is Wyatt Blaise. He is the brother of the previous witness.'

'Thank you,' says the judge. 'Let's have him sworn.'

Charles examines Wyatt carefully as the oath is administered. He does look remarkably like his older brother, although he is slightly shorter and skinnier. His face is blotchy and his eyes red, and it is obvious he has been crying. Charles takes out from his notebook a Xerox of Wyatt's handwritten statement, obtained only minutes ago by Olney. Fortunately, the handwriting is clear.

'Please give your name and address to the court,' he says.

'I'm Wyatt Blaise,' replies Wyatt quietly, 'and I'm presently staying at a big house in Kingston. I don't know the full address.'

'Were you born Wyatt Blaise?'

Wyatt shakes his head. 'No. I was christened Mark Edgar Robinson.'

'What were the circumstances of your change of name?' asks Charles.

'Johnny and I ran away from home. We had to get away from our father, who was violent and —' his voice drops further — 'and did things to us. We went all over, busking. I played the mouth organ and Johnny sang. In Detroit we started to get gigs in bars and I was frightened our father would track us down, so we changed our names.'

'On the witness box in front of you, there should still be a sheet of paper which records the conviction of a Mark Robinson in Georgia in 1959. Is that still there?'

Wyatt picks it up. 'Yes, sir.'

'Was that you?'

Wyatt nods. 'Yeah. That was me.'

'Thank you. Now, please look at the men sitting behind prosecuting counsel.'

Charles points.

'Mr Pilcher, yeah?'

'Yes, Mr Pilcher. Do you recognise the taller man with very pale skin sitting next to him?'

'Yeah. I met him the night Christine died.'

'Okay. Tell us how you first met Mr Pilcher.'

'He was our dealer. He supplied me 'n' other guys in the group with drugs.'

'What drugs?'

'Mainly weed, but some other stuff too. Whatever we wanted, really,' replies Wyatt.

'Did you know he was a police officer?'

'Not the first time I met him, but after that, yeah. He had the stuff delivered by another officer, a guy called Feder. I knew Fed was police, and I put two and two together.'

'How did they get the drugs into the property? Wasn't there security?' asks Charles.

Cartledge rises to object again. 'What's the relevance, my Lord? None of this is relevant to the issue in this case, which is whether the prisoner killed Christine Bailey.'

It's a hopeless objection, and all the lawyers present know it. *He's really rattled*, thinks Charles.

'Of course it's relevant!' retorts Charles impatiently. 'Our case is that Pilcher, through the agency of Feder and on the orders of Quigley, supplied the drugs that killed Christine Bailey. I'm coming to that now. It's also relevant to the credibility of these officers.'

Cartledge has sat down again even before Pullman gives his ruling.

'I agree,' says the judge. 'You may continue, Mr Holborne.'

'So, how did the drugs get in?' repeats Charles.

'Mr Pilcher had some deal going with Frankie Perry, the guy who ran the security. He allowed Fed to come in and out without it being recorded.'

'And did Fed deliver the drugs directly to you?'

'Sometimes. If I wasn't around, one of the roadies would take them for me.'

'Thank you. Did any of these police officers tell you where the drugs were coming from?'

'Yeah. Mr Pilcher joked once that they'd made a huge coke bust the night before, so they were starting a special offer on cocaine. They were street drugs they'd seized.'

'Thank you. Now, I'm going to ask you some questions about Christine Bailey. When did you first meet her?'

'Backstage, after the Astoria concert. There was a long line of kids, and she wanted Johnny's autograph.'

'Did you get the autograph for her?'

'I took her with me to the green room, got her the autograph and then offered her a drink.'

'What happened then?'

'We were talking, drinking and so forth. The buses were being loaded and I asked if she wanted to come back to Kingston Grange.'

'Did you know her age?'

'No. I swear. She said her name was Karen and she showed me ID. I thought she was eighteen.'

'What happened then?'

'We got on the bus, still talking. She was nice. We got on well.'

'What happened when you got back to Kingston Grange?' asks Charles.

The atmosphere in court changes again. The levity caused by the judge's joke has gone altogether. The jury members, the crowds in the public gallery, the journalists and everyone else in the packed room are leaning forward, listening intently. Several jury members have pens poised over notebooks. Everyone senses that, finally, the truth may be about to emerge.

'We were drinking, dancing, having a good time.'

'Did you and Christine take any drugs?'

'Here we are again,' intervenes Pullman.

'My Lord?' queries Charles.

'I have to give this witness the required warning too, don't I? If it carries on like this I'm going to start handing out printed sheets to all your witnesses.'

'I agree, it is unusual for witnesses to implicate themselves in serious criminality to prevent a miscarriage of justice to someone else, especially a virtual stranger,' replies Charles with a touch of irony. 'Perhaps that's something the jury will take into account when considering if these witnesses are truthful.'

Charles is well aware that Wyatt's sudden public-spiritedness has nothing to do with protecting Bobby Gold. He has been forced to choose the lesser of two evils: a charge of murder against him personally, or coming clean. But Charles will take the win, however it may be delivered.

'I've already had to warn Mr Cartledge about making speeches during the course of the evidence,' says Pullman, 'so that's enough of that.'

Pullman turns to Wyatt in the witness box and gives him the same warning he gave his brother. Wyatt acknowledges that he has understood.

Charles repeats his question. 'So, Mr Blaise, did you or Christine take any drugs?'

A few seconds pass before Wyatt answers. 'Yes. I made a pot of mandrake tea.'

'Mandrake tea?' asks Charles.

'Yeah. The police had seized some leaf but Pilcher didn't know what it was, so I got it real cheap. It looks like dried tree leaves and you soak 'em in hot water.'

'And what's the effect of drinking this tea?' asks Charles.

'It relaxes you and you see these incredible visions like, you know, hallucinations. I've used it a couple of times in the past. I thought it was safe.'

'What happened then?'

'Well, we were getting kinda friendly so we went upstairs to one of the bedrooms.'

'Did you have sex with her?'

'Yeah. But I thought she was eighteen, right? And she was drinking and smoking with the rest of us. I swear, I had no idea she was only fifteen. And, honest to God, she needed no persuasion. I mean, I began to get suspicious when I realised … well…' He looks up at the public gallery, embarrassed. 'You know, when I saw evidence that maybe this was her first time.'

'I see,' says Charles. 'Did you take heroin?'

'No.'

'Did you give heroin to Christine?'

'Absolutely not.'

'Have you taken heroin in the past?'

'Yeah, but I've been clean for a coupla years. Johnny paid for me to have rehab.'

'Okay. Carry on.'

'We both fell asleep … or, maybe, passed out. I woke at around three, real thirsty, so I went downstairs to get some water. I was kinda out of it, and when I came back up I got into the bed from the other side and tripped over something. I put on the light, and saw it was Christine. I thought at first she'd just fallen out of bed.'

'You said that was around three. Are you sure it wasn't nearer four?'

'I'm sure. I looked at the bedside clock.'

'Okay. Then what?'

'I tried to wake her up, to get her back into bed. She was cold, and the floor was wet. But I couldn't wake her. Then I started to get frightened, so I checked her breathing.'

'And?'

'She was alive.'

There is a communal gasp of surprise from the onlookers.

'Are you sure?' asks Charles.

'Yeah. I also felt her pulse, in her neck. She was unconscious, but she was definitely alive. And there was no hypodermic in her arm.'

'No hypodermic?'

'Absolutely not. I woulda seen it.'

'Okay. What happened then?'

'I ran to get Johnny and told him what had happened. I tried to drag him to see Christine, but he resisted. He didn't want to go. He gets wound up very easy. He panics and hyperventilates. He's no good in an emergency, so I told him to go back to his room, that I would deal with it.'

'What were you going to do?'

'I knew she needed an ambulance, but I was worried about the drugs. So I called Mr Pilcher. He was the only cop I knew, and I thought he'd help. His ass was on the line too.'

'Did you speak to him?'

'No. He wasn't available, but I was put through to Mr Quigley. I didn't know what to say to him. I was hanging up when he said he was a close colleague of Mr Pilcher and he knew we were in business. He said I could talk freely. So then I knew he was in on it. I told him what had happened and he said to do nothing, he was on his way. He asked me to put Frankie Perry on the phone, which I did.'

'Do you know what he and Perry said?'

'No, but Perry went down to the gate.'

'What happened next?'

'I stayed with Christine. She was breathing, but I still couldn't wake her and I was starting to panic. It took ages for Mr Quigley to get there and all the time I kept thinking I should call an ambulance. But I was scared.'

'What happened when Mr Quigley arrived?'

'He came upstairs and into the bedroom. He bent down by Christine. Then he said he wanted to talk to Mr Gold. I said Bobby had gone home ages ago and we had to get an ambulance. He said "All in good time" but he'd speak to Johnny first. So I took him to Johnny's bedroom.'

'What did he say?'

'I don't know. He told me to wait outside. Then he came out and said everything was going to be okay. He got on the phone and started making arrangements.'

'What did you do?'

'I went back to the library.'

'Why?' asks Charles.

'I needed a drink and there was a drinks cabinet in there, with brandy and whisky.'

'What happened next?'

'I must've fallen asleep.'

'You fell asleep?' says Charles, astonished. 'With an unconscious girl in the house?'

Wyatt hangs his head. 'I know it looks bad, but I was totally wasted. I'd done booze and weed even before the tea.'

'Very well. And then?'

Charles risks a glance at the jury. All twelve of them are leaning forward, eyes glued to Wyatt, transfixed by his evidence.

'I was woken up by someone screaming.'

'Time?'

''Bout four, I guess.'

'What did you do?'

'I ran back to the bedroom where Christine and I…' Wyatt shies away from finishing that sentence. He starts again. 'Mrs Gonzales was there, her hands over her mouth, standing between Christine and the bed. I looked around, 'cos I sorta expected Mr Quigley to be there, but he wasn't.'

'What did you do?'

'I pretended it was the first time I'd seen Christine.'

'Why?'

'Because I could see immediately that she had a syringe in her arm, and she was dead. Also the room had been cleared. So all the bottles, glasses and ashtrays had gone, and the surfaces had been wiped down. The room was clean. Mrs Gonzales was very upset. I told her I'd call the police and she should go back to bed. I found Perry and asked him where Mr Quigley had gone. He said not to worry, he'd call him.'

'Do you know where Mr Quigley had gone?' asks Charles.

'No, but he was back again five minutes later. He came up the stairs and pretended to go into the bedroom for the first time. Johnny was on the landing. Quigley came out of the room. He looked at Johnny and said he was very sorry, but Christine had died.'

Charles allows that piece of evidence to sink in with the jury before speaking again.

'Thank you, Mr Blaise. Now, at any time while you were staying at Kingston Grange, were you aware of any other members of the crew taking heroin?'

'No. I guess a couple of the guys may have shot up in the past, and a few smoke every now and then, but I wouldn't say any of the guys on the tour had a habit, know what I mean?

But it's possible, I guess. I wasn't the only one dealing with Fed. Others put in orders every now and then.'

'So it's possible that one of them might have ordered some heroin, assuming the police property store had some in stock?'

'It's possible, yeah.'

'What happened then?'

'Quigley started making calls and soon the place was full of police.'

'Did you recognise any of the other officers who arrived that night?'

'Yes. Mr Pilcher. He was the next to arrive. Mr Quigley gave him a holdall and he left again.'

'Do you know what was in the holdall?'

'No, sir.'

Charles runs his finger down the handwritten statement to make sure he has missed nothing. He looks up. 'One last question, I think, Mr Blaise. Since these events, have you had an opportunity to speak to your brother about them?'

'Sure.'

'Have you discovered who your brother thinks was responsible for Christine Bailey's death?'

'I object,' intervenes Cartledge, getting to his feet. 'Who Johnny Blaise believes was responsible for Christine Bailey's death is completely irrelevant. That's a question for the jury alone, not this witness or his brother.'

'Mr Holborne?' invites Pullman.

'I'm leading this evidence not because of its truth. Indeed, just the contrary. My case is that Johnny Blaise's supposition was actually wrong. So I'm leading it to establish only his state of mind and to explain his actions.'

'Yes, I thought so. Mr Cartledge, it would be admissible, would it not, if it was made clear to the jury that this opinion has nothing to do with Mr Gold's guilt or innocence, which is a matter for them only, but to explain something Mr Johnny Blaise did?'

'But, my Lord, this witness is being asked to speculate on who a different witness thought was responsible for a crime! It's opinion evidence, it's double hearsay, and it usurps the function of the jury!'

'No, sorry, Mr Cartledge, I'm against you. Mr Holborne is leading this evidence purely for the purposes of establishing Johnny Blaise's state of mind. I'll give the jury a suitable warning, but it's admissible according to the rules of evidence and I'm going to allow it.' He turns to Wyatt. 'You may answer the question.'

'He thought I'd done it,' says Wyatt, simply. 'Johnny thought I'd killed her. That's why he paid the money.' He turns to his brother who sits, still handcuffed to Sloane, behind the defence barristers. 'But I swear on my life, Johnny, it ain't true. That girl was alive when I first saw her. And I ain't touched heroin for nigh-on three years!'

Again, Charles waits for the import of the words to sink in.

'Yes, thank you, Mr Blaise,' he says. 'Please remain there.'

# CHAPTER THIRTY-NINE

'So, you are an admitted rapist then, Mr Blaise?' starts Cartledge, his voice dripping with scorn.

'She was fifteen, that's true, and I was just too old for the Romeo and Juliet defence,' replies Wyatt evenly.

'Romeo and Juliet defence?'

'Yeah. It ain't a felony if you're within three years of the girl. She was a fortnight short of her sixteenth birthday, and I was a coupla months past nineteen. We should've waited another two weeks.'

'But it was a crime, wasn't it?'

'According to the judge.'

'And you admit dealing illegal drugs?'

'I don't know what you mean by dealing.'

'You acquired drugs which you then supplied to other members of the group, the crew and, on the night in question, to Christine Bailey. Correct?'

'I guess.'

'Well, that's a serious criminal offence, both here and in the US. And, of course, you knew that, right?'

'I guess.'

'You guess,' says Cartledge wryly. 'And you were perfectly happy to take part, so you say, in a cover-up regarding Miss Bailey's death.' Wyatt does not respond. 'Well, Mr Blaise? You've just admitted it. I don't for one second accept that DCI Quigley *did* offer to cover up Mr Gold's crime. I'm looking at what *you* were prepared to do. You tell us you were willing to cover up the entire thing, yes?'

'At first. Not now.'

'You were happy to lie your way out of the death of an underage girl to whom you'd supplied illegal drugs and with whom you'd just had sex, right?'

'I wasn't happy about any of it.'

'Perhaps not. But the cover-up was designed to protect you from the consequences of your crimes, right?'

'Yes, and the consequences of Mr Pilcher and Mr Quigley's crimes.'

'And to carry that off, you'd have told lies to a court of law, right? You'd have had no choice.'

'I don't know. I didn't think that far ahead. I was frightened, and there was Mr Quigley telling me it was all gonna be okay. So I agreed.'

'Keeping your name out of it was going to require you to tell lies,' insists Cartledge.

'I guess.'

'Thank you. Finally. So, to summarise: on one side we have an ex-heroin junkie; a convicted rapist; a drug dealer; and someone who admits he was perfectly prepared to lie to a court to keep himself out of trouble. On the other side we have a very senior, distinguished and courageous member of the Metropolitan Police with a long career of public service behind him, corroborated by another senior officer. Why on earth should this jury believe *you*?'

Wyatt colours. 'I know it looks bad, but I'm telling the truth.'

'So you say. Let's go back to your heroin addiction,' says Cartledge.

'That was years ago.'

'Of all the people at Kingston Grange, can you give us the name of any other person who was using heroin?'

*That's a clever question,* thinks Charles. *Even if he knows of someone, he's not going to name them. Which leaves Wyatt the only one with a history of heroin use.*

'No, sir, I can't. But I'm clean. I ain't touched heroin for three years.'

'You see, Mr Blaise, I suggest this is all a smokescreen to divert attention from the person who actually supplied the drugs and allowed young girls into the property to be abused.' Cartledge points dramatically to Gold in the dock. 'Bobby Gold, the defendant.'

'No, that's not right. I've told you the truth.'

'It was Bobby Gold who allowed these young women in, and who permitted the use of drugs. He didn't care about the risk to Christine Bailey. He was responsible for her death, isn't that right? Even if he didn't administer the heroin himself.'

Charles jumps up. 'Is the Crown abandoning the charge of murder, then?' he challenges.

'I will address that question in my final speech, my Lord,' replies Cartledge. 'Until then, the Crown's position remains as set out in my opening.'

'Please repeat the question to the witness,' orders Pullman, apparently unwilling to be sidetracked from the evidence.

'Certainly, my Lord.' Cartledge turns to Wyatt again. 'I suggest it was Bobby Gold who allowed these young women into the property, and who condoned the use of drugs. I suggest that it was Bobby Gold who was responsible for Christine Bailey's death. I suggest the story you've just trotted out is a complete fabrication.'

'No. He had nothing to do with it. He was just the fall guy Mr Quigley and Mr Pilcher chose.'

Cartledge resumes his seat.

The judge looks over his bench at Charles, awaiting his decision on re-examination, but Charles is busy writing in his notebook. Despite his resistance, Cartledge does indeed appear to have abandoned the suggestion that Gold actually administered the heroin, which destroys the last vestige of his murder case. Charles is making a note to remind him to focus on this in his final jury address.

Bateman leans forward and touches his shoulder. 'Pullman's waiting.'

Charles looks up and stands. 'I apologise, my Lord.'

He hesitates a moment longer before addressing Wyatt. 'Mr Blaise, I've only one further question for you. I suspect it's a question the jury would like answered, too.'

Charles does this occasionally when he wants to be absolutely certain the jury are particularly focused on his next question. However, in this case, it isn't a ploy. He genuinely believes the jury want to know one last thing.

'Mr Cartledge pointed out that in the course of your evidence you admitted serious offences: underage sex with Christine Bailey, and supplying illegal drugs to her and certain group members. The judge explained that you were under no obligation to answer, and yet you did so anyway. So, just to be absolutely clear about this: you do realise, don't you, that you are likely to face criminal charges as a result of your giving evidence here today?'

'Yeah, of course I do.'

'Why then? Why have you admitted these offences, when you were told by the judge you didn't have to answer such questions?'

Wyatt looks across the court towards his brother. 'Johnny thought I'd killed her. And that guy there, the one who arrested me, Mr Olney, he also thought I'd killed her. I don't see I have a choice. I have to tell the truth, whatever the consequences. I don't know what's going to happen to Mr Gold, but I sure don't want to be next in line to be accused of Christine's murder!'

'Thank you, Mr Blaise. Does your Lordship have any questions?'

'No, thank you. Any further witnesses?'

'I'd like a quick word with my junior to decide. May I have a few seconds? It won't require your Lordship to rise.'

'Yes,' replies the judge.

Charles turns to Bateman and leans close to him.

'Gold?' asks Bateman.

Charles frowns. 'I suppose so. I was hoping we might get away without calling him.'

He casts a glance towards Gold in the dock. For the first time since the trial began five days earlier, the promoter doesn't look as if he has the weight of the world on his shoulders. He is looking up at the public gallery towards his wife and daughters, and smiling. They are grinning down at him and one of the girls, the younger one, is giving her father a shy thumbs-up.

'It's just that I was hoping —' starts Charles.

He stops. There, standing at the back of the court by the doors, is the imposing form of Billy Munday. He nods at Charles and inclines his head to the left. Standing next to him is a man of middling height with a round face, a flop of straight brown hair hanging over his forehead and a cleft chin. He wears a brown duffel coat and looks like an art student.

Without seeking permission, Charles leaves counsel's benches and hurries up the aisle towards the door. He has a quick whispered word with Munday, takes a scrap of paper from him, and returns to his seat.

'Sorry about that, my Lord. The defence calls…' He looks down at the paper in his hand. 'Vinnie Todman.'

The young man next to Munday looks puzzled at his name being called and seems reluctant to move. Munday gives him a gentle shove to set him off down the aisle. He reaches halfway before his footsteps falter and halt. The usher, waiting by the witness box, beckons him to continue. Charles sees that the young man has something in his hands.

'Stand there,' says the usher, indicating the witness box, and the young man steps tentatively up. 'Religion?' she asks.

'I … I don't know why I'm here,' says the man, to no one in particular.

Pullman leans over and addresses him. 'Don't you worry about that. Just answer the usher's question.'

'Erm … I don't really have a religion, actually.'

'Affirmation, then,' directs the judge, and the usher swaps laminated cards and holds out a different one.

'Read the words from the card, please,' she directs.

The young man reads the words off the card and hands it back. He gazes around the court, looking for the person who is going to tell him what's going on.

'Your name is Vinnie Todman, is that right?' says Charles.

The man looks around, identifies Charles as the origin of the question, and replies, 'Vincent. Vincent Robert Todman.'

'What's your profession, please, Mr Todman?' asks Charles.

'I'm a photographer,' replies Todman. There is a fresh-faced, naïve air about him.

'And your professional address, please?'

'Fourth floor, sixteen Denmark Street.'

'Do you know anything about this case?'

'Not really,' replies Todman in a Cockney accent. 'Course, I know Bobby's on trial. What I don't understand is how it involves me. A bloke came to the studio this morning, said I had to come to court and more or less dragged me down here.'

'Are you saying you're not here voluntarily?' intervenes Pullman.

'No … not really. It's all a bit of a surprise, that's all,' says Todman.

'Do you specialise in any particular type of photography work?' asks Charles, anxious to keep going in case Pullman takes it into his head to prevent Todman giving evidence.

'I work in the music industry. I do photo shoots of groups, stills mainly, but occasional thirty-five mill.'

'And in that capacity have you been photographing Johnny Blaise and the Hellraisers during their tour?' asks Charles.

'Yeah. Bobby took me on for the whole tour. I did the publicity shots, and I've been backstage at all the gigs.'

'Did you ever go to Kingston Grange?'

'Yeah. I've been there quite a lot the last few weeks. I usually go back on the bus after the concerts.'

'And were you there on the night that Christine Bailey's body was discovered?'

'Well, I didn't know about it at the time, but yeah. I wasn't allowed upstairs, but I was there when the police arrived.'

'Did you stay at the property after that?' asks Charles.

'Not for long. They didn't want a statement from me, so I went home.'

'What time did you leave?'

'I dunno. It was very late. The police took a while to decide who to talk to. A bit before five, maybe?'

'That's five in the morning?'

'Yeah.'

'As you were leaving, did you speak to anyone?'

'Only Frankie Perry. He was standing in the porch having a smoke.'

'And did you speak to him?' repeats Charles.

'Briefly. He said "You still here?", and I explained I'd been taking fly-on-the-wall pics, shots of the group and the crew having fun in the pool. Got some good 'uns. But I was still there when the fuzz turned up, and they wouldn't let me leave at first.'

'Anything else?'

'I asked him what was going on upstairs and he tapped his nose, you know, like it was a secret.'

'Did you have your camera with you?'

'I had everything with me, in a big case. I never leave it. It's too valuable.'

'So, what happened then?'

'Well, actually, I realised I needed the loo, so I asked him if he could keep an eye on my stuff while I popped back in.'

'Did he agree?'

'Yeah, he was fine. He said he was waiting for someone.'

'So, you left your case with him while you went back inside the house?'

'I did. Only for a minute.'

'Did that include your camera?'

'Yes. I handed it to him.'

'Thank you. Now, before you came here this morning, did that man —' Charles nods towards the back of the court where Billy Munday still stands — 'ask you to do anything?'

'Yeah. He asked to see the last roll of film I took that night. I told him I hadn't developed it yet.'

'Why not?'

'The stuff I took that evening, round the pool, was for fun, really. I mean, I thought I'd find a home for the photos, but I'd not been commissioned to take 'em. I was sort of moonlighting.'

'So, have you now developed that last roll of film?'

'I have,' replies the photographer, and he holds up what he was carrying, a sheaf of photos.

'May I see them, please?' asks Charles.

Todman hands them to the usher, who brings them to Charles. Charles skims through them. Some are blurred and show only indistinct moving figures around a swimming pool. Others show musicians posing, grinning at the camera, raising glasses in toasts. Charles comes across several showing naked figures, male and female, running, diving and swimming in the pool. He leafs through until he reaches the middle of the glossy bundle and then halts. He studies one photo for a moment, discards the rest on the bench and approaches Cartledge. Giving the QC the professional courtesy which the prosecutor has failed completely to show him, he offers the photograph. Cartledge half-rises from his position, looks briefly, and resumes his seat without a word or even a glance at Charles himself.

'Please would you show this photograph to the witness,' says Charles to the usher.

While that is happening Charles addresses the judge. 'There is only one copy at present, but I will endeavour to get more as soon as possible,' he says.

He returns his attention to the photographer. 'Mr Todman, would you please describe for us what that photograph shows?'

'Yeah. sure. But I should explain that I never took this photo.'

'Did you take the others?'

'Oh, yes. The ones before it on the roll were taken that night at the house and by the pool. I took the ones after it over the next couple of days.'

'Right, then. What does that particular exposure show?'

'It's a picture of the inside of a holdall, a leather bag of some sort.'

'And can you see what's in the holdall?'

'Yeah, money. Tons of money. You can make out fivers, tenners and twenties. It's stuffed. There's got to be thousands in there.'

'Perhaps the photograph could be shown to the jury, my Lord?'

'Yes, certainly. We'll call it defence exhibit VT1.'

Charles waits as the photograph is taken to the first jury member and examined. Charles feels a tug on his gown and spins round.

'How did you know?' whispers Bateman hoarsely. 'You couldn't possibly have known!'

Charles bends to reply quietly. 'No, I didn't *know* but I thought it a fair chance. Remember Perry saying he kept a full account of every time Pilcher took him hooky clothes? How much he got for them, how much he paid Pilcher? He's a meticulous man, and that was his insurance policy.'

'Yes, but —'

'I asked myself what I'd have done in his place, being told to hand over a heavy holdall to Pilcher that night, and knowing there were stolen police drugs that I'd let in, and a dead girl upstairs. I'd have wanted insurance, more than ever. And what did he have to hand? A photographer with a camera.'

The photograph is passed slowly along the top rank of jurors and then back along the bottom rank. Several of them, having seen the photograph, look up and nod directly at Charles.

*Game over*, he thinks.

He asks his final question of Vinnie Todman. 'Do you have any idea how that photograph, the one of the money, came into existence?'

'Not at first. I couldn't understand it. It was a surprise when I developed the roll this morning. But there's only one explanation. The only time the camera was out my hands was when Frankie was looking after it, on the porch, that night. The only person who could have taken it … is Frankie Perry.'

There is a sudden noise from behind Charles. He looks round. DCI Quigley is pushing past the solicitors and others sitting on his bench, trampling on feet, disturbing their papers and shoving them out of the way in his haste to get out.

*He's bolting!* thinks Charles.

He has time to register that, for a split-second, DI Pilcher looks shocked, his eyes wide, before he too leaps to his feet and starts pushing his way out of the row at the far end.

The commotion has attracted the attention of everyone in court, but at first no one seems capable of reacting.

'Stop them!' shout Charles and Pullman simultaneously, but it is unnecessary.

Sloane steps in front of the hurrying Quigley and two uniformed officers appear immediately behind him. There is a hitch in Quigley's stride as he realises his route to the door is blocked, but he accelerates again.

'Get out of my way!' he shouts. Sloane stands firm. 'That's an order!' he says, and he shoves the Irishman hard in the shoulder.

He almost gets past but Sloane recovers, grabs a handful of his senior officer's departing arm and hangs on. Quigley spins round, aiming a punch at Sloane's head, but the DS sways backwards and the blow passes harmlessly in front of his face.

Before Quigley knows what is happening, he's at the bottom of a rugby scrum and Sloane's handcuffs have been snapped around his wrists.

'Denis Quigley,' says Sloane, slightly breathlessly, 'I am arresting you on suspicion of corruption, attempting to pervert the course of justice, the murder of Christine Bailey and the unlawful supply of drugs. You are not obliged to say anything unless you wish to do so, but anything you say will be taken down and may be used in evidence against you.'

At the same time, on the other side of the courtroom, DCI Olney and two others have got hold of Pilcher and are still attempting to wrestle him to the floor. He is a lot stronger than his superior officer and it's taking more effort, but they eventually subdue him and Olney administers the caution.

Charles hasn't moved.

Cartledge sits heavily in his seat and throws his pen onto the bench. 'Fuck,' he says, loudly enough to be overheard by everyone close by.

'Game over,' repeats Charles, this time out loud.

# CHAPTER FORTY

'Come!'

His Honour Judge Pullman's associate stands back and Charles steps into the judge's chambers, the door closing softly behind him.

It is two days since Pullman directed the jury to acquit Bobby Gold. It isn't unusual for counsel to be invited into a judge's chambers for a cup of tea or perhaps a drink at the end of a difficult case. It's a way of ensuring the barristers are no longer still spitting fire at one another when they leave court. However, Charles was not surprised when Pullman extended no invitation after Gold's acquittal. Firstly, he was obviously unwell and, despite his vigour in the courtroom, the case clearly took a lot out of him. Secondly, nothing could have persuaded Charles to bury the hatchet with the supercilious and arrogant Cartledge, and he guessed Pullman was aware of that.

So the parties left court and dispersed, some to old lives and some to new. Bobby and his cousin, Serban, headed to Brixton for a family celebration; Wyatt departed in a police car for further interviews and consideration of charges; Johnny, minus his passport, was taken back to Kingston Grange on police bail, with instructions not to leave the country; and the Team members, Quigley, Pilcher and Feder, together with two others who didn't feature in the Gold frame-up, disappeared altogether, presumably into police interview rooms and cells, from whence they were shortly charged with multiple offences, from conspiracy to burgle all the way up to murder.

Operation Coathanger went public and was splashed across the newspapers and broadcast news. DCI Olney resumed his former role, happy in the knowledge that his pension was safe but disappointed that it would cost him a further eighteen months in post before he could claim it. And Sean Sloane resumed life at West Hendon police station (with a commendation), where he looked forward to a period of less exciting routine police work.

As for the barristers, Charles and Bateman shared a celebratory carafe of claret in El Vino's to honour their victory, and then each headed home, Bateman to a date with someone called Samantha (of whom he revealed very little, except that she had "sensational legs") and Charles back to Wren Street to pick up where he and Sally had left off wedding planning.

The case had lasted only four court days, but it seemed much longer.

It was therefore something of a surprise when Charles received Pullman's late invitation, after the dust had settled.

This isn't the first time Charles has been in this behind-the-scenes room at the Old Bailey. Several years earlier he was on the verge of being suspended, probably disbarred, on disciplinary charges threatened by Pullman himself. Charles hated him then with such a visceral fury that even thinking of the man kept him awake at night and brought him out in a sweat. But a lot of water has gone under that particular judicial bridge, and Charles enters the room with genuine sadness that the Gold prosecution will mark the end of Pullman's illustrious career.

'Ah, Holborne, thanks for popping in,' says the judge.

He is wearing a simple grey suit, a shirt and a tie. Without his court robes he looks diminished, older and frail. Charles sees for the first time that, without his wig, Pullman is now totally bald, his scalp shiny and blotched.

*Cancer treatment, I guess*, thinks Charles.

On the desk behind the judge Charles notes a glass bottle with a rubber pipette dispenser. He has seen them before, in Sunshine Court, on the dressing tables of terminally ill residents in need of relief from severe pain.

'May I introduce you to my sister, Margaret?' says the judge.

Charles spins round, unaware that anyone else was in the room. Sitting beneath the tall window is an angular lady of similar age to Pullman, perhaps in her early seventies, wearing a hat and clutching a handbag on her lap. Charles strides over and shakes her hand.

'How do you do?' he says.

'Margaret is here to help me pack up my last few things and drive me to my new home.' He indicates the cardboard boxes behind his desk. 'I'm going to have a little brandy, and wondered if you'd like to join me,' offers Pullman.

'I'd be very happy to, Judge,' replies Charles.

'Pull up a chair, then.'

Charles does so while the judge pours amber liquid into shot glasses. Pullman drags another chair out, so the two men are facing one another, their knees almost touching.

'I hear on the grapevine that the Gold case is likely to be your last,' opens Charles.

'Yes, I'm afraid so,' replies Pullman. 'I thought I might be able to continue for a little longer, but it took it out of me and I sense in my waters that I haven't very long. I've been defying my doctors' predictions for some weeks. Margaret has insisted that sea air is what's required, and I know she'll make me comfortable. I'm not as lucky as you, Holborne; I've never had a "little woman" at home to care for me.'

Charles smiles, knowing exactly how Sally would have responded to his characterisation of her as "a little woman". He's also surprised that Pullman knows anything at all about his home circumstances. That must have shown in his expression, because Pullman smiles knowingly.

'You can't keep secrets at the Bar, or the Bench,' he says. 'And as you know, there's little to do on circuit in the evenings except drink too much and gossip. You won't be surprised to learn that you and your … situation … was a fertile topic of conversation.'

Charles sips his brandy which, he notes in passing, is very good, and says, 'I suppose you disapprove, Judge.'

'Well, it wasn't how we did things in my day, but my day is almost done. It's a new world, I can see, and sometimes I'm not sorry I won't be around to experience much more of it. But, no, I don't actually disapprove. One of the things I admire about you, Charles — I hope you'll allow me a little familiarity, given the circumstances — is your refusal to compromise who you are. I know you've had a lot of additional hurdles to clear compared to your peers, and yet you have succeeded without changing your nature.'

'That's very kind of you to say, Judge, but it's not entirely true. I changed my name from Horowitz at the beginning of my career to camouflage my background. My mother had much to say on that subject, and in one respect she was undoubtedly right: it made absolutely no difference to how I was perceived at the Bar; it merely upset my family. Her in particular.'

'Because you remained the same person, despite the change of name. True to yourself.'

'Perhaps.'

There is a prolonged silence. Margaret has not spoken or moved from her position since Charles entered the room.

Pullman coughs and clears his throat. 'I wanted to say something to you which I hope you won't misinterpret. Please forgive me if this comes out a little clumsily.' He pauses, apparently unsure how to proceed. 'I am a product of my generation and of my class. I see now that many of the attitudes which were current when I grew up, and which I never questioned, are ... outdated. One of them relates to the Jewish race.' He looks down and Charles notes that his grey complexion has reddened slightly. The judge is embarrassed. 'I took those attitudes into my professional life. I never met a Jew until I came to the Bar, and I feel I did not give you or your co-religionists a fair hearing.'

Charles, now extremely embarrassed and wishing to bring this odd confession to an end, is himself blushing. 'Really, Judge, you owe me no —'

Pullman interrupts. 'No, please allow me to finish. I was really very unfair to you when we had that difficult case, you remember, the solicitor, Robeson? I know I apologised afterwards; I think I may even have said something in open court —'

'You did.'

'But I never apologised in person, like this. It continues to bother me and I am, truly, sorry about some of the things I said. You exemplify some of the finest attributes of the independent Bar, and I didn't want us to part, for what will probably be the last time, without telling you that. You are a first-rate advocate — sometimes with a novel approach, it must be said — but a first-rate advocate, and you are entirely honest, both in how you present yourself and also in the discharge of your professional duties.'

Charles wonders if Pullman would be so fulsome in his praise if he was aware of some of the darker moments in Charles's past. Nonetheless, he replies with as much grace as he can muster, while conscious of no little hypocrisy. 'That's very kind of you to say so, Judge. I appreciate it.'

'And so —' the judge reaches behind him to his desk and picks up a sealed envelope — 'I want you to have this.' He hands it to Charles. 'No, don't open it yet. It's a bit of forward planning. I know you considered applying for silk a year or two ago, and it's none of my business whether you apply again. If you do, I can think of few barristers who deserve it more, but I shan't be available in April to say so. So that envelope contains two letters, the first to Gerald Gardiner, and the second to Hubert Parker.'

Pullman has just named the Lord Chancellor, the judge and member of the Cabinet in charge of silk appointments, and the Lord Chief Justice, the most senior criminal judge in the country.

'If you don't apply, so be it. Many very talented advocates choose to remain juniors until ripe old age. In that case, you may open the envelope and frame the contents for your grandchildren, if you're so minded. On the other hand, I hope you will apply, because the world has changed and we need independent-minded chaps like you, drawn from a more diverse pool of talent. And the contents of that envelope might be of some assistance.'

Charles turns it over in his hands. He doesn't know how to answer, and he doesn't trust his voice.

'I don't know what to say, Judge. That is uncommonly kind of you. And, in fact, I am thinking of applying this year.'

'Excellent,' replies the judge, standing rather unsteadily. 'Now, we must get on if we are to miss the rush-hour traffic and reach Bournemouth tonight. And Margaret is a very cautious driver.'

Charles drains his glass and puts it on the desk. The judge has his hand out to shake Charles's. Legal etiquette prevents barristers shaking one another's hands and, although Pullman is a judge, he also remains a member of the Bar. Nonetheless, Charles envelops the judge's skeletal hand in his great paw, and shakes it warmly.

'Best of luck,' concludes Pullman.

'And you, judge,' replies Charles, a twinkle in his eyes. 'Whatever the future may hold.'

'Ah, the last and final judgment. Yes, well, I'm moderately optimistic on that score.'

He takes a couple of steps towards the door before his knees buckle. He gets a hand to his desk and Charles manages to grab him from the other side, preventing him from falling to the carpet. Charles steadies him as Margaret jumps up and drags over the chair Pullman has been using. He sinks gratefully into it, his entire body shaking.

'Are you all right, Judge?' asks Charles redundantly.

It takes Pullman a moment or two to gather the strength to answer. He waves Charles's concern aside. 'Fine, fine,' he gasps. His grey face shines with perspiration and he is panting. He flutters his hand again in a dismissive gesture, indicating that Charles should depart. Charles suddenly feels like an intruder.

'Of course,' he says, taking his leave.


It is the last time Charles sees His Honour Judge Pullman. As he arrives in Chambers two days later, Barbara takes him to one side and tells him quietly that the judge died the night before.

As is the custom following the death of prominent members of the Bar or Bench, a eulogy is given in open court, and Charles joins other barristers from Chambers and from the Inn generally who knew Pullman, to walk in procession from the Temple to the Old Bailey.

Both Bar and Bench are packed and there is standing room only. Charles has never seen so many senior judges in one place at the same time, all wearing formal ceremonial robes. The Bar is also very well represented, with some members of Pullman's former chambers wearing mourning bands.

As a junior from different chambers, Charles is not given an opportunity to speak and would not, in any event, have considered it appropriate. Nonetheless, he listens to and agrees with everything said by Richard Marven Hale Everett QC, the Leader of the South-Eastern Circuit, who leads the tributes.

'My Lords. Many of the members of the Bar attending this eulogy will remember His Honour Judge Pullman as a tenacious and vigorous prosecutor, as prosecutors should be. Indeed, some of us remember the spontaneous celebration that broke out at HM Prison Wormwood Scrubs when it was learned that His Honour had been appointed to the Bench and would no longer be prosecuting at the Bar. Although, it must be said, the celebration ended prematurely when the inmates discovered that he was destined to be the criminal judge on their patch.

'His Honour Judge Pullman was always a demanding judge. Rather like the brandy he so enjoyed, in his early days on the Bench he was very robust, perhaps a little unrefined around the edges, and he could give advocates quite a headache. However, years of experience prompted a distinct softening on the palate, although the unwary were liable still to be caught out.

'It is not the job of a judge to be friendly. It can be a difficult office. His Honour Judge Pullman had a lightning-quick intellect and gave all his cases, both at Bar and Bench, careful consideration. He remained rightly scornful of those advocates he found unprepared or, worse still, cavalier about their responsibilities.

'At a eulogy it is very easy to cloak a judge's reputation in angels' wings and overlook the range of opinion that was held about his qualites. It is the habit, however, of the Bar to meet with colleagues at lunch or after court hours and, over a cup of tea or something stronger, to reflect on the day's business. That often includes the wisdom of the judge who would occasionally succumb to what might be called an optimistic submission; the insensitivity of the judge who always did the opposite; the judge who came into court looking to pick a fight; or the most courteous of judges who nonetheless for some reason takes against you, your client, your case and every submission you make from the minute you first open your mouth.

'His Honour Judge Pullman was not exempt from such discussions. But the pretty much universal opinion of the Criminal Bar was that his rulings were impeccable and his sentences unimpeachable. If a judge, after many years on the Bench, has acquired and kept the reputation of just about getting it right just about all of the time, he and the members of his family should rightly be very proud, as we all pay tribute to a great servant to our profession, whom we have lost too soon.

'On behalf of this court and all who have gathered here today, I extend our deepest condolences to his family and loved ones, in particular his twin sister, Margaret, who some of us had the pleasure to meet over the years. Their loss is shared by all of us in the legal profession, and we honour his memory with profound gratitude and respect.

'We now observe a moment of silence to reflect on the life and service of His Honour Judge Pullman.'

# CHAPTER FORTY-ONE

Sally opens the curtains in the master bedroom and gazes out onto the gated gardens opposite. For most of the month it has been cooler than would be expected for the end of September, with cold sunny days interspersed with grey, drizzly spells. Today, however, the skies are clear and it is warm, without a breath of breeze. They have been lucky.

She leaves the bedroom and pads along to the spare room where Charles is sleeping. She knocks on the door.

'Charles? Are you awake?'

'Yes,' comes the answer.

'Can I come in?'

'Course you can. It was you who banished me here.'

She opens the door  Charles is sitting up in the spare bed, reading that morning's newspaper, a mug of tea in his hand.

'I didn't banish you,' she protests, sliding into bed and snuggling up to him. 'I thought we should give a nod to tradition, and not sleep together on the night before our wedding.'

'Tea?' he asks, folding his paper and preparing to get out of bed.

'In a mo. Do you still want to walk to the town hall?'

This has been the subject of some discussion, but Charles had thought the issue closed. For some reason that he could not fully articulate, he liked the idea of walking to the Registry where they were to be married, situated in Camden Town Hall. It would only take fifteen minutes, he said, and it's a pleasant walk.

Sally was reluctant. She knew, of course, that apart from his years in the RAF, Charles had spent his entire life in London and loved the city — he knew its byways and backwaters as well as any cab driver — but she hadn't appreciated the extent to which he drew comfort from its streets, its people, even its smells. The intensity of his connection with the city was something she had never encountered before. He actually loved it in the same way she loved the house on Wren Street. He felt completely at home and comfortable there, as if he drew strength from its busy streets, narrow alleyways and cobbled yards.

However, she pointed out that her dress — a flared A-shape in ivory silk with a boat neckline and an orange taffeta underskirt — was hardly suitable for busy London streets, and her heels were quite high. Furthermore, she didn't want to risk her hair being messed up when a cab would take four minutes and would deposit her, looking as perfect as the moment she left Wren Street, outside the town hall's main doors. Charles accepted that it was impractical, booked taxis and didn't mention it again.

'I thought you didn't want to,' he says.

'I know how important it is to you, although I'm not sure I understand why. But it's a lovely day, so if you still want to walk, I'm happy to take a little stroll with you.'

'Really?'

'As long as it doesn't start pelting the minute we step out the house, yeah.'

He throws back the covers and gets out of bed. 'Wait there,' he orders. 'Got something for you.'

He runs back to the master bedroom and she hears cupboard doors being opened. He returns a minute later with what looks like a shoebox.

'What's that?' she asks.

'Open it, and you'll see.'

She does so, and peels back several layers of tissue paper, revealing a pair of white plimsolls.

'They're your size,' he says. 'I got them in case you changed your mind. So you don't have to walk in high-heels.'

'These are Golas,' she says. 'They wear them at Wimbledon.'

He shrugs. 'Really? Didn't know that. But they're white and quite smart. So I thought they wouldn't look too bad with your dress.'

'My wedding dress? Oh, Charlie, you are a twit. But a lovely twit. Thank you.'

She kneels on the bed and kisses him.


The wedding party begins to assemble at Wren Street later that morning. Sally's change of mind persuades several guests also to make the journey on foot. As Sean Sloane points out, parking on Euston Road is impossible and the streets behind it are controlled by meters and residents' parking permits; finding spaces would be something of a lottery. Others in the party, such as Harry Horowitz and Nell Fisher, Sally's mother, will still travel by cab, together with others who can't manage or don't fancy the walk. That includes Leia, who will be brought by Sonia and David with their son, Jonathan.

Charles and Sally depart Wren Street shortly before everyone else. Charles wears a simple three-piece suit (an existing one, as he ran out of time to buy something new) and he carries Sally's wedding shoes by their straps. After a few minutes he glances behind him. The wedding party in its finery is following them at a respectful distance. They are laughing and talking.

'Feels like an old-fashioned Sicilian village wedding,' he comments.

'Yeah, but we forgot the brass band,' replies Sally.

The sun emerges from behind a cloud and, on impulse, Charles pulls her into Argyle Square Gardens. 'Let's go this way,' he says.

'Charlie! I can't go on the grass! I'm wearing white shoes!'

'We're not going on the grass. There's a path, see?'

The railed and tree-lined gardens are in the centre of a beautiful Georgian square surrounded by four-storey properties.

'They're just like ours,' says Sally, pointing.

'Yeah, but posher,' adds Charles.

They walk in silence, hand in hand.

'Charles?'

'Yes?'

'You sure about this?' she asks. 'There's still time to do a runner.'

'I have never been more sure of anything in my entire life,' he replies, giving her hand a squeeze. 'Do you remember what I said, after our first time, at Fetter Lane?'

'Course I do. You said being with me felt like coming home.'

'It still feels like that, except it's got better, every day. I can't imagine living another moment without you by my side.'

She smiles up at him, radiant.

They arrive at the neoclassical town hall built of white Portland stone, almost painfully bright in the sunshine, climb the Judd Street steps and enter beneath the huge Corinthian columns. Another wedding party is just leaving, and Sally and Charles almost get caught in the hail of rice and confetti.

Sally changes into her heels and, within a further few minutes, their wedding party has assembled. Sally holds out her arms to take Leia from Sonia, who has been carrying her.

'You sure?' Charles nods to her ivory dress.

Sally hesitates. 'Good point. Perhaps not,' she says.

'I'll take her,' he says, and Leia reaches out towards her father. He takes hold of her and inclines her carefully towards Sally, so she can kiss her daughter's cheek.

Sloane approaches. 'They say they're ready for us, and we need to follow that chap,' he says, nodding towards a man who is already moving off along a dark wood-panelled corridor. The wedding party follows.

He shows them into a modest-sized room with tall ceilings, large windows and half a dozen ranks of polished chairs facing forwards. The Registrar, a surprisingly young woman with long black hair shot through with grey, awaits them. There are vases of fresh cut flowers on the windowsills and Pachelbel's Canon in D is playing unobtrusively from speakers somewhere.

Charles seeks out Sally's gaze with an enquiring expression.

'It's lovely,' she confirms.

Later, Charles will struggle to remember precisely what happens over the next twenty minutes. It's as if the events have been imprinted on some emotional memory but not his rational, analytical memory. He has a strong feeling of being surrounded by everyone in his life whom he loves and who love him. He remembers Sean Sloane, Irenna and Peter Bateman, the three tallest people in the room, sitting towards the back, smiling over the heads of the Jews nearer the front. He remembers Maria and all the members of her current jazz sextet sitting in a row with broad smiles. He remembers Sally's sisters, one on either side of their mother, grinning broadly, and his father sitting in the front row between David and Sonia, holding Jonathan on his lap as the toddler wriggles. He even catches sight of his soon-to-be father-in-law, the disgraced solicitor, Harry Robeson, standing unobtrusively at the back of the room, which was strange because neither Sally nor he invited the old rogue. He remembers feeling confused about the only notable absence, his mother Millie, who would not have approved of this marriage, but who loved Sally.

At some point he must have handed Leia back to Sonia because he has been instructed to stand up, and he and Sally are facing one another before the Registrar.

She gives a few words of welcome, evidently including something funny because everyone laughs, although he can't remember what it was she said. He is aware that the Registrar is making some formal statements about the town hall being sanctioned for the celebration of marriages, and asking if any person present knows of any lawful impediment to the marriage, but all his focus is on Sally, facing him, her hands in his, looking up at him with love and tears in her eyes.

The Registrar asks questions and the two of them answer without breaking their locked gaze. They then each repeat the words dictated to them by the Registrar, and David (who, to Charles's surprise and pleasure, specifically asked to be given a role in the ceremony) steps forward with rings to be exchanged.

In what feels to be no time at all, the register has been signed and witnessed and the Registrar pronounces that they are now husband and wife. To cheers, Charles and Sally are invited to kiss their new spouse, which they do. Sonia steps forward and hands Leia, dressed in a white dress with an orange bow in her scant hair, to the two of them, and they each, simultaneously, place kisses on her cheeks. Someone takes a photograph of that moment, and the couple will cherish that image more than any other over the years that follow.

Then there are multiple camera flashes and, within what seems only to be moments from when they entered the building, they are walking back down the steps onto Judd Street.

'Well, Mrs H?' Charles asks, turning to Sally in the sunshine.

'Very well indeed, Mr H,' she replies with her familiar cheeky grin.

'Let's get back and get the party started then, shall we?'

'Good idea,' says Sally. 'I could murder a cuppa.'

# HISTORICAL NOTE

As some readers may know, I have a sort of one-man show entitled "My Life in Crime" which I take up and down the country and perform as often as fifty times each year. One of the questions I am most frequently asked at those events is: *"Surely the police corruption we read about in the newspapers and see on television now is worse than it was then, in the 1960s?"*

While I believe that most police officers are genuine public servants doing an almost impossible job, and that the current leadership of the Met (and other forces such as the Greater Manchester Police) are genuinely trying to redress the balance, there certainly still exists an alarming amount of criminality and misbehaviour scattered around the police forces of this country. Nonetheless, I always answer the questions in the same way: it is currently nothing like as bad as what was happening in London in the 1960s and 1970s. As evidence, I offer the subject matter of this book.

There were corrupt Met police officers who were indeed selling licences to commit crime, just as DCI Quigley and DI Pilcher were doing. Their modus operandi were as set out herein, namely, framing innocent people (or people who were, at least, innocent of the crimes for which they were fitted up) and then blackmailing them into committing further crimes from which the police took their shares. The extent and depth of the corruption is terrifyingly portrayed in *The Fall of Scotland Yard* by Barry Cox, John Shirley and Martin Short. Published in 1977 by Penguin, it is now out of print but can be acquired second-hand. Anyone wishing to see the exact parallels between *The Fall Guy* and historical fact is invited to find a copy. It will make your hair curl.

Some readers may remember the name Pilcher. DS Norman ("Nobby") Pilcher was a member of the Drugs Squad who became infamous for planting drugs on high-profile pop stars and then arresting them. Musicians he arrested included Mick Jagger, Keith Richards, Brian Jones, George Harrison and John Lennon. When he was eventually convicted of perverting the course of justice, Mr Justice Melford Stevenson (who appears elsewhere in this series in *Nothing But The Truth*) sentenced him to four years' imprisonment, stating that the corrupt Drugs Squad officer had *"poisoned the well of criminal justice, and set about it deliberately."*

Operation Coathanger is the actual name of the operation by honest coppers to uncover the ring of their dishonest colleagues who provided skeleton keys and information to allow burglars to steal huge quantities of fashion clothing. The operation was led by Detective Chief Inspector Irvine of the Kent Constabulary and his team of eleven detectives, drawn mostly from more reliably "straight" provincial forces. It was he who provided the template for my honest but (temporarily) discouraged DCI Olney.

One of the principal problems with investigating dishonest Metropolitan policemen was the fact that it was written into law that no outside agency could investigate the Met. If any investigation was to occur it had to be "in-house", with the predictable results of obfuscation and cover-up. The traditional defence of coppers who got too close to the criminals they were supposed to apprehend was that they had no choice. If they wanted to learn what was going on in the underworld, they needed to foster close relationships with many of the men they should have been arresting. That inevitably led to backhanders and the mutual scratching of dishonest backs. These relationships had existed for generations, and were ingrained in the very DNA of the CID. As I think I may have mentioned elsewhere, the Commissioner Sir Robert Mark, who was appointed two years before the events in this book, is on record as having said that the CID in London was at that time "*the most routinely corrupt organisation*" in the Metropolis. It was.

Having reached book ten in the series, I realised that I had paid too little attention to the burgeoning pop scene. I frequently refer to songs and groups in the charts at the time of the events I portray, but the British version of Tin Pan Alley, Denmark Street, was intrinsic to the rise of British pop culture. It was the musical revolution of that decade that we (or at least I) remember when recalling the "Swinging Sixties".

In this book I have tried to remedy that omission. Those who know anything about British pop culture might recognise certain similarities between my Bobby Gold and Don Arden, the late father of Sharon Osbourne, father-in-law of Ozzy and manager of several world-renowned groups, including Black Sabbath and ELO. Mr Arden, a Manchester Jew, was born Harry Levy and had an early variety career not dissimilar to that of Bobby Gold. Having featured a Jewish defendant in the previous book, *Death, Adjourned*, I decided I needed a change, but it was still important for Bobby Gold to be an outsider, hence his Romanian past.

I am much indebted to Don Arden's autobiography (written with Mick Wall) *Mr Big*. It's an interesting read, full of half-believable music business anecdotes, although careful cross-checking reveals that sometimes Mr Arden's recollections differ from others who lived through the same events. Nonetheless, whether it is true or not, I couldn't resist borrowing the infamous story of what happened when Robert

Stigwood allegedly attempted to entice one of Arden's most important discoveries, the Small Faces, into changing their representation. Mr Arden denies being responsible for hanging Mr Stigwood out of the window of his office block until he promised to leave the group alone, but seems to admit that he was there when the event occurred.

I managed to resist the temptation to populate the book with the musicians whose careers started in and around Denmark Street. Indeed, the list of groups and solo performers discovered is in fact longer and more illustrious than mentioned here. However, those who know their pop trivia might have recognised the pianist, Reg, as Elton John (born Reginald Dwight) who did indeed work as a delivery boy at one of the publishers on the street, Mills Music. If anyone is interested in this fascinating aspect of London history, I strongly recommend Peter Watts's *Denmark Street, London's Street of Sound*, a brilliantly researched history of Tin Pan Alley, littered with the names and histories of some of the greatest musical acts of the last sixty years.

# A NOTE TO THE READER

Dear Reader,

Thank you for taking the time to read the tenth Charles Holborne legal thriller. I hope you enjoyed it.

Nowadays, reviews by knowledgeable readers are essential to authors' success, so if you enjoyed the novel I shall be in your debt if you would spare the few seconds required to post a review on **Amazon** and **Goodreads**. I love hearing from readers, and you can connect with me through my **Facebook page**, via **Bluesky** or through my **website**, where you can sign up for my newsletter. If you find any mistakes in these pages I shall be delighted to hear from you. I always reply, and if you're right, I will make sure future editions are changed.

I hope we'll meet again in the pages of the next Charles Holborne adventure.

Simon

**www.simonmichaelauthor.com**

**Sapere Books** is an exciting new publisher of brilliant fiction and popular history.

To find out more about our latest releases and our monthly bargain books visit our website:
**saperebooks.com**

Printed in Dunstable, United Kingdom